DO YOU REMEMBER?

When everybody said it was impossible to make a film out of *The Exorcist?*

DID YOU KNOW?

That in the original screenplay there were shocking scenes of Christ's crucifixion, of a lynching, of Dachau, Auschwitz and Buchenwald, and no scenes at all of Father Merrin in Iraq?

That, originally, Father Karras's mother died before the opening credits?

That there was a subplot involving another suspect in the murder of Burke Dennings?

It's fascinating to compare the differences between the two screenplays—the original and the shooting script—and to read William Peter Blatty's detailed commentary on how and why all the changes were made.

This book is for everyone—the millions who've seen or read *The Exorcist,* plus anyone who's interested in filmmaking. Here is the primary source of information on what seems sure to be the most successful film in history.

WILLIAM PETER BLATTY ON
THE EXORCIST
FROM NOVEL TO FILM

Bantam Books by William Peter Blatty

THE EXORCIST
WILLIAM PETER BLATTY ON *THE EXORCIST*
FROM NOVEL TO FILM

William Peter Blatty on
The Exorcist
from Novel to Film

WILLIAM PETER BLATTY

BANTAM BOOKS
TORONTO · LONDON
NEW YORK

I would like to express my deep gratitude
for the talent and the intelligence of my
editor on this book, Nancy Hardin.

WILLIAM PETER BLATTY ON
THE EXORCIST FROM NOVEL TO FILM
A Bantam Book / published June 1974

Bantam Books are published by Bantam Books, Inc. Its trade-
mark, consisting of the words "Bantam Books" and the por-
trayal of a bantam, is registered in the United States Patent
Office and in other countries. Marca Registrada. Bantam
Books, Inc., 666 Fifth Avenue, New York, New York 10019.

CONTENTS

Introduction

It is Friday, July 13, 1973. As I write, Billy Friedkin, the director of *The Exorcist,* is returning from northern Iraq where he filmed at Nimrud and the ruins of Nineveh; William Kaplan, our production supervisor, is in Baghdad under armed guard because a Warner Brothers check to the Iraqi government has bounced; and I sit here thinking of many things: of the chain of disturbing and mysterious events that have haunted this project from its inception; of a little girl in demon makeup weeping because her pet mouse has died; and of a day in the fall of '71, when as I dozed in a hammock on the backyard patio of my agent, Noel Marshall, I heard the piping voice of Jane Fonda say in guarded tones from within the house, "There's someone out there." I believe she meant me and not the full-grown lion beneath the hammock whom Noel had raised, along with over fifty others, for use in a lion film. Noel and Miss Fonda were about to have a business meeting in the yard. I clenched my eyelids, feigning sleep: for Billy Friedkin and I had offered Miss Fonda the role of Chris MacNeil in *The Exorcist,* and after reading the novel Miss Fonda had reacted, according to her agent, with the following statement telephoned from Paris: "Why would any studio want to make this capitalist ripoff bullshit?" Which, when I'd heard it, I'd understood to mean that she didn't want to do the part. Now I heard a screen door sliding open; then footsteps. I opened my eyes and saw Miss Fonda approaching the hammock. I shifted a covert glance to the lion and pondered the efficacy of a "Sic 'em!" But it seemed that Miss Fonda had come to say something nice. She had heard the report of her comment on my novel and wanted to tell me that it wasn't true. "The reason I didn't want to do it," she explained sincerely, "was because I don't believe in magic."

Well, I do. For I've felt the firm warm touch of a

Providence that protects me from what I want; and I've witnessed the making of a film that not only is faithful to the novel but, on certain levels is better.

Let me give you the background—the history of the novel and of the film right up to the moment Mr. Friedkin was hired. As producer of the film this involves intrigue; and as the author of the novel and the script—possession.

In 1949, while a junior at Georgetown University in Washington, D.C., I read in the August 20 edition of the *Washington Post* the following account:

> In what is perhaps one of the most remarkable experiences of its kind in recent religious history, a 14-year-old Mount Rainier boy has been freed by a Catholic priest of possession by the devil, it was reported yesterday.
>
> Only after 20 to 30 performances of the ancient ritual of exorcism, here and in St. Louis, was the devil finally cast out of the boy, it was said.
>
> In all except the last of these, the boy broke into a violent tantrum of screaming, cursing and voicing of Latin phrases—a language he had never studied—whenever the priest reached those climactic points of the 27 page ritual in which he commanded the demon to depart from the boy.
>
> In complete devotion to his task the priest stayed with the boy over a period of two months, during which he witnessed such manifestations as the bed in which the boy was sleeping suddenly moving across the room.
>
> A Washington Protestant minister has previously reported personally witnessing similar manifestations, including one in which the pallet on which the sleeping boy lay slid slowly across the floor until the boy's head bumped against a bed, awakening him.
>
> In another instance reported by the Protestant minister, a heavy armchair in which the boy was sitting, with his knees drawn under his chin, tilted slowly to one side and fell over, throwing the boy on the floor.
>
> The final rite of exorcism in which the devil was cast from the boy took place in May, it was reported, and since then he had had no manifestations.
>
> The ritual of exorcism in its present form goes back 1500 years and from there to Jesus Christ.

4

But before it was undertaken, all medical and psychiatric means of curing the boy—in whose presence such manifestations as fruit jumping up from the refrigerator top in his home and hurling itself against the wall also were reported—were exhausted.

The boy was taken to Georgetown University Hospital here, where his affliction was exhaustively studied, and to St. Louis University. Both are Jesuit institutions.

Finally both Catholic hospitals reported they were unable to cure the boy through natural means.

Only then was a supernatural cure sought.

The ritual was undertaken by a Jesuit in his 50's.

The details of the exorcism of the boy were described to The Washington Post by a priest here (not the exorcist).

The ritual began in St. Louis, continued here and finally ended in St. Louis.

For two months the Jesuit stayed with the boy, accompanying him back and forth on the train, sleeping in the same house and sometimes in the same room with him. He witnessed many of the same manifestations reported by the Protestant minister this month to a closed meeting of the Society of Parapsychology laboratory at Duke University, who came here to study the case, was quoted as saying it was "the most impressive" poltergeist (noisy ghost) phenomenon that had come to his attention in his years of celebrated investigation in the field.

Even through the ritual of exorcism the boy was by no means cured readily.

The ritual itself takes about three quarters of an hour to perform. During it, the boy would break into the fury of profanity and screaming and the astounding Latin phrases.

But finally, at the last performance of the ritual, the boy was quiet. And since then, it was said, all manifestations of the affliction—such as the strange moving of the bed across the room, and another in which the boy's family said a picture had suddenly jutted out from the wall in his presence—have ceased.

It was early this year that members of the boy's family went to their minister and reported strange goings on in their Mount Rainier house since January 18.

The minister visited the boy's home and witnessed some of the manifestations.

But though they seemed to the naked eye un-explainable—such as the scratchings from the area of the wall in the boy's presence—there was always the suggestion, he said, that in some way the noises may have been made by the boy himself.

Retaining his skepticism in the matter, the minister then had the boy stay a night—February 17—in his own home.

It was there, before his own eyes, he said, that the two manifestations that he felt were beyond all natural explanation took place.

In one of these the boy's pallet moved across the floor while his hands were outside the cover and his body rigid.

In the other the heavy chair, with the boy immobile in it, tilted and fell over to the floor before the minister's amazed eyes, he said. The minister tried to overturn the chair while sitting in it himself and was unable to do so.

The case involved such reactions as neighbors of the boy's family sprinkling holy water around the family's house.

Some of the Mount Rainier neighbors' skepticism was startlingly resolved, it was reported, when they first laughed it off, invited the boy and his mother to spend a night in their own "unhaunted" homes, only to have some of the manifestations—such as the violent, apparently involuntary shakings of the boy's bed—happen before their eyes.

The article impressed me. And how coolly under-stated that is. I wasn't just impressed: I was *excited*. For here at last, in this city, in my time, was tangible evidence of transcendence. If there were demons, there were angels and probably a God and a life everlasting. And thus it occurred to me long afterward, when I'd started my career as a writer, that this case of posses-sion which had joyfully haunted my hopes in the years since 1949 was a worthwhile subject for a novel. In my youth I had thought about entering the priesthood; at Georgetown had considered becoming a Jesuit. The notion of course was unattainable and ludicrous in the extreme, since with respect to the subject of my worthiness, my nearest superiors are asps; and yet a novel of demonic possession, I believed—if only I could make it sufficiently convincing—might be token fulfillment of deflected vocation. Though let me make clear, if I may—lest someone rush to have me canonized—that I would never write a novel that I thought would not engross or excite or entertain; that I thought would have a readership of fifteen people. (It has often worked out that way, yes; but I didn't plan it.) If walking out of church you should pick up a Daniel Lord homiletic treatise from the vestibule pamphlet rack, you will not, I can virtually assure you, see "as told to Bill Blatty" under Father Lord's name. But if one has a choice among viable subjects and one can do good along the way by picking *that* one . . . well, that is the little one can say of my motive.

As the years went by, I continued my studies in possession, but desultorily and with no specific aim. For example, I made a note about a character on a page of a book called *Satan:*[1] "Detective—'Mental Clearance Sale.' " The words, in quotes, would turn up eventually very deep in the story, as a thought of Kinderman, the homicide detective in the novel; but at the time I made the note, I knew nothing of its context. Finally, however—I think it was in 1963—the notion of possession as the basic subject matter of a novel crystallized and firmed.

But the problem was that no one else liked the idea. Not my agent (then). Not Doubleday, my publisher (then). Even my dentist thought the notion was rotten.[2] So I dropped the idea. See how strong and persevering I am in my convictions? But then, I rationalized, I was a comedy writer; I had never written anything "straight," except a few forged letters of excuse from my mother when I'd been absent from school the day before. ("Well, it hurt right here, Sister Joseph. Pardon? How could I have cancer for just one day?") I was doubtful I could do it; even more doubtful than Doubleday, perhaps, which would extend us from doubt into negative certitude.

---

[1] Frank Sheed, New York: Sheed & Ward, 1952. I cannot recommend this book too highly for those interested in studying certain aspects of possession.

[2] He endeavored instead to seduce my interest, the cosmic rays being strong that day, toward fictionally exploiting "the romance of dentistry."

But sometimes something, someone helps. In December 1967, at a New Year's Eve dinner at the home of novelist Burton Wohl, I met Marc Jaffe, editorial director of Bantam Books. He asked me what I was working on. Finding the shortest line at the unemployment office, I told him; and then spoke of possession. He warmed to the subject matter instantly. I wondered if he was drunk. He suggested publication of the book by Bantam. I was then supporting the entire cast of Birnam Wood and requested an advance large enough to carry me for a year. He said, "Send me an outline."

What could I send him? The small scrap of paper with the cryptic notation about the detective? I had no plot. I had only the subject matter, some hazily formulated characters, and a theme.

So I wrote him a long letter. I began by detailing what I knew of the incident of 1949, including some rather bizarre phenomena that had been bruited about on the Georgetown campus at the time; for example, a report that the exorcist and his assistants were forced to wear rubber windjammer suits, for the boy, in his fits, displayed a prodigious ability to urinate endlessly, accurately, and over great distances, with the exorcists as his target.[3]

I went on to discuss the position of the Church on the matter:

It cautions exorcists that many of the paranormal phenomena can be explained in natural terms. The speaking in "unknown tongues" (unless it is part of intelligent dialogue), or possession of hidden knowledge, for example, can be explained in terms of telepathy—the possessed may simply be picking the knowledge out of the brain of the exorcist or someone else in the room. And as for levitation, Hindu mystics reputedly can manage it now and then, and what do we really know about magnetism and gravity? The "natural" explanations are, of course, somewhat mystical themselves. But the occurrence of one or two of these phenomena, exorcists are cautioned, does

---

[3]This report was false and later proved to have been a distortion of a similar and factual phenomenon whereby the boy could *spit* in such a manner, even with his eyes shut tight, or, as they sometimes were, physically shielded from his targets.

not justify assuming one is dealing with true possession. What the Church does tell its exorcists is to go with the laws of chance and probability which tell us that it's far less fanciful to believe than an alien entity or spirit has control of the possessed than to believe that all or most of these paranormal phenomena are likely to occur all at once through purely natural causes. When all of them occur, and psychological causes are eliminated, then try the cure.

Still loftily avoiding such crass considerations as a discussion of plot, I nimbly leaped to the next sure peak —my intended theme:

Is there a man alive who at one time or another in his life has not thought, Look, God! I'd *like* to believe in you; and I'd really like to do the right thing. But twenty thousand sects and countless prophets have different ideas about what the right thing is. So if you *are* out there, why not end all the mystery and hocus-pocus and make an appearance on top of the Empire State Building. *Show me your face.*

We follow through by thinking that God doesn't take this simple recourse, this *reasonable* recourse, and therefore isn't there. He isn't dead, and he isn't alive in Argentina. He simply never lived.

But I happen to believe—and this is part of the theme of the novel—that if God *were* to appear in thunder and lightning atop the Empire State Building, it would not affect (for long, at least) the religious beliefs of anyone who witnessed the phenomenon. Those who already believed would find the incident a reinforcement of their faith; those who did not already believe would be impressed for a while, but with the passage of time would convince themselves that what they saw was the result of either autosuggestion, mass hypnosis, or hysteria, or massive charlatanism involving nuclear energy and NASA. On a theological level, I happened to believe that if there is a God who is somehow involved with us and our activities he would *refrain* from appearing on top of the Empire State Building, because he would ultimately only cause trauma for those who *did not will* to believe, and thereby increase their guilt. The Red Sea's parting and the raising of Lazarus are not viable entries to religious belief. The trick to faith lies not in magic but in the *will of the individual.*

9

The novel would ask, I went on to explain, what effect a confrontation with undisputed paranormal phenomena would have on the book's main characters: the atheist mother of the boy (as I then intended the victim should be; I had named him Jamie), and the priest of weak faith called in for the exorcism, whom I first named Father Thomas.[4] This thematic aspect would prove only a suggestion of what it would become in the book I eventually wrote, expressed by Father Merrin as follows:

I think the demon's target is not the possessed; it is us . . . the observers . . . every person in this house. And I think—I think the point is to make us despair, to reject our own humanity, Damien: to see ourselves as ultimately bestial; as ultimately vile and putrescent; without dignity, ugly, unworthy. And there lies the heart of it, perhaps: in unworthiness. For I think belief in God is not a matter of reason at all; I think it finally is a matter of love; of accepting the possibility that God could love us . . .

And perhaps even this would seem merely an insight compared to the stronger, more encompassing theme that would spring from the Jesuit psychiatrist's act of ultimate self-sacrifice and love: the theme I call "the mystery of goodness." For in a mechanistic universe, where the atoms that make up a human being should logically be expected, even in the aggregate, to pursue their selfish ends more blindly than the rivers rush out to the seas, how is it there is love in the sense that a God would love and that a man will give his life for another?[5]

Because it is true and embedded in reality, this theme

---

[4]Later on I renamed him John Henry Carver. I thought this aspect of the theme would work better if the priest were black and had come to the priesthood to escape from the slums and his boyhood identity; for then his resistance to the notion of possession in the face of levitating beds could be partly ascribed to his rejection of what he thinks are the superstitions related to his Haitian parents. The reason I abandoned this characterization was my fear of falling into the trap of writing Sidney Poitier.

[5]It is useless to argue that unlike atoms, men have a higher intelligence, for this merely serves to help us rush all the more quickly.

would appear of itself in the inevitable developments of my plot, that plot which at the time of my letter to Jaffe was a beast as mythical as the unicorn and an even bigger pain in the ass. And so I "vamped," as we mental swindlers often say. And then a murder, predicted long ago before by my subconscious[6] when I scribbled that note about a "detective," indeed did appear to me. "The killer is the boy;[7] the mother knows this, and against the eventual arrest of her son," I wrote to Jaffe:

The mother seeks psychiatric help to establish the boy was deranged at the time of the murder. The effort proves unpromising. She then seizes upon the device of calling in the psychologically intimidating forces of the Catholic Church in an effort to prove (although she doesn't believe it for a moment) that her son is "possessed"—that it was not Jamie but an alien entity inhabiting his body who commited the murder. She resorts to the church and requests an exorcism; and soon it is arranged for a priest to examine the boy. She grasps at the desperate and bizarre hope that if the exorcist concludes that the boy is possessed and is able to restore him to a measure of normalcy, she will have a powerful psychological and emotional argument for securing both the release of the boy and the equally important release (even if the boy is imprisoned) from humiliation and degradation. The exorcist selected for the task is, by the one coincidence permitted us, the priest who has lost his faith.

---

[6]I believe that my subconscious, once it has the necessary raw material (data and research) and sufficient prodding (sweat), does most of my plotting; and that it knew, by the time I had made that notation, almost the entire plot of *The Exorcist*, slipping portions to my conscious mind a little bit at a time. I remember, for example, being so surprised at the moment it occurred to me that Burke Dennings, and not an offstage character as originally planned, would be the demon's murder victim, that from my desk I cried out aloud, "My God, Burke Dennings is going to be murdered!" Yet an early and seemingly accidental detail—Denning's habit of tearing off the edges of pages of books or scripts and then nervously twisting and fiddling with them—would later prove vital to a major piece of plotting. What we often call inspiration, I think, are in fact subconscious disclosures.

[7]I wish to make it clear that in the 1949 case no killings or deaths of any kind were involved. Two priests were injured, however, one to the extent that for weeks he could only use one hand for the lifting of the chalice when saying mass.

11

Ultimately, the boy is exorcised. Although his fate at the hands of the law is not the concern of this novel. Our concern is the exorcist. Has his faith been restored by this incredible encounter? Yes. But not by the exorcism itself, for finally, the exorcist is still not sure what really happened. What restores—no; *reaffirms*—his faith is simple human love, which is surely the fact of God made visible.

Virtually none of this plot survived; nor did my notion that "the alien entity possessing the boy should be a woman who claims to have lived in some remote period of history, possibly Judea in the time of Christ; and who attacks the exorcist psychologically by claiming an acquaintance with Christ, then proceeding to describe him in demythologizing, disillusioning terms."

My letter ended the way it had begun: with a truly dazzling display of whorishness which summoned up the powers of rhetoric and logic acquired in eight years of Jesuit education and shamelessly invested them in a theorem proving that the book would sell millions of copies and that Bantam should support me for a year.

Jaffe shopped my letter at some hardcover houses, hoping to bring them in on the deal and thus share in producing the required advance. But a book about possession by a writer of comedy? Whose books, while they didn't sell fewer copies than *The Idylls of the King* in its Tibetan translation, certainly didn't sell any more? No one was interested, a phenomenon to which I'd grown accustomed, but which surely should have given Marc Jaffe second thoughts. But Jaffe held fast, and Bantam, on its own, at last came up with the advance. Only then did I begin to believe that perhaps I could write the book.

After some intervening screenplay assignments, I undertook a period of intensive research early in 1969. From the outset I was biased by training and religion in favor of belief in genuine possession. Furthermore, replace the word "demon" with the words "disembodied malevolent intelligence," and one has a concept not repugnant to reason or in apparent contradiction to the laws of matter, whatever they happen to be this year. Aldous Huxley's *Devils of Loudun* makes a devastating argument to the effect that the seventeenth-century epidemic of demonic possession in a convent of Ursuline nuns in France was a fraudulent, hysterical manifestation; yet even Huxley observes:

> I can see nothing intrinsically absurd or self-contradictory in the notion that there may be non-human spirits, good, bad and indifferent. Nothing compels us to believe that the only intelligences in the universe are those connected with the bodies of human beings and the lower animals. If the evidence for clairvoyance, telepathy and prevision is accepted (and it is becoming increasingly difficult to reject it), then we must allow that there are mental processes which are largely independent of space, time and matter. And if this is so, there seems to be no reason for denying *a priori* that there may be nonhuman intelligences, either completely discarnate, or else associated with cosmic energy in some way of which we are still ignorant.[8]

Teilhard de Chardin, the Jesuit philosopher-paleontologist, once proposed that what we think of as matter and spirit are but differing aspects of something else, some third and fundamental reality in which matter and spirit commune. And indeed, the views of modern physicists on the ultimate nature of matter seemed to be leaning toward support of Chardin, seemed increasingly to be edging toward something like mysticism, a paradoxical consequence of the steadily deeper probings into the Chinese box of the atom. Consider the neutrino. It can speed through a planetary thickness in a twinkling, yet has no mass and no magnetic or electrical charge. Real, yet lacking fundamental properties of matter, the neutrino is a ghost.[9]

All well and good. Possession is possible, I thought. But where were the documented cases? Where was even *one* well-documented case? 1949. I thought of that. The

---

[8] *The Devils of Loudun* (New York: Harper & Row, 1952).

[9] Physics now tells us that on the subatomic level matter as we know it does not exist; that on the subatomic level there are no "things," only processes; and that the clockwork universe of the mechanists has been destroyed. We have the additionally mystical notion, which won for its discoverer the Nobel Prize, that a positron "is an electron *moving backward in time.*"

story in the *Washington Post* seemed factual; and yet, finally, how could I tell? Only an eyewitness could corroborate it for me. In an earlier try at tracing the exorcist, I had queried the *Washington Post,* but couldn't find the reporter who had written the story; and the names of the exorcist and the fourteen-year-old boy who was the victim had never been known. I'd also queried the Jesuits I'd known while at Georgetown who were still on the campus. None could help.

So I searched the literature of possession. To begin with, though in time they reached back to ancient Egypt, the published sources, notably those in which the insights of psychiatry were fully reflected, were not only few in number, but also repetitious. And of the cases cited, over 90 percent were conceivably attributable to fraud, delusion, a combination of both, or misinterpretations of the symptoms of psychosis, particularly paranoid schizophrenia, or of certain neuroses, especially hysteria and neurasthenia. Eighty percent of the victims were women, moreover, a ratio so disproportionate as to suggest, as opposed to possession, a common disorder once alluded to as *furor uterinus,* an expression that speaks, I would think, for itself. This would surely account for the extraordinary lewdness of speech and behavior that I found to be present, without exception, in every case of so-called demonic possession. And it surely is significant that LaTourette's syndrome, a still mysterious neurological disorder only recently isolated and labeled, is primarily characterized by the sudden, apparently unmotivated and unpredictable onset of a usually irresistible compulsion to shriek out a torrent of verbal obscenities not noticeably lacking in nauseating grossness.

A few of my findings were intriguing: the reporting of a common symptomology in cases widely separated with respect to both time and place; and cases where the victims were very young children. Both tend to make hysteria, fraud, or delusion more remote as explanations of possession. How would an eight-year-old boy, for example, come to know its classic symptoms? It is possible. But likely?

And consider what happened to four of the exorcists

sent to deal with the outbreak at Loudun. Three of them, Tranquille, Lactance, and Lucas, successively appeared to be possessed themselves, and while in that state, died, perhaps from cardiac exhaustion. The oldest of these men was forty-three. The fourth, Surin, a noted intellectual and mystic, a truly good man, only thirty-three, became totally insane and so remained for twenty-five years. If these exorcists were faking, they carried it far; if temporarily hysterical, they were so in defiance of a psychiatric principle that tells us that hysterics do not blossom overnight; and if hysterical beforehand, though of differing backgrounds, then their hysteria must surely have been the determining criterion employed by the cardinal who picked them for the mission, for how could we otherwise account for the coincidence involved in his selecting four closet hysterics? I do not find these possibilities alluring to reason. And it was certainly known well before the events at Loudun that symptoms suggesting possession could in fact be caused by mental illness: "The too credulous," the Church warned would-be exorcists in the Acts of the Synod of Rheims, "are often deceived, and . . . lunatics often declare themselves to be possessed and tormented by the devil; and these people nevertheless are far more in need of a doctor than of an exorcist." That statement was made in 1583.

Moreover, what was I to think of cases of possession in which the subject's personality, voice, and mannerisms altered so radically that people around them actually believed they were dealing with someone else? It is useless to resort to "dual personality" as an explanation. The competent psychiatrists[10] who authored *The Three Faces of Eve* make the candid admission that while Eve's disorder disappeared in apparent response to treatment based upon a certain diagnosis of the problem, that diagnosis depended on the interaction within equations of concepts like "mind," "personality," and "hysteria"; but in fact the reality back of these labels is still unknown. In physics, when working certain equa-

10Corbett H. Thigpen and Hervey M. Cleckley (New York: McGraw-Hill, 1957).

tions, one assumes that light is composed of particles; but in working other equations, the assumption is that light is composed of waves. It probably is neither.[11] But it cannot be both. And that either type of equation "works" does not prove either assumption concerning light; it only proves that the equation works. So in attempting to explain possession, one might as well say "demon" as "dual personality." The concepts are equally occult.

Before Eve Black's case, the great psychiatrist Morton Prince had treated a case of dual personality in which one of the newcomers, hardy "Sally," who knew everything her other personalities were doing whereas they knew nothing of her activities, claimed to be a "spirit" and refused to be therapeutically murdered, so that Prince at last resorted to "exorcism." By taking her on her own terms he was able to argue her into returning whence she had come. In a like vein, following publication of *The Exorcist* I was to hear from a noted psychologist that he believed that some of his former patients had been "obsessed," the second stage of possession in which the attack is from the exterior. This psychologist, Dr. Alan Cohen, a Ph.D. from Harvard who practices in San Francisco and coauthored *Understanding Drug Use*,[12] told me that in paranoid schizophrenic subjects experiencing auditory hallucinations, the verbal patterns of association of ideas should be identical to the patterns in the content of what is hallucinated, since both patterns have a common source. But in certain of his patients, Cohen told me, these patterns were totally dissimilar, thereby suggesting separate intelligences. Cohen alluded to the two little boys, aged ten and eleven, who killed by crucifixion a three-year-old boy in San Francisco, each explaining independently that "a voice" had told him to do it; he told me further that the former chief psychologist at Mendocino State Mental Hospital in northern California, Dr. Wilson Van Deusen, believed that many patients in the disturbed

---

[11]Or, like the neutrino, evidence that matter is finally spirit?

[12]*Understanding Drug Use: An Adult's Guide to Drugs and the Young*, Alan Cohen and Peter Marin, Harper and Row, 1971, New York.

ward in that institution were possessed;[13] and that he went so far as to practice therapeutic exorcism on occasion.

All interesting, indeed. Any yet all these findings taken together did not constitute the slimmest reed of evidence. The case for demonic possession had finally to rest on what was plentifully lacking at Loudun: the reliably witnessed and reported occurrence of so-called paranormal phenomena. Levitating mattresses are very out front.

Of course I found many such cases reported in the literature. And at times the eyewitness observer—the noted ethnologist Junod, for example—surely had to be counted as reliable. So too must William James, the great psychologist, who investigated the case of a girl in Watseka, Illinois, who underwent a total and abrupt transformation of personality and identity, claiming for months to be someone named Mary Roff who turned out to be a real person whom she had never met: a sixteen-year-old girl who had died in a state insane asylum years before. James declared the "spiritist explanation" of the case "the most plausible" one available. And Carl Jung, it is perhaps little known, was connected with another case of possession for almost a year.[14] The case involved a fifteen-year-old girl, the daughter of friends. Normally dull-witted, she manifested three distinct personalities, one of them a chatty and eloquent old man who spoke high German, a dialect completely unknown to the girl. She demonstrated tele-

---

[13]As reported in *Newsweek* (February 11, 1974, p. 61) other psychiatrists agree: ". . . there are some psychiatrists who no longer dismiss exorcism as a crude, pre-Freudian method of handling emotional disturbance. Milwaukee psychiatrist Alan Reed Jr. says he will not rule out possession as an explanation for some forms of extreme psychic disorder. 'In the whole field of spiritualism, mysticism, religion and the human spirit,' says Reed, 'there are things so minimally understood that almost anything's possible.' 'I believe in all that stuff,' admits Dr. Walter Brown, a psychiatrist at Mount Sinai Hospital in New York City. 'In a way, all psychoanalysis and psychotherapy are forms of exorcism, of getting rid of demons.' "

[14]Fully described in his "On the Psychology and Pathology of So-Called Occult Phenomena," *Psychiatric Studies,* in the Collected Works of C. Jung, Bollingen Series XX (Princeton, N.J.: Princeton University Press, 1957).

pathic abilities and an astoundingly accelerated intelligence, all of which phenomena were frequently witnessed firsthand by Jung, who found in them no possibility of fraud.

But the case involving James lacked paranormal phenomena, and the case involving Jung, while it apparently did exhibit such phenomena, was however totally lacking in the fits of rage, the malevolent activity, and the demonic self-identification that characterize so-called demonic possession. And of all the other cases of demonic possession I studied, almost all exhibiting paranormal phenomena had occurred no later than 1900, with some dating back several centuries. I constantly found myself asking: Who were the witnesses? Who had written the report I was reading? Could I trust his veracity and judgment? Did he witness the phenomena himself? If so, how much time intervened between events and the preparation of the report? Or was the record based on hearsay? and if so, how far removed was it from the eyewitness source?

In an ordinary circumstance when there is continuing and universal testimony that such-and-such a thing has occurred, we allow for inaccuracies and falsehood but accept the main core. There are extant a number of differing Deluge stories. There are those who cannot accept the Old Testament account of a massive ark that bore animals two by two in its hold. And who can take literally the Gilgamesh epic? The point is that we do accept the *core* of these stories: that at some point in history mankind experienced a devastating flood.

Yet I could not apply that kind of thinking to possession. Not that such reasoning is invalid, for in life— and sometimes in science, especially physics—very little is "proved" before we give it assent; instead, what we do is make prudent judgments. But prudent judgments do not satisfy when dealing with the supernatural; for the ultimate issue is too important; the issue is God and our hope of resurrection. Thus, on hearing a secondhand report from Martha and Mary to the effect that the tomb is empty, that "He is risen," I would first stroll over to the tomb and examine it myself; and then, if the women claimed to have personally witnessed the actual resurrection,[15] I would have a little chat with them to try to determine if they had been stoned at the time. I would also pull their files from Roman Intelligence to check out their character, their integrity, and their record of "prowler" calls to the police. Only then would I begin to formulate a prudent judgment based on what they had said.

And so with possession. I felt that if I couldn't write the novel with conviction I probably wouldn't want to write it at all; for how could it possibly turn out well? A hollow heart cannot excite.

I found a case that was relatively recent: 1928. In Earling, Iowa. There was only one account of the event, a printed pamphlet written by a monk. The pamphlet carried photographs of the principals. Paranormal phenomena were cited. One in particular gave me pause. It was stated that the victim, a forty-year-old woman, would repeatedly and forcefully fly up from her bed as if hurled like a dart, head first, at a point above the bedroom door, where she would hang suspended by her forehead, as if tightly glued to the spot. An extraordinary image! I instinctively felt that it could not have been invented. Moreover, while phenomena tended to repeat themselves in the cases I had studied, this was one I had never before heard the likes of. And yet my overall reaction to the pamphlet was a shrug. Perhaps some who are familiar with the pamphlet were impressed, by which I do not imply that my threshold of credulity is higher than theirs, as should be evident to anyone who examines my record of box-top mail-ins at the Post Toasties plant, notably the one in response to an offer of a Dick Tracy two-way radio ring. But the tone of the pamphlet seemed so overly credulous, so replete with pietistic asides and exclamations, that it turned me off. I reacted illogically, I suppose, as the basic phenomena might still have been factual; but the pamphlet made me think of "Crazy Mary," a friend of my mother's who during my boyhood visited seven churches a day and saw Our Lady of Fatima in the

---

[15]Merely a "for instance." According to Gospel accounts, they did not.

alphabet soup. I simply didn't trust it. And the people involved were unfortunately dead. That ended Earling, at least for me.

Next I called upon numerous Jesuit friends in the hope that they might lead me to someone now living who had actually performed an exorcism: maybe someone from the foreign missions, for in Asia and Africa possession is common. But I had no luck. I came closest with Father Thomas Bermingham, who had taught me at Brooklyn Prep and was master of studies at St. Andrew's-on-Hudson, a Jesuit seminary, at the time I sought him out. He recalled that in his earliest years in the priesthood a Jesuit quartered at the seminary was known to have performed an exorcism. Withdrawn and never known to speak, he haunted the wooded walks alone, a blank, burned-out look in his stare. He was late into his thirties. His hair was shock-white. It had happened in the exorcism, I was told.

The story caused my pilot light to flicker back on: and in the back of a book that I used in my research, I have recently discovered a small notation that it doubtless inspired: "Exorcist white-haired man called out of retirement to do it again. He dies early and assistant takes over." But Father Bermingham couldn't remember the original model's name.

So I tried something utterly illogical: instead of asking more Jesuits who'd been in the neighborhood when the incident had taken place, I called a Jesuit friend of mine in Los Angeles, thousands of miles away from the event. He gave me the exorcist's name and address.

I wrote to him. He answered with the following letter, from which I have deleted certain information for reasons that will be apparent:

Your letter, addressed to me at the ———— Retreat House at ————, was forwarded to me here, where I have been stationed for the past year. We have a mutual friend in Father ————, S. J.

As you stated in your letter, it is very difficult to find any authentic literature on cases of possession; at least, I could not find any when I was involved in such a case. Accordingly, we (a priest with me) kept a minute account each day of the happenings each preceding day and night, one reason being that our diary would be most helpful to anyone placed in a similar position as an exorcist in any future case.

My hesitancy in giving you the details of the case of possession is due to two facts. First, ———, who delegated me as the exorcist, instructed me not to publicize the case. I have been faithful to his instructions. Secondly, it would be most embarrassing, and possibly painfully disturbing to the young man, should he be connected in any way with a book detailing events that took place in his life some years ago. Since a case of possession is a very rare occurrence, he would certainly connect his own experience with any such account.

Some Jesuits living with me at ——— at the time were conversant with some of the events in the case; and, as often happens, as a story passes on, events are not correctly reported.

My own thoughts were that much good might have come if the case had been reported, and people had come to realize that the presence and the activity of the devil is something very real. And possibly never more real than at the present time. But I submitted my judgment to the instructions which I received from ———.

I can assure you of one thing: the case in which I was involved was the real thing. I had no doubt about it then and I have no doubts about it now.

Should I be of any assistance to you within the limitations I have set forth in this letter, I would be glad to accommodate you.

I wish you every success in the important apostolate of the pen. You can do so much good with that gift.

The letter was electrifying. For at last I felt I was in touch with reality, with a good and sensible man. I wrote again and asked permission to see his diary, not for the purpose of reproducing any of its details in the novel I would write, but because I am Thomas and needed to put my own fingers in the wounds. But again the exorcist declined, citing the need to protect the boy; he would only assure me that the case had indeed involved unambiguous paranormal phenomena.

I later would learn that even a priest who had requested the material from the Washington archdiocese was told in 1952 that "His Eminence [the Cardinal] has instructed me to inform you that he does not wish the case of exorcism of the boy in Mount Rainier discussed publicly. The parents of the boy made a very strong request to that effect and we have tried to shield them and the boy from any embarrassing publicity." After *The Exorcist* was published, a number of periodicals and newspapers resurrected the original account of the case given out by the victim's minister; I had changed the boy in my story to a girl, although more to ease the exorcist's anxiety than from fear of doing any real harm to the boy, inasmuch as the specific locations, the characters, and the story in my novel were not taken from the actual case, there being, as I have said and now repeat, no murders or deaths of any kind in the latter; and in addition, I utilized no paranormal phenomena peculiar to only *this* case of possession. Nevertheless, all this being said, it is a fact that the diary maintained by the exorcist was submitted, for their guidance, to two other people who were in contact with the boy and were to keep a watchful eye on the course of his recovery, to the archives of two arch-dioceses; and that it came somehow to be in the files[16] of a city hospital where the boy for a time was confined and where some of the exorcism was performed. And it is also a fact that I have read it; that I have long known the name of the boy and where he lives; and can attest that the diary kept by the exorcist is in part, and beyond any doubt, the thoroughly meticulous, reliable—even cautiously understated—eyewitness report of paranormal phenomena.

The story in the *Post* proved accurate, except where it implied that the boy knew Latin. It is true that he was able to parrot long phrases, and even sentences, in Latin just spoken by the exorcist as part of the ritual; and that he always burst into fury at the exorcist's command of *"principio tibi . . .,"* the beginning of the first of the stern adjurations of the Catholic ritual of exorcism. But the parroting is easily attributable to the heightened unconscious intellectual performance—sometimes fifty times normal—that is cited by Jung as

---

[16]*Not* via the exorcist, who to this day has continued to exhort me never to reveal the boy's identity.

a possible concomitant of certain forms of hysteria. And the rages were doubtless cued by the abruptly loud and commanding tone recommended for delivering the adjurations in the Catholic "Instructions to Exorcists." The "unknown language" specification used by the Church as a sign of possession requires that the person allegedly possessed by able to engage in *intelligent dialogue* in that language. I cannot vouch for what may have happened prior to the exorcist's appearance on the scene; but certainly no intelligent dialogue in Latin was ever in evidence thereafter, even though the exorcist frequently demanded it of the alien intelligence controlling the boy's response in Latin to certain questions required by the ritual ("What is your name? When will you depart?"); and although the "demon" (whatever ultimate reality may lie behind that name) protested at one point, "I speak the language of the persons," a seemingly childish, if not fraudulent, evasion.[17] But there was nothing evasive about the levitation of a hospital nightstand beside the boy's bed, which was witnessed by a physics professor from Washington University; nor could one so characterize a repeated and striking phenomenon not mentioned in the *Post* account: the various markings—described in the diary as "brandings"—that appeared spontaneously and without apparent cause on various parts of the victim's skin. Many times they were words clearly etched in fiery red block letters that were usually a little over two inches tall; other times they were symbols; at still others, pictorial representations. One of the words that appeared was SPITE. One symbol was an arrow that pointed directly at the victim's penis. And a very clear picture was that of a hideous satanic visage. But by far the most frequent and alarming of the brandings were lengthy lines that at times broke the skin, as if the boy had

---

[17]Although an identical claim in two earlier cases of possession was further explained by the possessing entities as relating to the absence, in the bodies of their hosts, of the muscular formations in the physical speech apparatus that develop with the use of a language; thus their efforts to speak another language not known to the host would be halting, if not laughable. In the cases cited, however, the languages were French and German; whereas Latin has never posed any such problem for high-school freshmen, with the possible exception of myself.

been raked with the prongs of an invisible miniature pitchfork. Or, one could say, claws.[18]

During brandings, the boy wore only his undershorts. No bedcovers hid his movements. His hands were at all times in view of the exorcist and his assistants and others in the room. One branding that ran from the boy's inner thigh to the top of his ankle, drawing blood, occurred while the exorcist was seated on the edge of the bed, his eyes on the boy, and no more than about a foot away. Other of the brandings were on the boy's back. And one, the word SPITE, did not fade from his skin for over four hours.

The physics professor from Washington, having seen the hospital bedstand levitate rapidly upward from the floor to the ceiling, later remarked that "there is much we have yet to discover concerning the nature of electromagnetism," an observation impervious to challenge. But when we are confronted with the paranormal, is it valid, in this age of scientific awareness, to resort at the

---

[18]In both the novel and the film the levitation of the bedstand would translate into the levitation of the bed itself. Other phenomena taken from the actual case would be: the rappings; lesser manifestations of telekinesis, such as the drawer popping out and objects flying around the room; the "brandings" (the words on the victim's flesh, as just described); the transformation of the voice; new abilities (such as perfect pitch) never before manifested by the subject; paranormal strength; the bellowings; and a few lesser and more ambiguous phenomena, such as the accurate "blindfolded" spitting. The transformation of Regan's face, the furring and lengthening of the tongue, did not come from the actual case, but were taken from countless other cases, and in fact are no less marked than occurs in certain types of hysterical disorders. The icy cold, the shaking of the room, and the cracked ceiling did not occur in *any* of the cases I studied. Neither, of course, did the turning of the head, at least to the extent depicted in the film. As this scene was first shot, Regan's head turned 360 degrees! When I pointed out to Billy Friedkin that in such an eventuality the head would likely fall off and that "supernatural" was not synonymous with "impossible," the head turn was modified in the editing room. I still believed it to be excessive and unreal, but audiences loved it, proving me an idiot once again. Moreover, there is *some* factual basis for it. In the state of possession, and among hysterics, you will find one medical case after another in which the subject—no acrobat—was nonetheless able to perform such incredible physical contortions as bending over backward and touching his heels with his head. What distinguishes possession—and pseudopossession—from hysteria in this context is that the possessed subject, when performing these actions, seems to be doing so involuntarily, for throughout he shrieks in pain.

last to "unknown forces"? We do not know all of the positive efficiencies of natural forces; however, we do know some *negative* limitations. In the words of the Jesuit Joseph Tonquedec, "By combining oxygen and hydrogen you will *never* get chlorine; by sowing wheat you will never get roses . . . If anyone, sowing wheat, should believe that 'perhaps' he might get roses, he must be in an abnormal state of mind."[19]

I wrote the novel. It was finished by the summer of 1970.[20] As soon as I had made several Xerox copies (for I never make carbons, which must mean I have a death wish), I took one to my neighbor, Shirley MacLaine. I had always felt inadequate and insecure in my handling of female characterizations, a bulletin certain not to stun like oxen any of the women in my life. And so when starting the novel, I had looked about for a model for Chris MacNeil, one who lived in a milieu that I knew very well and who also had a mental set and personality that would make the story work: a flipness of manner (masking vulnerability) and an earthiness of tongue that would help to keep the situation rooted in reality; whose "I'm from Missouri" attitude would serve initially as the reader's point of view. This device would later provide what Anthony Burgess has called the "nice irony" of *The Exorcist:* an atheist heroine who comes to believe that her daughter is possessed, in opposition to a Jesuit hero who does not. Though Shirley leans more to agnostic than atheist, she'd have been perfect as the model for Chris. And now I was bringing her the novel because I hadn't seen her in a very long time and because I'd had a little bit[21] too much wine and hoped to give her a happy surprise with Chris

---

[19]*Les Maladies nerveuses ou mentales et les manifestations diaboliques,* p. 230; also *Satan,* op. cit.

[20]Had it not been for a friend, William Bloom, it might not have been finished until the following year; for on an evening in June, when I allowed him to read what I had written thus far—which was up to the point of Merrin's death—my plan was for Karras to continue the exorcism for one or two more months. Bloom said the reader would kill me if I did that; the action was crying out to be at an end. This conversation convinced me to have Karras perform the actual exorcism in less than a minute of time.

[21]Staggering quantities.

MacNeil. I lasted twenty minutes. I think my line about "saving her career" must have done it, though it could have been my effort to show her some card tricks that I told her I had learned from Roy Rogers's horse. She steered me gently to my car after giving me a bag full of rocky road candy, which has always had an instantly sobering effect upon me, a reflex triggered by my need to be alert to defend the rocky road from aggressors, namely anyone at all who might ask me to share it. The candy was decidedly better than the dog food I'd once spied on a daintily wrapped dish in her refrigerator just before she conned me into taking several bites of it, calling it "White-fang Pâté Parisien"; but I felt a bit glum at her fluffing off the novel as something she would read when she had "a little time." Four days later, though, she called me to tell me she had read it. She seemed touched by the characterization of Chris. There were even lines of dialogue scattered through the novel that she recognized as having said many years ago. How did I come to remember them? she asked me.

She asked me to drop by. I did; and at her home she spoke more about my memory. And then said that she would like to do the book as a film. Of course when I had brought her the book I had imagined that it might be a film; and certainly Shirley would play Chris Mac-Neil. But I had no idea how such a film could be made; and now Shirley, who had entered into a partnership for the making of feature films wih Sir Lew Grade, an English producer, was talking of canceling the first of the films in which she was set to star, and going with *The Exorcist* in November.

It was all too sudden. I had labored nine months, often fourteen hours a day, every day, at a novel that had to be convincing to work. To achieve this texture of reality, I had resorted to techniques such as setting up a situation (Chris's party) where the reader would assume that Chris and Karras would finally meet, that seemed designed in fact, just in *order* that they meet, and then after this buildup *not* having them meet; to having Chris called "Mrs. MacNeil" by some characters and "Miss MacNeil" by others; and even to writing in varying styles, each matched to the major character being dealt with.[22] So now I was tired and, as I said, unsure that a script could be done at all, at least by me. There were so many problems involved in adapting the novel to the screen. First, the internalizing by Karras. And how could the paranormal happenings be shown? How could Regan's demonic transformations be managed? How could the complex events of the novel be accomplished in a film less than eight hours long? Finally, how could I write such a script by September in order to shoot it in November?

I thought it was impossible. And immediately agreed to do it. My creditors were restless.

But the wearier part of me set conditions. First, we had to make a satisfactory deal; and second, I wanted to produce the film. Have you any idea why I insisted on the latter, or what can happen to a screenplay when it leaves the writer's hands? Film is an industry[23] in which writers are either broken or wind up senselessly murdering strangers in the streets. For example, Ivan Tors, the creator of the *Flipper* series, had, in addition to the dolphin, a monkey and a pelican in subordinate roles in his "pilot" (establishing) script. The head of NBC television called Tors to his office and assured him that the project was "fantastic." In fact, it was going on the air that fall with a guaranteed run of thirty-nine weeks. Tors was elated but—"There's just one little change that I'd like you to make," the head of the network went on to tell him. "Get rid of the dolphin and build up the part of the pelican." And when *The Wizard of Oz* was first screened for studio heads,

---

[22]Merrin, complex and poetic and filled with concrete images of nature. Chris, simple, and direct and ordinary as a supermarket shopping cart. Karras, elegiac and haunted by images resonating pain in the minor particular. The styles blended with the appearance of Kinderman.

[23]I use the word advisedly and in a sense that could be sobering to some. For a film is made with stockholders' money. Its purpose is profit. When an artist isn't using someone else's money, he is free to create his art for art's sake. But when his creation is financed by a studio, which borrows the money from a bank, the loan must be repaid; otherwise the value of the stock goes down and some pensioner may lose her life's savings. Simple decency therefore dictates that the artist not make a silent film in which the actors all meditate for seventeen hours.

MGM's Louis B. Mayer recommended that the Kansas sequence, in which "Over the Rainbow" is sung, be cut from the picture because it was "boring," an act which was followed by Paramount's head of production, Marty Rackin. At the cocktail party celebrating the showing of the "rough cut" of *Breakfast at Tiffany's,* Rackin remarked to Blake Edwards, the film's director: "Well, I can tell you one thing, Blake: the song has got to go." The song in question being "Moon River." ("Are you running with me, Jesus?")

Fortunately, none of this advice was followed. But too often the producer or the director or the actor or his wife will commit more obscenities of change upon a script than Launce's dog wrought against the gentlewoman's farthingale in *Two Gentleman of Verona.* Oh, there are times when it can work in reverse: when direction and editing and performance can transform a weak script into something wonderful and essentially other than it was. But more often, and especially in the area of comedy, substantial tampering with the script inevitably leads to its destruction. I once wrote a caper script, for example, in which the first two acts built to an effort by talented rogues to rob "the unrobbable bank of the West," a bank constructed by bank robbers specifically for storing their stolen loot, since in no other bank would it be secure. For two whole acts we are showing the bank's impregnable defenses. We come to like the rogues, and hope they will succeed, since if they don't they will die. For two whole acts we watch them make elaborate preparations, while being kept in the dark about the specifics of their plan. How will they do it, the audience wonders. And that was what the film was supposed to be about. But the director,[24] known in the business as a genius with comedy, suggested "just one little change" in the script: namely, that the leader of the rogues do a "High Hopes" type of song with a bunch of kids, complete with choreography. Never mind that it paralyzed the momentum of the plot and utterly destroyed the pace; far worse, it put us on *overtime.* And the

---

[24]Whom I do not name, for he has suffered enough, his crime having served as his punishment as well.

film would run long. To solve this problem, the director suggested[25] that we cut out the entire robbery sequence. The robbery! "We just see them coming up on the bank and then dissolve to them loading the gold on the cart," he explained. The advice wasn't followed, thanks to Malcolm Stuart, the producer. But the role that was written to be played by Rex Harrison ended up being played by Zero Mostel, and the role intended for Melina Mercouri was played instead by the ever-iridescent Kim Novak.

I was determined that this wasn't going to happen with the script of *The Exorcist*. Thus, my insistence on producing it. But we never came to terms. In spite of Shirley's great enthusiasm, Lew Grade's offer for rights to the film was very low. In my straitened circumstances I probably would have accepted it except that in that case the producer would not be me but Robert Fryer, then most recently the producer of *Myra Breckenridge*. Shirley was upset that I'd rejected this offer, and instead took the lead in a rival work, *The Possession of Joel Delaney*. That decision ended, if for no other reason,[26] any chance of her playing Chris MacNeil. Chris still haunts her, however.[27] Since *The Exorcist* was published, she has several times told me of her conviction that the very blurred photo representing Regan MacNeil that appears on the jacket of the book is in fact a photograph of her daughter which I'd "lifted" surreptitiously from her house. "Have you ever seen 'baba au rhum in a blender' written in lipstick on your bathroom mirror?" I asked her the last time she made the accusation. I explained that whenever I burglarize movie stars' homes to steal photographs of their children, I write those words in lipstick on a mirror. "It's my mark," I told Shirley. In reality the jacket art and

---

[25]On three separate occasions in my presence, which eliminates the possibility that he wasn't really serious.

[26]Billy Friedkin preferred Ellen Burstyn for the role of Chris. Ellen got the part and proved to be magnificent.

[27]As the novel in a way haunts Sachi, her daughter; for various columnists, hearing that Shirley was the model for Chris, have published irresponsible innuendoes that Sachi was "possessed" at the time, and that the novel is her story, an absurdity cruelly put to use by Sachi's schoolmates. I repeat, there is not a shred of truth in the report.

photo were created by Harper & Row. When first I saw the photo, in fact, I thought that it strongly resembled *my* daughter.

Around the time the Lew Grade negotiation ended, Bantam put the novel out to bid for publication by a hard-cover house. Of the four good firms to whom it was submitted, two became active, if not vigorous, bidders, with Harper & Row at last bravely doubling the previous last bid that had been made by Random House. A third house receiving a submission, Knopf, had Thomas Tryon's *The Other* upcoming on its schedule; and a four-person editorial staff at McCall Publishing (now defunct) unanimously rejected the novel altogether, which may prove some consolation to frustrated writers.

I went to New York and heard Harper's suggestions for revisions of my first draft. I was asked to drop the prologue, which I considered but didn't do; and to make the ending less obvious, which I did. In my original version of the epilogue, both Chris and the reader realized fully what Karras has done: that he has lured the demon out of Regan's body into his, and after doing so is aware that the demon, when in total control of his body, will murder Regan and anyone else in the household and then leave him, once more in control of his body, to face the horror he has wrought. Karras, apprehending this, makes a superhuman effort to regain full control of his body and battles the demon's will just long enough to hurl himself out the window in a final, saving act of love. But the ending, as I'd written it, flirted with bathos, and perhaps even married it. You may judge for yourself. Here is the relevant section of the original epilogue:

> Chris went upstairs to Regan's bedroom. She looked in from the doorway and saw her standing at the window, staring out. Her hands were clasped lightly behind her back. Chris paused. She felt a twinge of worry. Slowly she moved forward to the window. There she stopped. She examined the child's face. Regan was lightly frowning as at sudden remembrance of forgotten concern. She looked up at her mother. "What happened to the man?"
>
> "The man?"

Regan nodded. "The one who jumped out of the window. Ya know? The man in the funny black dress."

Wide-eyed, Chris sagged to one knee. She took hold of her daughter's hands and held them firmly. "You saw a man jump?"

Regan nodded solemnly. "Is he all right?"

Chris held her breath. "Honey, tell me." She paused, controlling her voice. "Can you remember— can you remember what happened?"

"Well, he jumped."

"Honey, why? Do you know?"

Regan frowned.

"Do you remember why he jumped?"

"Well, it's kind of . . . well, funny." Regan looked off. "I mean, I think I might have dreamed it."

Regan shrugged. "Well, it sort of was crazy."

"Just tell me, honey! Tell me whatever you remember!"

"Well, the man . . . well, he was saying . . . I mean, talking to some animal or something . . ."

"An animal?"

"Well, something . . ." Regan bit her lip, her brow furrowed. "He was telling it to go, like—to get out. You know? And then he said . . ." She paused, as if groping for the memory. "He said—if it came out it could go inside *him*. And then—well, it seemed like it *did* go inside him. This animal or something. It went in him." She looked at her mother. "I think that part I *must've* been dreaming. Don't you think?"

Chris stared numbly. "Honey, tell me what else!"

"Well, this man started acting real crazy an' stuff. Like he was fighting with someone."

"Fighting?"

"Uh-huh. But there was nobody there, though. Just him. An' he was saying . . ." She squinted at the forming recollection. She turned to her mother. "I remember. He was saying that he wouldn't let it hurt you."

"Let it hurt me?"

"Well, hit you, sort of. And me. I mean, all of us. He said he wasn't going to let it hurt us. And that's when he jumped." Regan pointed to the window. "I mean, he ripped off the coverings, first. *Then* he jumped." Regan frowned. "Mother, why are you crying?"

"Because I'm happy that you're well again, baby. I'm just crying 'cause I'm—happy—that you're well."

"Is the man all right, Mom?"

Chris looked down: "Yes, honey. The man is— all right. He's resting."

"In the hospital?"

Chris nodded.

"Can we go and see him, Mom?"

Chris lifted her face. The tears ran freely. "Yes, honey," she smiled. She clasped Regan's hands. "Someday . . ."

And so I rewrote it. The basic elements remained the same but I made the exposition more oblique.[28]

While still in New York and in the midst of revising the manuscript, I received a call from a William Tennant, representing Paul Monash, who had just produced *Butch Cassidy and the Sundance Kid.* Would I enter an exclusive negotiation with his client for an option on the book? Tennant asked. I would. For Monash offered to meet my terms. We made a deal whereby Monash would have six months to get a major studio to make the film. If he failed, all rights to the property reverted to me and I would keep the money he had advanced. If he succeeded, I would write the script and produce, with Monash acting as executive producer. And he did succeed. He made a deal with Warner's to make the film.

But soon we had some disagreements. Paul, a bright man and a writer himself, was in favor of changing the locale of the action from Washington, D.C., as it was in the novel; didn't like the "colorful" treatment of Kinderman; thought that Chris shouldn't be an actress; said we shouldn't use the prologue of the novel, which introduces Merrin in Iraq;[29] and wanted to eliminate

---

[28]In view of widespread misunderstandings of both the novel and the film, I now wonder if I made the correct decision. And I certainly do miss the implication of Chris accepting faith, indicated in her "Someday . . ."

[29]As an archaeologist working on a dig at the ruins of Nineveh; for Merrin was modeled on Pierre Teilhard de Chardin, even to his self-confessed frailties, which are taken from letters that Chardin wrote to his friend Madame Zonta; his love of matter; and his view of the relationship existing between matter and spirit, which he thought to be merely differing aspects of some third, more fundamental reality.

Merrin entirely. None of this pleased me. Then came further disagreements involving the studio. I don't remember what I did then; I must have blacked out. But according to a rumor abroad in some circles, I pilfered some documents (Shirley MacLaine just sat up and paid attention) relating to my deal that showed a lack of . . . well, shall we just call it due regard for fair business practice?[30] According to the rumor, which of course is preposterous, I picked a day to go to Warner's when I knew that Paul Monash would be at Universal. And it being the lunch hour, and Monash's temporary secretary busy chatting in an office opposite, it is said that I entered the reception area of Monash's office; and that the secretary then returned to ask me who I was; and that I told her, "William Faulkner," requested some coffee, the urn being visible in Monash's office, and then inquired if I might use the phone; and while using the phone—now being seated behind the reception desk and in view of the secretary, who'd gone back across the hall—I rummaged through drawers for a key, found it, went into Paul's office for another cup of coffee, lunged at a file drawer labeled "A to E," unlocked it, found some documents filed under "Exorcist" that I thought of unusual interest, tucked them in a copy of *Fortune* magazine, went out the office and two doors down to the Warner Brothers Xeroxing room, made copies of the documents, tucked them back inside the copy of *Fortune,* returned the originals to the file, locked it, sat down again at the desk, picked up the phone and dialed "time and temperature" while returning the key to where I'd found it; and then disappeared into the Burbank fog with a clutch of documents which seemed to prove conclusively that crimes against the author had indeed been committed and which, because they were in my possession, impelled the studio to buy Monash out and make me sole producer of the film. Monash did, in fact, bow out and I did in fact become sole producer. But the rumor about how it happened is, I repeat, on its face an absurdity. I do not know how "baba au rhum in a blender" ever came to be written on a studio mirror.

---

[30]More commonly known as "screwing the author."

I began the script. I compressed the first third of the book into only thirty-three pages. And then I further decided to eliminate the subplot relating to Elvira, the servant Karl's daughter. I hated to do that. The Elvira subplot not only added a dimension to Karl, but was intended to illustrate Merrin's belief that out of evil there finally always comes good; for Kinderman's relentless investigation of Dennings's murder results in Elvira, a heroin addict, at last being hospitalized and on the road to cure. But there simply wasn't time and the subplot had to go. So too did the novel's subtle hints that the killer and desecrator might be Karras. Though I did insinuate it, at first, in the sequence that begins in the Jesuit refectory at Georgetown and ends with Karras and a young Jesuit on a platform at the top of the steps from which Dennings was probably[31] pushed to his death. Karras says he always tries to make it to the platform around that time to watch the sunset. The Georgetown University clock booms the hour: 7:00 P.M. Dennings plunged to his death at 7:05. And Karras, who once blacked out at a time when a desecration was taking place, is surely a candidate for somnambulism produced by an "unconscious rebellion" against the Church; for not only is he filled with compulsions of guilt but he was refused in his request for a transfer to New York so that he might be close to his mother, who since that time has died alone.

Again, though, there wasn't time and most readers of the novel had failed to pick up on the suggestion anyway. And so finally I cut the scenes. Even so, I wound up with a first-draft script that ran to over two hundred pages. If shot, it would result in a four-hour film. But I decided, like Scarlett O'Hara, that I would "worry about that tomorrow."

It was June and by now the novel had been published. I could tell by the mail I was getting. Some of it was nice. Some was not. And some of it, letters from a number of readers seeking help because they thought themselves to be possessed, was very pathetic.[32]

---

[31] The likely assumption at that point in the story.

[32] Although one from a woman who complained she had an incubus

I heard from Jack Douglas, the humorist, who began his letter with the comment, "I sure wish Karras was still alive—I've got a couple of kids I'd like to have him take a look at." Another who wished that Karras had lived was my friend the exorcist. For in a letter which remarked on the authenticity of the book, he decried the impression that Karras had "lost." I was stunned. For he thought it was the *demon* who impelled Karras out through the window to his death. It was a view shared by many other readers, I learned, and accounted in part for my hate mail. With such an interpretation, my novel was received by the reader as a definite "downer" and construed by many to mean that evil finally triumphs. I really don't know what to do about "speed readers."[33] Shooting them certainly comes to mind. Although most of the hate letters that I received —and by far the most virulent—had nothing to do with sloppy reading, but came instead from those who presumed to lecture me obscenely about obscenity. Useless explaining to them that obscenity lies not in words but in every contravention of the Sermon on the Mount; useless citing favorable reviews in a number of religious periodicals, among them the *Civiltà Cattolica,* the Vatican literary journal.[34] One woman to whom I had pointed out the latter, in fact, wrote again to me, screeching: "If the pope likes your book that *proves* it's rotten." And that helped. Until then the attacks had hurt a bit. But at that point I realized that they had come, in the main, from people who hated themselves.

Not so with some others, perhaps mainly those who felt the book's shocking aspects were unnecessary. I did

---

(demon lover) seemed not only rational but touched with humor. She'd taken her complaint to a psychiatrist who told her "most women would give their right arm" to have her problem.

[83]One reviewer thought the action took place in Boston. Another complained that I knew nothing about construction, citing my introduction of a character in the prologue (Merrin) whom one "never sees again." And the *Saturday Review* somehow got the notion that Karras was Jewish.

[34]Religious press reactions to the film have been widespread and equally favorable. Among them is a review in the *Catholic News,* the official newspaper of the archdiocese of New York, which stated that "*The Exorcist* is a deeply spiritual film"; and the arch-conservative *Triumph* magazine, which published a rave review.

not share their belief. To begin with, the descriptions of demonic behavior are authentic (as are also the descriptions of rites at Black Mass; and everything else in the book that relates to satanism or possession). Furthermore, and purely apart from dramatic considerations—the need for something so unthinkably horrible (the crucifix masturbation scene) that it drives an atheist to a priest—if you're attempting to present possession as possible evidence of an unutterably evil and malevolent intelligence, then you must back it up both in concrete detail and in the viscera. You cannot say, "Regan then did something awful"; for if demons exist, that is not the way to argue it; and not the way to make us abhor what is evil. Oddly—and significantly, I think—the only blast at the novel, in print or in the mail, from any formal religious source, emanated from a Jesuit named Raymond Schroth who assailed me in *Commonweal,* basing his attack not on "obscenity" but on his feeling that *The Exorcist* fostered belief in Satan, thus prompting a return to "the superstitions of the Middle Ages." He suggested I ought to be writing about social action. Perhaps he was right.[35]

I myself, in considering the question of Satan's existence, reflect upon the fact that every primitive culture has had a myth about an evil being or "magician" who comes to earth and spoils the work of the Creator; who introduces hatred, disease, and death. Then I think of the soldier who deliberately throws himself atop a freshly hurled enemy grenade in order to shield his comrades from the blast. Not his children;

---

[35]Though not about everything; for in the article in *Commonweal,* he asserted that "Pere de Tonquedec, the old Parisian Jesuit, one of the most renowned exorcists of recent times, reportedly told his fellow Jesuits that he had never encountered an authentic case of diabolic possession." But another Jesuit who read Schroth's article wrote to me stating: "In 1961 I stayed for a few days at the Jesuit residence on the rue de Grenelle in Paris. After dinner I was sitting next to Father de Tonquedec in the recreation room. In the course of the conversation, I asked whether he had ever been involved in a real case of possession. I kept a diary during my trip with no thought that what I recorded would ever be of any significance. I just checked it and I find this entry under date of October 23, 1961: 'Father de Tonquedec told me that he certainly had encountered one real case of diabolical possession, and possibly two others.'"

not his sweetheart; not his mother: fellow soldiers. And I cannot help feeling, when I consider these things, that the world holds far more monstrous evil than can be accounted for solely by man, who is essentially good. I have not reasoned to this. I *feel* it.

But is Satan a single personal intelligence? Or Legion, a horde of evil entities? Or even, as has been conjectured, the stuff of the universe: matter itself, Lucifer working out his salvation through the process of physical evolution that ends in Teilhard de Chardin's "omega point." I surely do not know, nor can I even make a prudent judgment. Whatever my beliefs concerning Satan's existence, however, we have no record of reliable data that would link him to possession. I know that will surprise many readers and reviewers. But historically, the "demons" involved in possession and pseudopossession only rarely identify themselves as Satan. And surely the chief of the fallen angels has far worse things that he could be doing. Even in terms of my novel, I have never known the demon's identity. I strongly doubt that he[36] is Satan; and he is certainly none of the spirits of the dead whose identity he sometimes assumes. If I had to guess, I would say he is Pazuzu, the Assyrian demon of the southwest wind. But I'm really not sure.[37] I know only that he's real and powerful and evil and apparently one of many— and aligned with whatever is opposed to love.

Now I put away the mail. It was time to select the film's director. My contract with Warner's called for a form of mutual approval whereby, before the signing of my contract, we were to shape a list of directors agreeable to both. The list we had agreed upon finally included Arthur Penn, Stanley Kubrick, and Mike Nichols.

I had also suggested Billy Friedkin. I had met him years before. I'd been working with Blake Edwards on the script of a Peter Gunn feature called *Gunn*. Billy

---

[36] Perhaps the one instance of dreaded male chauvinism not bound to irritate woman's liberationists.

[37] The novel is ultimately what Billy Friedkin calls a "realistic look at inexplicable events." And only in fantasy can the author be omniscient. We can get inside the heads of humans; not of demons.

was up for the job of directing it; in first position in fact. Billy had never directed a full-length feature film. But all he had to do to change that fact was to read the script and then tell us he liked it.

He read the script and met with Blake and me for lunch at the Paramount commissary. Straight-on and very articulate, he was only twenty-six and with his horn-rimmed glasses looked like *Fiddler on the Roof*'s Tevye as a boy. But he wasn't about to ask God for any favors and proceeded to tangle with Blake on a sequence in the script that he thought should be cut, a sequence I had written. It was a very small point and he might have let it slide. But he didn't. And blew the assignment, of course. But I never forgot him. My previous experience with most directors had been that they would tell you your script was sensational, their only reason for taking low money, because frankly, they would confide, they needed a hit; and then when they'd been hired and were safely under contract, they would give your script to the FBI chief, instructing him, "This should never see the light of day." Friedkin, in that context, was a wonder.

Years later, I saw his *The Night They Raided Minsky's*. I thought it had movement and grace and sensitivity. It wasn't commercially successful but I liked it very much. I had a pet script in my trunk at that time. It was based on the novel I had written before *The Exorcist, Twinkle, Twinkle, "Killer" Kane,* my first exploration of the mystery-of-goodness theme, although, despite the lurid jacket copy on the Curtis paperback edition, it had nothing at all to do with the occult.[38] It was set in a military rehabilitation center and centered on a war of nerves between the psychiatrist in command of the center and a number of inmates led by

---

[38]Let book people never cast stones at Hollywood. Compare the quotes that were used on the *first* Curtis edition of *Twinkle, Twinkle, "Killer" Kane*—"Nobody can write funnier lines than Blatty" (Martin Levin, *New York Times*) and "Wild . . . with the verbal virtuosity of S. J. Perelman" (Richard Armour, *Los Angeles Times*)—with their jacket copy and front matter on the edition published following *The Exorcist:* "The nerve-twitching chiller from the author of *The Exorcist*" and "INVITATION TO EVIL! A grotesque old mansion that once used to belong to a silent horror movie star, and now was home to shrieking terror . . ."

an astronaut who refuses to go to the moon on the grounds that it might be bad for his skin. Just prior to being committed, he is observed, while dining in the officers' mess, as he picks up a plastic catsup squeeze bottle, squeezes a thin red line across his throat, and then staggers over to a table where the head of the Space Administration is dining, falls across it in front of him and gurgles, "Don't—order—the swordfish." Another of the inmates, to round it out for you, is adapting the plays of Shakespeare for performance by a cast of dogs and "cannot abide a Dalmatian that lisps." ("Shrieking terror"!) It was what you might call bizarre material. I had hoped to direct it myself. But after seeing *Minsky's* I thought that the script would be safe with Friedkin. I sent it along to him. He liked it. But we couldn't find a studio that liked it. We'd put it away. Now, with *The Exorcist* film in preparation, his name leaped to mind and I submitted it to Warner's for inclusion in the list. They turned it down. But then one by one the directors on the list were penciled out. Some had commitments that would keep them unavailable for almost a year. Arthur Penn was teaching at Yale. Stanley Kubrick could produce for himself, thank you kindly. And Nichols said he didn't want to hazard a film whose success might depend upon a child's performance.

Then there were none. So I suggested Friedkin again. Again they said no. And they asked if instead I'd be willing to consider another director whom I personally liked and who was talented and sensitive but whose work I nonetheless loathed. He'd been critically acclaimed for a film that consisted in the main of interminable reaction shots in which the characters stared at each other piercingly, thinking presumably staggering thoughts. Let us say that the name of that film was *Hypnosis* and the name of the director, Edmund de Vere. If he were to wind up directing *The Exorcist,* with a script of over two hundred pages, its running time couldn't be under three weeks. However, I agreed—to be fair[39]—to screen a rough cut (generally, the first edited version, but minus music and finished sound, and in some cases optical effects) of de Vere's most recent

---

[39]I lie. It was to give the *appearance* of being fair.

work which, I was assured, would "change my mind"; it was "absolute dynamite," "so sensitive," I was told.

I screened it alone at the studio while a studio executive sat awaiting my reaction. And yes, it was sensitive. But so were Leopold and Loeb. And I felt that I was watching another murder, the victim in this case being pace. Entire novenas could be said during pauses in the dialogue.[40] This was all very well at Cannes, I supposed, but would surely be deadly for *The Exorcist*. Thinking the locale of the novel was Boston was but one indication of how readers often flew through the pages of the novel to gulp down further developments of plot. Slow pacing on screen would result in frustration and diminishing tension. Furthermore, de Vere always tried for Art.

And now I suppose I will be branded a philistine, and I also suppose that I'm sorry; but I think that art in motion pictures is something one never can *consciously* strive for, as the very appearance of striving defeats it. Let the artist just attend (isn't this insufferable?) to the rudiments of his craft, and if he is a genius the result will be art in spite of himself.[41] He will not give us *Hypnosis*.

Midway through the screening I thanked the projectionist and left. I returned to the executive's office. On seeing me back an hour early he did a little leap about an inch off his chair, and I imagined his hair standing straight up on end just like Little Orphan Annie about to say, "Yike!" when the news isn't really all that great.

He asked that I return to the screening room. The ending, he insisted, "was the picture." And how could I judge after seeing only half of it? There was also the need to forestall "bad word of mouth," which would start with the projectionist's report to his friends that "Blatty walked out on it halfway through, and he isn't

---

[40]Directors who come up from the ranks of cameramen sometimes subordinate other considerations in a scene to what will make the best-composed "picture." De Vere had been an actor (and though never a star, was truly outstanding), and thus no doubt tended to indulge his casts.

[41]In researching my master's thesis on *T. S. Eliot's Shakespearean Criticisms* I discovered in Eliot a strong vein of jealousy of Shakespeare, because, unlike Eliot, Shakespeare was not "a conscious artist."

even *bright*"; and which is how the public comes not to queue around the block on opening night for a film that hasn't been reviewed yet.

The executive had his secretary call the projectionist. She told him I'd had a headache but was feeling much better now and would be back to see the rest of the film. I returned to the screening room. And liked the second half of the film only very little more than I had liked the first. I didn't return to the executive's office. Depressed, I had dinner and then went to a movie. I went for diversion, not to study. But the film was Friedkin's *The French Connection*. And I went berserk. The pace! the excitement! the look of documentary realism! These were what *The Exorcist* desperately needed.

I called the head of the studio. And soon the executives at Warner Brothers were screening *The French Connection*.

Billy Friedkin was hired. I gave him my first-draft screenplay, which follows.

The First Draft
Screenplay of
The Exorcist

FADE IN:

EXTERIOR SERIES OF VERY EARLY MORNING, CLOUDY-DAY MOOD SHOTS OF GEORGETOWN UNIVERSITY CAMPUS AND ENVIRONS IN WASHINGTON, D.C.:

1. CAMPUS VIEW OF THE POTOMAC RIVER, FEATURING KEY BRIDGE AND JEFFERSON MEMORIAL IN FAR BACKGROUND.

2. THIRTY-SIXTH STREET, SHOOTING PAST HOLY TRINITY CATHOLIC CHURCH AT A BROODING BRICK HOUSE WHERE THIRTY-SIXTH DEAD-ENDS INTO PROSPECT STREET.

3. ANGLE FEATURING THE SAME HOUSE, BUT WITH CAMERA SHOOTING DOWN PROSPECT STREET TO INCLUDE THE JESUIT RESIDENCE HALL DIAGONAL TO THE HOUSE.

4. UP ANGLE (WITH CAMERA POSITIONED ON M STREET BELOW) TYING IN HOUSE TO A LONG AND PRECIPITOUS FLIGHT OF OLD STONE STEPS IMMEDIATELY ADJACENT TO IT.

5. SHARP DOWN ANGLE AT STEPS.

6. UNIVERSITY BELL TOWER.

7. COPLEY RESIDENCE HALL.

8. ANGLES AT MOTION-PICTURE DRESSING-ROOM TRAILERS AND EQUIPMENT STRUNG OUT ON DRIVEWAY BESIDE MAIN ADMINISTRATION

BUILDING. EXTRAS. THE CREW. SPEC-
TATORS. AMONG THE LATTER, A
JESUIT PRIEST (DAMIEN KARRAS). IN
HIS FORTIES. POWERFULLY BUILT.
HIS FACE IS SAD AND CHIPPED LIKE
A MELANCHOLY BOXER'S, AND SEEMS
TO HARBOR SECRET PAIN. BESIDE
KARRAS STANDS A FEY, DIMINUTIVE
YOUNGER PRIEST (FATHER JOE DYER)
WEARING STEEL-RIMMED SPECTACLES
AND DEADPAN EXPRESSION.

At the outset of this series of shots, we hear the voices
of a man with a British accent (Burke Dennings) and
a woman (Chris MacNeil) engaged in spirited argument. Up through shot #5, the voices are indistinct, as
if coming from afar, but from shot #6 on, they are
closer and we clearly hear, though in lowered and
guarded tones:

> CHRIS (*off scene*)
>
> . . . *not* being difficult. The line doesn't make
> any (sense)—

> BURKE (*off scene*)
> (*overlapping "sense"*)
>
> Darling, you're the leader of the rebels, and you
> (have)—

> CHRIS (*off scene*)
> (*overlapping*)
>
> Burke, I can *read*. She yells "Let's tear it
> down," but I (don't)—

> BURKE (*off scene*)
> (*overlapping, giggling*)
>
> My baby, you want to tear it down because it's
> *there!* You—

> CHRIS (*off scene*)
> (*overlapping*)
>
> Because it's there in the *script*?

> BURKE (*off scene*)
> (*giggling harder*)
>
> Because it's there on the *grounds*!

CHRIS (*off scene*)

Yeah, well, this kind of character just wouldn't do that.

BURKE (*off scene*)

She would.

CHRIS (*off scene*)

No, she wouldn't and I think we should change it.

The scene is bucolic, the camera now trained on the campus athletic field and astronomical observatory through the branches of a tree as we hear off scene:

BURKE (*off scene*)

Shall we summon the writer? I believe he's in Paris.

CHRIS (*off scene*)

Oh, yeah? What's he doin' there? Hiding?

BURKE (*off scene*)

Fucking.

We hear a splutter, then laughter from Chris as we go to:

EXTERIOR ADMINISTRATION BUILDING— AREA OF GEORGETOWN UNIVERSITY CAM- PUS—FULL HIGH DOWN SHOT

We now see clearly that a motion-picture company is filming on campus and that Chris and Burke are alone except for a young assistant director (Chuck) in the center of the silently observing cordon of cast, crew, and a few spectators. Chris has collapsed with laughter against Burke. She is attractive and gaminlike, and looks to be in her middle thirties. She is costumed in jeans and a sweatshirt. Burke, the director, is in his fifties, is very slight of frame, and has an elfin quality accented by the large red pimple on the end of his malmsey nose. He seems perpetually flushed with gin, even at this hour of the morning, and always on the verge of either a giggle or a guffaw, as if all is a game and actors and actresses merely children who must be humored. He is nervously nibbling on a thin strip of

47

paper. Chuck has a rolled-up script in his hands and stands to the side, arms folded, head bent, as he waits.

THREE-SHOT—CHRIS, BURKE, CHUCK

CHRIS (*laughing*)
Oh, Burke, you're impossible, dammit!

BURKE (*proudly*)
Yes.

Then Chris swiftly turns to check something off scene.

CHRIS'S POINT OF VIEW—KARRAS AND DYER

Karras is nodding, giving Chris a slight but warm smile as if to reassure her that he has not been offended. The tower clock is booming out the hour and Dyer has been looking at Karras with concern.

DYER
Damien?

Karras turns to him.

DYER
Your train.

Karras checks his wristwatch, the grave look returning to his face, but now deeper; and after gripping Dyer's wrist with a nod of farewell, he moves away somberly, the camera pivoting to cover him.

AT CHRIS—BURKE—CHUCK

Chris watches Karras leave, a look of pleasant surmise and curiosity on her face as:

BURKE
Now then, shall we get on with it?

CHRIS (*in a light fog*)
Hm?
(*disengaging*)
Oh, yeah. Yeah, let's do it.

BURKE (*turning to Chuck*)
Thank heavens.

CHRIS

No, *wait.*

BURKE

Oh, good Christ!

CHRIS

But—

BURKE

What is it?

CHRIS (*meekly*)
Can I go to the bathroom?

He swats her behind, sending her off.

BURKE

Oh, *go.*
(*at Chuck*)
Call a ten-minute break.

CHUCK (*to company*)
Take ten.

CHRIS (*off scene*)
Fifteen!

BURKE (*at Chuck*)
Make it twenty and we'll have us a gin.

TRACKING SHOT

Chris approaching trailer dressing room. We hear:

CHUCK (*off scene*)
(*over bullhorn*)
Make it twenty!

As Chris passes a grip:

GRIP

How ya feelin', Chris?

CHRIS

Fine, Eddie. You?

In the meantime the second assistant director has fallen in beside Chris. He carries a clipboard from which he has detached a shooting schedule. As he hands it to her:

SECOND ASSISTANT

Well, you get the morning off tomorrow, kid.
You're not in any of the scenes.

CHRIS

Shit, movies *are* better than ever. Hey, what's all
this—?

She has reached the trailer and now breaks off (the
second assistant moving away, oblivious), as she spots
something off scene. A pixieish expression comes over
her, and with a mock-threatening "Ahhhhh . . ." sound
deep in her throat, she crooks out her arms, as if
intent on capturing someone. She is looking toward:

POINT-OF-VIEW SHOT—SHARON AND REGAN

Regan is a pretty eleven-year-old girl. Freckles. Hair
in ponytails. Braces and a missing front tooth. Sharon
Spencer is a blonde in her late twenties to early thirties.
Her manner and looks are fresh and direct. Regan,
holding her hand, has been skipping along, but now she
stops, grinning slyly as she sees that her mother has
spotted her.

FULLER ANGLE—THE TRAILER

In a scene for which the dialogue, if any, should be
spontaneously generated by the actors, Chris and Regan
play a game that seems a combination of touch-tag and
hide-and-go-seek, Chris the pursuer and Regan the pur-
sued. When at last Chris captures Regan she gets her
down on the lawn and tickles her. When it is over they
both sit back, panting, as:

CHRIS

So whadjya do today, Stinkpot?

REGAN

Oh, stuff.

CHRIS

So, what *kind* of stuff?

REGAN (*thoughtful; index finger to mouth*)
Well . . .

50

CHRIS (*imitating her voice and gesture*)
Well . . .

REGAN
Well, I studied, of course.

CHRIS
Of course.

REGAN
An' I painted.

CHRIS
Whadjya paint?

REGAN
Oh, well, flowers. Ya know, daisies? Only pink.
An' then— Oh, yeah! This horse!
(*excited, eyes widening*)
This man had a *horse,* ya know, down by the
river? We were walking, see, mom, and then
along came this *horse!* He was *beautiful!* Oh,
mom, ya should've *seen* him, and the man let
me *sit* on him! *Really!* I mean, practically a
minute!

Chris twinkles up at Sharon (off scene).

CHRIS
The big spender?

ANOTHER ANGLE AT SHARON

SHARON (*smiling mischievously*)
Um-hmm.

REGAN (*off scene*)
It was a *gray* horse!

ANOTHER ANGLE AT CHRIS AND REGAN

Regan is now kneeling and has her arms around her
mother's neck.

REGAN
Mother, can't we get a horse? I mean, could we?

CHRIS
We'll see, baby.

51

REGAN

When can I get one?

CHRIS

Lemme up, hon, I gotta go tinkle.

REGAN (*rising*)

Me, too.
(*starting to run off scene toward the trailer
steps*)
And me *first!*

CHRIS (*rising and chasing after*)

No, *me!*
(*and from off scene*)
I'm your *mother!*

REGAN (*off scene*)

No, *me!*

CHRIS (*off scene*)

I'm a *star,* you creepy kid!

ANGLE AT BURKE

He is sitting in a camp chair and holds a glass into
which Chuck pours from a bottle of gin. Behind them,
activity, as:

BURKE

Yes, that's fine, love. Now, then, let's have a
munch.

Burke sips at his drink, then puts it aside as Chuck
hauls out a script from his back pocket, opens it and
offers it to Burke as an altar boy offers the missal to a
priest at solemn mass. The edge of the script looks
gnawed, with narrow strips ripped off. During this, a
still photographer passes behind Burke, momentarily
touching a hand to his shoulder with:

STILL PHOTOGRAPHER

How's it goin'?

BURKE

Oh, twiddles and twaddles.

Burke has begun to surgically shave off a narrow section from the edge of a page of the script. His fingers shake alcoholically. During this:

> BURKE (*scanning the page as he tears*)
> My God, you know she's absolutely right about this scene. It's really *mad;* it's simply absolutely *hideous;* just *vomit.*

> CHUCK (*warily squinting up at the sky*)
> More clouds.

INSERT—CLOSE AT BURKE'S SHAKING FINGERS TEARING PAPER

> BURKE (*off scene*)
> Please hold still, love.

> ASSISTANT DIRECTOR
> We're losing the light.

BACK TO SCENE

> BURKE
> Yes, I know. They're going out all across the fucking world.

He puts the end of the strip into his mouth and begins to chew it, then worriedly squints up at the sky.

POINT OF VIEW—AT SKY

A rolling mass of windswept black clouds. Distant rumble of thunder; faint flash of lightning in the distance. During this, superimposed are the words:

> ". . . As Jesus stepped ashore, He was met by a man possessed by devils . . . Jesus asked him, 'What is your name?' "

QUICK CUT TO:

INTERIOR HOLY TRINITY CHURCH—FULL HIGH SHOT FROM ALTAR—NIGHT

Dim lighting. Shadows. A scrubwoman mops the floor, advancing slowly toward the rear of the church. As we come in, she briefly pauses to wipe sweat from her brow, the small action explaining why the doors of the church are seen to be wide open in the far background.

53

Outside, it is still. A late hour. We hear only the mopping as we superimpose:

> ". . . 'Legion,' he replied, 'for we are many . . .' "

CLOSE (AND FULL) AT THIRD STATION OF THE CROSS

We hear the mopping off scene as over the descriptive narrative on the plaque below the station ("Jesus Falls the First Time") we superimpose:

> *James Torello:* "Jackson was hung up on that meat hook. He was so heavy he bent it. He was on that thing three days before he croaked."

The camera shifts over to the next station and we superimpose onto the plaque:

> *Fiore Buccieri* (giggling): "Jackie, you shoulda seen the guy. Like an elephant he was, and when Jimmy hit him with that electric prod . . ."

The camera shifts to the next station and we superimpose onto the plaque:

> *Torello* (excitedly): "He was floppin' around on that hook, Jackie. We tossed water on him to give the prod a better charge, and he's screamin' . . ."

LOSE SUPERIMPOSURE AND QUICKLY SUPER:

> *Excerpt from an FBI wiretap of*
> *a Cosa Nostra telephone conversation*

And now the camera makes rapid cuts to the tenth (Christ stripped by executioners), eleventh (Christ nailed to the cross), and twelfth (Christ dies on the cross) stations as we superimpose on the plaques, in order:

> Dachau
>
> Auschwitz
>
> Buchenwald

On each, a jolting stab of the score. Then silence and

the mopping sound as the camera drifts down from the last station to the rear of church . . . pokes into the foyer . . . past the pamphlet rack . . . then holds on the holy-water font as abruptly the mopping sounds cease and we hear a gasp from the scrubwoman off scene. The camera now swishes to and holds on a statue of the Blessed Virgin. We hear the mop falling to the floor, the scrubwoman racing away down aisle toward the priests' residence. The statue of the Virgin has been desecrated: rouged, lipsticked, and painted harlotlike, effecting a dissolute appearance.

SCRUBWOMAN (*off scene*)
Father Toomey!

We now hear muffled and ominous rapping sounds that are irregular, yet rhythmically clustered, like alien code tapped out by a dead man. They grow louder (and seemingly closer) as the camera moves down the church front steps and out into:

EXTERIOR 36TH STREET—NIGHT

Deserted. The camera follows the rappings, moving closer to the house beside the steps at the corner of 36th and Prospect, where a single light is on in an upstairs bedroom. During this, superimpose:

"They said, 'What sign can You give us to see, so that we may believe You?' "

The rappings grow louder and swifter, and the camera rushes to the front door of the house as we:

QUICKLY CUT TO:

INTERIOR MACNEIL HOUSE—NIGHT

Heavily paneled colonial. We are in the entry hall, and the camera is still in motion, slowly climbing the staircase to the second-floor hall. The rappings are now much clearer and more immediate. Coming to the open door to the bedroom, the camera stops, looking in, as Chris MacNeil, in bed studying a script, abruptly peers over it, frowning at the rappings. She looks down to the script again; then irritably slams it down on her lap, flouncing out of bed. She exits into the hall, frowns, looking around for the source of the sound; locates it. The camera tracks with her as she moves toward the door to another bedroom. And now the rappings accelerate and come regularly, much louder, building to a crescendo as Chris throws open the door.

INTERIOR REGAN'S BEDROOM—AT DOOR—CHRIS—NIGHT

The rappings have abruptly ceased. Chris looks baffled.

POINT OF VIEW—THE ROOM—CAMERA SHIFTING

to follow Chris's scrutiny. It is a typical child's bedroom, with large stuffed animals, paintings, and sculptures executed by Regan placed all about, among them a green clay sculpture of a turtle on the window seat in front of the large bay window overlooking the steps outside the house. Regan is asleep in her bed, her blankets kicked off and askew. She is lightly perspiring. Chris moves to her bedside.

> CHRIS (*a whisper*)
> Baby bear? You awake?

No response. Heavy breathing, regular and deep.

> CHRIS (*louder tone; weary*)
> OK, Rags. Old mother's ass is draggin'. Say it: "April Fool."

Still no response. Chris considers, then abruptly notices goose pimples on her arms. She rubs at them, shivering as if at an icy coldness and frowning in puzzlement as she looks at:

REGAN

The blankets tossed off; perspiration on her brow.

AT CHRIS

She squints her eyes in consternation and vague apprehension; looks back down at her goose pimples. Now she hears a scraping sound from above, like tiny claws scratching at the edge of a galaxy. Arms folded

56

for warmth, while still trembling uncontrollably from the cold, she lifts her puzzled stare to the ceiling as we:

FREEZE THE FRAME AND REPRISE THE RAPPINGS

SUPERIMPOSE: FEMALE STAR'S CREDIT

INTERIOR NEW YORK SUBWAY STATION— NIGHT

Silence. Points of light stretch down the darkness of the tunnel like guides to hopelessness.

SUPERIMPOSE (IN GOTHIC):

". . . You do not believe although you have seen."

ANGLE AT PLATFORM—MAN

The station appears to be deserted. The man stands close to the edge of the near platform. Black coat, hat and trousers. Powerfully built. He carries a valise resembling a doctor's medical bag, and stands with his back to us, head down, as if in dejection. Near him, a vending machine on a pillar. We hear echo chamber voices, remembered whispers of conversations.

OLD MAN'S VOICE (TOM)
A transfer to the New York province, Damien?

KARRAS'S VOICE
It's my mother. I never should have left her. She's alone, Tom. At least here I could look in now and—

WIDE-ANGLE DOWN SHOT AT MAN—PLAT-FORM

We hear the distant hum of an incoming train and a new voice (Uncle John) that is old and heavy with some accent, likely Mediterranean.

UNCLE JOHN'S VOICE
You know, if you wasn't be priest, you be famous psychiatrist now on Park Avenue,

Dimmy. Your mother, she be livin' in a pent-house instead of da—

MIRROR SHOT IN VENDING MACHINE

Reflected is an old derelict lying drunk in a pool of his own urine, his back against the station wall.

> DERELICT
>
> Hey, Faddah.

MEDIUM-LONG FRONT SHOT AT MAN

from opposite platform. The camera is pushing in closer as:

> KARRAS'S VOICE
>
> No, it's more than a transfer. I want reassign-ment. I can't go on counseling other priests.

> TOM'S VOICE
>
> But you're—

> KARRAS'S VOICE
>
> Tom, I'm unfit. I've got problems of my own.

> TOM'S VOICE
>
> Who doesn't?

> KARRAS'S VOICE
>
> Mine's bad.
> (*a long pause; then:*)
> I think I've lost my faith.

By now, the camera is full on the man.

> DERELICT (*off scene*)
>
> Couldjya help an old altar boy, Faddah? I'm Cat'lic.

The man looks up with dismay, disclosing the round Roman collar and the face of Damien Karras, now filled with an even deeper pain than when we met him. He shuts his eyes against this intrusion and clutches at his coat lapels, pulling them together to hide the collar. The train sound is up full now, and the camera reverse zooms so that the train rushes across the frame, block-ing our view of Karras and the derelict.

EXTERIOR HIGH SHOT—EAST TWENTY-FIRST STREET IN NEW YORK CITY—NIGHT

Between First and Second avenues. Karras walks despondently along the south side of the street, which is studded with decrepit tenement buildings. As he passes the open entry doors of the police station situated there, we hear from within the station:

> POLICEMAN'S VOICE
> Father Karras?

Karras wearily halts. A middle-aged police sergeant (Mike) appears in the doorway, leaning on one hand, a cigarette in the other. His manner is leisurely.

> MIKE
> Thought it was you. How ya been?

Karras does not want this encounter; rather, he endures it, patient and subdued.

> KARRAS
> Oh, not bad, Mike. And you?

Mike's attention is diverted to an approaching squad car as:

> MIKE
> Can't complain.

Karras nods, starting to move on, but must stop as:

> MIKE
> You gonna be here for a while?

> KARRAS (*shakes head; then:*)
> Just in to give a talk.

> MIKE
> To them nuns again?

> KARRAS
> No. To some other psychiatrists.

Mike comes down off the stoop to the street, his attention returning to—*and staying with*—the squad car, which contains two officers and a prisoner. The latter is handcuffed. On Mike's move:

MIKE

Wouldn't hurt 'em. Well, your mother will be sure glad ta see ya.

KARRAS

How's she been?

MIKE

Oh, OK. I mean, at least she ain't still in that hospital. Right, Father?

Karras again lowers his head and glumly nods.

MIKE

I see her leanin' out the winda most of the time, ya know, watchin' the traffic go by. I dunno how people do that, Father; livin' all alone. I couldn't do that. She don't seem to complain, though.

KARRAS (*sotto; head still down*)

No.

MIKE (*flipping away cigarette butt*)

She'll sure be glad ta see ya.

Karras glumly nods, then starts away.

KARRAS

Good night, Mike. Take it easy.

MIKE

You too, Father.

The prisoner, as he is hustled past to the station entry, spits into Mike's face, and Mike instantly, savagely cuffs his head with an almost automatic backhanded slap. As he does:

FRONT SHOT AT KARRAS

MIKE (*off scene*)

Keep the faith.

The priest halts with lowered head and shuts his eyes. Mike's words have pierced his soul. We hear a metallic rattling off scene and Karras raises his head.

POINT OF VIEW—AT RAT SCUTTLING AWAY

A garbage-can lid still quivers on the sidewalk.

AT KARRAS

looking up at the apartment window.

FREEZE THE FRAME

SUPERIMPOSE MALE STAR'S CREDIT

INTERIOR HALLWAY OF TENEMENT BUILD-ING—NIGHT

The camera is stationed by an apartment front door and is trained on Karras mounting the steps at the far end of the hall. He approaches and lightly raps. From within we hear the faint sound of a radio tuned to an all-news station. Karras waits a moment, then digs out a key from his pants pocket, opens the door, and enters.

INTERIOR TENEMENT APARTMENT—NIGHT

The radio is now more audible. We are in a railroad-flat kitchen. Tiny. Cracking plaster and peeling wallpaper. Unkempt. Sparse and ancient furnishings. In the kitchen, a small tub for bathing. Faded old newspapers are spread on the uncarpeted floor. As Karras enters, he breathes in an aching sigh as his gaze brushes lightly over painful reminders of his impoverished boyhood. Then he glances to the right, whence we hear the sounds of the radio.

KARRAS

Mama?

No response. He puts down his valise and the camera follows him into the bedroom and then into the squalid living room. Karras now sees his mother, fully dressed, lying on a torn and grease-stained sofa. He observes her for a moment, then sighs as he removes his raincoat and drapes it over a chair. He turns off the radio, stands looking down at his mother; then the camera comes in close on his face as he bends and kisses his mother's forehead, his eyes closed. He freezes and opens his eyes wide in alarm. Lifting his head back, he clutches quickly for his mother's pulse as:

61

Mama?

Swiftly, he lifts her eyelid and starts to say "Mama" again; but the word catches and is lost in the convulsion of grief in his throat. He straightens, then begins to crumple, his face contorting, breaking up with unbearable anguish. Here, the camera is close on his face as we freeze the frame and superimpose:

THE EXORCIST

MAIN TITLE MUSIC. LOSE *THE EXORCIST* AND SUPERIMPOSE FEATURED CAST CREDITS. THEN ABRUPTLY TO:

INTERIOR MACNEIL HOUSE—KITCHEN—DAY

Chris finishes dictating a letter to Sharon. Regan takes a cookie from a jar and munches.

> CHRIS
> OK, honey, run upstairs and get dressed and we'll go out for some pizza.

> REGAN
> *Great!*

As Regan races upstairs:

> REGAN
> Can I wear my new dress?

> CHRIS (*calling*)
> Yes.
> (*at Sharon*)
> Got a date?

> SHARON
> Yes, I do.

> CHRIS
> You go on, then.
> (*indicating mail*)
> We can catch all this stuff in the morning.

Sharon rises, but Chris abruptly recollects something.

CHRIS

Oh, hey, wait. There's a letter that's got to go out tonight.

SHARON (*reaching for her dictation pad*)

Oh, OK.

Chris starts to dictate:

CHRIS

"Dear Mr. Gable . . ."

Sharon reacts, amused; then Chris dictates in earnest: a letter to her agent. As she gets into it:

REGAN (*off scene*)

Moth-theeeeeerrrr! I can't find the dress!

CHRIS (*starting out*)

Shar, wait'll I come down.

SHARON (*eyeing her watch*)

Gee, it's time for me to meditate, Chris.

CHRIS (*after a beat; muted exasperation*)

You really think that stuff is going to do you any good?

SHARON

Well, it gives me peace of mind.

CHRIS (*after a long pause*)

Terrific.

INTERIOR SECOND-FLOOR HALLWAY—MAC-NEIL HOUSE—DUSK

Chris heads for Regan's bedroom and enters.

INTERIOR REGAN'S BEDROOM—DUSK

The scene is odd: Regan is standing in the middle of the room, silently staring up at the ceiling, frowning.

CHRIS

What's doin'?

REGAN (*still staring up*)

Funny noises.

Chris looks up at the ceiling and we freeze the frame and reprise the rappings. Briefly, superimpose additional credits, then go to:

EXTERIOR FULL SHOT—MACNEIL HOUSE—NIGHT

In an upper-floor gabled window we see the glow of a moving flashlight.

INTERIOR MACNEIL HOUSE—NIGHT

Down shot at Chris as she climbs the narrow steps to the attic with a flashlight.

INTERIOR ATTIC—ANGLE AT DOOR—NIGHT

The door is pushed slowly open. Chris enters, tries the light switch. It doesn't work. She pans the flashlight beam about the attic, searching for something and slowly advancing toward the camera. Behind her looms an enormous, shadowy figure: a tall, brawnily muscled man (Karl) in dark trousers, white shirt, and black tie. In his forties and totally bald, he reminds us of Savonarola: eagle eyes and hawk nose. Coming up silently behind Chris:

> KARL (*Nordic accent*)
> I can help?

He doesn't quite get through the "help" as Chris leaps three feet out of her skin and emits a startled yelp of fright, spinning around and practically into Karl's arms. Putting a hand to her fluttering heart, while shading her eyes with her other hand:

> CHRIS
> Jesus H. *Christ,* Karl, don't *do* that!

> KARL
> Sorry, madam. I can help?

> CHRIS (*recovering*)
> Yeah, you can help. We've got rats in the attic.
> (*moving toward door*)
> Set some traps in the morning, would you, Karl?

64

KARL

There are rats?

CHRIS

I just said that.

KARL

No rats, madam. Attic is clean.

CHRIS

Well, OK, we've got *tidy* rats. Will you please get the traps and quit arguin'?

KARL

Yes. But no rats.

CHRIS

No rats. Terrific.

INTERIOR MACNEIL HOUSE—SECOND-FLOOR HALL—NIGHT

Chris comes down the attic steps and into view as she rounds a corner. She enters her bedroom. The camera follows. There is no illumination except for the glow of a night-light. Chris gets into bed, then turns, realizing that Regan is in her bed. Regan is staring at her, wide-eyed.

CHRIS

Wha—?
(*with a faint chuckle*)
Hey, what are *you* doin' in here?

REGAN

My bed was shaking.

As the camera zooms tight to Regan, we freeze the frame and reprise the rappings. Briefly superimpose additional credits. Then go to:

INTERIOR MACNEIL HOUSE—KITCHEN—NIGHT

Activity. Willie cooking; Karl lugging in a fresh purified-water jug; Sharon standing with a note pad by the door to a half bath just off the kitchen. The bathroom door is slightly ajar. Chris's suit jacket and wig box are on the breakfast-nook table.

CHRIS (off scene)

. . . and get hold of that real-estate agent and tell him we're staying through June. I want Rags to finish up the semester at school.

We hear off-scene toilet flush, and Chris exits the bathroom, still pulling up skirt and zipping as:

SHARON (making note)

Oh, I'm glad.

CHRIS

I'm euphoric. Hey, where's Rags?

SHARON

In the playroom.

INTERIOR BASEMENT PLAYROOM OF MAC-NEIL HOUSE—NIGHT

The camera is fixed at a steep up angle at the bottom of the steps, and reminiscent of the earlier mood shots of the stone steps beside house.

Chris opens the door and starts down.

CHRIS
(at Regan, who is off scene in playroom)

Whatchya doin' there, Stinkpot?

REGAN (off scene)
(depressed and subdued)

Oh, playin'.

CHRIS

Take your pills today, honey?

REGAN (off scene)

Um-hmm.

Chris comes to the bottom of the steps and halts, deep concern in her eyes. Then she frowns as she thinks she sees . . . What? She walks forward and out of the frame to check it out. We hear her footsteps halt. The camera remains fixed on the steep up angle at the steps, then switches to a steep down angle from the top of the stairs as:

> CHRIS (*off scene*)
> Honey, where'd you get the Ouija board?

> REGAN (*off scene*)
> I found it.

> CHRIS (*off scene*)
> Found it where?

> REGAN (*off scene*)
> Oh, over there in the closet.

FRONT SHOT—CHRIS—REGAN

In the background, playroom decorations: a ping-pong table, a jukebox, a framed blowup of Chris and Regan on a magazine cover. Regan, dark sacs beneath her eyes, is dressed in pajamas and robe. She is seated at a small game table. Before her is a Ouija board. She is staring with brow-furrowed concentration at the planchette, which, resting beneath the fingertips of both hands, is moving from letter to letter in swift, agitated jerks.

> CHRIS
> Wheredjya learn how to play it?

> REGAN
> Oh, it says on the back. On the box.

> CHRIS
> Oh, yeah.

Chris turns and stares in the direction of an odd creaking sound off scene. The planchette stops moving, and Regan stares at it, her body fidgety and alive with small, restless movements.

> REGAN
> Captain Howdy, you're a poop.

Chris turns back to Regan, puzzled.

> CHRIS
> What'd you say?

(*she puts her hands on Regan's shoulders*)
Hey, quit twitchin'.

REGAN (*looking up at some point in space*)
He said daddy went away because of me. He
didn't want me.

CHRIS
Baby, what . . . ? Honey, *who* said those
things?

REGAN (*looking to Chris*)
Captain Howdy.

Chris crouches down to Regan's level.

CHRIS
Captain *who?*

REGAN
Captain Howdy.

Chris puts a hand to Regan's cheek with loving and
grave concern.

CHRIS
Honey, who's Captain Howdy?

REGAN
Oh, ya know: I ask questions and he does the
an—

Regan is cut off as a sharp and strong movement of
the planchette jerks her around to the board. Her eyes
grow wide as with helpless fear and fascination she
follows the planchette, which is moving in rapid and
savagely powerful circular movements while Chris
looks on with alarm. As the camera comes in close
on the planchette:

Freeze the frame. Reprise the rapping sounds. Superimpose additional credits. Then go to:

INTERIOR SECOND-FLOOR HALL OF MACNEIL
HOUSE—DAY

The camera looks down from a high angle that includes the staircase at the edge of the frame as Chris,

yawning as she sleepily knots the belt of her bathrobe, exits her bedroom, and heads for the stairs. From Regan's bedroom (off scene), we hear the sound of heavy furniture being moved. Passing Regan's doorway, Chris halts, arrested by the sounds and what she sees inside.

INTERIOR OF REGAN'S BEDROOM—CHRIS'S POINT OF VIEW

The items of furniture are in positions different than when last we saw this room. Karl, pushing a dresser back to its former position, pauses a moment to give Chris a dark and inscrutable look. He then continues his work.

FRONT ANGLE—CHRIS AND REGAN

looking into the bedroom, Regan a little ahead of Chris and to the side. Regan's brow is furrowed in puzzlement, and her face is wan, her eyes dark as if from lack of sleep. Chris looks from Karl to Regan.

CHRIS

What's doin'?

Regan looks up and in a flat, somewhat frightened tone:

REGAN

I dunno. In the night someone moved all my furniture around.

Freeze the frame. Reprise the rappings and superimpose the next credit.

INTERIOR DOCTOR'S EXAMINING ROOM—DAY

A nurse is leaning with her back against an examining table, her expression part puzzled and part disturbed as she observes Regan, who is in her slip and in constant motion: stepping, twirling, touching, with nervous movement; aimlessly humming.

INTERIOR DR. KLEIN'S OFFICE—DAY

Klein is bald, owlish, and wears glasses. He is seated

69

behind his desk, writing out a prescription. Chris sits opposite him. We catch him in the middle of a statement:

KLEIN

. . . hyperkinetic behavior disorder.

CHRIS

A what?

KLEIN

A disorder of the nerves.
(*ripping off a prescription sheet*)
You often see it in early adolescence.

CHRIS

Oh, you do?

KLEIN (*handing her prescription*)
That's for Ritalin.

CHRIS (*eyeing it*)
What is it, doc? A tranquilizer?

KLEIN

No, it's a stimulant.

CHRIS

Are you kidding? She's higher'n a kite right *now!*

KLEIN

Her condition isn't quite what it seems. It's a form of—well, overcompensation. She's over-reacting to depression.

CHRIS (*glum*)
Depression.

KLEIN

Well, her love for her father. The divorce.

CHRIS

Do you think I should take her to see a psychiatrist?

KLEIN (*swiveling to rise*)
Oh, no.

CHRIS

But those things she's been doin' to get attention. You know, all of that knocking and moving her furniture and stuff and then actin' like it's someone else doin' it.

KLEIN (*rising*)

Well, let's wait and see what happens with the Ritalin. I think that's the answer.

Chris rises, nodding and downcast.

KLEIN

Wait two or three weeks.

CHRIS (*looks down, frowning*)

Boy, she never used to lie to me.
(*eyes the prescription sheet*)
Never.

KLEIN

Well, in certain disorders of the nerves you see what look like personality changes.

He is opening the door for her.

INTERIOR HALL OF KLEIN'S SUITE OF OFFICES—DAY

As Chris and Klein exit, the camera tracks along the hall with them and:

KLEIN

For example, have you ever known your daughter to use obscenities?

CHRIS (*moody, her thoughts elsewhere*)

Oh, no, never.

KLEIN

Well, you see, that's very much like her lying—uncharacteristic, from what you tell me, but in certain disorders of the nerves it can—

They have come to the door of an examining room, and Klein has put a hand on the doorknob, when he halts, interrupted by:

CHRIS

Wait a minute, wait a minute, hold it. Tell me, where'd you get the notion that she uses obscenities? I mean, is that what you were saying?

KLEIN

Well, yes. Yes, I'd say that she uses obscenities. Weren't you aware of it?

CHRIS

I'm *still* not aware of it! What are you talking about?

KLEIN

Well, she let loose quite a string while I was examining her, Mrs. MacNeil.

CHRIS

What? You're kidding! Like what?

KLEIN (*evasive*)

Well, I'd say her vocabulary's rather extensive.

CHRIS

Well, for instance. I mean, give me a specific example.

He shrugs, still reluctant and uneasy.

CHRIS

You mean "shit"? Or "fuck"?

KLEIN (*relaxing*)

Yes, she used those words.

CHRIS

And what else did she say, Dr. Klein? *Specifically.*

KLEIN

Well—specifically, she called me a cocksucker, Mrs. MacNeil. Then she—

Chris interrupts as she moves to open the examining room door.

CHRIS

Jesus!

72

Chris looks in at Regan who sits solemnly, head bowed, on an examining table. Regan looks up with haunted eyes and the camera zooms to full on her as we:

Freeze the frame. Reprise the rappings. Superimpose additional credits. Then go to:

INTERIOR MACNEIL HOME—LIVING ROOM— NIGHT

Spacious and heavily beamed with dark old wood. Bay windows. A crowded cocktail party is in progress. We detect faces of the cast and crew from the motion picture being shot on the Georgetown University campus. A vibrant hum of conversation; Burke, an empty glass in his hand, stands chatting with a silver-maned senator and the senator's wife. Back of them, and to the side, Chris is visible, chatting with the Jesuit dean of the college. Karl is moving about with a drinks tray, and the camera picks him up as he passes. Sharon and Mary Jo Perrin are seated somewhere in the room. A bubbly personality, Mary Jo is reading Sharon's palm.

> PERRIN
> Well yes, your work line is longer than your heart line. There, you see? And you've recently broken up with a boyfriend. Right?

> SHARON
> Wrong.

> PERRIN
> I'm really famous for predictions, not palms. (*dropping Sharon's hand*)
> Where's the bathroom?

> SHARON
> Upstairs.

> PERRIN (*rising*)
> Oh, by the way, I brought that witchcraft book you asked for.

> SHARON
> Oh, thanks.

ANGLE AT BURKE—SENATOR AND WIFE

In the background, Chris, conversing with the dean, is close to Burke, her back to him.

> BURKE
>
> No, no, *her* part is finished, all the parts with the principal actors, you see, but *I* stay on to finish the second unit; you know, the less important scenes.

> SENATOR
>
> I understand.

Karl has approached Burke's group.

> BURKE
>
> Oh, how splendid.
> (*reaching for a fresh drink*)
> Yes, let's have another for the road.

> CHRIS
>
> (*brief over-the-shoulder shot at Burke*)
> The Lincoln Highway?

> BURKE
>
> Oh, now, don't be so silly.

> SENATOR'S WIFE
>
> Great party, Chris.

> CHRIS
>
> Thanks, Martha.

Chris returns to her conversation with the dean. During the preceding exchange, the senator has mutely refused another drink, but Burke now takes one in his *other* hand as well.

> BURKE
>
> Oh, tell me, Karl, was it *public* relations you did for the Gestapo, or *community* relations? I believe there's a difference, is there not?

> KARL (*grimly uptight*)
>
> I am Swiss.

> BURKE
>
> Yes, of course. And you never went bowling with Goebbels, I suppose.

SENATOR'S WIFE
(*a guarded aside to the senator*)
We should be going.

BURKE (*at Karl as the servant moves on*)
So superior, aren't you! Nazi!

FRONT TRACKING SHOT—KARL

His face is impassive, yet his eyes seethe with fury as we hear:

BURKE (*off scene*)
Bloody damned butchering Nazi pig!

AT BURKE—SENATOR—WIFE

The senator is turning away from his wife, nodding.

SENATOR
All right, dear.

BURKE
(*composed; blandly, as he stares down into his gin glass*)
There seems to be an alien pubic hair in my gin.

SENATOR (*as his wife leaves hurriedly*)
I beg your pardon.

BURKE (*defensive*)
Never seen it before in my *life!*

ANGLE AT CHRIS AND THE DEAN

In the background we see the senator walking away from Burke. Chris is listening intently.

DEAN
Well, that was one; and then another desecration happened yesterday.

CHRIS
What?

Willie passes, offering a canapé tray. As he takes one:

DEAN
No, it's disgusting.

CHRIS

Oh, no, tell me. What was it?

DEAN (*reluctant*)

Well, a mound of human excrement was found on the altar in front of the tabernacle. It's very reminiscent of what went on at Black Mass. You know, satanism.

CHRIS

You mean that kind of thing still goes on?

DEAN (*looking off scene*)

Oh, well, Joe knows much more about those things. I'll get him over.

CHRIS

Joe?

DEAN (*beckoning off scene*)

Joe Dyer, Father President's assistant.

Dyer enters the frame, his face expressionless, his eyes fey. He carries a heaping platter of food.

DYER

Can I come back in just a minute, Roy? I've got something going with the astronaut.

DEAN

What?

DYER

Would you believe—first missionary on the moon?

AT SHARON

She is still on the couch, but a male guest now sits beside her.

GUEST

And you're her secretary?

SHARON

Well, sort of half and half. I'm Regan's nurse part-time, part governess.
(*looking down into empty highball glass*)
I think I'll freshen this. How's yours?

GUEST
Oh, I'm fine.

SHARON
Excuse me.

The camera tracks with Sharon and as she passes Chris, Chris grabs her arm, halting her.

CHRIS
Hey, Shar. Take a look in on Rags, would you, honey?

SHARON
Just did. She's in bed with a book. She's OK.

TRACKING SHOT—MAIN STAIRCASE

A hand-held camera, representing the point of view of a very short, unseen person, is slowly descending the steps from the second floor down to the main floor. It enters the hall outside the living room; then enters the living room and picks a steady path through the guests. One guest does a double take at the camera; we hear a gasp; and amid stifled reactions of startlement, the conversation gradually fades to silence. Now we reach:

UP ANGLE—DYER, ASTRONAUT

The astronaut is chuckling and Chris is walking up to join them as:

DYER (*to astronaut; deadpan*)
No, I'm really not a priest. I'm a terribly avant-garde rabbi.
ASTRONAUT (*still chuckling*)
Do you—?
(*sees Chris*)
Hi. Say, you know what he's been—?

He breaks off as Chris stares down at the camera, and in the now total silence, gasps in shock and dismay at what she sees, her hand flying to her cheek. The camera zooms quickly to a tight shot of the astronaut's face as he, too, looks down and we hear:

REGAN (*off scene*)
You're going to die up there.

77

As the astronaut's face turns gray with dismay and chilling apprehension, we hear:

> CHRIS (*off scene*)
> (*anguished*)
> Oh, Rags! Oh, my—

AT REGAN

From the astronaut's point of view, we see Regan, in a nightgown, staring up at him. She is urinating gushingly onto the rug while surrounding guests stare at her, dumbfounded.

> CHRIS (*off scene*)
> —baby! Oh, God! Oh, my—!

CLOSE SHOT

of the astronaut staring, shaken.

Freeze the frame. Superimpose final credits.

INTERIOR REGAN'S BEDROOM—NIGHT

Moonlight streams in through the open window.

Regan is in bed, dully staring at a point in space. Chris is tucking in the bedcovers. Through the window, from the street below, we hear off scene the sounds and voices of departing guests.

> SENATOR'S WIFE (*off scene*)
> Oh, well, sleepwalking's common at that age.

> SENATOR (*off scene*)
> Come along, dear.

> SENATOR'S WIFE (*off scene*)
> Please tell her we hope Regan feels better.

> CHUCK (*off scene*)
> Hey, tell Chris I had a really great time.

> SHARON (*off scene*)
> Yes, I'll tell her.

During this, Chris sits on the edge of Regan's bed and puts her hand tenderly to Regan's cheek.

CHRIS (*softly*)
How ya feelin'?

No response.

CHRIS
Would you like me to read to you?

Regan shakes her head slightly, staring at the wall.
After a pause:

CHRIS
Honey, why did you say that?

REGAN
Are you going to marry Mr. Dennings?

CHRIS
Am I going to—? Baby, where'd you get that
idea?

REGAN
You don't like him?

CHRIS
I like pizzas, but I wouldn't want to marry one,
honey. He's a friend, just a crazy old friend.

REGAN
You don't like him like daddy?

CHRIS
I *love* your daddy, honey. I'll *always* love your
daddy. Now where did you get an idea like that?

REGAN
Well, I heard . . .

CHRIS
You heard what? From who?

Regan turns her head and stares out of the window.

REGAN
I don't know.

For a few beats, Chris sits still, staring at Regan. Then:

CHRIS
Try to sleep.

Regan mutely nods. Chris rises, leans over and kisses her.

> REGAN (*still looking out of the window*)
> I made that bear for you, mom.

> CHRIS

The bear?

> REGAN
> You know. With the daisies in his hand, like you wanted.

She has laboriously reached over to the nightstand to pick up a gaily painted sculpture of a bear. It has a sweet expression on its face and is sniffing at a cluster of daisies in its paw. Chris reaches, too, and takes it from Regan's uncertain grasp.

> CHRIS (*examining the bear fondly*)
> Oh, you angel.

> REGAN
> I hope you like the colors. I—

But Chris smothers her words as she stoops to embrace Regan in a spontaneous outburst of love.

> CHRIS
> Oh, Rags, hon, I love you so much.

> REGAN

I love you, mom.

> CHRIS

OK.
> (*kisses Regan's cheek, straightens up*)
> Now go to sleep, babe. Can you sleep?

Regan turns her head aside to stare out of the window again, and nods. We hear car doors being closed off scene and for a few beats, Chris stares down at the sculpture in her hand and starts quietly out of the room. As she gets to the door and gently opens it, she is stopped by:

> REGAN (*off scene*)
> (*haunted, flat tone*)
> Mother, what's wrong with me?

Chris is rocked by this. She makes flustered and silent false starts at a reply. Then:

>CHRIS (*lamely*)
>Why, honey, it's nerves.

FULL SIDE ANGLE—THE ROOM

Chris at the door, Regan with her head still averted.

>CHRIS
>That's all. I mean, it's just like the doctor said. You keep taking those pills and you'll be fine. Just fine.

A long wait for a reaction from Regan; but Regan neither moves nor speaks.

>CHRIS
>OK, Baby Bear?

Chris waits. Still nothing. Troubled and despondent, Chris leaves the room.

INTERIOR SECOND-FLOOR HALL OF MACNEIL HOUSE—NIGHT

The camera is fixed at one end of the hall, and at the other end we see Chris exit from Regan's bedroom. Head down, thoughtful, she starts toward us, then seems to remember something and moves back to lean over the balustrade railing to observe some activity below for a moment or two. We hear off-scene scraping sounds, like a brush against carpeting.

>CHRIS (*softly*)
>Comin' out, Willie?

>WILLIE (*off scene*)
>(*from below*)
>Yes, madam. I think so.

>CHRIS
>Good.

Chris continues to stare down for a moment more, then comes toward the camera again until she reaches the door to her bedroom. She enters. She closes the door. A beat. Then from off scene, within Regan's bedroom, we hear loud metallic sounds, like bedsprings violently quivering.

> REGAN (*off scene*)
> (*with mounting apprehension*)
> Mother?

Two beats. The bedspring sounds. Then, much louder, in a voice filled with terror:

> REGAN (*off scene*)
> Mother, come *here!* Come *here!*

Chris's door shoots open as she dashes out into the hall, racing for Regan's bedroom.

> CHRIS
> Yes, I'm coming! All right, hon! I'm coming!

> REGAN (*off scene*)
> Mothhhheerrrrrrrrrr!

> CHRIS
> Oh, my baby, what's—

INTERIOR REGAN'S BEDROOM—AT DOOR— NIGHT

Chris bursts in, and as she reaches for the light switch we hear massive metallic sounds as:

> CHRIS
> —wrong, hon? What is it? What's—?

The lights are on and, as Chris stares at Regan's bed, off scene, she breaks off, electrified.

> CHRIS
> Jesus! Oh, Jesus!

POINT-OF-VIEW SHOT OF REGAN

She lies taut on her back, her face stained with tears and contorted with terror and confusion as she grips at the sides of the narrow bed. It is savagely quivering back and forth!

> REGAN
> Mother, why is it *shaking?* Make it stop! Oh,

I'm scared! Make it stop! Oh, I'm scared,
Mother, please make it stoooooooo—

We break off her elongated, fearful cry before hearing
the *p* sound as we:

Freeze the frame. Superimpose the writer's credit, the
producer's credit, the director's credit. Main title score.
Then:

CUT TO:

INTERIOR KARRAS'S OFFICE-QUARTERS IN THE JESUIT RESIDENCE HALL—DUSK

A second-floor room facing out to Prospect Street. It is
sparsely furnished: a narrow bed with a crucifix above
it, desk, chairs, bookcase, connecting bathroom. Karras is seated behind his desk, his face reflecting sadness
and the strain of attempting to keep his mind on what
is being said by a troubled-looking young Jesuit scho-
lastic in his mid-twenties who is sitting opposite him in
a straight-backed chair. The camera is in a full down
shot as:

> YOUNG JESUIT (*thoughtfully nodding*)
> . . . well, partly that . . . partly . . . I suppose
> so. But that's not the main thing, I don't think
> —the main problem.

> KARRAS
>
> What is?

ANGLE AT YOUNG JESUIT

> YOUNG JESUIT
> Well, I know it sounds . . .

He trails off.

> KARRAS (*off scene*)
>
> What?

The young priest hesitates, then looks down, shaking
his head.

ANGLE AT KARRAS

Go ahead.

> YOUNG JESUIT (*off scene*)
> Well, it's loneliness, I guess . . .

Karras's gaze shifts over to the window.

> YOUNG JESUIT (*off scene*)
> Just plain . . .

ANGLE AT WINDOW—KARRAS'S POINT OF VIEW—MATTE SHOT

Diagonally across the street, one can see the MacNeil house and a beautiful sunset-dappled sky as:

> YOUNG JESUIT (*off scene*)
> . . . loneliness. Do you know what I—?

QUICK CUT TO:

INTERIOR HALL OF BELLEVUE HOSPITAL

This is a flashback, and the color process should be a grainy black and white to set it off from the scenes that take place in the present. The camera is fixed at one end of the hall, and Karras and his Uncle John are approaching from far down the opposite end; but their dialogue is clearly audible at all times, and their voices are metallically reverberant. Karras has his head down, sorrowful and dismayed, as he listens to his uncle. Karras is ruefully shaking his head, and the uncle is gesturing helplessly, defensively.

> UNCLE
> But, Dimmy, da edema affected her brain! You understand? She don't let any doctor come near her! She was all da time screamin', even talkin' to da radio! Listen, regular hospital not gonna put up wit' dat, Dimmy! So we give her a shot an' bring her here 'til da doctors, dey fix up her leg! Den we take her right out, Dimmy. Two or t'ree month, and she's out, good as new. Dimmy—

> KARRAS (*gently*)
> Couldn't you have put her someplace else?

Like what?

A private hospital?

Who got da money for dat, Dimmy? You?

EXTERIOR JESUIT RESIDENCE HALL—DUSK

Back to the present.

We are shooting through the window at Karras and the young priest. As we come in, Karras lowers his head with guilt at the recollection of his uncle's words. Meantime, continuing from before:

YOUNG PRIEST
—like I'll start to put my arm around another guy's shoulder, and then have to catch myself —you know?—I'm afraid he might think that I'm queer. You know you hear so many theories about "latents" in the priesthood. Well, that's always on my mind, Father, always on my—

During the above, at the last, Karras has again lifted his head and turned to stare moodily at the window (and camera point of view), so that after the move we break the young priest's speech and:

QUICK CUT TO:

INTERIOR BELLEVUE HOSPITAL

Again, a flashback, the film process grainy black and white. Karras and his uncle stand outside a locked door above which is posted the legend: NEURO-PSYCHIATRIC: WARD 3. Karras's head is lowered despondently. The uncle is pushing a buzzer to summon a nurse to open the door. Then:

UNCLE
You go in, Dimmy. I wait out here.

Karras nods, still downcast. Now the uncle stares at the floor, lost in ironic thought.

Dat's funny. You know, if you wasn't be priest, you be famous psychiatrist now on Park Avenue, Dimmy. Your mother, she be livin' in a penthouse instead of—

INTERIOR WARD 3—AT PADDED ENTRY DOOR

as a corpulent nurse waddles into the frame and with a large iron key unlocks the door. Off screen, we hear the demented screams, moans, and fragmented chatter of mental patients. The door comes open, disclosing Karras and his uncle. Karras slowly lifts his head at the sounds.

INTERIOR WARD 3—INVALIDED PATIENTS' ROOM

The camera, hand-held, is the eyes of Karras as he walks down an aisle of an enormous ward containing eighty beds. The patients are mostly elderly, and the sound of their cries increases as the camera first scans from bed to bed while Karras walks, then halts as it fixes on a bedded patient far down the row: Karras's mother. Gaunt and hollow-eyed, she looks confused, helpless, disoriented. She has spied her son and is gripping at the sidebars of her bed, trying to raise herself as the camera now moves forward again, trained on the mother. As Karras gets closer, a tear rolls down the camera lens, then another, and by the time Karras halts beside her bed, his mother, looking frightened and pathetic, eyes wide and pleading, has raised herself up, pulling weakly, hands trembling.

MOTHER
Why you do dis, Dimmy? Why?

Now the frame seems to blur with tears and the eyes (lens) close twice, blinking. With this, we go back to the present and:

INTERIOR KARRAS'S OFFICE-QUARTERS— ANGLE AT KARRAS—DUSK

He uses the pretext of reaching for his cigarettes in

order to angle away from the young priest and thus conceal a wetness in his eyes as:

> YOUNG PRIEST (*off scene*)
> . . . so I just don't do it. I won't even go to someone's room to listen to records. It's not that I'm worried about *him,* Father Karras, I'm worried about him getting worried about *me.*

> KARRAS
> I understand.

ANGLE AT THE YOUNG PRIEST

> YOUNG PRIEST (*lowering head*)
> Well, I know it must sound awfully petty—

AT KARRAS LIGHTING CIGARETTE

> YOUNG PRIEST (*off scene*)
> —compared to the problems you must usually have to cope with.

The wetness still in his eyes, Karras flicks up his gaze at something off scene on the near wall as:

> KARRAS
> Not at all, Jim.

POINT-OF-VIEW SHOT OF WALL PLAQUE

The inscription reads:

> "MY BROTHER HURTS.
> I SHARE HIS PAIN.
> I MEET GOD IN HIM."

Once again, we have the effect of watering eyes blinking, and the inscription seems blurred and clouded by cigarette smoke; then it quickly clears. During this:

> KARRAS (*off scene*)
> Go on, Jim. Please go on.

> YOUNG PRIEST (*off scene*)
> Well, the thing that I find most upsetting is the—

ABRUPTLY CUT TO:

EXTERIOR DOWN SHOT AT STEPS BESIDE MACNEIL HOUSE—NIGHT

We hear the voice of Karras, but thicker and slightly slurred, as if from exhaustion or a numbing of the senses—or from drinking. He seems to be continuing the young priest's unfinished line in the preceding scene.

> KARRAS'S VOICE
> . . . problem of evil; yeah, yeah, that's a part of it. Part. Just a part.

EXTERIOR PROSPECT STREET—FULL SHOT—NIGHT

The angle includes the MacNeil house and the Jesuit residence hall. It is late in the night. No traffic. There is a light on in only one room in the Jesuit residence hall.

> KARRAS'S VOICE (*continuing unbroken*)
> Pain and disease and the frailty of the body . . .

INTERIOR KARRAS'S OFFICE-QUARTERS—ANGLE AT DYER—NIGHT

Dim desk lamp lighting. Dyer is sitting in back of Karras's desk, wearing a "Snoopy" T-shirt. He holds a drinking cup, and is staring at Karras off scene. He is nodding with compassion and understanding: a perfect reversal of Karras and the young priest in the scene before.

> KARRAS (*off scene*)
> The suffering of children, and the fucking outrageous corruption of death.

ANGLE AT KARRAS

He is sitting on the edge of a cot, his eyes fixed low in haunted stare. In his hand is another cup containing a small amount of Scotch. His eyes and voice are fogged by heavy drinking and chronic sleeplessness.

> KARRAS
> But there's more than that, Joe. There's ugliness.
> (*lifting gaze to Dyer*)
> Tell me, where is that spark of the Divine in

the human gastrointestinal system? In having to rip food with your teeth and then defecate? In stinking socks and in pus?

ANOTHER ANGLE INCLUDING DYER AT DESK

DYER

You're rejecting your own humanity, Damien.

KARRAS

Maybe. No, not maybe. I am. I reject it. But most of all, Joe—most of senseless, incredible all: (*lifting gaze to Dyer*)
Why does God hide? With us, His creatures standing in front of Him, lost, tormented, screaming for help, can you believe He wouldn't show Himself and tell us where it's at? Why the hell not put an end to all the doubts and confusion?

DYER

"Lord, give us a sign . . ."

KARRAS (*looking down into his cup*)
Joe, the raising of Lazarus was long, long ago. Long . . . long . . . time . . .

Dyer has pedaled his chair over to Karras, bottle poised to pour, but holds it for:

KARRAS

And now when I lift up the Host in consecration, it's like an unexpected glimpse in a crowd of a girl you once loved. That pain . . . that funny little stabbing in your heart.

A pause. Then Dyer starts to fill Karras's cup.

KARRAS

Joe, where'd you get the money for Chivas Regal? Did you rob the poor box?

DYER

Don't be an asshole, that would be breaking my vow of poverty.

As Dyer pedals the chair back to his desk:

KARRAS

Where did you get it then?

DYER

I stole it.

KARRAS

I believe you.

As Karras gulps the contents of the cup:

DYER

College presents shouldn't drink. It tends to
set a bad example.

Dyer sees that Karras is staring at a small framed
photograph of his mother. Dyer drops the empty bottle
into a wastebasket, intentionally jarring Karras's attention away from the photo.

DYER

Incidentally, did I tell you about the screenplay
I'm writing?

KARRAS (*lying back on cot*)

No, you didn't.

Dyer begins rummaging through Karras's desk drawers.

DYER

Well, I really haven't written it yet, but I'm
going to. It's part of my plan for when I quit
the priesthood.

KARRAS (*briefly alert*)

Who's quitting the priesthood?

DYER

Faggots. In droves. Basic black has gone out.

Karras relaxes again. The trace of smile and the warmth
in his eyes tells us that he knows that Dyer is merely
trying to distract him, to cheer him up. He intermit-
tently opens and closes his eyes as:

DYER

I met Chris MacNeil—you know, the famous
movie star—at a— Hey, incidentally, she asked
about you at her party.

KARRAS (*eyes closed*)

Never met her.

DYER

I know, but she saw you on the campus one day
and she liked you.

KARRAS (*eyes closed*)

Why was that?

DYER

Her director said "fuck" and you smiled. She
got the notion from that that you were human.

KARRAS

Well, tell her she's wrong. I reject my humanity.

The empty cup still in his hands, Karras opens his eyes
and watches Dyer as the latter closes a drawer and rises
to inspect some containers on various shelves, searching
for something. During this:

DYER

Getting back to my plan: I figure she can find
me a backer for the screenplay which I'm basing
on the life of St. Ignatius Loyola. Would you
like to hear the title?

KARRAS

Joe, what do you need?

DYER (*continuing the hunt*)

I'm looking for a lemon drop. Got any lemon
drops, Damien?

That warmth and the slight smile on the tortured face
again tell us Karras appreciates what Dyer is doing.
He closes his eyes as the camera moves to follow Dyer.
During this:

DYER

Boy, I really crave one. I once spent a year
hearing children's confessions, and I wound up
a lemon-drop junkie. I got hooked. The little
bastards keep *breathing* it on you along with all
that pot. Between the two, I've got a feeling it's
probably addictive.

Dyer has lifted the lid of a clear glass jar containing pistachio nuts and has his nose low to the jar's mouth. He sniffs, then:

DYER
What are these? Dead Mexican jumping beans?

The sound of a cup falling to the floor and rolling makes Dyer turn, deadpan, to Karras, and then look relieved at what he sees.

POINT-OF-VIEW SHOT OF KARRAS

He has turned over to a sleeping position, his eyes closed. Dyer moves quietly into the shot and picks Karras's cup off the floor. Then:

DYER (*whispering*)
Do you think you can sleep now, Damien?

Karras nods his head along with a throat sound of affirmation. Dyer moves to the foot of the bed, undoes the laces, and then removes Karras's shoes. As he does:

KARRAS
Gonna steal my shoes now?

DYER (*softly*)
No, I tell fortunes by reading the creases. Now shut up and go to sleep.

KARRAS
You're a Jesuit cat burglar.

DYER
Someone's got to worry about the bills around this place.
(*moving quietly to desk*)
All you other guys do is just rattle your beads and pray for the hippies down on M Street.

Dyer has just flicked off the desk light.

KARRAS
(*unmoving, eyes still closed; he is almost asleep*)
No, leave the light on. Someone might need me. If they see that the light's not on, they won't knock.

Dyer looks at him with enormous affection in his expression, nods, then:

> DYER
> OK.

He flicks on the light.

> KARRAS
> And leave the door open.

> DYER
> Right.

Dyer moves to the side of the bed.

> DYER
> I'll leave it open. Go to sleep.

> KARRAS (*a whisper*)
> I'm asleep.

Dyer nods and touches a hand to Karras's shoulder in good night, and, as he starts to move toward the door, Karras's hand reaches out and grips his wrist, squeezing, a gesture of gratitude and deep friendship. Dyer stares down and the camera follows his gaze to a tight shot of the hands again as sleep at last comes to Karras. The sleepy Jesuit's grip slackens; his hand slowly falls.

> DYER (*off scene*)
> (*whisper*)
> Good night, Damien. Sleep tight.

EXTERIOR RESIDENCE HALL—SHOT AT KARRAS'S ROOM THROUGH WINDOW—NIGHT

We see Dyer adjusting the lamp to lessen the beam; then he silently walks from the room. He closes the door from outside. Now the camera pushes in to a closer angle at Karras as he opens pained eyes and stares hauntedly into space. We hear the opening line from the mass:

> KARRAS'S VOICE
> "I will go to the altar of God . . ."

CAMERA HALTS CLOSE

and Karras's lips move to complete it:

93

KARRAS (*a murmur*)
". . . unto God Who gives joy to my youth."

INTERIOR HOLY TRINITY CHURCH—VERY EARLY MORNING

Only two or three worshipers. Karras, in black vestments, is at the main altar saying mass. While washing at a small table to the side of the altar:

KARRAS
"O Lord, I have loved the beauty of Thy house and the place where Thy glory dwelleth. Take not away my soul, O God, with the wicked, nor my life with men of blood . . ."

ANOTHER ANGLE (TIME LAPSE)

KARRAS
"Remember also, O Lord, Thy servant, Mary Karras, who has come before us with the sign of faith, and sleeps the sleep of peace. To her, O Lord, and to—all—"
(*he's fighting tears*)
"—who rest in Christ, grant her we pray Thee, a place of—refreshment—of light—and—"

ANOTHER ANGLE (TIME LAPSE)

KARRAS
"Peace I leave you; my peace I give you. Look not upon my sins but upon the faith of Thy church . . ."

ANOTHER ANGLE (TIME LAPSE)

KARRAS (*hands extended*)
"O Lord, I am not worthy. Speak but the word and my soul shall be healed."

ANOTHER ANGLE (TIME LAPSE)

With upraised hands, Karras turns to read from one of the three altar cards which contain some of the prayers most frequently used at mass. He starts to murmur the Latin aloud; then reacts with extreme puzzlement which, as he slowly picks up the card and brings it closer to his face, gives way to disbelief and then shocked revulsion.

KARRAS (a whisper)

God!

INTERIOR KLEIN'S EXAMINING ROOM—DAY

Chris has her head down, shielding her eyes while in a *silent shot* Karl uses all his strength to restrain a struggling, kicking Regan while Klein stands by ready to administer an injection. During this we hear:

KLEIN'S VOICE

It was actually moving?

CHRIS'S VOICE

Maybe ten, fifteen seconds. I mean, that's all I saw. Then she sort of went stiff and wet the bed and passed out.

KLEIN'S VOICE

Has she ever had a fall?

CHRIS'S VOICE

No, not that I know of.

As Klein leans over to administer the injection, Regan spits in his face and he pauses, leaning back, then tries again. During this:

KLEIN'S VOICE

Any sleepwalking history?

CHRIS'S VOICE

Well, not until now. But I'm sure she was walking in her sleep at the party. She still doesn't know what she did that night.

KLEIN'S VOICE

Then perhaps she wasn't lying about the moving of the furniture. What I mean is, she might have been doing those things in one of those states that we call "automatism." It's similar to a state of trance.

CHRIS'S VOICE

You know, something just occurred to me, doc.

95

There's this great big heavy bureau in her room made out of teakwood. I mean, trance state or not, how the hell could she move *that,* come to think of it?

Now, Chris turns and stares speculatively, even suspiciously, at Karl. as we hear:

CHRIS'S VOICE

How could she?

KLEIN'S VOICE

Well, extraordinary strength is not uncommon in pathology.

As the injection is plunged home, Karl looks to Chris and she looks away.

ANOTHER ANGLE (SILENT)

Regan is now calm, on her back on the table, arms and legs bowed outward.

Chris and Karl stand to the side, observing as Klein repeatedly takes Regan's foot in both his hands and flexes it toward her ankle, holds it there for several moments in tension, then abruptly releases it. Each time, the foot relaxes into normal position, and Klein reacts with puzzlement.

During the above, meantime, we hear:

KLEIN'S VOICE

Well, all right now: the untidiness, the pugnacity, the automatism, and the seizures that made the bed shake. Anything else that you've noticed in the way of bizarre behavior?

CHRIS'S VOICE

Well, you remember that Ouija board she's been playin' with? Captain Howdy?

KLEIN'S VOICE

Yes, the fantasy playmate.

CHRIS'S VOICE

Well, now she can hear him, and I think even *see* him.

Again, Chris has turned to stare at Karl with brooding speculation.

INTERIOR LARGER EXAMINING ROOM—(SILENT SHOT)—DAY

Karl is now absent, but Chris is present, observing as Klein assists a nurse in attaching EEG machine saline-tipped electrodes to Regan's scalp. During this we hear:

> KLEIN'S VOICE
> It's sometimes the symptom of a type of disturbance in the chemicoelectrical activity in the forward part of the brain. We call it "temporal lobe" disorder . . . Now it's rare, but it does cause bizarre hallucinations, and usually just before a convulsion. It's produced by a lesion.

ANOTHER ANGLE

Time lapse. The electrodes are now attached and Klein is operating the EEG as he and Chris observe the graph depicting Regan's brain waves. He shakes his head, as if puzzled.

> CHRIS'S VOICE (*apprehensive*)
> You know, you keep on saying that, doc— "convulsion." What exactly is the name of this disease?

> KLEIN'S VOICE
> Well, it isn't a disease; it's a disorder. You know it as epilepsy, Mrs. MacNeil.

INTERIOR RADIOLOGY LAB—(SILENT SHOT)—DAY

Regan is again lying on her back on an examining table while Chris watches a radiologist take skull X rays of Regan.

A series of angles. During them:

> CHRIS'S VOICE
> But how could her whole personality change?

> KLEIN'S VOICE
> In temporal lobe, that's extremely common, and

97

can last for days or even weeks. It isn't rare to find destructive or even criminal behavior. There's such a big change, in fact, that two or three hundred years ago people with temporal lobe disorders were often considered to be possessed by a demon.

CHRIS'S VOICE

They were what?

KLEIN'S VOICE

Taken over by a demon, or sometimes the spirit of someone dead. A sort of superstitious version of dual personality.

INTERIOR SMALL MEDICAL LAB AND X-RAY ⚹
ROOM—DAY

Klein and a consulting neurologist (Dr. Samuel Arnold) are thoughtfully studying Regan's skull X rays, which are pinned up to a fluorescent screen. Arnold, shaking his head, removes his eyeglasses and tucks them into the breast pocket of his jacket with:

ARNOLD

There's just nothing there, Sam.

KLEIN (*frowning, still studying X rays*)

I know. It doesn't figure.

ARNOLD

Want to run another series?

KLEIN

I don't think so. I'll try an LP.

ARNOLD

Good idea.

KLEIN

But in the meantime, I'd like you to—

The telephone buzzer interrupts. He picks up the phone:

KLEIN

Excuse me.

(*into the phone*)
Yes.

RECEPTIONIST'S VOICE (*filter*)
Chris MacNeil's calling, doctor. Says it's urgent.

INTERIOR SECOND-FLOOR HALL—MACNEIL HOUSE—DAY

The camera is by the door to Regan's bedroom, from which emanate Regan's moans of pain and screams of terror. Rushing up from the steps onto the landing is Sharon, followed by Klein and Arnold. Sharon cracks the door open and calls in:

SHARON
Doctors, Chris!

Chris immediately comes to the door and opens it. She is extremely distraught and bewildered, her voice quavering:

CHRIS
Oh, God, come in! Come in and see what she's doing!

INTERIOR REGAN'S BEDROOM—ANGLE AT DOOR—DAY

Karl stands beside the door, staring numbly, and as the doctors enter, we hear, over Regan's cries, an off-scene sound of something slamming onto the bedsprings repeatedly.

KLEIN (*introducing to Chris*)
This is Dr. Arnold, the consulting neurologist I told you I would—

He breaks off, staring off scene at Regan. He takes a step or two closer toward the bed, startled. He stops.

REGAN (*off scene*)
(*hysterical wail*)
Moooooooootheeerrrrrrrr!

POINT-OF-VIEW SHOT OF REGAN

Her arms flailing, her body seems to be flinging itself

99

up horizontally about a foot into the air above her bed, and then is slammed down savagely onto her mattress, as if by an unseen person. This happens repeatedly and rapidly as:

> REGAN
> Oh, Mother, make him stop! Please *stop* him! *Stop* him! He's trying to kill me! He's—! Oh, please stoopppppppppp himmmmmmmmmm, Motherrrrrrrrrrr!

ANGLE AT CHRIS AND DOCTORS

> CHRIS (*at doctors*)
> What *is* it?

> KLEIN (*awed, still staring off scene*)
> I don't know.

ANGLE AT REGAN

The up-and-down movements abruptly cease. Now Regan twists feverishly from side to side, her eyes rolling upward into their sockets so that only the whites are exposed. Her legs keep crossing and uncrossing rapidly.

> REGAN (*moaning*)
> Oh, he's burning me! I'm burning! I'm—! *Uhh!*

With this sudden sound of pain, Regan has abruptly jerked her head back, disclosing a bulging, swollen throat. She begins to mutter incomprehensibly in a strangely deepened, guttural tone.

ANOTHER ANGLE

as the doctors approach. Reaching the bedside, Klein reaches down to take Regan's pulse.

> KLEIN (*soothingly*)
> All right, now, let's see what the trouble is, dear. I'm just going to—

And abruptly Klein is reeling across the room, stunned and staggering from the force of a vicious backward swing of Regan's arm as she suddenly sits up, her face contorted with hideous rage. In a coarse and powerful,
100

deep male voice, she bellows first at Klein and then at the others:

REGAN

The sow is mine! She is mine! Keep away from her!

AT KLEIN

He stares off scene, stunned, as Karl and Arnold kneel to help him.

KLEIN

No, I'm all right.

AT REGAN

She leans her head back and a yelping, demonic laugh gushes up from her throat; then she begins to caress her own arms sensually as she croons in that same guttural voice:

REGAN

Ah, yes, my flower . . . my pearl . . . my . . .

Abruptly, she falls onto her back as if shoved, and cries out with a wrench of breath. Then abruptly she is sitting up again, as if pulled by the hands.

REGAN

Oh, mother! Mother—!

Another sudden cry, and then she is bending at the waist, whirling her torso around in rapid, strenuous circles.

REGAN (*weeping*)

Oh, *stop* him, mother! It *hurts!* Oh, I can't breaaaaaaathe!

Before she finishes her cry, she again appears to be shoved savagely onto her back, and as Dr. Arnold comes beside her bed and observes, her eyes roll upward into their sockets and again she begins muttering incomprehensibly in that thickened voice. Arnold leans his head closer to try to make it out, frowning.

AT KLEIN

He is by the large window overlooking the steps. He is

hastily dipping into his medical bag and preparing a hypodermic injection. During this, he looks to the neurologist.

KLEIN

Sam!

He beckons Arnold over to him with a movement of his head and continues preparing the hypo. We hear the off-scene fevered gibberish from Regan. Arnold comes into the frame.

KLEIN (*guardedly*)
I'm giving her Librium, but you're going to have to hold her.

Arnold nods, looking preoccupied, and stares over at Regan, off scene.

KLEIN
What's she saying?

ARNOLD (*at Klein*)
I don't know. Just gibberish. Nonsense syllables.
And yet—
(*turning to Regan again*)
It's got cadence. She certainly *says* it as if it has—

The off-scene gibberish is replaced by:

REGAN
Oh, *no!* No, Captain Howdy, don't—!

AT REGAN

slamming up and down off the bed again, emitting a prolonged scream of pain and terror.

QUICK CUT TO:

CHRIS

Fists to her temples, she turns to shriek at the doctors over Regan's cry.

CHRIS
God almighty, will you do something!
Help her! Help—!

AT THE DOCTORS

Klein is ready, and over:

> CHRIS
>
> —herrrrrrrrrr . . . !

and Regan's continuing scream from off scene, he grimly tells Arnold:

> KLEIN
>
> Let's go.

As they start toward the bed, and with Chris and Regan's cries persisting, we:

> QUICKLY CUT TO:

INTERIOR DEN—STUDY OF MACNEIL HOUSE —DAY

Blessed silence. Chris sits in a chair, shaken, while Arnold, his head bent in frowning thought, leans against the fireplace facade. Klein is in the background at the bar. He fills a glass with water, then walks slowly to Chris. Reaching her, he offers her a small green pill in his upturned palm. Chris looks up.

> CHRIS
>
> That a tranquilizer?

> KLEIN
>
> Yes.

> CHRIS (*taking pill*)
>
> I'll have a double.

> KLEIN
>
> One's enough.

> CHRIS
>
> Big spender.

She swallows the pill and as Klein takes the glass from her hand:

> CHRIS
>
> I could fix you some coffee, if you'd like. It's just instant. I gave the housekeepers off. Would you like some?

KLEIN

Not for me, thanks.

CHRIS

Dr. Arnold? It'll only take a minute.

ARNOLD

No, I'll have to be leaving very soon. I have a patient waiting. Thanks, though.

CHRIS

Yeah. So what's next?

ARNOLD

I would think a lumbar tap.

CHRIS (*alarmed*)

A *spinal*?

KLEIN

What we missed in the X rays and the EEG could turn up there. At the least, it would exhaust certain possibilities. I'd like to do it now, right here, while she's out. I'm going to give her a local, of course, but it's movement that I'm trying to eliminate.

CHRIS

Doc, how could she jump off the bed like that?

KLEIN

Well, I think we discussed that before. Pathological states can induce abnormal strength and accelerated motor performance.

CHRIS

But you don't know why.

ARNOLD

Well, it seems to have something to do with motivation. But that's all we know.

KLEIN

Well, now, what about the spinal? OK?

Chris exhales, sagging, staring at the floor. Then, softly:

CHRIS

I don't know what you're doing or why. Guess I'm dumb. But go ahead. Do whatever you have to. Just make it well.

INTERIOR REGAN'S BEDROOM—DAY

Regan is supine on her bed, unconscious, her face away from the camera. Klein carefully extracts spinal fluid into a tube. Chris watches anxiously and Sharon, who is assisting Klein, has an eye on the manometer. A cotton swab and a bottle of alcohol are at the ready.

SHARON

Pressure's still normal.

Klein nods, removing the needle. Chris exhales with relief. Sharon rubs the swab at the needle puncture and bandages it, while Klein detaches the hypo from the fluid, putting away the needle. Glancing briefly up at the large shuttered window (shutters are open), then back to stowing the needle:

KLEIN (*a murmur*)

Best put a lock on those window shutters.
(*holding up the fluid to the light*)
If she's walking in her sleep, she could go through.

CHRIS

Yeah.
(*moves to window, closes and locks it*)
That's right. I'd better lock it right now. Keep this closed, Shar.

KLEIN

The fluid's clear.
(*carefully stowing the tube in his medical bag*)
Now between the sedation and the usual aftermath of convulsion, I would guess she'll be out until tomorrow noon or even longer.
(*closing his bag, then reaching for his prescription pad*)
But just in case, I'm going to give you a prescription for soluble Thorazine.

As Sharon dresses Regan's bedding, etc.

CHRIS

So what's next?

KLEIN (*writing prescription*)
Well, I'm going to run tests on the fluid.

CHRIS (*frowning*)
What kind of tests, doc?

KLEIN
Well, a number of—

CHRIS (*anxiously, cutting in*)
When ya gonna run 'em?

KLEIN
Right away. I'm going to run them myself.

CHRIS
Well, now tell me how you—

SHARON (*cutting in*)
Chris, why don't you go along with Dr. Klein?
(*indicating Regan*)
She'll be sleeping. Go ahead.

Chris turns from Regan to Klein.

CHRIS

Would you mind?

KLEIN
No, I know how you feel. The way I do when
I talk to mechanics about my car.

CHRIS (*eyeing him steadily; a pause; then:*)
Not exactly. Regan's kid brother was killed
when his doctor prescribed some new antibiotic.
No offense. But I'd really like to see what's
goin' on.

INTERIOR MEDICAL LABORATORY—NIGHT

Chris and Klein are alone. Chris watches intently as
Klein completes the spinal sugar test with an air of
resignation and bafflement.

CHRIS (*worriedly*)

So what's wrong, doc?

KLEIN

Nothing. It's negative.

She sighs and bows her head.

CHRIS

Well—
(*a bleak murmur*)
—here we are again, folks.

Klein stares down, shaking his head and frowning in perplexity. Then he looks up at Chris.

KLEIN

Are you planning to be home soon? LA, I mean.

CHRIS

No. No, I'm building a new house and the old one's been sold. We were going to Europe for a while after Rags finished up with her school here.

Klein nods, staring down.

CHRIS

Why'd you ask?

KLEIN

I think it's time you started looking for a local psychiatrist.

EXTERIOR CHRIS'S CAR—HIGH MOVING DOWN SHOT—NIGHT

as Chris drives back across Key Bridge.

INTERIOR CHRIS'S CAR—ANGLE FROM DRIVER'S SEAT—NIGHT

Through the windshield, dead ahead, a crowd has gathered by the base of the steep steps beside the house. An ambulance is pulling out into traffic. As Chris rounds off the bridge onto Prospect Street, the ambulance cuts in just ahead of her, siren wailing. We follow the ambulance for two beats, then

CUT TO:

INTERIOR MACNEIL HOUSE—ANGLE AT FRONT DOOR—NIGHT

We are shooting down from the second-floor landing as, in the silence, Chris enters despondently. Closing the door behind her, she leans back against it. Looking down in thought, her hand still clutches the doorknob. A beat. Then the lights in the house blink out for a beat. Chris looks up. They blink out again, this time for longer.

> CHRIS
>
> Sharon?

The lights come back on.

> CHRIS
>
> Shar?

Still no response. Chris starts up the staircase, frowning apprehensively.

INTERIOR SECOND-FLOOR HALL—MACNEIL HOUSE—NIGHT

The camera is fixed by the door to Regan's bedroom. As Chris reaches the landing, the lights blink out again, briefly, then on. Chris has halted, her eyes warily scanning around; then she continues down the hall toward us. She opens the door to Regan's bedroom.

INTERIOR REGAN'S BEDROOM—FULL SHOT—NIGHT

Silence. Chris stands by the door a moment, then goes to Regan's bedside where she rubs at her arms, as if from extreme cold. She examines Regan, who is still sound asleep.

> CHRIS (*a perplexed whisper*)
>
> Shit.

She looks toward window and frowns in consternation.

FULL SHOT—THE ROOM

The window is open. Chris moves to it and stares for a moment.

CHRIS

Hmh.

She closes and locks the window. But she still feels cold. She hears the front door opening from off scene, below, and turns toward the sound. We follow her out into:

INTERIOR SECOND-FLOOR HALLWAY—MAC-NEIL HOUSE—NIGHT

Chris exits and carefully closes Regan's door. She starts toward the stairs and calls softly:

CHRIS

Sharon?

INTERIOR FOYER-LIVING ROOM AREA—MAC-NEIL HOUSE—NIGHT

Sharon has just come in with a white paper pharmacy bag in her hand. Chris appears at the upper-floor balustrade and starts down the stairs.

CHRIS (*hushed tone*)
Hey, what the hell's wrong with you, Sharon?
(*Sharon looks up*)
You go out and leave Rags by herself? Where've you been?

SHARON
I went out for the Thorazine, Chris. Burke's here.

CHRIS
No, he's not. *No* one's here.

SHARON
Are you—?
(*does a take, slapping hand to brow*)
That nut!

TRACKING SHOT—CHRIS AND SHARON

as they join and head for the kitchen.

SHARON

He came by about twenty minutes after you
left and I asked him to stay while I went for
the stuff. Do you *believe* that man?

CHRIS

That's Burke.

SHARON

Hey, what happened with the tests?

Sound of front door being opened and closed. Willie
arriving.

CHRIS

Not a thing. All negative.

SHARON

So what now?

INTERIOR KITCHEN OF MACNEIL HOUSE—
NIGHT

Chris and Sharon are entering.

CHRIS

A psychiatrist.

Chris goes to the refrigerator.

SHARON

Oh.

Chris turns for an afterthought.

CHRIS

Hey, Sharon, are you the one who opened up
the window?

SHARON

What window?

Chris opens the refrigerator.

CHRIS

Forget it. Want a sandwich?

Willie has entered and heard. Sharon eyes the evening
paper.

WILLIE

I fix. You sit down.

CHRIS (*dully*)

Hi, Willie. Any fun today?

WILLIE (*continuing toward her room*)

Shopping. Movies.

SHARON

Where's Karl?

Willie stops and makes a gesture of dismissal.

WILLIE

He lets me see the Beatles this time, by myself, while he goes to see Shakespeare movie.

Willie makes a "phew" gesture, gripping her nose with her thumb and forefinger, while Chris, still staring into the refrigerator, absently lifts two fingers in the "V for Victory" sign. Willie is by the doorway which leads to the pantry and then to her room and above, on the wall, is a kitchen clock. As Willie starts toward the room, the camera drifts up to a close shot of the clock. The time is 8:01. We hear the sound of the refrigerator door closing.

CHRIS

Guess I'm not hungry. Hey, better call Herb in LA, would ya, Shar, and get the name of a psychiatrist around here in this area.

DOWN ANGLE FROM WALL CLOCK POINT OF VIEW

Chris sits at the breakfast table practicing hypodermic injections on a grapefruit. Not doing too well. Sharon comes quickly to the table and sits. Off scene, from Willie and Karl's room, we hear the sound of bath water running. Fragments of a sandwich and an emptied glass of milk on a table indicate the passage of time.

SHARON

Still asleep.

Chris nods glumly, makes a pass at the grapefruit.

111

SHARON

Not bad.

CHRIS

Not good.

SHARON

Are you going to tell Howard?

CHRIS (*still practicing*)

That's using a crisis to get him back.

Sharon shrugs diffidently. Then Chris looks up, thoughtful.

CHRIS

Humhh. Funny. "Howard"—"Captain Howdy."

The wall phone rings. Sharon rises to answer.

SHARON

Say, that's right. I never thought of that. Do you suppose that there might be some kind of a—?

Sharon breaks off to answer the insistent ringing of the phone, signaling Chris to hold on for the rest.

SHARON

Hello, Chris MacNeil's residence.

The front-doorbell chimes have sounded.

CHRIS (*calling out*)

Willie?

No response. Chris rises and leaves the kitchen to answer the door, the camera following. She pays no heed to Sharon on the phone.

SHARON

Yeah, hi, Chuck, it's Sharon. What's happening? . . . Oh? No. No, I haven't . . . *What?*
(*she turns ashen*)
Oh, no! Oh, my God, Chuck, how'd it . . . ?

We are now approaching the front door and are out of range. The chimes sound again.

CHRIS

Hold your horses.
(*opens door, disclosing Karl*)
Oh, it's you.

KARL

Sorry, madam. I forget my key.

As she closes the door and heads for staircase to check in on Regan.

CHRIS

Christ, next thing you know you'll be losing at chess to Reshevsky.

KARL

(*heading for kitchen without looking back*)
Never.

CHRIS

Tell me, how was the movie?

KARL

Exciting.

THE CAMERA IS TRACKING FRONT WITH CHRIS

as she reacts, then climbs the stairs; and halts, looking down at a stunned Sharon coming out from the kitchen.

SHARON

Chris!

CHRIS

Yeah, what?

Camera zooms past Chris to Sharon.

SHARON

Burke's dead!

EXT. STEPS BESIDE MACNEIL HOUSE—DOWN SHOT—NIGHT

The camera is already in motion, drifting downward as a very portly, late-middle-aged man (Kinderman) in a floppy hat and an oversized, old-fashioned overcoat, comes up the steps. He holds a flashlight and is shining its beam along the rococo iron railing running along the side of the steps. As he reaches the last landing before the top, the camera meets him and holds while he examines the landing, and then the railing. He is breathless and wheezes as if from emphysema. His eyes are moist and droopy, as are his cheeks. He finishes his careful examination and shakes his head. Then he stares up at something off scene.

UP ANGLE AT HOUSE FROM LANDING—NIGHT

Kinderman raises the flashlight. He trains it on Regan's window.

QUICK CUT TO:

INTERIOR JESUIT RESIDENCE HALL REFECTORY—ESTABLISHNG SHOT—DAY

Bright sunlight streams in through the windows. A hum of chatter. Jesuits in various modes of dress, many casual, are filtering into the dining room.

ANGLE AT TABLE

Dyer is loading his plate with food as Karras approaches, stands back of a chair, says a quick grace, then sits.

> DYER
> Hi, Damien.

> KARRAS
> What's lunch?

A Negro waiter is approaching close with a tray of knockwurst and sauerkraut.

> DYER
> Can't you smell it?

> KARRAS (*reaching for a pitcher of milk*)
> Oh, shit, is it "dog day" again?

> DYER
> (*eyeing a slice of bread as he butters it*)
> I wouldn't do that. See the bubbles? Saltpeter.

KARRAS (*pouring*)
I need it.
(*eyes haggard as he looks up*)
Any news on reassignment?

DYER
Not yet.

KARRAS
Have you asked him?

Dyer nods glumly and Karras looks down, depressed.
An elderly priest, the pastor of Holy Trinity, sits between them. He looks very Irish and speaks with a
slight brogue. Karras proceeds with lunch.

PASTOR
Damien, have ya got any notions on that altar
card yet?

DAMIEN
No, I really haven't studied it, Father.

DYER
What card?

PASTOR
Oh, another desecration that Damien found.

DAMIEN
An altar card. Somebody typed up a filthy new
text and inserted it inside the plastic casing.

DYER
How filthy?

DAMIEN (*sighing*)
Oh, it more or less describes a homosexual
encounter between—

PASTOR (*interrupting*)
Well, all right now, that's enough of that.

DYER
Yeah, watch that, I'm a minor and easily
corrupted.

PASTOR

And enough of your lip, Joseph Dyer.

DYER

I'm *old* and *not* easily corrupted?

PASTOR

You know, your tongue in itself is an occasion
of sin.

KARRAS (*to Dyer*)

It was written in a very fluent Latin. It had style.

PASTOR (*back to Karras*)

Yes, Church Latin style, don't ya think?

KARRAS

At first glance.

PASTOR

Well, a sergeant of police came by again, ya
know, the one took away the card in the first
place. Well, he says that he talked to some
fellow, a psychologist, and he says that the
person's doin' these desecrations, well, he could
be a priest, ya know, a very sick priest. Do ya
think?

KARRAS (*thoughtful*)

It could be. Yes, it could. Acting out a rebellion against the Church, perhaps, in a state of
complete somnambulism.
(*resumes eating*)
I don't know. Maybe. Could be.

PASTOR

Can ya think of any candidates, Damien?

KARRAS

I don't get you.

PASTOR

Well, now, sooner or later they come and see
you, wouldn't ya say? I mean, the sick ones, if
there are any, from the campus. Do ya know any
like that?

DYER (*staring at pastor incredulously*)
Do you think he'd ever *tell* you?

PASTOR (*aside at Dyer*)
You be still. Do ya have any candidates, Damien?

Dyer is looking at Karras and pointing a finger at the pastor as:

KARRAS
No, I don't.

Without turning to look, the pastor grips Dyer's finger and squeezes it, drawing a brief yelp of pain from the younger priest. Karras smiles, looking down and shaking his head in reaction to their antics. The pastor is rising.

PASTOR
Well, think about it, Damien.

Another Jesuit (Second Jesuit) sits at the table as:

KARRAS (*head still lowered*)
I will.

DYER (*at Karras*)
Will you show me the C-A-R-D later on or should I try to get the——?

The pastor cuts him off with a backhand swat, which causes Dyer to laugh. The pastor turns to him, smiling good-naturedly.

PASTOR
You scoundrel.

He makes a small gesture of farewell to Karras.

PASTOR
Said a mass for your mother this morning, Damien.

Karras grows somber. As the pastor leaves:

KARRAS (*a murmur*)
Thank you, Father.

SECOND JESUIT (*helping himself to food*)
Pretty shocking about that director.

KARRAS
What director?

DYER
Dennings.

SECOND JESUIT
Hadn't you heard?

KARRAS
What happened?

SECOND JESUIT
He's dead. He apparently was drunk and fell down from the top of the "Hitchcock" steps across the street.

DYER
God have mercy on his soul.

SECOND JESUIT
Amen.

We are close at Karras as we hear Third Jesuit joining the table off scene. Karras still staring at his plate, not moving.

THIRD JESUIT (*off scene*)
Hi, I read that book you gave me, Father.

Karras slowly looks up and we see a familiar burden falling upon him.

KARRAS'S POINT OF VIEW

It is the young Jesuit whom Karras had counseled in an earlier scene.

YOUNG JESUIT
Heavy going.

TWO-SHOT—KARRAS AND DYER

As Karras tugs himself up to answer the call for help.

KARRAS
I know. And what did you think of it?

118

Show him the card.

INTERIOR SECOND-FLOOR HALL—MACNEIL HOUSE—DAY

We are down the hall from Regan's bedroom. Chris, red-eyed from weeping, a handkerchief balled in her hand, leans against the banister beside a neuropsychiatrist. Off scene, from inside Regan's bedroom, we hear Regan's howls of pain and terror alternating with obscenities bellowed in that coarsened, deeper voice which grows less intense through:

PSYCHIATRIST
And when was the divorce?

CHRIS
Oh, a year ago. Ten months. I don't know. Is this April?

PSYCHIATRIST
Yes, April 22.

CHRIS
Ten months.

PSYCHIATRIST
Was she close to her father?

CHRIS
Yes, very.

PSYCHIATRIST
Any history of hysterical disorder?

Chris shakes her head.

PSYCHIATRIST
Is she—

They both look down the hall at the sound of Regan's door opening. Klein leans out, nodding for them to come. The furious sounds have ceased, and are replaced by the sound of Regan softly crying, like any normal little girl who is confused and frightened by something she doesn't understand. Then we hear:

REGAN (*off scene*)
(*weeping*)
Where's mom? I want my mom!

CHRIS
Oh, baby!

Chris races the rest of the way and disappears into the bedroom.

REGAN (*off scene*)
Mom!

INTERIOR REGAN'S BEDROOM—ANGLE OVER BED TOWARD DOOR—DAY

As the doctors enter, we see Chris rushing to the bed where she hugs and kisses Regan.

CHRIS
Oh, honey! Oh, Rags! It's really you! You're back! It's you!

As the doctors approach the bed:

REGAN
Oh, mom, he hurt me! Make him stop hurting me! Please? OK?

Chris looks with bewilderment and distress at the doctors.

KLEIN
She's been heavily sedated.

CHRIS
You mean she's—?

PSYCHIATRIST
We'll see.
(*he sits on the edge of the bed, and Regan withdraws from him, uncertain*)
There, there, it's all right, dear. I'm a doctor. I'm here to try to help you. All right?

Regan nods. She is wide-eyed and crying a little again. The camera picks up and follows Klein who moves to a teakwood bureau, turns, and rests an elbow atop it.
120

About a foot distant from his elbow is a large, square-based clay pot. During this:

> PSYCHIATRIST (*off scene*)
> Do you hurt?

> REGAN (*off scene*)
> Yes.

> PSYCHIATRIST (*off scene*)
> Where?

> REGAN (*off scene*)
> Just everyplace! I'm all achy! I don't know why he does it! He was always my friend before.

> PSYCHIATRIST (*off scene*)
> Who's that?

AT BED—CHRIS, REGAN, AND PSYCHIATRIST

> REGAN
> Captain Howdy! And then it's like somebody else is inside me! Making me *do* things!

> PSYCHIATRIST
> Captain Howdy?

> REGAN
> I don't *know!*

> PSYCHIATRIST
> But it's a person?

Regan nods.

> PSYCHIATRIST
> Who?

> REGAN
> I don't knowwwwww!

> CHRIS
> It's OK, honey. It's OK.

> PSYCHIATRIST
> Regan, let's play a game. Would you like to play a game? Here, look at this. See this?

He has reached into his pocket and withdrawn a shiny bauble attached to a length of silvery chain. Regan's sobbing abates. Like any child, she stares with fascination at the bauble.

PSYCHIATRIST
Have you ever seen movies where someone gets hypnotized?

She nods. He is already swinging the bauble gently back and forth.

PSYCHIATRIST
Well, I'm a hypnotist, Regan. Oh, yes! I hypnotize people all the time. That's of course if they'll let me. Now I think that if I hypnotize you, dear, it will help you to get well very soon. Yes, that's right. And that person inside will come right out. Would you like to be hypnotized, Regan? See, your mother's right here, right beside you.

Regan is doubtful. She looks questioningly to Chris.

CHRIS
Go ahead, honey. Do it. It's fun.

REGAN
Well—OK.
(at psychiatrist)
But only a little.

The psychiatrist smiles. Then he and Chris glance toward the sound of pottery breaking behind them.

AT KLEIN

resting his elbow atop the teakwood bureau. He looks at his arm in puzzlement and then looks down at the pot that has just fallen off the top of the bureau and shattered into pieces. As he stoops to pick them up:

ANOTHER ANGLE

CHRIS
Never mind, doc. Willie'll get it.

PSYCHIATRIST
Would you close those shutters for me, Sam? And pull the drapes?

Chris gets up to help him, then comes back and sits on the bed. The room is dark. The psychiatrist gently swings the bauble back and forth. He shines a penlight on it and it glows.

PSYCHIATRIST

Now watch this, Regan, keep watching, and soon you'll feel your eyelids growing heavier and heavier, heavier and heavier, and then you will sleep, you will want to go to—

AT KLEIN

He picks up some shards of the pottery then straightens up. He looks at the bureau again. He is still puzzled as to how it came to fall. During this:

PSYCHIATRIST (*off scene*)

—sleep because your eyes are feeling heavy, feeling heavier and heavier, and now you have to close them. And now you have to close them, and as soon as they are closed you are going to be asleep. As soon as they are—

AT BED

PSYCHIATRIST (*off scene*)

—closed you are going to be asleep and you will do what I say and you will answer my questions. You will do what I say and you will . . .

He halts, inclining the penlight beam up to Regan's eyes. They are closed. She appears to be in trance. In a murmur:

PSYCHIATRIST

Extremely suggestible.

CHRIS

Yeah?

He turns off the penlight.

PSYCHIATRIST

Are you comfortable, Regan?

123

REGAN (*her voice soft and whispery*)

Yes.

PSYCHIATRIST

How old are you, Regan?

REGAN

Twelve.

PSYCHIATRIST

Is there someone inside you?

REGAN

Sometimes.

PSYCHIATRIST

When?

REGAN

Different times.

The camera is angling around to varying views of the scene as:

PSYCHIATRIST

It's a person?

REGAN

Yes.

PSYCHIATRIST

Who is it?

REGAN

I don't know.

PSYCHIATRIST

A man?

REGAN

I don't know.

PSYCHIATRIST

But he's there?

REGAN

Yes, sometimes.

PSYCHIATRIST

Now?

REGAN

I don't know.

PSYCHIATRIST

If I ask him to tell me, will you let him answer?

REGAN

No!

PSYCHIATRIST

Why not?

REGAN

I'm—afraid.

PSYCHIATRIST

If he talks to me, I think he will leave you. Do
you want him to leave you?

REGAN

Yes.

PSYCHIATRIST

Let him speak, then. Will you let him speak?

A pause. Finally:

REGAN

Yes.

The camera is now so positioned that we have only a
side view of Regan's face as, in a new and firm tone:

PSYCHIATRIST

I am speaking to the person inside of Regan
now. If you are there you, too, are hypnotized
and must answer all my questions:
(*pause; then he repeats:*)
If you are there, then you, too, are hypnotized
and must answer all my questions. Come forward and answer, now: Are you there?

No response. Three beats and we hear Regan's breath
coming loud and raspy. It is the sound of a rotted putrid
bellows. The psychiatrist flicks on the penlight and
shines it up into Regan's face.

CHRIS

(*with a sudden intake of breath, a whispered:*)
Oh, my God!

CLOSE AT REGAN

Her features have contorted into a malevolent mask, the lips pulling tautly into opposite directions while a tumefied tongue lolls wolflike from the side of her mouth. Her eyes gleam hatred and unthinkable spite. The sight is unbearable for Chris. She lowers her head and grips the psychiatrist's arm very tightly. This causes him to lower the penlight beam so that it is not directly on Regan's face as he looks with concern to Chris.

CHRIS
It's all right. You go ahead.

He looks quickly back to Regan. Her face is shadowed.

PSYCHIATRIST
Are you the person inside of Regan?

From Regan comes that coarse and guttural voice from an earlier scene.

REGAN
Say.

PSYCHIATRIST
Did you answer?

REGAN
Say.

PSYCHIATRIST
If that's yes, nod your head.

He has flicked up the beam to the face again. Regan nods. The psychiatrist quickly flicks the penlight beam down.

PSYCHIATRIST
Who are you?

REGAN
Nowonmai.

PSYCHIATRIST

That's your name?

REGAN

Say.

PSYCHIATRIST

Are you a woman?

REGAN

One.

PSYCHIATRIST

Is that no?

REGAN

Say.

A pause.

PSYCHIATRIST

Where do you come from?

REGAN

Dog.

PSYCHIATRIST

A dog?

REGAN

Dogmorfemocion.

PSYCHIATRIST

Are you speaking in a foreign language?

REGAN

Say.

PSYCHIATRIST

Are you someone whom Regan has known?

REGAN

One.

Slowly, the psychiatrist has inclined the penlight up again to the face. It is as before.

HIGH OVERHEAD SHOT

PSYCHIATRIST
Are you someone she's invented?

REGAN
One.

PSYCHIATRIST
You're real?

REGAN
Say.

PSYCHIATRIST
Part of Regan?

REGAN
One.

A pause.

PSYCHIATRIST
Do you like her?

REGAN
One.

PSYCHIATRIST
Do you hate her?

REGAN
Say.

PSYCHIATRIST
Over something she's done?

REGAN
Say.

PSYCHIATRIST
Are you punishing Regan?

REGAN
Say.

PSYCHIATRIST
You wish to harm her?

REGAN
Say.

The camera is drifting steadily lower and to a side angle as:

> PSYCHIATRIST
>
> To kill her?

> REGAN
>
> Say.

Over a stifled gasp from Chris:

> PSYCHIATRIST
>
> But if she died, wouldn't you die, too?

> REGAN
>
> One.

> PSYCHIATRIST
>
> Is there something she can do to make you leave her?

> REGAN
>
> Say.

> PSYCHIATRIST
>
> Do you blame her for her parents' div—?

He never gets it out, and his question elides into a prolonged gasp of startled pain and horror as we go quickly to a full shot of Regan, mad, evil glee in the eyes as the psychiatrist drops the penlight.

CLOSE AT PSYCHIATRIST

In the darkness, we see his mouth agape in horrible pain, his eyes wide-staring. What has happened—*and which we must not see,* but now mention for the benefit of the actor and director—is that Regan has gripped his scrotum in a hand that is squeezing like talons of iron.

> PSYCHIATRIST
>
> Sam! Sam, help me!

QUICKLY AT CHRIS

leaping up and away from the psychiatrist as he struggles to wrench away Regan's hand.

Oh, my God!

Kaleidoscopic montage of very quick cuts, mixing: (1) Klein racing forward; (2) Chris running in panic for the light switch; (3) Psychiatrist in agony, struggling; (4) The Regan "creature" with head tilted back, cackling demonically, then howling like a wolf; and (5) Chris's hand slapping at light switch. Then:

AT CHRIS TURNING FROM LIGHT SWITCH

Karl and Willie open the door, looking in. The lights are on now. Sounds of the struggle; the wolf cry. Chris stares in anguish and disbelief as she sees:

POINT OF VIEW AT BED

Cackling demonically, Regan is rolling around on the bed struggling with Klein and the psychiatrist, who still cannot dislodge Regan's grip. Grimaces. Gasps. Curses. *The bedstead is quivering violently from side to side.* We glimpse the scene blurrily and briefly. But the focus clears when we leave the point-of-view shot and go to:

OVERHEAD SHOT—THE ROOM

Regan jerks upright. As her face becomes her own again, her eyes roll upward into their sockets and she wrenches up a keening shriek of terror, torn raw and bloody from the base of her spine. At the start of the scream, the camera descends quickly to a tight shot of her face. Holds for two beats. Then Regan falls backward in a faint and out of frame.

SIDE VIEW OF BED

Stillness. Regan unconscious. Two beats. One of the doctors makes a small feeble move at extricating himself from the tangle but stops as he looks up at a point just to the side of camera point of view. Instantly, Chris crumples into the edge of the frame, falling down out of sight in a dead faint.

HIGH OVERHEAD SHOT OF THE SCENE—FREEZE THE FRAME

FADE OUT

FADE IN:

INTERIOR MACNEIL HOUSE—STUDY—AT
KLEIN—DAY

He is at the bar, dialing the telephone as we hear:

> PSYCHIATRIST (*off scene*)
> No, hysteria is a form of neurosis in which
> emotional disturbances are—

AT CHRIS

Sitting in a chair, she is still stunned, nodding and staring off scene at the psychiatrist and trying with difficulty
to comprehend. She nervously and absently fumbles
with a handkerchief in her lap. We hear, off scene,
Klein's indistinct phone conversation with his office,
delaying an appointment.

> PSYCHIATRIST (*off scene*)
> —converted into bodily disorders and in what
> Freud used to call the "conversion" form of
> this neurosis, the primary feature—

FULL SHOT

disclosing the psychiatrist sitting in a chair near Chris
as:

> PSYCHIATRIST
> —is "dissociation," a kind of splitting off of
> certain material from the basic personality, the
> primary consciousness. This sometimes results
> in schizophrenic psychosis. But where the—
> (*Chris puts head into hand, unable to grasp
> this*)
> —dissociated material is strong enough to some-
> how come glued together, why then it's been
> known, at times—though very rarely—to func-
> tion independently as a separate personality,
> you see, and take over the bodily functions. Do
> you follow?

FULL DOWN SHOT

with Klein hanging up phone and slowly approaching
them to listen.

CHRIS (*looking up*)
No, I don't, but go ahead.

PSYCHIATRIST
I'm sorry. It's quite technical.

CHRIS
Never mind that, I'm listening.

Camera begins slowly circling around them as:

PSYCHIATRIST
In addition, the syndrome of conversion
hysteria might also include epileptoidlike con-
vulsions, hallucinations, and abnormal motor
excitement.

CHRIS
Like Regan.

PSYCHIATRIST
Right. And possibly like Regan, conversion
hysteria grows out of unconscious feelings of
guilt and the need to be punished.

CHRIS
For what? I mean, what would she be guilty
about?

PSYCHIATRIST
Well, a cliché answer might be the divorce.
Children often feel *they* are the ones rejected
and assume the responsibility.

CHRIS (*lowering head to hand despondently*)
Oh, Christ.
(*looking up*)
So OK, then; what's the bottom line?

The camera is now on the psychiatrist as he answers.

PSYCHIATRIST
At the moment, a blank. I think she needs an
intensive examination by a team of experts, two
or three weeks of really concentrated study in
a clinical atmosphere, Mrs. MacNeil. Getting
down to specifics, I think you should take her
to the Barringer Clinic, in Dayton, Ohio.

INTERIOR REGAN'S BEDROOM—DAY

Regan is in bed, unconscious. She is facing away from the camera while Sharon takes her pulse. A beat. Chris enters the room quietly, goes to Regan's closet, and removes some of her clothes from the rack. Then she turns, looks at the bed. She moves to the bedside. She looks down at Regan with pain and compassion. Softly, slowly:

> SHARON
> I'm giving her the Sparine just before we leave. It'll last six hours.

Chris nods, still sadly staring. She reaches a tender hand down to Regan's unseen face; then pulls herself together before tears can come and exits the room with the clothes.

INTERIOR SECOND-FLOOR HALL—MACNEIL HOUSE—DAY

As Chris exits and starts toward her bedroom, Willie comes from the direction of the staircase.

> WILLIE
> Madam!

> CHRIS
> Yeah, Willie. What's doin'?

> WILLIE (*handing her a calling card*)
> Detective downstairs wait to see you.

> CHRIS
> Detective?
> (*eyeing card*)
> Jesus, homicide.
> (*looking up*)
> Homicide?
> (*a moment's thought; she looks disturbed, then hands dresses to Willie*)
> Here, Willie, would ya pack these for me?

> WILLIE (*as Chris moves away*)
> Yes, madam. Surely.

I'd better see what he wants.

As Chris starts down the stairs, the camera follows, disclosing Kinderman waiting below.

CHRIS

Hello there. What's doin'?

As she reaches him, he extends his hand and speaks in a wheezing, husky whisper.

KINDERMAN

I'd know that face in *any* lineup, Miss MacNeil.

CHRIS

Am I *in* one?

KINDERMAN

Oh, my goodness, oh, no! No, it's strictly routine. Routine. Look, you're busy? Tomorrow. I'll come again tomorrow.

CHRIS

What is it? Burke Dennings?

KINDERMAN

What a shame.

CHRIS (*her concern mounting*)
Was he *killed?*

KINDERMAN

God forbid! No, it's strictly routine. But a man so important, we just couldn't pass it. You know?
(*pleading; a helpless look*)
We just couldn't. At least one or two questions. At the least. One or two.
(*he is always gesturing, moving his hands*)
Did he fall? Was he pushed?

CHRIS

Was he robbed?

KINDERMAN

No, not robbed, Miss MacNeil, never robbed, but then who needs a motive in times like these? Why, today, for a murderer a motive is only an encumbrance. A *deterrent*. These drugs, this LSD.

(*tapping his chest with a fingertip*)

Look, believe me, I'm a father and when I see what's going on . . . ahh, boy. You've got children?

                    CHRIS

Yes, one. Listen, why don't we go—(into)

                    KINDERMAN

Please, miss, I could trouble you for something?

(*hand to stomach, grimacing*)

My stomach. Do you keep a little Calso water, maybe?

                    CHRIS

(*heading toward kitchen, Kinderman following*)

Yeah, I think there's a bottle in the fridge. C'mon in.

Kinderman walks with a listing waddle. The camera tracks with them to the kitchen as:

                    KINDERMAN

I'm such a bother. How I hate to be a bother.

                    CHRIS

No bother.

                    KINDERMAN

You've got children? No, that's right; yes, a daughter; you told me; just the one.

                    CHRIS

Just the one.

                    KINDERMAN

And how old?

                    CHRIS

She just turned twelve.

INTERIOR KITCHEN—DAY

In the kitchen we find Karl hard at work polishing the stove and oven racks. Chris gets the Calso for Kinder-

135

man and pours. Throughout the scene, Kinderman's glance keeps flitting to Karl's back. During this:

> KINDERMAN
> Then you don't have to worry.

Chris briefly reacts, then opens the refrigerator as:

> KINDERMAN
> No, not yet. Later on, though.
> (*shaking head*)
> Ah, my God, when you see all the sickness day in and day out. Unbelievable. *Crazy.* You know, I looked at my wife just a couple of days ago— or weeks ago—my memory—but, I said, I said, "Mary, the world—"
> (*he is gesturing globally as Chris comes with the glass and he takes it*)
> Oh, yes, thank you. "The entire world is having a massive nervous breakdown."

> CHRIS
> Yeah, I know.
> (*indicating the table and moving to sit*)
> Come on, sit down.

> KINDERMAN
> You're very kind. Incidentally, that film you made called *Angel?* You know, I saw that film six times.

> CHRIS (*as they sit*)
> If you were looking for the murderer, arrest the director.

> KINDERMAN
> No, the film was just lovely. Really. So touching. But just one thing . . . one minuscule point . . . the score—it seemed to me a little intrusive. Incidentally, was it stolen perhaps from Mendelssohn?

> CHRIS
> I really wouldn't know.
> (*impatient, she indicates the Calso with a move of her head*)
> Better drink that, it tends to get flat.

KINDERMAN
Yes, of course. I'm so garrulous. Forgive me.
(*he drinks it down*)
Ah, good. That's much better.
(*reaching into his pockets for a crumpled high-school play program and a stub of a pencil*)
Now, then, one or two questions, routine, and we're done. In fact, only one question.

His eye catches Regan's sculpture of the bear. It is now the centerpiece of the table. He reaches for it, slides it closer.

KINDERMAN
Ah, look, that's so lovely. So cute. Who's the artist?

CHRIS (*impatient*)
My daughter.

KINDERMAN
So cute.
(*he hunts out paper and pencil again as:*)
Now to business. A nuisance but it has to be done. Now since poor Mr. Dennings had been filming in this area, we wondered if he might have been visiting someone in the neighborhood the night of the accident.

CHRIS
Oh, he was here that night.

KINDERMAN (*eyebrows arching upward*)
He was? Near the time of the accident?

CHRIS
What time did it happen?

KINDERMAN
Seven-oh-five.

CHRIS
I think he was.

Kinderman, nodding, turns in his chair and tucks the paper back in his pocket, as if preparatory to leaving.

Well, that settles it then. He was drunk, he was leaving the house, and he fell down the steps. Yes, that settles it. Definitely.
(*settles back again*)
Oh, no, wait a second, listen, though—just for the sake of the record—can you tell me approximately what time he left the house?

CHRIS

I don't know. I didn't see him. He left while I was out. I was over at a doctor's lab in Rosslyn.

KINDERMAN

Ah, I see. But then how did you know he was here?

CHRIS

Oh, well, Sharon said—

KINDERMAN (*cutting in*)
Sharon?

CHRIS

Sharon Spencer, my daughter's nurse. She told me she was here when Burke dropped by. My daughter was sick and Sharon left him here while she went to pick up some prescriptions. By the time I got home, though, Burke was gone.

KINDERMAN

And what time was that, please?

CHRIS

Seven fifteen or so, 7:30.

KINDERMAN

And what time had you left?

CHRIS

Maybe six fifteenish.

KINDERMAN

What time had Miss Spencer left?

CHRIS

I don't know.

KINDERMAN

And between the time Miss Spencer left and the
time you returned, who was here in the house
with Mr. Dennings besides your daughter?

CHRIS

No one.

KINDERMAN

No one? He left her alone?

CHRIS

Yes, he did.

KINDERMAN

No servants?

CHRIS

No, Willie and Karl were—

KINDERMAN

Who are they?

Chris reacts, abruptly realizing that the nuzzling inter-
view has turned into a steely interrogation. Motioning
with her head:

CHRIS

Well, Karl's right there. And Willie's his wife.
They're my housekeepers. I'd given them the
afternoon off and when I got home they weren't
back yet.

She has reached for a cigarette and Kinderman lights
it as:

KINDERMAN

So then only your daughter would know when
Dennings left the house.

CHRIS

It was really an accident?

KINDERMAN

Of course. Routine. Just a minute and we're
done. Now your daughter, she would know
when Mr. Dennings left the house?

CHRIS

No, she wouldn't. She's been sick and she was heavily sedated.

KINDERMAN

Ah, what a shame. Is it serious?

CHRIS

I'm afraid so.

KINDERMAN

Watch out for drafts. A draft in the winter when a house is hot is a magic carpet for bacteria. My mother used to say that. Well, maybe that's folk myth, for sure I don't know. But a myth, plainly speaking, is like a menu in a fancy French restaurant: glamorous, complicated camouflage for a fact you wouldn't otherwise swallow like maybe the lima beans.
(*gesturing up at the ceiling*)
That's her room there, your daughter, with that window looking down on the steps?

CHRIS (*alert and frowning*)

Yeah, that's hers.

KINDERMAN

Keep the window closed, she'll get better. Drafts.

CHRIS (*relaxing*)

Yeah, I'll watch that.

KINDERMAN

Good. Well, we're finished. Just a note for the record—routine—we're all done.
(*pencil poised*)
Now that's Spencer with a *c*?

CHRIS

Yes, *c*.

KINDERMAN

A *c*.
(*painstakingly writing the name in the margin of the program*)
And the housekeepers? John and Willie?

CHRIS

Karl and Willie Engstrom.

KINDERMAN

Karl. That's right, it's Karl. Karl Engstrom.
Now, the times I remember,
(*turns the program around in search of space
to write on*)
I—oh. Oh no, wait. I forgot. Yes, the housekeepers. You said they got home at what time?

CHRIS

I didn't say. Karl, what time did you get in last
night?

Karl turns around, his face inscrutable.

KARL

Exactly 9:30, madam.

CHRIS

Yeah, that's right, you'd forgotten your key. I
remember I looked at the clock in the kitchen
when you rang the doorbell.

KINDERMAN (*at Karl*)

You saw a good film? I never go by reviews. It's
what the people think, the audience.

KARL

Paul Scofield in *Lear*.

KINDERMAN

Ah, I saw that; that's excellent.

KARL

Yes, at the Crest. The six o'clock showing. Then
immediately after I take the bus from in front of
the theater and—

KINDERMAN

Please, that's not necessary. *Please.*

KARL

I do not mind.

KINDERMAN

No, no, no.

KARL

I do not mind.

KINDERMAN

If you insist.

KARL

I get off at Wisconsin Avenue and M Street.
Nine twenty, perhaps. Then I walk to the house.

KINDERMAN

Look, you didn't have to tell me, but anyway,
thank you, it was very considerate. You liked
the film, by the way?

KARL

It was excellent.

KINDERMAN

Yes, I thought so, too. It was excellent.
(*dotting the final* i)
All right, now, we're finished; finished; done.
Oh, no, wait! Mrs. Engstrom.
(*indicating Karl*)
They came and went together?

CHRIS (*as Karl turns to reply*)
No, she went to see a Beatles flick. She got in
a few minutes after Sharon.

Kinderman tucks away the pencil and program, then
rises, as does Chris. During this:

KINDERMAN

Well, that's that. When I'm back in the office
I'll doubtless remember some question I forgot.
Well, never mind. I can call you.

CHRIS

I'm going out of town for a while, so you'd
better ask it now.

KINDERMAN (*gesture of dismissal*)
Never mind. It doesn't matter.

With smiling fondness, he stares at the sculpture of the
bear.

KINDERMAN

Ah, cute. So cute.

He picks it up, rubbing his thumbnail back and forth along it in a silent, scraping movement as Chris glumly picks a rubber band off the table and listlessly fingers it.

KINDERMAN

I mean, really, it's so lovely. You must be proud.

He sets it back on the table and starts out of the kitchen with Chris, the camera following.

KINDERMAN

Do you have a good doctor? I mean, for your daughter?

CHRIS

Well, I've sure got enough of them. Anyway, I'm checking her into a clinic.

KINDERMAN

Ah, the *clinic* is the out-of-town trip. In New York?

CHRIS

No, in Dayton.

KINDERMAN

It's a good one?

CHRIS

It's supposed to be the best.

KINDERMAN

In the meantime, keep her out of the draft.

INTERIOR FOYER BY FRONT DOOR—DAY

KINDERMAN

Well—I would say it's been a very great pleasure, but under the circumstances . . .

Hat in hand, he holds the doorknob while Chris stares down at the rug with folded arms. Kinderman bows his head and shakes it.

KINDERMAN

I'm sorry. Really. So sorry. I know he was a friend.

143

Chris nods glumly. Kinderman opens the door and steps outside. He turns for:

> KINDERMAN
> Good luck with your daughter.

> CHRIS (*soft and sad-eyed*)
> Good luck with the world.

Chris watches as Kinderman nods and waddles away toward a squad car parked in front of a fire hydrant. The squad car engine turns over. Just before stepping into the car, Kinderman notices the hydrant. He stops. He stares. He looks up to Chris. Then he looks away, shaking his head, starting to enter the squad car on the passenger side.

EXTERIOR MACNEIL HOUSE—AT CHRIS IN DOOR—DAY

She smiles wanly, then slowly closes the door.

INTERIOR SQUAD CAR—DAY

The driver is a detective sergeant. As Kinderman reaches into the glove compartment to extract a small penknife and a specimen envelope:

> KINDERMAN
> In front of the hydrant you parked?

The sergeant eases the car forward a few yards, the initial movement causing a rough lurch. Kinderman gives the sergeant a look, then proceeds to use the smaller blade of the penknife to carefully scrape paint from under his thumbnail into the specimen envelope. Then he seals it and hands it to the sergeant, staring thoughtfully ahead through the windshield. During this:

> KINDERMAN
> All right, this to the lab for a spectrum analysis, and have them compare it with the paint on the statue from the church. Holy Trinity. The new paint, not the old underneath.

> SERGEANT
> Right, I've got it.

144

Kinderman lowers his head and rubs his face wearily.

> KINDERMAN
> Ah, God, what a life, what a life.

The sergeant slowly pulls out into the street. Kinderman looks up through the windshield.

> KINDERMAN
> What a puzzle. Couldn't happen. It happened. How could it?

> SERGEANT
> Back to headquarters?

> KINDERMAN
> No. I have to see again. District Morgue.

INTERIOR RECEPTION AREA—DISTRICT MORGUE—DAY

A young attendant has his feet propped up on a desk. He is munching at a dripping sandwich while working a newspaper crossword puzzle. As we come in, the camera is the eyes of Kinderman approaching the attendant. As the attendant looks up, the camera halts.

ANOTHER ANGLE DISCLOSING KINDERMAN SHOWING I.D.

> KINDERMAN
> Dennings.

The attendant rises, filling in a word, then consults a list before proceeding languidly down a corridor, chewing his sandwich. Kinderman follows.

INTERIOR ROOM IN MORGUE—DAY

The camera is fixed at one end and angled, disclosing—as Kinderman and the attendant approach—the rows and banks of metal lockers used for the filing of sightless eyes. They stop at the other end. The attendant finds the proper locker and pulls it out full length; then he stands back. Kinderman takes his hat off, staring down as:

> KINDERMAN
> Pull the sheet back.

UP ANGLE AT KINDERMAN STARING DOWN

We hear the rustling sound of the sheet being drawn back.

CLOSE ANGLE—POINT OF VIEW AT HEAD OF DENNINGS' CORPSE

Eyes still opened and wide, the face is staring upward. After a quick beat, and with a stab of the score, the camera reverse zooms to disclose that Dennings's head is in fact *turned completely around and is facing backward!*

LONG ANGLE AT KINDERMAN AND ATTENDANT LOOKING DOWN

KINDERMAN

OK.

ATTENDANT (*still staring*)
Could that have happened from the fall?

KINDERMAN (*still looking down*)
Unlikely. But another human being could have done it. A man. An exceptionally powerful man.

EXTERIOR OUTDOOR TRACK IN A HOLLOW OF GEORGETOWN UNIVERSITY CAMPUS—DAY

FRONT MOVING SHOT AT KARRAS

In shorts and T-shirt, he is doing laps. The angle is sufficiently full to disclose his extremely powerful build.

HIGH SHOT—THE TRACK

Karras running. Parked on the road near the track is the squad car. Kinderman emerges and heads for the bench at the edge of the track. Sounds of baseball practice are heard from off scene.

FRONT TRACKING SHOT—KINDERMAN WATCHING KARRAS

ANOTHER ANGLE—AS KARRAS PASSES KINDERMAN

146

and, shortly thereafter, stops running, hands to hips as he walks, head down, panting.

KINDERMAN
Father Karras?

Karras turns, squinting into sun, his breath coming in great gulps. He waits for Kinderman to reach him, then beckons him to follow as he resumes walking.

KARRAS
Do you mind? I'll cramp.

KINDERMAN
Yes, of course.

FRONT TRACKING SHOT—KARRAS, KINDER-MAN

KARRAS
Have we met?

KINDERMAN (*fishing for one of his cards*)
No, we haven't, but they said I could tell; that you looked like a boxer; some priest from the barracks. I forgot. I'm so terrible, awful with names.
(*handing a card to Karras*)
Incidentally, mine is Kinderman, Father. William F.

KARRAS (*eyeing card*)
"Lieutenant" . . .

KINDERMAN (*pointing to a spot on the card*)
Yes, with Homicide.

KARRAS (*handing back the card*)
What's this about?

KINDERMAN
Hey, you know something, Father? You *do* look like a boxer. Excuse me, that scar, you know, there by your eye? Like Brando, it looks like, in that film, you know, *Waterfront*. Just *exactly* Marlon Brando. They gave him a scar . . .
(*illustrating by pulling at the corner of his eye*)

. . . that made his eye look a little bit closed,
just a little, made him look a little dreamy all
the time, always sad. Well, that's you. You're
Brando. People tell you that, Father?

KARRAS

No, they don't.

KINDERMAN

Ever box?

KARRAS

Oh, a little.

KINDERMAN

You're from here in the district?

KARRAS

New York.

KINDERMAN

Golden Gloves. Am I right?

KARRAS

You just made captain. Now what can I do for
you?

KINDERMAN

Walk a little slower, please.
(*gesturing at throat*)
Emphysema.

KARRAS (*slowing his pace*)

Oh, I'm sorry.

KINDERMAN

Never mind. Do you smoke?

KARRAS

Yes, I do.

KINDERMAN

You shouldn't. Incidentally, you're busy? I'm
not interrupting?

KARRAS (*bemused*)

Interrupting what?

148

KINDERMAN

Well, mental prayer, perhaps.

KARRAS (*smiling*)

You *will* make captain.

KINDERMAN

Pardon me, I missed something?

KARRAS

I doubt that you ever miss a thing.

Kinderman halts and mounts a massive and hopeless effort to look befuddled; but, glancing at the Jesuit's crinkling eyes, he lowers his head and ruefully chuckles.

KINDERMAN

Ah, well. Of course . . . of course . . . a psychiatrist. Who am I kidding?
(*he shrugs*)
Look, it's a habit with me, Father. Forgive me. Schmaltz—that's the Kinderman method: pure schmaltz. Well, I'll stop and tell you straight what it's about.

KARRAS (*nodding*)

The desecrations.

KINDERMAN

So I wasted the schmaltz.

KARRAS (*slight smile*)

Mea culpa.

KINDERMAN

Never mind, Father; that I deserved. Yes, the things in the church. Right. Correct. Only maybe something else, something serious.

KARRAS

Murder?

KINDERMAN

Yes, kick me again, I enjoy it.

KARRAS (*shrugging*)

Well, "Homicide Division."

KINDERMAN

Never mind, Marlon Brando, never mind. People tell you for a priest you're a little bit smart-ass?

KARRAS

Not often enough, I'm afraid. I'm sorry.

KINDERMAN

You should be. Now, look, Father, could we keep this between us? Confidential? Like a matter of confession, so to speak?

KARRAS

Of course.

KINDERMAN

You know that director who was doing the film here, Father? Burke Dennings?

KARRAS

Well, I've seen him.

KINDERMAN

You've seen him. You're also familiar with how a month ago he died?

KARRAS (*shrugging*)

Well, the papers . . .

KINDERMAN

That's *part* of it.

KARRAS

Oh?

KINDERMAN

Only part. Listen, what do you know on the subject of witchcraft, Father? From the witching end, please, not the hunting.

KARRAS (*smiling*)

Oh, I once did a paper on it—from the psychiatric end.

KINDERMAN

Oh, really? Wonderful! Great! That's a plus.

You could help a lot more than I thought. Much more. Listen, Father, now witchcraft . . .

He has reached up and gripped at the Jesuit's arm as they round a turn and approach a bench.

KINDERMAN

Now, me, I'm a layman and, plainly speaking, not well educated. Not formally. No. But I read. Look, I know what they say about self-made men, that they're horrible examples of unskilled labor. But me, I'll speak plainly, I'm not ashamed. Not at all, I'm . . .

Abruptly, he arrests the flow as he looks down and shakes his head.

KINDERMAN

Schmaltz. It's a habit. I can't stop the schmaltz. Look, forgive me, you're busy.

KARRAS

Yes, I'm praying.

The Jesuit's soft delivery was dry and expressionless, and Kinderman halts for a moment and eyes him uncertainly.

KINDERMAN

You're serious? No.

The detective faces forward again and they walk.

KINDERMAN

Look, I'll come to the point: the desecrations. They remind you of anything to do with witchcraft?

KARRAS

Maybe. Some rituals used in Black Mass.

KINDERMAN

A-plus. And now Dennings—you read how he died?

KARRAS

In a fall.

KINDERMAN

Well, I'll tell you, but please! Confidential!

KARRAS

Of course.

KINDERMAN (*wistfully, eyeing the bench*)

Do you mind? Could we stop? Maybe sit?

KARRAS

Oh, sure.

They move to the bench.

KINDERMAN

You won't cramp?

KARRAS

No, I'm fine now.

KINDERMAN

You're sure?

KARRAS

I'm fine.

KINDERMAN

Well, all right, if you insist.

Kinderman settles his aching bulk on the bench with a sigh of contentment. The Jesuit picks up his towel and wipes his perspiring face.

KINDERMAN

Ah, better. That's better. Middle age. What a life.

KARRAS

Burke Dennings, you were saying.

KINDERMAN

Yes, yes, Burke Dennings, Burke Dennings, Burke Dennings . . .

He is nodding down at his shoes, and now glances up at Karras.

KINDERMAN

Burke Dennings, good Father, was found at the

bottom of those steps down to M Street with
his head turned completely around and facing
backward.

Karras abruptly stops wiping his face; then he looks up
to meet Kinderman's steady gaze.

KARRAS

It didn't happen in the fall?

KINDERMAN

Sure, it's possible. Possible. However . . .

KARRAS (*nodding his head*)

Unlikely.

KINDERMAN

And so what comes to mind in the context of
witchcraft?

The Jesuit slowly sits down, looking pensive.

KARRAS

Well, supposedly, demons broke the necks of
witches that way. At least, that's the myth.

KINDERMAN

A myth?

KARRAS

Oh, largely.
(*turning to Kinderman*)
Although people did die that way, I suppose:
likely members of a coven who either defected
or gave away secrets.

KINDERMAN

Yes, that's right, Father. Right. I've done a little
research. So on the one hand, a murder, and
on the other, desecrations in the church, Holy
Trinity, identical with rituals they used in devil
worship, Black Mass.

Karras is slipping on a sweatshirt and khaki pants over
his shorts as:

KARRAS

The killer and the desecrator, you think, are the
same?

KINDERMAN (*nodding*)

Maybe somebody crazy, Father Karras. Maybe someone with a spite against the Church. Some unconscious rebellion, perhaps.

KARRAS

Sick priest?

KINDERMAN

Listen, you're the psychiatrist, you tell me.

KARRAS (*thoughtfully*)

Well, of course, the desecrations are clearly pathological. And if Dennings was murdered; well, the way it was done would mean the killer's someone deeply disturbed.

KINDERMAN

And perhaps had some knowledge of witchcraft?

KARRAS

Could be.

KINDERMAN

Could be. And so who fits the bill, also lives in the neighborhood, and also has access in the night to the church?

KARRAS (*nodding gravely*)

Sick priest.

KINDERMAN

Listen, Father, this is hard for you—please—I understand. But for priests on the campus here, you're the psychiatrist; you'd know who was sick at the time, who was not. I mean, *this* kind of sickness. You'd *know* that.

KARRAS

No, not necessarily, lieutenant. It would only be an accident, in fact, if I did. You see, I'm not a psychoanalyst. All I do is counsel. Anyway, I really know of no one who fits the description.

KINDERMAN

Ah, yes; doctor's ethics. If you knew, you wouldn't tell.

KARRAS

No, I probably wouldn't.

KINDERMAN

Incidentally—and I mention it only in passing
—this ethic is lately considered illegal. Not to
bother you with trivia, but lately a psychiatrist
in sunny California was put in jail for not telling
the police what he knew about a patient.

KARRAS (*slight smile*)

That a threat?

KINDERMAN

Don't talk paranoid; I mention it only in passing.

KARRAS

I mention it only in passing, but I could always
tell the judge it was a matter of confession. I
mean, plainly speaking.

KINDERMAN

(*glancing up at him, faintly gloomy*)
Want to go into business, Father?
(*he looks away*)
Father—what "Father"? You're a Jew, I could
tell when I met you.

Karras chuckles.

KINDERMAN

Yes, laugh. Laugh.
(*he bows head, sighing*)
Ah, well. Strange things.
(*looking up, frowning*)
Listen, Father . . . Listen, *doctor*—am I crazy?
Or could there maybe be a witch coven here in
the District of Columbia? Right now, I mean.
Today.

KARRAS

Oh, come on.

KINDERMAN

Then there could.

I didn't get you.

KINDERMAN

Now *I'll* be the doctor. You didn't say *No,* but instead you were smart-ass again. That's defensive, good Father, defensive. You're afraid you'll look gullible, maybe; a superstitious priest in front of—
(*tapping index finger against his temple*)
—Kinderman the mastermind, the rationalist, the genius sitting beside you here, the walking Age of Reason. Right? Am I right?

KARRAS (*sincere*)

Why, that's very astute.

KINDERMAN (*looks away dismally*)

Whatever.
(*squinting back up at Karras*)
Listen, what am I looking for, Father? Tell me.

KARRAS

A madman. Maybe someone on drugs.

KINDERMAN

Or a member of a satanist cult?

KARRAS

Or all three.

Kinderman stares up at him for a moment; then he looks down again.

KINDERMAN

Strange. Strange things.
(*rising*)
Well, thank you very much, Father Karras.
(*takes Karras's arm*)
Come, we'll take you where you're going.

KARRAS

That's all right, thanks. It's just a short walk.

Kinderman takes Karras by the arm and walks him toward the car.

Never mind, Kirk Douglas. Enjoy. You can tell all your friends you went riding in a police car.

QUICK DISSOLVE TO:

INTERIOR SQUAD CAR—KINDERMAN, KARRAS IN BACK SEAT—DAY

KINDERMAN

You like movies, Father Karras?

KARRAS

Very much.

KINDERMAN

You saw *Lear*?

KARRAS

No, I don't see too many. Can't afford it.

KINDERMAN

I saw it. I get passes.

KARRAS

That's nice.

KINDERMAN

I get passes for the very best shows. Mrs. K., she gets tired, though; never likes to go.

KARRAS

That's too bad.

KINDERMAN (*staring out window*)

It's too bad; yes, I hate to go alone. You know, I love to talk film; to discuss; to critique.

Karras silently nods, looking down at his large and very powerful hands, now clasped between his legs. A beat. Then, hesitantly, Kinderman turns with a wistful look.

KINDERMAN

Would you like to see a film with me sometime, Father? It's free. I get passes. I've got passes for the Crest. It's *Othello*.

KARRAS

Who's starring?

157

Molly Picon, Desdemona, and Othello, Leo Fuchs. You're happy?

KARRAS

Well, I'll have to check my schedule. What night?

KINDERMAN (*happily*)

I'll call.

They have come to the Residence hall and parked. Karras puts a hand on the door and clicks it open.

KARRAS

Please do. Look, I'm sorry that I wasn't much help.

KINDERMAN

Never mind, you were help. In fact, for a Jew who's trying to pass, you're a very nice man.

Karras smiles faintly, nodding. Then he exits from the car.

EXTERIOR JESUIT RESIDENCE HALL ON PROSPECT STREET—AT SQUAD CAR—DAY

As Karras closes the car door, Kinderman slides over to the window.

KINDERMAN

Oh, one more thing. That card from the Church, with the dirty writing? You've seen it?

KARRAS

Yes, I've studied it.

KINDERMAN

Any conclusions?

KARRAS

I don't know. It doesn't look like the work of a prankster. At first, I thought maybe a student. But I doubt it. Whoever did *that* thing is deeply disturbed.

KINDERMAN

As you said.

KARRAS

And the Latin . . . It's just flawless, lieutenant, it's—well, it's got a definite style that's very individual. It's as if whoever did it is used to *thinking* in Latin.

KINDERMAN

Do priests?

KARRAS

Oh, come on!

KINDERMAN

Just answer the question, please, Father Paranoia.

KARRAS (*leaning closer; looking grave*)

Look, lieutenant, can I tell you who I really think did it?

KINDERMAN

No, who?

KARRAS

Dominicans. Go pick on them.

KINDERMAN

Listen, don't be so snotty. You should render unto Caesar just a little now and then. I'm the law. I could have you deported, you know that?

KARRAS

What for?

KINDERMAN

A psychiatrist shouldn't piss people off. Plus also the goyim, plainly speaking, would love it. You're a nuisance to them altogether, Father. No, I'm serious. Really. You embarrass them. They would love to get rid of you. Who needs it? A priest who wears sweatshirts and sneakers!

KARRAS (*smiling*)

Got to go. Take care.

Karras turns and walks toward the Residence hall entrance.

> KINDERMAN (*calling out after him*)
> I lied! You look like Sal Mineo!

INTERIOR SQUAD CAR

We hear a car pulling up and parking nearby, off scene. Kinderman watches as we see Karras give a small wave from the door and then enter the Residence hall. Now Kinderman looks toward the off-scene sound of car doors being opened. He stares intently at:

ANGLE THROUGH CAR WINDOW—KINDERMAN AT EDGE OF FRAME

A limo has pulled up to the MacNeil house. Karl is exiting from the driver's seat and opening the rear door while Sharon exits on the right rear side. Chris sits in the back seat, holding a small figure (Regan) wrapped in a blanket. Karl takes Regan from Chris and carries her toward the house where Willie stands, anxiously watching. Chris exits from the car. She is deeply depressed. She halts, staring at the ground, one hand in her coat pocket, the other shakily rising to her lowered head. During this, the camera zooms to a tight shot of her face and just as she touches her hand to the side of her brow, we:

FREEZE THE FRAME

as we hear:

> MALE VOICE (CLINIC DIRECTOR)
> ... fewer and fewer lucid—

AND QUICKLY CUT TO:

INTERIOR BARRINGER CLINIC—DIRECTOR'S OFFICE—DAY

A flashback and again a grainy black and white. The office is glass-enclosed on two sides, so that we have a view in the background of a steady traffic of doctors and nurses. The camera angle now features the clinic director, who leans against the edge of a desk, his arms folded, as he gravely addresses the camera (Chris). To the side is another doctor.

CLINIC DIRECTOR

—moments, and now there's a total blacking out of her consciousness during the fits, which would seem to eliminate hysteria. In the meantime, a symptom or two of "parapsychic phenomena" seem to have—

QUICK CUT TO:

INTERIOR SECOND-FLOOR HALL—MACNEIL HOUSE—DAY

The present. Chris is coming at us, toward the door to Regan's bedroom. Her manner is trancelike, numbed by pain.

INTERIOR HIGH OVERHEAD FULL SHOT—REGAN'S BEDROOM—DAY

Regan faces to the side. Sharon is adjusting a Sustagen flask used for a nasogastric feeding of Regan. Karl is affixing a set of restraining straps to the bed. Chris enters, stands by the door and observes. Karl lets the straps hang loose, nods at Sharon. Sharon starts out of the room, pausing by the door to look at Chris. Then she exits.

LONG ANGLE TOWARD DOOR AND PAST BED

Chris now slowly advances toward the bed, her gaze fixed on Regan's face, which is averted, and hidden from camera. As Chris halts, we zoom to a tight shot of her.

DIRECTOR'S VOICE (*echo chamber*)

—syndrome of a type of—

INTERIOR BARRINGER CLINIC—DIRECTOR'S OFFICE—DAY

Flashback. Grainy black and white.

CLINIC DIRECTOR

—disorder that you rarely ever see anymore, except among primitive cultures. We call it somnambuliform possession. Quite frankly, we don't know much about it, except that it starts with some conflict or guilt that eventually leads to the patient's delusion that his body and his mind have been invaded and are being controlled by an alien intelligence; a so-called "spirit," if you will. In days gone by, the possessing entity was usually a demon; an evil spirit. In relatively modern cases, however, it's mostly the spirit of someone dead, often someone the patient has known or seen and is able to mimic unconsciously. The voice, I mean, their mannerisms. Sometimes even the features of the victim's face seem to change into that of the invading personality. This type of possession is easier to cope with. You don't find the rages in most of those cases, or the hyperactivity and the motor excitement. However, in the other main type of possession, the new personality is always—well, hostile toward the first. Its primary aim, in fact, is to kill it. We—

QUICK CUT TO:

INTERIOR REGAN'S BEDROOM—TIGHT AT CHRIS'S HAUNTED EYES—DAY

They stare, then drop to:

POINT OF VIEW AT REGAN'S FACE AND ZOOM TO A TIGHT SHOT

The face is torn and bloated. Numerous scratch marks and scabs. Projecting hideously from a nostril is the nasogastric tubing.

CLINIC DIRECTOR'S VOICE (*echo chamber*)
The syndrome is—

INTERIOR BARRINGER CLINIC—OVERHEAD SHOT TO INCLUDE CHRIS—DAY

Flashback. Grainy black and white.

CLINIC DIRECTOR
—only the manifestation of some conflict, of

some guilt, so we try to get at it, find out what it is. Well, the best procedure in a case like this is hypnotherapy; however, we can't seem to put her under. So then we took a shot at narco-synthesis—that's a treatment that uses narcotics—but, frankly, it looks like another dead end.

CHRIS

So what's next?

CLINIC DIRECTOR

Mostly time, I'm afraid; more time. We'll just have to keep trying and hope for a change. In the meantime, she's going to have to be hospitalized for a . . .

CHRIS

You want me to put her away?

CLINIC DIRECTOR

But it isn't an—

CHRIS (shouting)

I'm not going to do it!

CLINIC DIRECTOR

Well, I'm sorry.

CHRIS

Yeah, sorry. Christ, eighty-eight doctors and all you can tell me with all of your bullshit is—!

QUICK CUT TO:

INTERIOR REGAN'S BEDROOM—TIGHT AT CHRIS'S EYES—DAY

Back to the present.

KARL (off scene)

She is going to be well?

Chris flicks up her gaze.

OVERHEAD SHOT TO INCLUDE REGAN, KARL

Karl is sitting in a straight-backed chair by Regan's bed, looking up anxiously at Chris. She bows her head.

163

CHRIS (*low*)

I don't know.

ANOTHER ANGLE

A beat. Then Chris leans over and tenderly adjusts Regan's pillow. In the process, she discovers a white bone crucifix underneath it. Frowning, she lifts it out and examines it.

CHRIS

Who put this crucifix under her pillow?

INTERIOR BARRINGER CLINIC—INTERCUT CHRIS AND DIRECTOR—DAY

Flashback. Grainy black and white. Through the glass wall, we see a doctor and a nurse having a flirtatious encounter in the hallway.

CLINIC DIRECTOR (*dossier in hand*)

Now you stated "No religion" here, Mrs. Mac-Neil. Is that right? No religious education at all?

CHRIS

Yeah, that's right. I'm an atheist, I guess. Or agnostic.

CLINIC DIRECTOR

Odd. The content of much of her raving— when it isn't that gibberish she spouts—is definitely religiously oriented. Now where did she get that?

CHRIS

I don't know. Why'd you ask?

CLINIC DIRECTOR

Well, there *is* one outside chance of a cure, and possibly a very rapid cure. You see, possession *is* loosely related to hysteria insofar as its cause is almost always suggestion; or autosuggestion. At least that's what we think. So, if your daughter might have known about possession, knew some of its symptoms, and also believed in possession, her subconscious might simply be duplicating the syndrome. Now if all of those things can be established, you might take a stab at a form of cure that works through suggestion. I think of it as shock treatment in these cases, though most other therapists wouldn't agree, I suppose. Well, it *is* a very outside chance. But since you're so opposed to your daughter being hospitalized—

CHRIS (*interrupting*)
What is it?

CLINIC DIRECTOR
Have you ever heard of exorcism, Mrs. Mac-Neil?

INTERIOR MACNEIL HOUSE—STUDY—DAY

We are back in the present. Chris moves slowly to the bookshelves and begins looking for one book in particular. The camera is then trained on the books, Chris's finger slowly running along the titles, shelf to shelf, as we hear, continuing, the voices from the past.

CLINIC DIRECTOR'S VOICE (*echo chamber*)
It's a stylized ritual—mostly prayers—in which rabbis and priests tried to drive out the so-called invading spirit. It's pretty much discarded these days, although the Catholics still keep it on the books. But to someone who really believes in possession, the ritual can work, you see, through the power of suggestion: the counteracting suggestion to the one we think caused the disorder in the first place.

CHRIS'S VOICE
Are you telling me to take my daughter to a witch doctor?

Chris frowns and the camera tracks with her back into the hallway and then toward the kitchen as we continue with:

CLINIC DIRECTOR'S VOICE
Yes, I suppose that I'm saying just that: as a desperate measure, perhaps to a priest. That's a

165

rather bizarre little piece of advice, I know; even dangerous, in fact, unless we can ascertain whether Regan knew anything at all about possession, and particularly exorcism, before this all came on. Do you think she might have read it?

CHRIS'S VOICE

I don't know.

CLINIC DIRECTOR'S VOICE

Any books on possession in the house? Or on witchcraft that might have a chapter on the subject?

CHRIS'S VOICE

Gee, I think I might have seen one in the—

We have passed Willie wiping her hands on her apron while en route to answer the front door; and now we cut off the clinic director's voice and are finished with the dialogue flashback.

INTERIOR KITCHEN—MACNEIL HOUSE—DAY

Sharon is listlessly typing some correspondence at the breakfast nook table.

CHRIS

Hey, wasn't there a book on witchcraft in the study?

SHARON (erasing something)

Yes, I've got it in my room. Do you want it?

CHRIS

Is there something—I mean, a chapter on possession in it?

SHARON (blowing away eraser fragments)

I don't know. I'll go and get it, if you want. I haven't read it.

CHRIS

Yeah, wouldjya? And, Sharon, do you know if maybe Rags might have read it?

SHARON

Yes, she did, I think. Willie found it under her bed.

As Sharon exits, Willie appears at the kitchen door.

WILLIE

Please, madam. Detective come again. He want to see you.

CHRIS (*impatient*)

Oh, well, tell him to—!
(*arrested by a troubling thought*)
Tell him to come in.

We lose Willie, who leaves with a nod, and we come in closer at Chris. She is wrinkling her brow at a disturbing recollection, as we hear (echo chamber):

CLINIC DIRECTOR'S VOICE

Yes, Dennings. Burke Dennings. Who is he?

CHRIS'S VOICE

Why?

CLINIC DIRECTOR'S VOICE

Well, the name occurs frequently during her fits.

CHRIS'S VOICE

What's she say about him, doc?

CLINIC DIRECTOR'S VOICE

She doesn't like him.

The flashback exchange of echo voices is cut off by the return of Willie with Kinderman.

KINDERMAN (*off scene*)

Ah, sorry; you're busy.

ANOTHER ANGLE DISCLOSING KINDERMAN APPROACHING

KINDERMAN

You're busy. I'm a bother.

CHRIS

(*an edge of alertness in her manner; of foreboding*)
How's the world?

KINDERMAN

Very bad. How's your daughter?

CHRIS

No change.
(*sitting*)
Please sit down.

KINDERMAN

Oh, yes, thank you. That's better. Your poor
daughter. I'm so sorry.

CHRIS

What's doin'?

KINDERMAN

Well, I really wouldn't bother you at all, except . . .

He breaks off as Sharon returns. She puts the witchcraft
book on the table next to Chris; then sits and resumes
typing.

KINDERMAN (*eyeing the book*)

Witchcraft. For a film?

CHRIS

No, just reading.

KINDERMAN (*flipping through the pages*)

It's good?

CHRIS

I just started. Now—?

Sharon rips a page out of the typewriter platens and
crumples it, interrupting them.

SHARON

Darn it!
(*she sees they are looking at her*)
Oh, I'm sorry.

KINDERMAN

You're Miss Fenster?

SHARON (*tossing paper at wastebasket*)

Spencer.

Sharon has missed the basket, and makes as if to rise, but Kinderman leans down and retrieves the balled-up sheet. He toys with it through the rest of the scene.

KINDERMAN

Never mind.

SHARON

Oh, thanks.

CHRIS

Shar, this is—I'm sorry.

KINDERMAN

Lieutenant Kinderman, William F.

SHARON

Oh.

KINDERMAN

Maybe you can help me, Miss Spencer. Who knows? Now—on the night of Mr. Dennings's demise, you went out to a drugstore and left him alone in the house. That's correct?

SHARON

Well, no, Regan was here.

CHRIS

That's my daughter.

KINDERMAN

And you left at what time? You remember?

SHARON

Oh, quarter to seven or so. Around there.

CHRIS

Look, what's this all about, lieutenant?

KINDERMAN

Well, the matter—you'll forgive me—has now grown serious. The report of the pathologist, Mrs. MacNeil, seems to show that the chance that he died accidentally is still very possible. Possible. However—

CHRIS

Are you saying Burke was murdered?

Perhaps. The position of his head and a certain —well, shearing of the muscles of the neck would—

CHRIS (*wincing*)

Oh, God!

KINDERMAN

Yes, it's painful. I'm sorry. Truly. But, you see, this condition—we can skip the details—well, it never could happen, you see, unless Dennings had fallen some distance *before he hit the steps;* for example, some twenty or thirty feet before he went rolling down to the bottom. So a clear possibility, plainly speaking, is maybe . . . Well, first let me ask you this. Might your daughter remember if perhaps Mr. Dennings was in her room that night?

CHRIS

No, I told you before, she was heavily sedated and—

KINDERMAN

Yes, yes, you told me; that's true; I recall. But perhaps she awakened, not so?

CHRIS

Listen, why are you asking all this?

KINDERMAN

Well, a clear possibility, perhaps, is that maybe the deceased was so drunk that he stumbled and fell from the window in your daughter's bedroom.

CHRIS

No way. No chance. In the first place, the window was always—
(*remembers something; switches track*)
—well, Burke was *always* drunk, but he never got sloppy. Burke used to *direct* when he was smashed. Now how could he stumble and fall out a window?

Were you maybe expecting someone else here
that night?

CHRIS

No.

KINDERMAN

Have you friends who drop by without calling?

CHRIS

Just Burke. Why'd you ask?

KINDERMAN

The deceased comes to visit, stays only twenty
minutes without even seeing you, and leaves all
alone here a very sick girl. And, speaking plainly, Mrs. MacNeil, as you say, it's not likely he
would fall from a window. Besides that, a fall
wouldn't do to his neck what we found except
maybe one chance in a thousand.
(*he nods at the book on witchcraft*)
You've read in that book about ritual murder?

Chris shakes her head, wide-eyed with some presenti-
ment.

KINDERMAN

Maybe not in that book. However—forgive me
—I mention this only so maybe you'll think just
a little bit harder—but poor Mr. Dennings was
discovered with his neck wrenched around in
the style of ritual murder by so-called demons,
Mrs. MacNeil. Yes, some lunatic killed Mr.
Dennings. At first, I never told you to spare you
the hurt. And besides, it could technically still
be an accident. But me, I don't think so. My
hunch. My opinion. I believe he was killed
by a powerful man: point one. And the fracturing of his skull—point two—plus the various
things I have mentioned—would make it very
probable—not certain—only probable—the deceased was killed and then afterward pushed
from your daughter's window. But no one was

171

here except your daughter. So how could this
be? It could be one way: if someone came
calling between the time Miss Spencer left and
the time you returned. Not so? Maybe so. Now
I ask you again, please; who might have come?

CHRIS (*in shock*)

Judas priest, just a second!

KINDERMAN

Yes, I'm sorry. And perhaps I'm all wrong—I'll
admit. But you'll think, now? Who? Tell me who
might have come?

Chris has her head down, frowning in thought.

CHRIS

No. No, there's no one.

KINDERMAN

Maybe you, then, Miss Spencer. Someone comes
to see *you?*

SHARON

Oh, no, no one.

KINDERMAN (*to Chris*)

Then, the servants? They have visitors?

CHRIS

Never.

KINDERMAN

You expected a package that day? Some delivery?

CHRIS

Not that I know of. Why?

KINDERMAN

Mr. Dennings was—not to speak ill of the dead,
may he rest in peace—but, as you said, in his
cups he was somewhat—well, call it "irascible"
—capable, doubtless, of provoking an argument;
an anger; in this case, a rage from perhaps a
delivery man who came by to drop a package.
So were you expecting something? Like dry

cleaning, maybe? Groceries? Liquor? A package?

CHRIS

I really wouldn't know. Karl handles all of that.

KINDERMAN

Oh, I see.

CHRIS

Want to ask him?

The detective sighs, leaning back from the table and stuffing his hands in the pockets of his coat. He stares glumly at the witchcraft book.

KINDERMAN

Never mind, it's remote. You've got a daughter very sick and—well—never mind.
(*he makes a gesture of dismissal and rises from the chair*)
Very nice to have met you, Miss Spencer.

SHARON (*distantly*)

Same here.

KINDERMAN

Baffling. Strange.
(*at Chris, as she rises*)
Well, I'm sorry. I've bothered you for nothing. Forgive me.

CHRIS

Here, I'll walk you to the door.

KINDERMAN

Don't bother.

CHRIS

No bother.

FRONT TRACKING SHOT—KINDERMAN, CHRIS

KINDERMAN

If you insist. Incidentally, just a chance in a million, I know. But your daughter—you could possibly ask her if she saw Mr. Dennings in her room that night?

CHRIS

Look, he wouldn't have a reason to be up there
in the first place.

KINDERMAN

I know that; I realize; that's true; but if certain
British doctors never asked, "What's this fun-
gus?" we wouldn't today have penicillin. Right?
Please ask. You'll ask?

CHRIS

When she's well enough, yes; I'll ask.

KINDERMAN

Couldn't hurt. In the meantime . . .

They have come to the front door and Kinderman
falters, embarrassed. He puts his fingertips to his mouth
in a hesitant gesture.

KINDERMAN

Look, I really hate to ask you; however . . .

CHRIS (*tensing*)

What?

KINDERMAN

For my daughter . . . you could maybe give me
an autograph?

He has reddened, and Chris almost laughs with relief.

CHRIS

Oh, of course. Where's a pencil?

KINDERMAN

Right here!

He has whipped out the stub of a chewed-up pencil
from the pocket of his coat while dipping his other hand
into a jacket pocket and slipping out a calling card.

KINDERMAN

She would love it.

CHRIS (*taking the card and pencil*)
What's her name?

174

Chris presses the card against the door and poises the pencil stub to write. There follows a weighty hesitation. She glances around and in Kinderman's eyes we see some massive, terrible struggle that turns to desperation and defiance as:

KINDERMAN

I lied. It's for me.
(*he fixes his gaze on the card and blushes*)
Write "To William—William F. Kinderman"—
it's spelled on the front.

Chris eyes him with a wan and unexpected affection, checks the spelling of his name, and writes on the card. Then she gives it to him.

KINDERMAN (*sheepishly*)

You're a very nice lady.

CHRIS

You're a very nice man.

KINDERMAN (*opening door*)

No, I'm not. I'm a bother. Never mind what I said here today. It's upsetting. Forget it. Keep your mind on your daughter. Your *daughter*.

Chris nods, her despondency surging up again as Kinderman steps outside onto the stoop. He turns, donning his hat.

KINDERMAN

Well, good-bye. And take care.

CHRIS

You, too.

She closes the door softly, then instantly opens it again as we hear a knocking.

KINDERMAN

What a nuisance. I'm a nuisance. I forgot my pencil.

EXTERIOR MACNEIL HOUSE—DAY

Chris smiles faintly, staring at the stub in her hand. She gives it to Kinderman.

Oh, thank you. Well, all right, now, good— No. No, no, wait—one thing. It's pointless—I know —it's a bother—it's dumb—it's ridiculous— but I know I won't sleep thinking maybe there's a lunatic loose or a doper if every little point I don't cover, whatever. Do you think I could . . . ? No, no, it's dumb, it's a . . . Yes— yes, I should. Could I maybe have a word with Mr. Engstrom, do you think? The deliveries, the question of deliveries. I really should—

CHRIS (*wearily*)

Sure, come on in.

KINDERMAN

No, you're busy. I can talk to him here.
(*leaning against railing*)
Here is fine. Very nice.

CHRIS (*forcing a smile*)

If you insist.

Chris closes the door. A few beats later, Karl opens it and steps out. He is expressionless.

KARL

Yes?

Kinderman now speaks rapidly and with a flat and deadly cadence, his gaze locked to Karl's as we see a totally unexpected side of the detective.

KINDERMAN

You have the right to remain silent. If you give up the right to remain silent, anything you say can and will be used against you in a court of law. You have the right to speak with an attorney and to have an attorney present during questioning. If you so desire, and cannot afford one, an attorney will be appointed for you without charge prior to questioning. Do you understand each of these rights I've explained to you?

KARL

Yes.

KINDERMAN

Do you wish to give up the right to remain silent?

KARL

Yes.

KINDERMAN

Do you wish to give up the right to speak to an attorney and have him present during questioning?

KARL

Yes.

KINDERMAN

Did you previously state that on April 22, the night of the death of Mr. Dennings, you attended a film that was showing at the Crest?

KARL

Yes.

KINDERMAN

And what time did you enter the theater?

KARL

I do not remember.

KINDERMAN

You stated previously you attended the six o'clock showing. Does that help you to remember?

KARL

Yes. Yes, six o'clock show. I remember.

KINDERMAN

And you saw the picture—the film—from the beginning?

KARL

I did.

KINDERMAN

And you left at the film's conclusion?

KARL

Yes.

KINDERMAN

Not before?

KARL

No, I see entire film.

KINDERMAN

And, leaving the theater, you boarded the Capital Transit bus in front of the theater, debarking at M Street and Wisconsin Avenue at approximately 9:20 P.M.?

KARL

Yes.

KINDERMAN

And walked home?

KARL

I walk home.

KINDERMAN

And was back in this residence at approximately 9:30 P.M.?

KARL

I am back here *exactly* 9:30.

KINDERMAN

You're sure.

KARL

Yes, I look at my watch. I am positive.

KINDERMAN

And you saw the whole film to the end?

KARL

Yes.

KINDERMAN

Your answers are being electronically recorded, Mr. Engstrom. I want you to be absolutely positive.

KARL

I am positive.

You're aware of the altercation between an usher and a drunken patron that happened in the last five minutes of the film?

KARL

Yes.

KINDERMAN

Can you tell me the cause of it?

KARL

The man, he was drunk and was making disturbance.

KINDERMAN

And what did they do with him finally?

KARL

Out. They throw him out.

KINDERMAN

There was no such disturbance. Are you also aware that, during the course of the six o'clock showing, a technical breakdown, lasting approximately fifteen minutes, caused an interruption in the showing of the film?

KARL

I am not.

KINDERMAN

You recall that the audience booed?

KARL

No, nothing. No breakdown.

KINDERMAN

You're sure?

KARL

There was nothing.

KINDERMAN

There was, as reflected in the log of the projectionist, which shows that the film ended not at 8:40 that night, but at approximately 8:55,

which would mean that the earliest bus from
the theater would put you at M Street and
Wisconsin not at 9:20, but 9:45, and that, therefore, the earliest you could be at the house was
approximately five before ten, not 9:30, as
testified also by Mrs. MacNeil. Would you care
now to comment on this puzzling discrepancy?

KARL

No.

The detective stares at him mutely for a moment, then
sighs and looks down as he turns off the tape-activating
mechanism that is tucked in the lining of his coat. In a
tone that is weary with understanding:

KINDERMAN

Mr. Engstrom . . . A serious crime may have
been committed. You are under suspicion. Mr.
Dennings abused you, I have learned from other
sources. You were also once charged with theft
of drugs from a former employer, a Dr. Jennings
in San Francisco. The charges were dropped at
the doctor's insistence; who knows why? Still,
they are charges. And, apparently, you've lied
about your whereabouts at the time of Dennings's death. Now it sometimes happens—we're
human—why not?—that a man who is married
is sometimes someplace where he says that he is
not. You notice I arranged we are talking in
private? Away from the others? Away from your
wife? Now, I'm not recording. It's off. You can
trust me. If it happens you were out with a
woman not your wife on that night, you can
tell me. I'll have it checked out, you'll be out of
this trouble, and your wife, she won't know.
Now, then, tell me, where were you at the time
Dennings died?

KARL

At movies.

The detective eyes him steadily, silent and unmoving,
no sound but his wheezing as the seconds tick heavily
by. Then, his voice breaking:

You are going to arrest me?

The detective makes no answer, but continues to eye him, unblinking, and when Karl seems again about to speak, Kinderman abruptly pushes away from the railing, listing toward the parked squad car, his hands in his pockets. He walks unhurriedly, eyeing his surroundings to the left and the right like an interested visitor to the city. From the stoop, Karl watches, his features stolid and impassive as Kinderman opens the door of the squad car, reaches inside to a box of Kleenex fixed to the dashboard, extracts a tissue, and blows his nose while staring idly across the river as if considering where to have lunch. Then he enters the car without glancing back. Karl closes the door and we—

CUT TO:

INTERIOR SQUAD CAR—DAY

Kinderman closes the door and from his coat pocket he extracts Sharon's crumpled ball of typescript. As he eyes it:

KINDERMAN
Crime lab. Hurry. Break laws.

INTERIOR MACNEIL HOUSE—KITCHEN—DAY

Sharon is continuing her hunt-and-peck typing. Willie is at the stove. Chris sits at the table, the witchcraft book open before her. She is turning gaze from the left-hand page to the right when she freezes, turning ashen. A beat. Then, numbly, as Chris lifts the book to show to Willie:

CHRIS
Willie—did you find this under Regan's bed?

Willie examines the book, then turns back to her cooking with:

WILLIE
Yes, madam.

Chris's gaze is still fixed on the book.

181

CHRIS

When did you find it?

WILLIE

After all go to hospital, madam, when I vacuum.

CHRIS

You're sure?

WILLIE

I am sure.

Still numb, Chris runs a finger along edge of the right-hand page, and in a closeup we see that a narrow strip has been surgically shaved from along its edge—in the manner of Burke Dennings.

CHRIS (*off scene*)
(*whisper*)
He was up there in the room with her.

SHARON (*glancing up*)
What, Chris?

Then all look up toward Regan's bedroom at the sound of a blow, of someone staggering across the room, of someone crashing to the wall and falling heavily to the floor. Chris races out of the kitchen, the camera following as we hear an at first indistinct altercation between a tearful and terror-stricken Regan and someone else —a man with a powerful and incredibly deep bass voice. Regan is pleading, the man commanding in obscene terms.

ANGLE AT CHRIS FROM TOP OF STEPS (SECOND FLOOR)

She rushes up, frenzied, while Willie and Sharon stare up from the bottom of the steps. We hear:

REGAN (*off scene*)
No! Oh, no, don't! Don't—!

DEEP BASS VOICE (*off scene*)
Do it, damned piglet! You'll—!

REGAN (*off scene*)
No! Oh, no—!

And in this manner, the voices continue—*and never overlapping*—while camera tracks with Chris to the door of Regan's bedroom. She throws it open.

INTERIOR REGAN'S BEDROOM—DAY

Chris bursts in, then stands rooted in shock, as from off scene, we hear the sound of the bed shaking violently, and the continuation of dialogue between Regan and the thundering deep male voice.

<blockquote>
REGAN (*off scene*)
Please! Oh, please don't m(ake)—!
</blockquote>

<blockquote>
MALE VOICE (*off scene*)
You'll do as I tell you, filth! You'll—!
</blockquote>

Chris has turned her head to stare at:

POINT OF VIEW—AT KARL

Blood trickling down from his forehead, he lies unconscious on the floor near the bureau. The camera (Chris's eye) then swishes over to the bed, disclosing Regan sitting up in a side view, her legs apart and the bone-white crucifix clutched in raw-knuckled hands that are upraised over her head. She seems to be exerting a powerful effort to keep the crucifix up, away from her vagina, which we cannot (and *will not*) see, her nightgown pulled up to that point. Her face keeps altering expression to match each voice in the argument, *both of which are coming from her!* When the deep male voice speaks through her mouth, the features instantaneously contort into a demonic grimace of malevolence and rage. Blood trickles down from Regan's nose. The nasogastric tube has been ripped out. During the above:

<blockquote>
REGAN
Oh, no, don't make me! Don't.
</blockquote>

<blockquote>
REGAN/DEMON
You'll do it!
</blockquote>

<blockquote>
REGAN
No!
</blockquote>

REGAN/DEMON

Do it, stinking bitch! You'll do it or I'm going to kill you!

REGAN

Nooooo!

REGAN/DEMON

Yes, do it, do it, d—!

QUICK CUT TO:

CLOSE DOWN ANGLE AT REGAN

showing nothing from the waist down as with eyes wide and staring, Regan seems to be flinching from the rush of some hideous finality, her mouth agape and shrieking in terror as she stares up at the upheld crucifix. The shriek ends as the demonic face once again takes over her features, and the piercing cry of terror elides into a yelping, guttural laugh of malevolent spite and rage triumphant as the crucifix is plunged down and *out of sight* at Regan's vagina. The demonic face looks down, and we hear Regan/Demon roaring in that coarse deafening voice as the crucifix is repeatedly brought up into the frame and plunged down again, blood now spotting it as:

REGAN/DEMON

Yes, now you're *mine,* you stinking cow! You're *mine,* you're *mine,* you're—!

Chris has raced into the frame, screaming, grappling to take hold of the crucifix, and in a series of rapid cuts, the angles contrived so that we see blood on Regan's thighs (*but never the vagina*) the demon first turns on Chris with a look of fury. Then:

REGAN/DEMON

Ahhh, the little pig mother!

Regan/Demon smashes Chris a blow on the chest that sends her reeling across the room and crashing to a wall with stunning force while Regan/Demon laughs with bellowing spite. Chris crumples against the wall near Karl. Now the camera moves to the door to disclose Sharon and Willie arriving, staring in confusion and horror. We then go to Chris as she begins to pick herself up. Her head bloodied, she begins to crawl painfully toward the bed as we hear:

REGAN/DEMON (*off scene*)
Ah, there's my sow, my sweet honey piglet! Yes, mine! You are—!

MOVING SHOT AT BED—CHRIS'S POINT OF VIEW

as she crawls closer. Regan now has her back to the camera, looking down, and we know that the crucifix is being used for masturbation. The focus is blurry, swimming, shifting as we hear:

REGAN/DEMON
—mine, you are mine, you are—

The coarse voice breaks off and the Regan/Demon thing abruptly looks over its shoulder at the camera (Chris's point of view) which halts at the sight, for now, as the camera focus clears, the features of Regan's face seem to be those of Burke Dennings. Then it speaks in the British-accented giggly voice of the dead director.

REGAN/DENNINGS
Do you know what she *did* to me, your daughter?

CLOSE AT CHRIS SCREAMING IN HORROR

QUICK CUT TO:

EXTERIOR POTOMAC RIVER—KEY BRIDGE AREA

Above, on Key Bridge, automobile traffic clogs the lanes. The sound is muted and the camera is now trained on a college couple paddling along under the bridge in a canoe. The girl has her hand to her mouth, giggling at some naughtiness from the grinning boy, as the canoe passes out of frame and we cut to an overhead shot of Chris looking down at it. She is leaning over the parapet along the Key Bridge walkway. The sounds of traffic are now very loud. Chris wears oversized dark glasses. She is nervously smoking a cigarette.

185

as Chris stares down the D.C. side of the walkway, and sees approaching her a large, powerfully built man wearing khaki pants, a sweater, and scuffed white tennis shoes. Chris quickly looks away, turning her back three-quarters to him. Though she doesn't recognize him we see it is Karras. As he comes up beside her:

> KARRAS
>
> Are you Chris MacNeil?

> CHRIS
>
> (*unmoving, flipping cigarette over the side*)
> Keep movin', creep, or I'll yell for a cop.

> KARRAS
>
> I'm Father Karras.

Chris reddens and jerks swiftly around.

> CHRIS
>
> Oh, my God! Oh, I'm—! *Jesus!*

Flustered, she is tugging at her sunglasses, then immediately pushes them back as the Jesuit's sad, dark eyes probe hers.

> KARRAS
>
> I suppose I should have told you that I wouldn't be in uniform. I'm sorry. I thought it would be less conspicuous. You seemed so concerned about keeping this quiet.

> CHRIS (*fumbling through her purse*)
>
> Guess I should have been concerned about not making such an ass of myself.
> (*comes up empty*)
> Got a cigarette, Father?

> KARRAS (*reaching into shirt pocket*)
>
> Can you go a nonfilter?

> CHRIS
>
> Right now I'd smoke rope.

> KARRAS (*offering pack*)
>
> On my allowance, I frequently do.

Director William Friedkin and the author.

THE EXORCIST

Author on location at Georgetown University Campus.

The "Hitchcock" steps in Georgetown.

Interior of the MacNeil house.

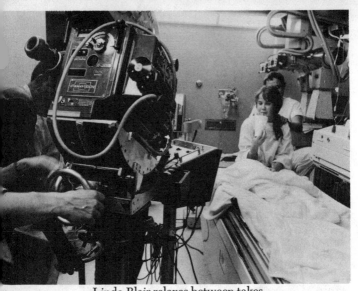
Linda Blair relaxes between takes.

Chris walking through Georgetown on
her way home from shooting the film within the film.

Jason Miller
as Damien Karras.

Max von Sydow
as Father Merrin.

Lee J. Cobb
as Detective Kinderman.

Kitty Winn
as Sharon Spencer.

Linda Blair as Regan MacNeil.

Jack MacGowran as Burke Dennings.

Ruins in Northern Iraq.

The medal is found.

Merrin examines the amulet of the demon Pazuzu
in the Mosul curator's office.

Merrin in the
Mosul bazaar
en route
to the ruins
of Nineveh.

Merrin confronts the statue of the demon Pazuzu.

Chris hears the rapping sounds.

Regan gives her mother a sculpture she's made.

"I'm so glad to see you, Dimmy."

"I wasn't there, I should've been there."

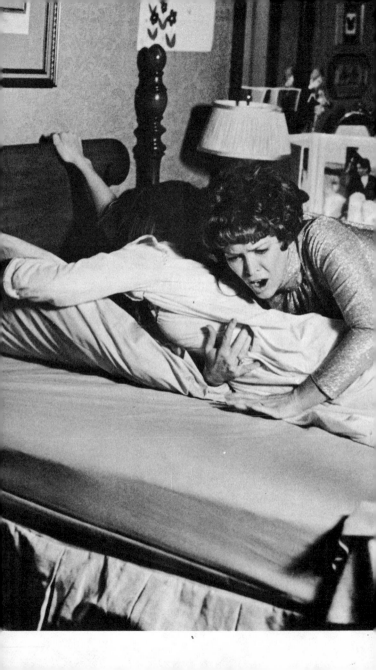

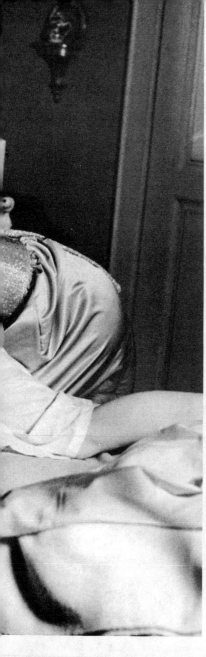

"*Please*, mother.
Mother, make it stop!"

Regan's first medical
examination—later edited
out of the film.

"I really don't
understand how her whole
personality
could change."

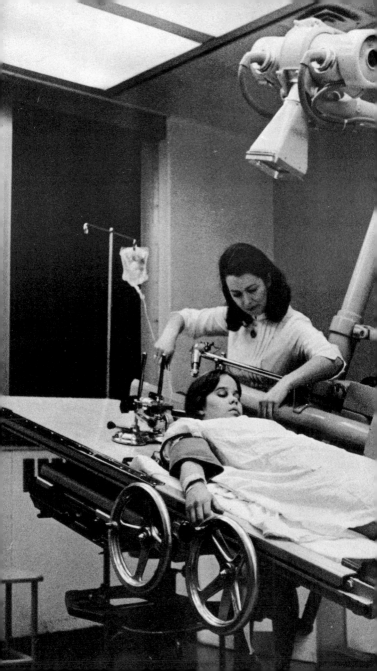

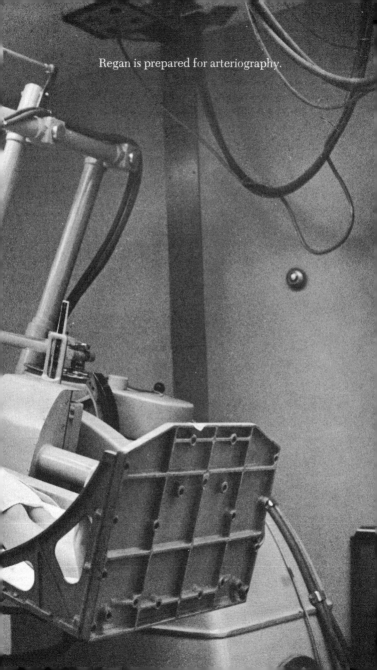

Regan is prepared for arteriography.

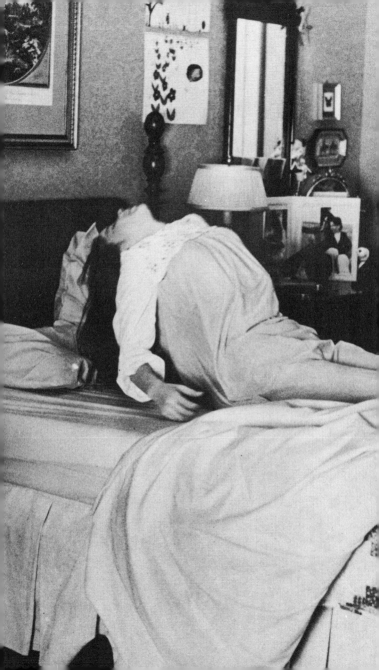

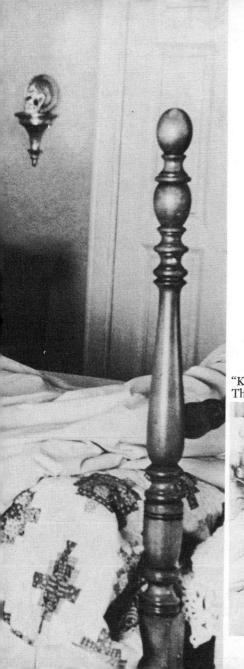

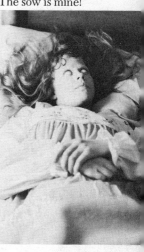

"Keep away!
The sow is mine!"

Hypnosis scene:
"Are you
comfortable, Regan?"

Doctor: "Do you
have any religious
beliefs?"
Chris: "No."

"This was under Regan's pillow. Did you put it there?"

Kinderman finds the fragment of clay.

"And, uh, how do you go about getting an exorcism?"

"She says she's the Devil himself."

Objects fly about
Regan's bedroom.

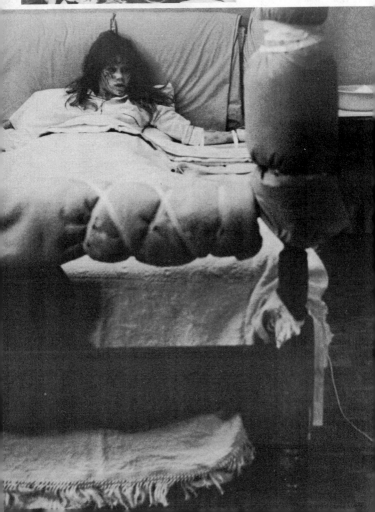

"What an excellent day for an exorcism."

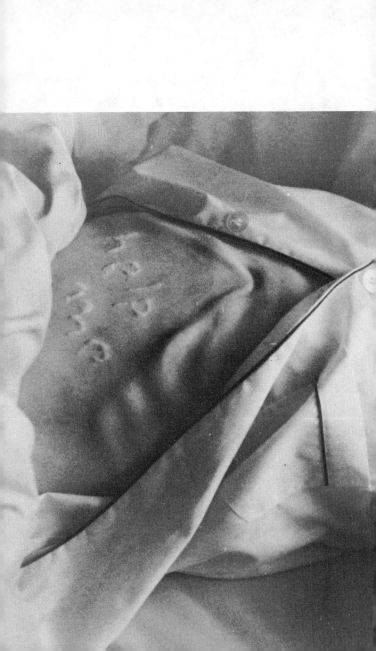

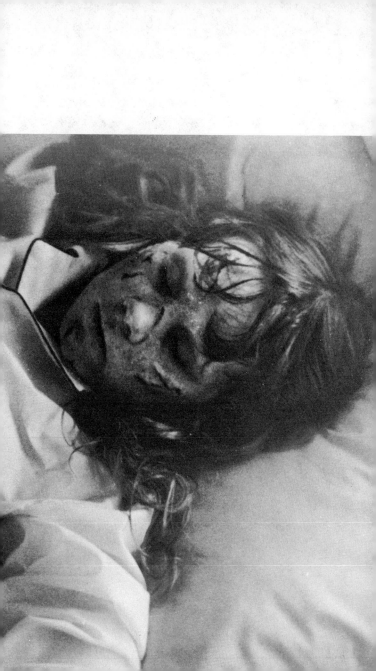

Father Karras hurries to the MacNeil house with supplies for the exorcism.

"Do you want to
hear the background
of the case first,
Father?" "Why?"

The exorcism begins.

"The power of Christ compels you."

The priests are stunned by an apparition of the demon Pazuzu.

The demon Pazuzu.

"Take me! Come into me!"

Father Karras triumphs.

Regan stares at Father Dyer's collar.

The medal: "I thought you'd like to keep this."

CHRIS (*taking cigarette*)
Vow of poverty, right?

KARRAS
It has its uses.

CHRIS
Like what?

KARRAS
Well, for one thing, it makes rope taste better.

He sees that her hand is trembling, takes the cigarette from her fingers and puts it in his mouth. He lights it, his hands cupped around the match. He puffs and gives the cigarette back to Chris, his eyes on the cars passing over the bridge. As he does:

KARRAS
Lots easier. Breeze from the traffic.

CHRIS (*appreciating his sensitivity*)
Yeah. How'd a shink ever get to be a priest?

KARRAS
It's the other way around. The Society—

CHRIS
Who?

KARRAS
The Society of Jesus. Jesuit is short for that.

CHRIS
Oh, I see.

KARRAS
The Society sent me through medical school and through psychiatric training.

CHRIS
Where?

KARRAS
Oh, well, Harvard, Johns Hopkins, Bellevue.

CHRIS
Not bad. Not bad.

KARRAS (*with a slight edge*)
We don't take vows of *mental* poverty.

CHRIS
Look, it's just that I don't know you, and . . .

She drags on the cigarette, long and deep, and then exhales. She crushes out the butt on the parapet.

CHRIS
You're a friend of Father Dyer's, that's right?

KARRAS
Yes, I am.

CHRIS
Pretty close?

KARRAS
Pretty close.

CHRIS
Did he talk about the party?

KARRAS
At your house?

CHRIS
At my house. Did he talk about my daughter?

KARRAS
No, I didn't know you had one.

CHRIS
She's twelve. He didn't mention her?

KARRAS
No.

CHRIS
He didn't tell you what she did?

KARRAS
He never mentioned her.

CHRIS
Priests keep a pretty tight mouth, then, that right? Look, I mean, like confession. You're not allowed to talk about it, right?

KARRAS

Yes, that's right.

CHRIS

And outside of confession? I mean, what if
some . . .
(*her hands are agitated, fluttering*)
I'm curious. I . . . No. No, I'd really like to
know. I mean, what if a person, let's say, was a
criminal, like maybe a murderer or something,
you know? If he came to you for help, would
you have to turn him in?

KARRAS

If he came to me for spiritual help, I'd say no.
No. I wouldn't. But I'd try to persuade him to
turn *himself* in.

CHRIS

And how do you go about getting an exorcism?

KARRAS

Beg pardon?

CHRIS

If a person's possessed by some kind of a demon, how do you go about getting an exorcism?

KARRAS

Well, first you'd have to put him in a time
machine and get him back to the sixteenth century.

CHRIS

What do you mean by that? I didn't get you.

KARRAS

Well, it just doesn't happen anymore.

CHRIS

Since when?

KARRAS

Since we learned about mental illness; about
paranoia and dual personality. Many educated
Catholics don't believe in the devil anymore,
Miss MacNeil. And, as far as possession is

concerned, since the day I joined the Jesuits, I've never met a priest who's ever in his life performed an exorcism. Not one.

CHRIS (*bitter disappointment*)
Are you really a priest, or from Central Casting? I mean, what about all of those stories in the Bible about Christ and Him driving out demons?

KARRAS
Look, if Christ had said those people who were supposedly possessed were schizophrenics, which doubtless they were, they would probably have crucified Him three years earlier.

CHRIS
Oh, really?
(*a shaking hand to her sunglasses*)
Well, it happens, Father Karras, that someone close to me is probably possessed. She needs an exorcism. Will you do it?

Chris has slipped off the glasses and Karras winces at the redness, at the desperate pleading in her haggard eyes.

CHRIS
Father Karras, it's my *daughter!* Please! She's only twelve.

KARRAS (*gently*)
Well, then, all the more reason to forget about exorcism, and—

CHRIS (*outburst in a cracking voice*)
Why? God, I don't under*stand!*

He takes her wrist in a comforting hand.

KARRAS
To begin with, it would make things worse.

CHRIS
But *how?*

KARRAS
The ritual of exorcism is dangerously suggestive. It could plant the notion of possession where

it actually never existed before, or, if it did, it could tend to strengthen it. And, secondly, Miss MacNeil, before the Church approves an exorcism, it conducts an investigation to see if it's warranted. And that takes time. In the meantime, your—

Her lower lip begins to tremble. Her eyes are filling up with tears.

> CHRIS
> Couldn't you do the exorcism yourself?

> KARRAS
> Look, every priest has the power to exorcise, but he has to have Church approval and, frankly, it's rarely ever given, so—

> CHRIS
> Can't you even look at her?

> KARRAS
> Well, as a psychiatrist, yes, I could, but—

Her features contorted with anger and fear, Chris suddenly cries out:

> CHRIS
> She needs a *priest!* I've taken her to every goddamn fucking doctor psychiatrist in the world, and they sent me to *you!* Now you send me to *them!*

> KARRAS
> But your—

HIGH OVERHEAD SHOT

> CHRIS (*shrieking*)
> Jesus *Christ,* won't somebody *help her!*

ANGLE AT RIVERBANK

as "help her" echoes and reverberates and startled birds shoot up into the air.

ANGLE AT BRIDGE—CHRIS, KARRAS

She crumples against Karras's chest.

Oh, my God, someone help her! Please! Please!
Oh, won't somebody . . .

The final "help" elides into deep, throaty sobbing.

HIGH ANGLE FEATURING THE NOISY, IN-DIFFERENT AUTO TRAFFIC

We see Chris eventually stop crying and begin to converse with Karras, who seems to be asking questions, Chris answering. Finally, Karras nods, puts his head down, and frowns. Then he turns, squinting thoughtfully as he looks in the direction of the house.

CUT TO:

INTERIOR MACNEIL HOUSE—STAIRCASE—DAY

Chris and Karras, with the camera tracking, are slowly ascending the staircase, Karras frowning in consternation at the off-scene sound from Regan's bedroom, of the demonic voice threatening and raging. When they reach the door to Regan's bedroom, we pick up Karl leaning against the opposite wall, arms folded, head bowed. He looks up to Chris with bafflement and fright.

KARL

It wants no straps still.

KARRAS (*to Chris*)
Who's in there with her?

CHRIS

No one.

Karras looks to the door, his consternation deeper. He thinks. Then he slowly begins to open the door.

INTERIOR REGAN'S BEDROOM—DAY

Karras enters, scanning the room; then he freezes, seeing:

POINT OF VIEW AT BED—REGAN

Arms held down by a double set of restraining straps,

it seems no longer Regan but the demonic entity that now lies on the bed and turns its head to stare at the camera. We instantly zoom to disclose a closer view of the eyes bulging wide in wasted sockets, shining with a mad and burning intelligence. The hair is tangled and thickly matted, the legs and arms spider-thin, a distended stomach jutting up grotesquely.

ANOTHER ANGLE

Stunned, Karras fights to recover himself. He closes the door behind him. In an everyday tone:

> KARRAS
>
> Hello, Regan.
> (*fetching a chair to bedside*)
> I'm a friend of your mother's. She tells me you're not feeling too well. Do you think you'd like to tell me what's wrong?

> REGAN/DEMON (*in that deep, guttural voice*)
> I am not Regan.

> KARRAS
>
> Oh, I see. Well, then, maybe we should introduce ourselves. I'm Damien Karras. Who are you?

> REGAN/DEMON
>
> The devil.

> KARRAS (*sitting*)
> Good. Now we can talk.

The Regan/Demon entity throws back its head and roars with yelping, spine-chilling laughter. It abruptly breaks off. Regan/Demon stares piercingly at him, drooling.

> REGAN/DEMON
> So it's you. After all, they sent you.

> KARRAS
> Yes, I've come here to help you.

> REGAN/DEMON
> Very well, then, begin by undoing these straps.

193

KARRAS
Are they very uncomfortable for you?

REGAN/DEMON
Extremely. Take them off.

KARRAS
I'm afraid you might hurt yourself.

REGAN/DEMON
Undo them!

KARRAS
You say you're the devil?

REGAN/DEMON
I assure you.

KARRAS
Then why don't you just make the straps disappear?

REGAN/DEMON
That's much too vulgar a display of power, Karras. Too crude. After all, I'm a prince! I prefer persuasion, Karras, togetherness, community involvement. Moreover, if I loosen the straps myself, I deny you the opportunity of performing a charitable act.

KARRAS
But a charitable act is a virtue and that's what the devil would want to prevent; so, in fact, I'd be helping you now if I *don't* undo the straps.
(*shrugging*)
Unless, of course, you're really *not* the devil. And, in that case, I *would* undo them.

REGAN/DEMON
Undo them. Undo them and I'll tell you the future.

KARRAS
But how do I know that you *can* read the future?

REGAN/DEMON
I'm the devil.

KARRAS

Yes, you say so, but you won't give me proof.

REGAN/DEMON

Of what sort?

KARRAS

Well, now, something very simple might do. For example: the devil knows everything, correct?

REGAN/DEMON

No, almost everything, Karras—almost. You see? They keep saying that I'm proud. I am not. Now, what are you up to, fox?

KARRAS

Well, I thought we might test the extent of your knowledge. For example, where is Regan? Do you know?

REGAN/DEMON

She is here.

KARRAS

Where is "here"?

REGAN/DEMON

In the pig.

KARRAS

Let me see her.

REGAN/DEMON (*leering*)

Why? You wish to top her? Loose the straps and I will let you go at it. However, she's a poor conversationalist, my friend. I strongly advise you to stay with me.

KARRAS

Well, it's obvious you really don't know where she is, so apparently you aren't the devil after all.

REGAN/DEMON

Did I say I was the devil?

KARRAS

Well, didn't you?

REGAN/DEMON

Perhaps. I don't know. I'm not well.

KARRAS

Well, are you the devil?

REGAN/DEMON

Not quite.

KARRAS

Not quite?

REGAN/DEMON

I am a demon. *A* devil, if you will.

KARRAS

Which one?

REGAN/DEMON (*ominous*)

I do not think you would wish to know.

A pause, as Karras stares. Then he half turns his head as if reacting to an invisible, chilling force at the back of his neck. Sustained sting of dramatic scoring.

REGAN/DEMON

Yes, Karras? Icy fingers at the back of your neck? And now colder—gripping tighter, now—tighter—

The score abruptly breaks off and Karras jerks out of an apparently hypnotic state. The demon laughs.

REGAN/DEMON

Yes, of course, Karras. Autosuggestion. Whatever would we do without the unconscious mind? Yet it does give you pause, does it not? Just a bit?

KARRAS (*wary now*)

Which demon are you? What's your name?

REGAN/DEMON

Karras, what's in a name? Call me "Howdy" if it makes you more comfortable.

KARRAS

Captain Howdy? Regan's friend?

REGAN/DEMON

Regan's *very* close friend.

KARRAS

If you're her friend, then why do you torment
her?

REGAN/DEMON

She likes it.

KARRAS

Likes it?

REGAN/DEMON

Adores it.

KARRAS

Why?

REGAN/DEMON

Ask her.

KARRAS

Well, all right. I'll do just as you say. Let me see
her for a moment and I'll ask her. All right?

REGAN/DEMON

Very sly. Let her in and push me out of control?

KARRAS (*feigning a sigh*)

There you go again with all these excuses and
evasions.

REGAN/DEMON

Loose the straps and I may let you see her.

KARRAS

No, you won't, because you don't even know
where she is. You're not a demon and you
haven't any powers whatsoever.

REGAN/DEMON

Undo the straps, Karras! Loose them! We are
restless!

KARRAS

"We"?

REGAN/DEMON

Oh, we are quite a little group in the piglet,
Karras. A multitude of wandering souls.

KARRAS

Like who?

REGAN/DEMON

Call us Legion. Later on I may see about dis-
creet introductions. As for now, however, loosen
the straps. They inhibit conversation. I'm accustomed to gesturing. I spend most of my time
in Rome.

KARRAS

How long are you planning to stay in Regan?

REGAN/DEMON

(*jerking head up, building to a fury*)
How long? Until she rots and lies stinking in
the earth! Until the worms have curled festering
garlands in her hair and come crawling through
the pus-oozing sockets of her eyes, the little—!

The demon breaks off, trembling with hatred and rage;
then falls back on the bed.

REGAN/DEMON

There, you see how these straps have upset me?
Take them off.

KARRAS

Well, as I said, I'll con—

Abruptly, Karras breaks off and flinches in shock as he
finds himself staring at:

CLOSE ANGLE AT REGAN

The features are now her own, the eyes filled with terror,
the mouth gaping open in a soundless, electrifying
shriek for help that is simulated by a piercing stab of
the dramatic score.

ANGLE AT KARRAS

reacting as we now hear:

DENNINGS' VOICE

Won't you take off these straps? They're *hurting* me! *Really!*

ANGLE AT REGAN

whose face is now demonic again.

REGAN/DEMON
(*in the voice of the derelict in the subway scene*)
Couldjya help an old altar boy, Faddah? I'm Cat'lic.

ANGLE AT KARRAS

reacting as we hear the off-scene mocking laughter of the demon.

ANOTHER ANGLE

as the laughter abruptly stops.

REGAN/DEMON
Incidentally, your mother is here with us, Karras. Would you like to leave a message? I will see that she gets it.

Karras turns, his expression ashen, and suddenly he is dodging a projectile stream of vomit. He leaps out of his chair so that only his hand and a portion of his sweater are hit. At the same time, Karl throws open the door, drawn by the sound of the chair toppling over as Karras leaps out of it.

CLOSE AT REGAN/DEMON

turning toward Karl in a fury, the face now that of Burke Dennings as the creature strains against the straps.

REGAN/DENNINGS
Damned butchering bastard! Hun! Get the bloody hell out of my—

EXTERIOR SECOND-FLOOR HALL—MACNEIL HOUSE—DAY

Karl rapidly exits, closing the door as the shrieking continues. Chris and Sharon are in the hall as:

REGAN/DENNINGS (*off scene*)
—sight! Get out! Get—!

And as Karl looks bloodlessly at Chris, the shouts from within yield abruptly to the demonic laughter.

CHRIS
Get out of the house, Karl.

KARL
No, I—

CHRIS
Do as I tell you, goddamn it! Get—!

She breaks off. Then she and Karl look to Regan's room as, simultaneously, Karras steps out and we hear the wall-shivering lowing of a steer. A glimpse into the room before Karras closes the door behind him discloses that the sound is coming from Regan.

KARRAS (*to Sharon*)
Have you got any Compazine?

SHARON
Yes, Father.

KARRAS
Give her half of a twenty-five-milligram suppository.

SHARON (*moving quickly away*)
I'll get it.

KARRAS (*to Chris*)
Is there someplace I can wash?

CHRIS
Yeah, come on.

INTERIOR CHRIS'S BATHROOM OFF BEDROOM —DAY

His sweater draped over the shower pole, Karras washes at the sink. Chris sits on the edge of the tub, anxiously fidgeting as she watches Karras. She holds a towel in her lap. From down the hall, off scene, we hear varied animal sounds.

CHRIS

And at the clinic, there were—well—
(*tracing a finger on her chest*)
—you know, like writing? Just letters. They'd show up on her chest, then disappear.

KARRAS

You said letters. Not words?

CHRIS

No, no words. Just an *M* once or twice, and an *L*.

KARRAS (*turning off taps*)
And what else?

CHRIS

Well, that's it. I mean, all I can think of.

KARRAS

(*as she hands him the towel and he dries his hands*)
Has she spoken any languages she's never known?

CHRIS

Well, that stuff when she was hypnotized, maybe. I don't know.

KARRAS

It's one of the primary signs of possession. But so far as you know, it's just gibberish.

CHRIS

I don't know.

KARRAS

Does Karl have a daughter?

CHRIS

Well, he did. But she died a few years ago. Why?

KARRAS

Did Regan know a priest was coming by?

CHRIS

No, she didn't.

KARRAS

Or that my mother had just died?

CHRIS

Huh-uh. No.

KARRAS

There was an—well, another personality that appeared just now, very briefly. It had a broad British accent. You've seen it?

CHRIS (*averting gaze*)

Yes, I have.

KARRAS

Is it someone that Regan might have known?

CHRIS

Yes, it was.

KARRAS

You said "was"?

Chris lifts her haunted gaze to meet his.

CHRIS

I think it's Burke Dennings.

EXTERIOR PROSPECT STREET—DAY

Karl is racing for a bus parked in front of the car barn near the MacNeil house. He boards and the bus pulls away.

INTERIOR CORRIDOR OF TENEMENT BUILD-ING—DAY

Crumbling plaster. Dank. Gloomy. Karl slowly climbs ancient, creaking stairs and approaches an apartment door. Scattered domestic sounds from various parts of the building.

From somewhere a baby crying. Karl comes to the door and for a moment lowers his head, a hand on the door frame. On the wall beside him, a penciled scrawl in a plaster heart: "Nicky and Ellen." Karl takes a deep breath and pushes the doorbell. From within the apartment, a squeaking of bedsprings—someone rising; then irritable muttering as someone approaches with an irregular sound: the dragging clump of an orthopedic shoe. Abruptly the door jerks partly open, the chain of a safety latch rattling to its limit as a woman (Elvira) in a slip scowls through the aperture. She has hard eyes and the ravaged face of what might have been a beautiful young woman. A cigarette dangles from the corner of her mouth and there are puncture scabs on her arm. She has a clubfoot.

> ELVIRA (*husky, coarse voice*)
> Oh, it's you.

As she takes off the chain, we hear from within:

> BOYFRIEND'S VOICE (*slurred*)
> Hey, tell 'im ta get lost!

> ELVIRA (*turning in*)
> Oh, shut up, ya asshole! It's pop!
> (*then at Karl*)
> He's drunk, pop; ya better not come in.

Karl nods. He reaches for his wallet. Elvira's eyes follow the move as:

> ELVIRA
> How's mama?

> KARL
> She's fine. Your mother is fine.

As he hands her bills from his wallet, she coughs rackingly, covering her mouth.

> ELVIRA
> Fuckin' cigarettes'll kill ya.

More coughing, then she takes the money.

> ELVIRA
> Thanks, pop.

> BOYFRIEND'S VOICE
> C'mon, hurry it up!

ELVIRA

Listen, pop, we better cut this kinda—

Karl reaches through the door, grasping her wrist. With whispered, urgent pleading:

KARL

Elvira! There is clinic in New York now for drug addict!

ELVIRA (*grimacing, trying to twist free*)

Oh, come on.

KARL

I will send you! You don't go to jail! It is—!

ELVIRA (*breaking free*)

Jesus, come *on,* pop!

KARL

No, no, please, it is—!

Elvira slams the door in his face. Karl stares mutely at the door for a moment, then lowers his head into quiet grief. From within the apartment, we hear the clubfoot dragging; muffled conversation; a cynical, ringing woman's laugh, followed by coughing. Karl turns away toward the camera, and, looking up, he halts, shocked.

KARL'S POINT OF VIEW—ANGLE AT KINDER-MAN

KINDERMAN

At the time Dennings died, you were here. Is that correct?

INTERIOR BASEMENT PLAYROOM—MACNEIL HOUSE—NIGHT

As Karras follows her movements, Sharon is rummaging through Regan's desk drawers and school books.

KARRAS

Compositions. Letters. Anything at all that I could use to check her patterns of speech in the normal state?

SHARON (*handing him a paper*)

Well, there's this.

(*another one*)

And I think maybe this.

(*picking out a tape reel*)

Oh, here's a tape she was making just before the recorder broke down. She was planning on sending it as a letter to her dad.

KARRAS

Yes, that's good. That's *very* good.

INTERIOR CORRIDOR—JESUIT RESIDENCE HALL—DAY

Coming at us down the hall is Karras, unpinning his Roman collar. He pushes open a door, and the camera moves around to disclose Dyer sitting at a desk, some papers before him, as:

KARRAS

Joe, is there a tape recorder here in the hall?

DYER

There isn't even a lemon drop here in the hall. You need it now?

KARRAS

I need it now.

DYER (*rising*)

Father President's got one, I think. Let's take a look.

KARRAS

I'd sure appreciate it, buddy.

DYER

Didn't see you at dinner, by the way. Where'd you eat?

KARRAS

I didn't.

As camera tracks with them from the rear as they go down the hall:

205

That's foolish. Why diet when you only wear frocks?

EXTERIOR RESIDENCE HALL—AT KARRAS'S WINDOW—NIGHT

Lights are out in all of the rooms but his. In casual dress, he is working on some papers on his desk. He lowers his head, wiping at his eyes. He rises and moves to a window, where he looks out toward the MacNeil house. Then he moves nervously back to his desk.

INTERIOR KARRAS'S ROOM—NIGHT

He lights a cigarette, exhales. He stares at a tape recorder; then activates the playback. At first we hear tape hiss. Then:

> REGAN'S VOICE (*normal*)
Hello . . .

Whining feedback. Then:

> CHRIS'S VOICE (*hushed in background*)
Not so close to the microphone, honey. Hold it back.

> REGAN'S VOICE
Like this?

> CHRIS'S VOICE
No, more.

> REGAN'S VOICE
Like this?

> CHRIS'S VOICE
Yeah, OK. Go ahead, now. Just talk.

> REGAN'S VOICE (*muffled giggling; then:*)
Hello, daddy? This is me.
(*giggling; then a whispered aside*)
I can't tell what to *say*.

> CHRIS'S VOICE
Oh, just tell him how you are, Rags, and what you've been doin'.

Karras's look grows more and more shaken as he listens to:

REGAN'S VOICE

Umm, daddy—well, ya see; I mean I hope you can *hear* me OK and—let's see. Umm, well, first we're— No, wait, now . . . See, first we're in Washington, daddy, ya know? It's— No, wait, now; I better start over. See, daddy, there's . . .

QUICK CUT TO:

INTERIOR CHURCH—KARRAS AT ALTAR—DAY

KARRAS

"Thou shalt turn again, O God, and quicken us. And Thy people shall rejoice in Thee. Show us Thy mercy, O Lord, and grant us Thy salvation. O Lord, hear my prayer. And let my cry come unto Thee."

ANOTHER ANGLE (TIME LAPSE)

Karras lifts the communion host in consecration. It trembles in his fingers with a hope he dares not hope.

KARRAS

"For this—is—My body."

INTERIOR REGAN'S BEDROOM—CLOSE ANGLE AT TAPE RECORDER—DAY

A full reel is just beginning to wind onto an empty reel. A microphone is propped in position. Karras sits at the foot of Regan's bed. He is wearing his clerical robes.

REGAN/DEMON

Hello, Karras. Flying your colors, I see. Ah, what an excellent day for an exorcism. Do begin it soon.

KARRAS (*puzzled*)

You would like that?

REGAN/DEMON

Intensely.

207

KARRAS

But wouldn't that drive you out of Regan?

REGAN/DEMON

It would bring us together.

KARRAS

You and Regan?

REGAN/DEMON

You and us.

Karras breaks off at a sound off scene. He turns and sees that a bureau drawer has apparently popped open, and as he watches, it slides back shut. The demon bursts into cackling laughter. Karras eyes the bureau for a beat, and then slowly turns back to Regan. He looks thoughtful, his brow furrowed. The laughter stops.

REGAN/DEMON

Yes, mind over matter. Underground springs. Magnetic forces and all of that. Ah, how pleasant to chat with you, Karras. I feel free. I can spread my great wings in the air like a wanton, for nothing would prove anything at all to you, Karras. That is why I cherish all reasonable men. For the truth only serves to increase their damnation. The trouble with signs in the sky, my dear morsel, is that once having seen them, one has no excuse. Have you noticed how few miracles one hears about lately? Not *our* fault, Karras. No, indeed. *We try!*

KARRAS

So you claim you made the drawer come open.

REGAN/DEMON

Yes.

KARRAS

Would you do it again for me, please?

REGAN/DEMON

Assuredly.

KARRAS

Do it again.

REGAN/DEMON

Yes, in time.

KARRAS

No, now.

REGAN/DEMON

In time, in time. But *mirabile dictu,* don't you agree?

KARRAS (*startled*)

You speak Latin?

REGAN/DEMON

Ego te absolvo.

The demon chuckles.

KARRAS (*excitedly*)

Quod nomen mihi est?

REGAN/DEMON

Bonjour.

KARRAS (*persistent*)

Quod nomen mihi est?

REGAN/DEMON

Bon nuit. La plume de ma tante.

The demon laughs full and mockingly. Karras holds up a small vial of water.

REGAN/DEMON (*warily*)

What is that?

KARRAS

Holy water.

Karras has uncapped the vial and now sprinkles its contents over Regan. Instantly Regan/Demon writhes to avoid the spray, howling in pain and terror.

REGAN/DEMON

Ahhhhhhhhhh! It burns me! It burns! It burns! Ah, cease, priest, bastard! Cease! Ahhhhh!

Karras looks disappointed. The howling ceases and Regan's head falls back onto the pillow, eyes rolling upward into their sockets, exposing the whites. Regan/ Demon is now moving its head feverishly from side to side, while muttering an indistinct gibberish:

REGAN/DEMON

Idrehtellteeson. Dobetni tee siti. Leafy. Tseerpet reef. Emitsuvig.

Karras is intrigued and moves to the side of the bed. He turns up the volume on the recorder, then lowers his ear to Regan's mouth. He listens and he straightens up.

KARRAS

Who are you?

REGAN/DEMON

Nowonmai . . . Nowonmai . . .

KARRAS

Is that your name?

The lips move. Fevered syllables, slow and unintelligible. Then silence. Only the eerie sound of breathing. Karras waits a little; then he shakes his head, disappointed. He grips Regan's wrist to check her pulse; then he draws back her nightgown top and winces with pained compassion at the sight of her skeletal ribs.

INTERIOR STUDY IN MACNEIL HOUSE—NIGHT

Chris has her head propped in a trembling hand as Karras somberly enters the study and closes the door quietly behind him. She keeps her head averted as Karras comes up beside her.

CHRIS

So what's doin'?

KARRAS

I don't want to alarm you, but your daughter's condition is already close to critical. She's in danger of shock or even cardiac exhaustion. She ought to be hospitalized immediately.

CHRIS

I can't do that, Father.

KARRAS

Why not?

Chris at last turns her face to him, the red-veined eyes revealing she's been crying as:

CHRIS

Listen, what about the exorcism, Father? Can't you do it?

KARRAS

I could never get permission from the bishop.

CHRIS

Why not?

KARRAS

There's no evidence.

CHRIS

Well, what about those rappings and things?

KARRAS (*gently*)

I'm afraid that we'd hardly need a devil to explain them. Poltergeist phenomena are pretty much accepted today, and they happen outside of possession, almost always with disturbed adolescents, in fact. Call it mind over matter. But it isn't supernatural. The same with telepathy. And so far as the writing on her skin is concerned, just the power of the mind can control your blood flow. We know that from experiments under hypnosis. So Regan's unconscious mind may be controlling the differential of blood flow to her skin, sending more to the parts that it wants raised up. And so you have letters. Or words. Do you see?

CHRIS

Father, that's so far out of sight that I think it's lots easier to believe in the *devil!*

KARRAS

If—

CHRIS (*intense, building*)

Look, I don't know anything about any of

these theories, but I'll tell you *one* thing, Father Karras! You show me Regan's identical twin! Same face! Same voice! Same smell! Same everything down to the way she dots her *i*'s and I'd know in a second it wasn't Regan! I'd know it! I'd know it in my gut and I'm telling you I know that thing upstairs *is not my daughter!*

Karras holds up the almost empty vial.

> KARRAS
>
> I just told her this was holy water, Mrs. Mac-Neil, and when I sprinkled it on her, she reacted very violently.

> CHRIS (*building to hysteria*)
>
> So?

> KARRAS
>
> It isn't anything but ordinary tap water.

> CHRIS
>
> Christ, who *gives* a shit! She's *dying!*

> KARRAS
>
> But—

> CHRIS (*hysterical; fists to temples*)
>
> She killed Burke Dennings! Is that evidence enough for you, Father? She killed him! *She killed Burke Dennings!*

QUICK CUT TO:

INTERIOR CAMPUS LANGUAGE LAB—NIGHT

Karras and a professor (Frank) listen to a tape-recorded playback of the gibberish. After a few beats, over the recording:

> KARRAS (*tense*)
>
> Well, what do you think, Frank? Could it be a language?

> FRANK
>
> Sure, it's a language.

> KARRAS
>
> *What?*

It's English—English in reverse. Here, listen.

As Frank pushes the start button on a second tape recorder, we:

QUICK CUT TO:

INTERIOR KARRAS'S ROOM—NIGHT

Karras sits in front of the borrowed tape recorder, listening to an eerie, unearthly series of various whispered voices.

TAPE RECORDER
(*First Voice*)

Let her die!

(*Second Voice*)

No, no, sweet! It is sweet in the body! I feel!

(*Third Voice*)

Fear the priest.

(*Second Voice*)

Give us time.

(*Third Voice*)

He is ill.

(*Fourth Voice*)

No, not this one. The other. The one who will—

(*Second Voice, interrupting*)

Ah, the blood! Feel the blood! How it sings!

(*Karras's Voice*)

Who are you?

(*First Voice*)

I am no one.

(*Karras's Voice*)

Is that your name?

(*Second Voice*)

I have no name.

(*First Voice*)

I am no one.

213

(*Third Voice*)

Many.

(*Fourth Voice*)

Let us be. Let us warm in the body.

(*Second Voice*)

Leave us.

(*Third Voice*)

Karras, let us—

(*First Voice*)

Merrin . . . Merrin.

The phone rings. Karras leaps for it.

KARRAS (*urgently*)

Hello, yes? . . . Be right over.

EXTERIOR PROSPECT STREET—NEAR THE HOUSE—NIGHT

Very late. No traffic noise. Karras is hastily crossing, throwing on a sweater.

INTERIOR ENTRY OF MACNEIL HOUSE—NIGHT

Sharon, wearing a sweater and holding a flashlight, has the door open, waiting as Karras comes up the steps. At the door, she puts a finger to her lips for quiet. She beckons him in and closes the door, very carefully.

SHARON (*whispering*)

I don't want to wake Chris. I don't think she ought to see this.

She beckons for him to follow.

INTERIOR SECOND-FLOOR HALL—BY RE-GAN'S DOOR—NIGHT

The house is darkened. Karras and Sharon are silently approaching. Sharon carefully opens the door, enters, and beckons Karras into the room.

INTERIOR REGAN'S BEDROOM—AT DOOR—NIGHT

As he enters, Karras reacts as if to extreme cold. His breath, like Sharon's, is frostily condensing in the chill air of the room. He looks at Sharon with wonder.

ANOTHER ANGLE

as Karras and Sharon approach the bedside. The room is dark except for a night-light glow. Sharon has the flashlight on now, trained low. They stop by the bed. Regan seems to be in a coma, the whites of her eyes glowing eerily in the dim light. Heavy breathing. Karras takes Regan's wrist to check her pulse. The naso-gastric tube is in place, Sustagen seeping into her motionless body. Beads of perspiration on Regan's forehead. Sharon is bending, gently pulling Regan's pajama tops wide apart, exposing her chest. Karras wipes a little perspiration off Regan's forehead, then stares at it on his fingers, rubbing them together with consternation. Then he looks up at Sharon, feeling her gaze upon him.

> SHARON (*whispering*)
> I don't know if it's stopped. But watch. Just keep looking at her chest.

Karras follows her instructions. One beat. Two. Then, flipping the flashlight beam onto Regan's chest:

> SHARON (*whispering*)
> There! There, it's coming!

Karras leans his face in closer to observe, then halts, shocked at:

POINT OF VIEW—REGAN'S CHEST

Rising up on her skin in blood-red, bas-relief script are two words:

help me

CLOSE AT SHARON

> SHARON
> That's her handwriting, Father.

EXTERIOR SUNRISE SHOT—GEORGETOWN UNIVERSITY SPIRES FROM ACROSS THE PO-TOMAC IN ROSSLYN

As the camera begins slowly moving across the river toward the steps beside the MacNeil house, we hear echo chamber voices:

BISHOP'S VOICE

You would want to do the exorcism yourself?

KARRAS'S VOICE

You know my problem, Your Excellency. Judging from accounts in the gospels, the faith of the exorcist, or the lack of it, seems to affect the eventual outcome. And in case that's so . . .

BISHOP'S VOICE

I see.

KARRAS'S VOICE

I'm sorry.

BISHOP'S VOICE

Well, you can assist. We've got to have a psychiatrist present in any case. Meantime, Lankester Merrin's in the area.

KARRAS'S VOICE (*awed*)

Merrin!

BISHOP'S VOICE

He's just back from Iraq. He's been digging in some temples around Nineveh or some such. It's fortunate he's here. It's rare you find experience in this kind of thing.

KARRAS'S VOICE

Oh?

BISHOP'S VOICE

Did an exorcism years ago in Africa. It lasted several months, I understand.

KARRAS'S VOICE

Several *months?*

BISHOP'S VOICE

Yes, I hear it almost killed him.

The camera has reached the steps and we freeze the frame. Stab of dramatic score.

INTERIOR REGAN'S BEDROOM—NIGHT

While Karras and Karl hold Regan/Demon still, Sharon plunges home an injection, then wipes the puncture with a swab. During this, Regan's head is averted toward the shuttered window.

> REGAN/DEMON
> (*weakly croaking, filled with hate*)
> Yes! I am here! I await you!
> (*Regan spits toward window*)
> Come! Come, bastard! Come! I await you! I—!

As the tirade continues, Karras eyes Regan with puzzlement, then follows her gaze to the window.

EXTERIOR PROSPECT STREET IN FRONT OF HOUSE—NIGHT

A cab has pulled up, and out steps a tall old priest carrying a battered black valise. A hat obscures his face. As the cab pulls away, Merrin stands rooted, staring up at Regan's bedroom window like a melancholy traveler frozen in time.

INTERIOR MACNEIL HOUSE—KITCHEN—NIGHT

Chris sits dejectedly at the table, pondering Regan's sculpture of the bear with the daisies. She holds it tenderly between her hands as Karras wearily enters and slumps down opposite her. From off scene (Regan's bedroom) we hear the continued croakings of demonic epithets. Karras puts his head into his hands. After a beat:

> CHRIS
> She made this for me.

Karras looks up, sees the bear, takes it from her hands, and eyes it. Then he looks up at Chris, who rises from the table and heads for the stove, stifling incipient tears.

> CHRIS
> Would you like some coffee, Father?

> KARRAS (*softly*)
> No, thanks.

A beat. Then both look upward. Silence. The demonic croakings have ceased.

KARRAS

I guess the Librium finally took hold.

CHRIS (*wiping at a sniffle*)

Yeah. Father, why don't you go home and get some sleep. I'll give you a call when Father Merrin gets in in the morning.

Karras shakes his head with an air of disbelief.

KARRAS

Merrin!

Chris looks up at him. Then:

CHRIS

That's some big deal, I gather.

KARRAS

Yes.

Chris looks toward the sound of the doorbell chime, then meets Karras's worried gaze. She leaves the kitchen. Karras notices an open scrapbook on the table where Chris was sitting. He slides it over, examines it. In a close point-of-view shot we see a candid photo of Regan. In one photograph she is blowing out candles on a birthday cake. In another she is sitting on a lake-front dock in shorts and T-shirt with "Camp Brown Ledge" stenciled on the front. Karras sighs deeply as he riffles through the pages.

ANGLE AT KARRAS

lifting his gaze in haunted remembrance.

INTERIOR ENTRY TO MACNEIL HOUSE

Chris opens the door, disclosing Merrin. His face is obscured by his black felt hat, and his coat, which is buttoned at the top, hides his collar.

CHRIS

Yes, hello, can I help you?

From the shadows, a voice that is gentle yet as full as a harvest:

MERRIN
Mrs. MacNeil? I'm Father Merrin.

He's removed his hat, and Chris is momentarily taken aback by the eyes that shine with intelligence and kindly understanding, with serenity and unearthly power. Flustered, Chris flings wide the door.

CHRIS
Oh, my gosh, please come in! Oh, come. in! Gee, I'm—! Honestly, I don't know where my—!

He's entered and she closes the door behind him.

CHRIS
I mean, we weren't expecting you until tomorrow!

MERRIN
I'm sorry. I hope I haven't inconvenienced you.

As she turns to him after closing the door:

CHRIS
Oh, no, no, it's just—

She halts, puzzling at Merrin's posture. He is standing with his head angled sideways, glancing up toward the second floor as if listening; no, more like probing at the vibrations of some presence out of sight. After a moment:

CHRIS
Can I take that bag for you, Father?

MERRIN (*his attention still elsewhere*)
It's all right. It's like part of my arm: very old ... very battered.
(*now he looks down at her with a warm, tired smile in his eyes*)
I'm accustomed to the weight. Is Father Karras here?

Yes, he's in the kitchen. Have you had any dinner, by the way?

Flicking his glance sharply upward again at the sound of Regan's door being opened:

MERRIN
Yes, I had some on the train.

CHRIS
Are you sure you wouldn't like something else?

Sound of the door being closed. Then Merrin's gaze drops back to Chris.

MERRIN
Thank you, no.

As they move into the house:

CHRIS
Gee, if only I'd known you were coming to-night I could have met you at the train.

MERRIN
That's all right.

CHRIS
Did you have to wait long for a cab?

MERRIN
A few minutes.

Karl has appeared and reaches for Merrin's bag.

KARL
I take that, Father.

Karl takes the bag toward the study.

CHRIS
We put a daybed in the study for you, Father. I'll show you where it is. Or would you like to say hello to Father Karras first?

MERRIN
I should like to see your daughter first.

CHRIS

Right now you mean, Father?

He again glances up with that distant attentiveness.

MERRIN

Yes, now. I think now.

CHRIS

Gee, I think she's asleep.

MERRIN

I think not.

CHRIS

Well, if—

Suddenly, Chris flinches at a sound from above: the voice of the demon, booming, yet muffled.

REGAN/DEMON (*off scene*)

Merriiiinnnnnnnn!

It is followed by the sound of a massive jolt against Regan's bedroom wall that causes the frame to jerk and blur.

CHRIS

God almighty!

Merrin continues to stare upward, unruffled, even as a second jolt shakes the house. Merrin moves toward the staircase as:

REGAN/DEMON (*off scene*)

Merrin, come here, you scum! Come here!

As an incredulous Karl appears from the study, Karras races out from the kitchen. The camera tracks front with Merrin calmly ascending the staircase. The joltings and croakings of "Merrinnnnn" continue until finally the elderly Jesuit reaches Regan's bedroom and enters, closing the door behind him.

ANGLE AT CHRIS, KARRAS

staring up at the bedroom door, stunned.

POINT-OF-VIEW SHOT AT BEDROOM DOOR FROM BELOW

Silence. Then the off-scene hideous laughter of the demon. Merrin, ashen, steps quickly out into the hall, closing the door behind him. He heads for the stairs. Sharon reopens Regan's door, from within, pokes her head out and stares oddly after Merrin's retreating figure.

FULL SHOT—STAIRS, CHRIS, KARRAS

as Merrin comes quickly down and puts hand out to Karras.

> MERRIN (*warmly and serenely*)
> Father Karras.

> KARRAS
> Hello, Father. It's an honor to meet you.

Merrin takes Karras's hand in both of his, searching the younger Jesuit's face with a look of gravity and concern while upstairs the demonic laughter segues into vicious obscenities directed at Merrin.

> MERRIN
> You look terribly tired. Are you tired?

> KARRAS
> No, Father.

> MERRIN
> Very well. I should like you to go quickly across to the residence and gather up a cassock for myself, two surplices, a purple stole, some holy water, and your copy of *The Roman Ritual*. The full one. I believe we should begin.

> KARRAS
> Now?

> MERRIN
> Yes, now. I think now.

> KARRAS
> Don't you want to hear the background of the case first, Father?

Why?

Karras looks into those ingenuous, saintly eyes, is about to formulate an answer; then realizes none is possible.

KARRAS
OK. I'll go and get the things.

As he starts away, Karl rushes to get ahead of him and open the door for him. Karras gives him a look at the door, then steps into the night.

CHRIS (*to Merrin*)
You must be terribly tired, Father. Would you like a cup of coffee?

He sees her fidgeting hands, her nervous glances upward at the sound of demonic raging.

MERRIN
If you're sure it's no trouble.

INTERIOR KITCHEN OF MACNEIL HOUSE—
NIGHT

Merrin leans against the refrigerator door, his head lowered as he looks into the steamy blackness of his coffee mug. Chris picks the brandy bottle up off table.

CHRIS
Want some brandy in it, Father?

MERRIN
Well, the doctors say I shouldn't. But thank God my will is weak.

Chris looks uncertain until he gives her a gentle smile; she smiles back and pours brandy into his mug.

MERRIN
What a lovely name you have. Chris MacNeil. It's not a stage name?

CHRIS
No, Father, I'm really not Esmerelda Glutz.

MERRIN (*murmuring into his coffee*)
Thank God for *that*.

223

And what's Lankester, Father? So unusual.
Were you named after someone?

MERRIN (*staring absently*)
A cargo ship, I imagine.
(*sips*)
Or a bridge. Yes, I think it was a bridge. Now,
Damien! How I wish I had a name like Damien.
Do you know where it comes from?

She shakes her head.

MERRIN
It was the name of a priest who devoted his life
to the care of the lepers on Molokai.

CHRIS
Yeah, it is a nice name.

MERRIN
He finally caught the disease himself.

EXTERIOR HIGH SHOT—RESIDENCE HALL
AREA—NIGHT

Karras, in his cassock, is crossing swiftly toward the
house, carrying a cardboard laundry box.

INTERIOR UNMARKED POLICE CAR ON PROS-
PECT STREET—NIGHT

Kinderman sits behind the wheel, watching Karras.

INTERIOR MACNEIL HOUSE—HALL NEAR
STUDY—NIGHT

Advancing toward us are Karl and Merrin. Karl opens
the study door.

KARL
In here please, Father. Whatever you need,
please tell me.

MERRIN
Thank you. You're very kind.

INTERIOR STUDY OF MACNEIL HOUSE—AT
DOOR—NIGHT

Merrin enters, and the instant he closes the door behind him, he sags against it, a sharp pain expressed in his face as he takes a pillbox from his pocket, hastily extracts a nitroglycerin tablet, and carefully places it under his tongue.

INTERIOR KITCHEN—MACNEIL HOUSE—NIGHT

Sharon is reheating the coffee as Chris comes up beside her and studies the tightness and the distant, troubled look in her face.

> CHRIS
> What happened up there, Sharon?

> SHARON
> Happened where?

> CHRIS
> When Father Merrin walked in upstairs.

> SHARON
> I don't know. It was funny.

> CHRIS
> Funny.

> SHARON
> Strange. They only . . .
> (pauses)
> Well, they only just looked at each other for a while, and then Regan . . . that thing . . . it said . . . It said, "This time—"
> (turns an odd look to Chris)
> "—you're going to lose."

> CHRIS
> And that was all that—?

She breaks off, frowning; then they both flick glances upward. There has been a sudden cessation of the raging of the demon. And something more; something pulsing in the air. Chris lowers her gaze, meeting Sharon's expressionless stare.

> CHRIS
> You feel it, too?

225

Sharon nods, then looks up again, awed, with a whispered:

SHARON

Yes.

EXTERIOR FULL DOWN SHOT OF HOUSE—
NIGHT

Ominous dramatic scoring of thick, pulsing energies.

INTERIOR STUDY OF MACNEIL HOUSE—AT
KARRAS—NIGHT

slipping on a surplice over his cassock, then hauntedly
watching:

MERRIN

on his knees by the daybed, his head bowed in prayer.
The pulsing sound is reprised.

ANOTHER ANGLE

As Karras looks away, hearing Merrin rising, he picks
up a sweater from the open laundry box on the sofa.

MERRIN

Thank you, Damien.

KARRAS (*handing the sweater to Merrin*)

I thought you might wear this under your
cassock, Father. The room gets very cold at
times.

MERRIN

That was thoughtful of you, Damien.
(*starting to slip on the sweater*)
You're familiar with the rules concerning exorcism?

Karras takes two cassocks from the box and hands one
to Merrin.

KARRAS

Yes.

MERRIN (*donning the cassock*)
Especially important is the warning to avoid

226

conversations with the demon. We may ask what is relevant, but anything beyond that is dangerous. Extremely. Especially, do not listen to anything he says. The demon is a liar. He will lie to confuse us; but he will also mix lies with the truth to attack us. The attack is psychological, Damien. And powerful. Do not listen. Remember that. Do not listen.

Now Karras hands him a surplice.

> MERRIN
> Is there anything at all you would like to ask now?

> KARRAS
> No. But I think that it might be helpful if I gave you some background on the different personalities that Regan has manifested. So far, I'd say there seem to be three.

> MERRIN
> There is only one.

INTERIOR SECOND-FLOOR LANDING—DOWN SHOT AT THE STAIRS—NIGHT

Merrin and Karras, fully vested, *Roman Ritual*'s in their hands, slowly come to the stairs and ascend in single file, Karras following Merrin. The pulsing effect again.

ANGLE DOWN HALL FROM OUTSIDE REGAN'S BEDROOM

as the priests approach. Bundled in sweaters Chris and Sharon watch them. The priests halt by the door.

> KARRAS (*frowning at Chris's garb*)
> You're coming in?

> CHRIS
> Well, I really thought I should.

> KARRAS
> Don't! *Please,* don't. You mustn't see her in this state.

She looks questioningly to Merrin, who nods assent.

> CHRIS
>
> OK. I'll wait out here.

> MERRIN
>
> What is your daughter's middle name?

> CHRIS (*after a puzzled hesitation*)
>
> Teresa.

> MERRIN
>
> Teresa. What a lovely name.

He briefly lowers his gaze, then looks to the door. The others do the same.

> MERRIN
>
> All right.

Karras opens the door, disclosing Karl sitting in a corner wearing a heavy hunting jacket, a look of bewilderment and fear on his face as he looks toward us (camera point of view). Merrin hangs motionless for a moment.

INTERIOR REGAN'S BEDROOM

Merrin, just outside the door, is staring in at:

REGAN/DEMON

lifting head from pillow, staring at Merrin with burning eyes.

ANOTHER ANGLE

as Merrin steps into the room, followed by Karras and Sharon, who closes the door. Merrin goes to the side of the bed while Karras moves to its foot. They halt. A beat. Regan licks a wolfish, blackened tongue across dried lips with a sound like parchment being smoothed over.

> REGAN/DEMON
>
> Well, proud scum! At last!

Regan laughs mockingly and Merrin traces the sign of the cross above her, then repeats the gesture at Karras and Karl. As he plucks the cap from a holy-water vial in his hand, the demonic laughter breaks off.

REGAN/DEMON
Ah, yes, of course! The holy urine, now! The semen of the saints!

As Merrin uplifts the vial to sprinkle the bed, Regan's face contorts with rage and spite.

REGAN/DEMON
Ah, *will* you, Merrin! *Will* you!

Merrin begins sprinkling the holy water on Regan, and she jerks her head up, her mouth and neck muscles trembling with hatred.

REGAN/DEMON
Yes, sprinkle! Sprinkle, Merrin! Drench us! Drown us in your sweat! Your sweat is sanctified, St. Merrin! Bend and spew out clouds of incense! Bend and show the holy rump that we may worship and adore it!

There follows a wild roaring, cut off by:

MERRIN
Be silent!

The words are flung forth like bolts. Karras flinches, turning in wonder to Merrin, who stares commandingly at Regan. The demon has fallen silent, returning Merrin's stare with eyes now blinking and wary. Merrin caps the holy-water vial and gives it back to Karras, who slips it in his pocket and watches as Merrin kneels down beside the bed and closes his eyes in murmured prayer:

MERRIN
"Our Father Who art in . . ."

Regan spits and hits Merrin in the face with a yellowish glob of mucus. It oozes slowly down the exorcist's cheek. His head still bowed, Merrin continues the prayer without pause while taking a handkerchief out of his pocket and unhurriedly wiping away the spittle. As he ends the prayer:

KARRAS

"But deliver us from the evil one."

Karras briefly looks up. Regan's eyes are rolling into their sockets until only the whites are exposed. Karras seems uneasy. He returns to his text to follow as:

MERRIN

"God and Father of our Lord Jesus Christ, I appeal to Your holy Name, humbly begging Your kindness, that You may graciously grant me help against this unclean spirit now tormenting this creature of Yours; through Christ our Lord."

KARRAS

"Amen."

Now Merrin stands and prays reverently:

MERRIN

"God, Creator and defender of the human race, look down in pity on this Your servant, Regan Teresa MacNeil, now trapped in the coils of man's ancient enemy, sworn foe of our race, who . . ."

As Merrin continues reading, Karras again glances up as he hears Regan hissing. She is sitting erect, the whites of her eyes exposed, while her tongue flicks in and out rapidly and her head weaves back and forth like a cobra's. After another look of disquiet, Karras looks down again to his text as:

MERRIN

"Save your servant."

KARRAS

"Who trusts in You, my God."

MERRIN

"Let her find in You, Lord, a fortified tower."

KARRAS

"In the face of the enemy."

MERRIN

"Let the enemy have no power over her."

During Merrin's last response, Karras hears a gasp from Sharon, who is standing by the door. He looks back to see her staring toward the bed in stupefaction. Puzzled, Karras follows her gaze—and is instantly electrified.

ANGLE AT BED

The front legs are gently, rockingly rising up off the floor!

ANGLE AT KARL

rising and hastily blessing himself.

KARL
Gott im Himmel!

ANGLE AT BED

It comes up jerkily, inches at a time, until the front legs are a foot off the ground, at which point the back legs come up also. Then the bed hovers, gently bobbing and listing in the empty air as if floating on a stagnant lake. Regan still undulates and hisses.

ANGLE AT KARRAS, TRANSFIXED

MERRIN (*off scene*)
Father Karras.

Karras doesn't hear it; a beat.

MERRIN
Father Karras.

Karras turns to Merrin. The angle shifts to include him, and we see him watching Karras serenely as he motions with his head at a copy of *The Roman Ritual* in Karras's hands.

MERRIN
The response, please, Damien.

Karras, still dumbfounded, again glances at the bed, and as Sharon races from the room, Karras collects himself and looks down at his text.

231

KARRAS (*excited*)

"And the son of iniquity be powerless to harm her."

MERRIN

"Lord, hear my prayer."

KARRAS

"And let my cry come unto Thee."

MERRIN

"The Lord be also with you."

KARRAS (*looking up*)

"And with your spirit."

And now as Merrin embarks upon a lengthy prayer Sharon rushes into the room with Chris, who stops short and stares at the bed, incredulous. Merrin reaches up his hand in a routine workaday manner and unhurriedly traces the sign of the cross three times on Regan's brow while continuing to read:

MERRIN

". . . Almighty Father, everlasting God, Who sent Your only begotten Son into the world to crush that roaring lion . . ."

The hissing ceases and from the taut-stretched *O* of Regan's mouth comes a nerve-shredding lowing of a steer, growing shatteringly louder and louder as:

MERRIN

". . . snatch from ruination and from the clutches of the noonday devil this human being made in Your image."

For a time the prayer is drowned out by the lowing that shivers through the walls. Then Merrin, still reading aloud, reaches his hand up again and presses a portion of his purple stole to Regan's neck. Abruptly, the bellowing ceases and in the ringing silence a thick and putrid greenish vomit begins to pump from Regan's mouth in slow and regular, sickening spurts that ooze like lava over her lip and flow in waves onto Merrin's unmoving hand as:

232

MERRIN

"God and Lord of all creation, by Whose might
Satan was made to fall from heaven like lightning, strike terror into the beast now laying
waste Your vineyard. Let Your mighty hand
cast out this cruel demon from this Your creature, Regan Teresa MacNeil."

Chris bolts from the room as:

MERRIN

"Drive out this persecutor of the innocent . . ."

The bed begins to rock lazily, and then to pitch, and
then suddenly is violently dipping and yawing. During
this, the vomit still pumping from Regan's mouth, Merrin routinely makes adjustments, keeping the stole firmly to Regan's neck. During the above:

MERRIN

"Fill Your servants with courage to fight man-
fully against that reprobate dragon, lest he
despise those who put their trust in You, and
say with Pharaoh of old, 'I know not God nor
will I set Israel free.' Cast him out of Your
servant so he may no longer hold captive this
person whom it pleased You to make in Your
image, and to redeem through Your Son; who
lives and reigns with You in the unity of the
Holy Spirit, God, forever and ever. Amen.
Lord, hear my prayer."

During the latter part of the prayer, the bed has ceased
its movements and has floated to the rug with a cush-
ioned thud.

Karras stares mesmerized at Merrin's hand buried under the thick and mounded vomit.

MERRIN

Damien?

Karras turns to him blankly.

MERRIN (*repeating*)

"Lord, hear my prayer."

KARRAS (*turning to the bed*)
"And let my cry come unto Thee."

Merrin takes a step back and jolts the room with the lash of his voice as he commands:

MERRIN
"I cast you out, unclean spirit, along with every satanic power of the enemy! every specter from hell! every savage companion! It is He Who commands you, He Who flung you headlong from the heights of heaven! Depart, you monster! You robber of life! You corrupter of justice! Prince of murderers! You inventor of every obscenity! You enemy of the human race! . . ."

Regan has ceased vomiting, and as Merrin continues with the adjuration, Karras moves slowly around to the bedside and reaches down, checking Regan's pulse. Regan is silent and unmoving. Into icy air, thin mists of vapor waft upward from the vomit like a reeking offering. And now Karras lifts his eyes, staring, as with nightmare slowness, a fraction at a time, Regan's head turns toward him, creaking with the sound of a rusted mechanism until the dread and glaring whites of the eyes are fixed directly on Karras. Then Karras glances up warily as the lights in the room begin flickering and dimming, and then fade to an eerie, pulsing amber. Regan turns back toward Merrin, and a muffled pounding jolts the room, jerking and blurring the frame; then another; and another, and then steadily, the splintering sound throbbing at a ponderous rate like the beating of a heart that is massive and diseased.

MERRIN
"Depart, you monster! Your place is in solitude! Your abode is in a nest of vipers! Get down and crawl with them! It is God Himself Who commands you . . ."

Merrin continues and now the poundings begin to come steadily louder, faster, until Sharon cries out, pressing her fists against her ears as the poundings grow deafen-

234

ing, suddenly accelerating to a terrifying tempo. Merrin's words are blotted out. And then abruptly the poundings cease and Merrin's prayer comes through pure and clear in the silence.

> MERRIN
> "O God of heaven and earth, God of the angels and archangels . . ."

Over the continued recitation, we hear the return of the demon as:

> REGAN/DEMON (*raging at Merrin*)
> Scum! You are going to lose! Do you hear me? The piglet is going to die!

The flickering haze grows gradually brighter now as:

> MERRIN (*unruffled*)
> ". . . God Who has power to bestow life after death and rest after toil . . ."

> REGAN/DEMON (*over this*)
> Prideful bastard, will you not look on me? Will you not? Now turn and look!

Here Regan spits, the mucoid glob hitting Merrin's eye.

> REGAN/DEMON
> *Thus* does your master cure the blind!

> MERRIN (*calmly*)
> ". . . deliver this servant of Yours . . ."

> REGAN/DEMON (*over Merrin*)
> Ancient hypocrite! You care nothing at all for the piglet! Nothing! You have made her a contest between us! Your abode is in a nest of peacocks, Merrin! Your place is within yourself. Go back to the mountaintop and speak to your only equal! Speak to—!

Here, as Merrin continues with the ritual of prayer, the demon breaks off and jerks its head around to Willie as she enters the room with an armload of towels and sheets.

REGAN/DEMON

Willie, I bring you good news! I bring tidings of
redemption! Elvira is alive! She lives! She is—!

As Willie stares in shock:

KARL	REGAN/DEMON
(*shouting at Willie*)	—a hopeless drug addict,
No, Willie! No! Do not	Willie! Shall I tell you
listen!	where she lives? You can
(*rushing Willie out of the*	visit her tomorrow on
room)	Mother's Day, Willie! Sur-
Do not listen! It is lies!	prise her! Go and—!
Do not listen! Willie, no!	

Abruptly, the demon breaks off and fixes its gaze on
Karras, who has moved to Sharon, speaking to her
guardedly. Sharon crimsons, keeping her eyes downcast as:

REGAN/DEMON

Yes, Karras! Yes! Do you want her? She is
yours! You may ride her as you wish! She
fantasizes nightly concerning you, Karras! She—

Sharon has nodded, and with eyes still downcast, she
has started stiffly out of the room. As she passes the
bed, Regan jerks her head up.

REGAN/DEMON (*at Sharon*)

Slut!

And Regan hits Sharon's face with a projectile stream
of vomit. After a stunned moment, Sharon bolts from
the room while Regan laughs demonically. Meanwhile,
Merrin has not ceased to recite from the *Ritual,* and as
he again commences a lashing adjuration, the demon
stops laughing and eyes him with rage and hatred.

MERRIN

"I adjure you, ancient serpent, by the judge of
the living and the dead, by your Creator, by the
Creator of the universe . . ."

As Merrin continues, Karras moves to check Regan's
pulse again, and as he does, the Dennings personality
takes over in Regan, turning to plead with Karras:

236

What the hell are you *doing*, Karras? Can't you
see the little bitch should be in hospital? She
belongs in a madhouse! Now really. Let's stop
all this cunting mumbo-jumbo! If she dies, you
know, it's *your* fault! I mean, just because
he's . . .

(*indicating Merrin*)

. . . stubborn doesn't mean *you* should behave
like a snot! You're a *doctor!* You should *know*
better! And anyway, it simply isn't fair to drive
us out. I mean, speaking for myself, it's only
justice I should be here. Little bitch! I was
minding my business at the bar that night when
I thought I heard her moaning, so I went upstairs to see what was the matter and she bloody
well took me by the *throat!* Christ, I've never in
my *life* seen that kind of strength! She began to
scream that I was diddling her mother or something, or that I caused the divorce. Some such
thing. It wasn't clear. But I tell you, love, she
pushed me out the *window!* Yes, she *killed* me,
bloody *killed* me! Now you think it's really fair
to throw me out? You really—?

Abruptly, the demon entity replaces Dennings, staring
past Karras to Chris who has entered room with a swab
and a disposable syringe. Karras, disturbed, hastily
moves to intercept her as:

REGAN/DEMON

Ah! Now the sow comes! The mother of the
piglet with a dosage of Librium!

As Regan laughs demonically:

CHRIS (*at Karras*)

Sharon's changing her clothes and—

KARRAS

All right! Let's get it done. I'll hold her. Don't
look at her face, though! Come on!

Chris and Karras approach the bed.

237

REGAN/DEMON

Yes, come see your handiwork, sow-mother!
Come!

While Karras pins Regan's unresisting arms, Chris tries
desperately not to look or listen.

REGAN/DEMON (*at Chris*)

See the puke! See the murderous bitch! Are you
pleased? It is *you* who has done it! *You!* Yes,
you with your career before *her,* before her
father, before—!

Karras glances around, sees Chris standing paralyzed
by the demon's accusations. Simultaneously:

KARRAS	REGAN/DEMON
(*at Chris*)	—*anything!* The *divorce*
Go ahead! Don't listen!	is the cause of her illness!
Go ahead!	Go to priests, will you!
	Priests will not help! She
CHRIS	is mad! You have driven
(*staring at the syringe in*	her to madness and to
her shaking hand)	murder! You have driven
I *can't!*	her into her grave! She
(*shaking head*)	will—!
I *can't do it!*	

Karras plucks the syringe
from Chris's fingers.

KARRAS

All right, swab it! Swab
the arm! Over here!
(*as Chris moves*)
And don't listen! Don't—!

And now the demon, eyes bulging with fury, has jerked
its head around to Karras.

REGAN/DEMON

And *you,* bastard! *You!*

Chris has swabbed Regan's arm and as Karras flicks
the needle into wasted flesh:

238

KARRAS (*at Chris*)

  Now get out!

Chris flees the room.

REGAN/DEMON

  Yes, we know of your kindness to mothers, Karras!

ANGLE AT KARRAS

Head lowered, he pulls out the needle, and as we hear the off-scene mocking laughter of the demon, Karras blanches and for a moment does not move. The laughter ceases. Karras slowly looks up as from Regan there now comes the slow, lilting singing—in a sweet clear voice like a choir boy's—of a hymn sung at Catholic benediction: *"Tantum Ergo."*

ANGLE AT REGAN/DEMON

The whites of the eyes are exposed. The singing. Merrin's reading of the *Ritual* has ended.

ANGLE AT KARRAS

Slowly rising, his face is bloodless as he stares down at Regan. Then he looks up.

A FULLER ANGLE—REGAN, KARRAS

as Merrin comes into the frame with a towel in his hands. With a look of compassion that is almost painful, he wipes the vomit from Regan's face with tender, weary movements. Sharon enters the room and comes to the bed. She takes the towel from Merrin's hands.

SHARON

  I'll finish that, Father.

Karras gives her a look of concern. She responds to it.

SHARON

  I'm OK now. Let me change her and get her cleaned up before I give her the Compazine. OK? Could you both wait outside for a while?

Karras slowly turns to the bed.

POINT-OF-VIEW SHOT—REGAN/DEMON

The singing continues.

EXTERIOR HALL OUTSIDE REGAN'S BED-ROOM—NIGHT

From within the bedroom we hear the singing of the hymn. In the dimness of the hall, Merrin and Karras lean wearily against the wall opposite the door. Karras is staring at the door. After a beat, he begins a hesitant dialogue that will continue in hushed tones, almost whispers.

> KARRAS
> If it's possession, why her? Why this girl?

> MERRIN
> Who can know? Who can really hope to know? Yet I think—the demon's target is not the possessed; it is us . . . the observers . . . every person in this house. And I think—I think the point is to make us despair; to reject our own humanity, Damien; to see ourselves as ultimately bestial; as ultimately vile and putrescent; without dignity; ugly—unworthy. And there lies the heart of it, perhaps: in worthiness. For I think belief in God is not a matter of reason at all; I think it is finally a matter of love; of accepting the possibility that God could love *us* . . .

Merrin looks up at the door and listens to the singing for a moment. Then:

> MERRIN
> Yet even from this . . . from evil . . . will come good. In some way. In some way that we may never understand or ever see. Perhaps evil is the crucible of goodness. And perhaps even Satan . . . Satan, in spite of himself . . . somehow serves to work out the will of God.

It has an impact. Karras thinks. Then:

240

KARRAS

Once—the demon is driven out—what's to keep
it from coming back in?

MERRIN

I don't know. Yet it never seems to happen.
Never . . .

He puts a hand to his face tightly pinching at the corners
of his eyes.

MERRIN

Damien . . . what a wonderful name.

There is exhaustion in his voice. And something else.
Some anxiety. Something like repression of pain. Now
abruptly Merrin pushes himself away from the wall, and
with his face still hidden in his hand:

MERRIN

Excuse me.

Merrin hurries down the hall to the guest bathroom.
Karras watches him, wondering what is wrong. Then he
turns to the door as the singing stops. Sharon emerges
with a bundle of fouled bedding and clothing.

SHARON

She's sleeping now.

Karras nods. Sharon moves away. Karras takes a deep
breath and enters.

INTERIOR REGAN'S BEDROOM—NIGHT

Regan sleeps but Karras's frosty breath tells us that the
air in the room is still icy. Karras shivers. Then he
walks to the bedside, reaches down and grips Regan's
wrist to take her pulse. As he stares at the sweep-second
hand of his wristwatch, we are in a close shot of Karras
—and we hear the voice of Karras's mother.

REGAN/MOTHER (*off scene*)
(*mournful*)

Why you do this to me, Dimmy?

Karras freezes in shock. A beat.

REGAN/MOTHER (*off scene*)

You leave me to be priest, Dimmy. Send me
institution. Now you chase me away? Why?
Why you do this?

Karras is almost trembling with the effort to keep from
looking at Regan's face. And now the voice grows
frightened, tearfully imploring.

REGAN/MOTHER (*off scene*)

You always good boy, Dimmy. Please! I am
'fraid! Please don' chase me outside, Dimmy!
Please!

KARRAS (*vehement whisper*)

You're not my mother!

REGAN/MOTHER (*off scene*)

Outside nothing! Only dark, Dimmy! Lonely!

KARRAS

You're not my mother!

REGAN/MOTHER (*off scene*)

Dimmy, *please!*

KARRAS

You're not my—!

INTERCUT REGAN, KARRAS

as the demonic entity now returns, raging.

REGAN/DEMON

Won't you face the truth, Karras? Won't you?
You believe what Merrin tells you? You believe
him to be holy and good? Well, he is not! He is
not and I will prove it! I will prove it by killing
the piglet! Yes, Karras, she will die and Merrin's
God will not save her! *You* will not save her!
She will die from Merrin's pride and your in-
competence! Bungler! *You should not have
given her the Librium!*

Karras looks up. The demonic eyes are gleaming
triumph and spite as:

242

REGAN/DEMON (*grinning*)
Feel her pulse, Karras! Feel it!

Karras looks down at the wrist still gripped in his hand.

REGAN/DEMON
Somewhat rapid, Karras? Yes. But what else?
Ah, yes, feeble. Just a trifle. For the moment.
Ah, but wait!

As Karras dips in to his medical bag and hastily extracts a stethoscope:

REGAN/DEMON
Yes, yes, quickly, oaf, the stethoscope! Quickly!
Make haste!

REGAN/DEMON
(*a brief laugh; then as Karras puts the instrument to Regan's chest*)
I give you silence, Karras! Listen! Listen well!

We hear (echo chamber) Regan's heart tones. They
are distant and inefficient. Karras looks very worried.
Then the heart sound cuts out as:

REGAN/DEMON
I will not let her sleep!

Karras stares up at Regan numbly.

REGAN/DEMON
Yes, Karras! The piglet will not sleep until she
dies!

The demon puts back its head in prolonged and hideous
laughter. Karras stares. Merrin has appeared at the
bedside. He looks at Regan and then at Karras's
stunned expression.

MERRIN
What is it?

KARRAS
The demon—said he wouldn't let her sleep.
(*turns haunted gaze to Merrin*)
Her heart's begun to work inefficiently, Father.

243

If she doesn't get rest soon she'll probably die from cardiac exhaustion.

MERRIN (*alarmed*)
Can't you give her any drugs to make her sleep?

KARRAS
No, that's dangerous. She might go into coma. If her blood pressure drops any more . . .

MERRIN
What can be done for her?

KARRAS
Nothing. There's just nothing.

Merrin stares grimly at Karras for a moment. Then he picks up Karras's copy of *The Roman Ritual* from the floor, hands it to Karras, and then kneels by Regan's bedside. He makes sign of cross on himself.

MERRIN (*reading aloud*)
"Save Your servant."

KARRAS (*staring at Regan*)
"In the face of the enemy."

EXTERIOR ANGLE AT VIRGINIA SIDE OF THE POTOMAC RIVER

The sun is minutes away from setting. Orange and gold reflect on the waters.

INTERIOR REGAN'S BEDROOM

The two priests are standing by the bed, going through the ritual of exorcism. They now have blankets draped around their shoulders. Regan is lowing like a steer, then drops back exhausted onto the pillow. With the whites of the eyes exposed, Regan now begins to simulate the low grunting of a pig. At the end of a passage of the ritual, Merrin pauses while Karras listens to Regan's heartbeat, checks her pulse; and then wraps the black sphygmomanometer cloth around Regan's arm for a blood-pressure reading. He blinks repeatedly to clear the blurring of his vision.

ANGLE AT KARRAS

as we hear:

> REGAN/MOTHER (*off scene*)
> I not good to you, Dimmy? Why you leave me
> to die all alone?

This time Karras looks at the off-scene Regan, and
reacts with grief and shock at what we may suppose
he sees: his mother's features reflected in Regan's face.
At almost the same moment, Merrin is at his side,
clutching at his arm as he tries to draw him away.
Karras resists, his gaze fixed trancelike on the off-scene
face. During this:

> MERRIN
> Damien!

> REGAN/MOTHER (*off scene*)
> Why, Dimmy?

> MERRIN
> Go and rest for a little!

ANGLE AT REGAN

The features and eyes are reminiscent of Karras's
mother, and vividly evident is the large, circular mole
that the mother had on her right cheek.

> REGAN/MOTHER
> Dimmy, *please!*

> KARRAS (*a sudden agonized shout*)
> *You're not my motherrrrrrr!*

QUICK CUT TO:

INTERIOR KARRAS'S ROOM IN RESIDENCE HALL

Karras enters, exhausted, numbed. He removes a raincoat, revealing the vomit-stained cassock. He takes it
off, stumbles to a closet and finds a fresh one. Exhaling,
he lowers his face into his hand; then looks at his bed.
He sinks to it with bone-wrung weariness, starts to
stretch out, eyes closed. And his telephone rings. He
gropes for it, drops it, picks it up again. His eyes closed,
and in a husky whisper:

Yes.

RECEPTIONIST'S VOICE (*phone; filter*)
Someone waiting here to see you, Father Karras.

INTERIOR JESUIT RESIDENCE HALL RECEPTION ROOM—DAY

The camera is on Kinderman at the telephone switchboard counter. He is delicately rearranging a vase full of flowers. A camellia in his hand, he turns at the sound of a door opening.

KINDERMAN
Ah! Father Karras!

Kinderman quickly replaces the camellia and turns as Karras enters the scene.

KARRAS
Hello, lieutenant.

KINDERMAN
You look awful. What's the matter? That's what comes of all this schlepping around the track? Give it up!

Taking Karras by an elbow, Kinderman guides him to the door and steers him out into the street with:

KINDERMAN
Listen, come! You've got a minute?

KARRAS
What is it?

KINDERMAN
A little talk.

EXTERIOR JESUIT RESIDENCE HALL ENTRY —DAY

As they come through, the camera tracks with them.

KINDERMAN
I need advice, nothing more, just advice.

KARRAS

What about?

KINDERMAN

In a minute. Now we'll walk. We'll take the air.
We'll enjoy.

He has linked his arm through the Jesuit's and guides
him diagonally across Prospect Street. In the stillness
we hear the laughter and the talking-all-together of
Georgetown undergraduates in front of a drinking hall
near the corner of Thirty-sixth Street.

KINDERMAN

Ah, college, college . . . I never went . . . but I
wish . . . I wish . . . You know seriously, you
really look bad. What's the matter? You've been
sick?

KARRAS

No, just busy.

KINDERMAN

Slow it down, then. Slow. You know better. You
saw the Bolshoi Ballet, incidentally, at the
Watergate?

KARRAS

No.

KINDERMAN

No, me neither. But I wish. They're so graceful
. . . so cute!

KARRAS

What's on your mind, lieutenant?

KINDERMAN

Ah, well, Father, I'm afraid I've got a problem.

KARRAS

Professional?

KINDERMAN

Well, mostly it's . . .
(*hesitant*)

247

Well, mostly it's ethical, you could say, Father
Karras. A question . . .

They have come to the parapet in front of the car barn
near the house and steps and once again Kinderman
gropes for the words. He leans his back against the
parapet and stares down at the sidewalk, hands in his
pockets. He sighs, shaking his head. Karras flicks a
worried glance up toward Regan's window.

KINDERMAN

There's just no one I could talk to about it; not
my captain in particular, you see. I just couldn't.
I couldn't tell him. So I thought . . .
(*his face lights up with sudden animation*)
I had an aunt . . . you should hear this; it's
funny. For years she was terrified—*terrified* of
my uncle. Never dared to say a word to him.
Wouldn't even dare to raise her voice. *Never!*
So whenever she got mad at him for something,
for whatever, right away, she'd run quick to the
closet in her bedroom, and then there in the
dark—you won't believe this!—in the dark, by
herself, and the moths and the clothes hanging
up, she would curse—she would *curse!*—at my
uncle for maybe twenty minutes! Tell exactly
what she thought of him! Really! I mean, *yell-
ing!* She'd come out, she'd feel better, she'd go
kiss him on the cheek. Now, what *is* that, Father
Karras? That's good therapy or not!

KARRAS (*smiling bleakly*)

It's very good. And I'm your closet, now? Is
that what you're saying?

KINDERMAN

In a way. In a way. But more serious.
(*looks up at Karras*)
And the closet must speak this time, Father.

KARRAS (*hands shaking*)

Got a cigarette?

The detective looks up at him, blankly incredulous.

KINDERMAN

A condition like mine and I would smoke?
Some doctor! God forbid I should be sick in
some jungle and instead of Albert Schweitzer,
there is with me only *you!* You cure warts still
with frogs, Dr. Karras?

KARRAS (*a murmur*)

It's toads.

KINDERMAN

You're not laughing today. Something's wrong?

Karras mutely shakes his head.

KARRAS

Go ahead.

KINDERMAN

I was saying . . .
(*he scratches his brow with a thumbnail*)
. . . I was saying . . . well . . . let's say I'm
working on a case, Father Karras. A homicide.

KARRAS

Dennings?

KINDERMAN

No, purely hypothetical. You wouldn't be familiar with it. Nothing. Not at all. Like a ritual
witchcraft murder, this looks. And let us say,
in this house, this hypothetical house, there are
living five people—and that one of these five
must be the killer. Now I know this. I *know*
this, I know this for a fact. But then the problem . . . All the evidence . . . paint scraping . . .
things I can't mention . . . well, it points to a
child, Father Karras; a little girl maybe ten,
twelve years old . . . just a baby, she could
maybe be my daughter. Yes, I know: sounds
fantastic . . . ridiculous . . . but true. And now
there comes to this house, Father Karras, a
priest . . . and this case being purely hypothetical, Father, I learn through my also hypothetical genius that this priest has once cured

a very special type illness. An illness which is mental, by the way, a fact I mention just in passing for your interest. Now also there is . . . satanism involved in this illness, it happens, plus . . . strength. Yes, incredible strength. And this . . . hypothetical girl, let us say, then . . .

(*a pause*)

. . . could twist a man's head around, you see. (*nodding*)

Yes, yes, she could. Now the question . . .

(*he grimaces thoughtfully*)

You see . . . you see, the girl is not responsible, Father. She's demented. And just a child. A *child!* Yet the illness that she has . . . well . . . it could be dangerous. She could kill someone else. Who's to know? It's a problem. What to do? Hypothetically, I mean. Forget it? Forget it and hope she gets . . .

(*a pause*)

. . . gets well?

(*he reaches for a handkerchief*)

Father, I don't know . . . I don't know.

(*he blows his nose*)

It's a terrible decision. Awful.

(*searching for a clean, unused section of the handkerchief*)

Just awful. And I hate to be the one who has to make it.

(*he again blows his nose*)

Father, what would be right in such a case? Hypothetically? What do you believe would be the right thing to do?

Karras meets Kinderman's steady gaze.

KARRAS (*softly*)

I would put it in the hands of a higher authority.

KINDERMAN

I believe it is there at this moment.

KARRAS

Yes . . . and I would leave it there, lieutenant.

Their gazes are locked. Kinderman pockets the hand-kerchief.

KINDERMAN
Yes. Yes, I thought you would say that.

He tugs back his sleeve for a look at his wristwatch.

KINDERMAN
Ah, well, I have to go. Mrs. K will be *schrei*-ing now, "The dinner, it's cold!" Thank you, Father. I feel better. Oh, incidentally, you could maybe do me a favor? Give a message? If you meet a man named Engstrom, tell him . . . well . . . say, "Elvira is in a clinic, she's all right." He'll understand. Would you do that? I mean, if you should meet him.

KARRAS (*puzzled*)
Sure.

KINDERMAN
Look, we couldn't make a film some night, Father?

KARRAS (*looking down, nodding*)
Soon.

KINDERMAN
"Soon." You're like a rabbi when he mentions the Messiah: Always "Soon!" Listen, do for me another favor, Father.
(*looks gravely concerned*)
Stop this running round the track for a little. Just walk. Walk. Slow down. You'll do that?

Karras nods. The detective looks down at the sidewalk nodding in resignation.

KINDERMAN
I know. Soon. Well . . .

As Kinderman starts away, he reaches up a hand to the Jesuit's shoulder and squeezes.

KINDERMAN
Elia Kazan sends regards.

Karras watches Kinderman waddling away. There is surprise and then fondness in his look. His crusted eyes begin blinking repeatedly. He lowers face to his hand, rubbing at his eyes, trying to clear them. He looks at the hand and sees it is trembling. Then he looks up at Regan's window.

INTERIOR MACNEIL HOUSE—ENTRY AREA— DUSK

Coming down the stairs carrying a laundry basket filled with soiled bedding, Sharon moves to the front door to answer the chime.

She opens the door for Karras. He enters, looks up toward the sound of muted, indistinct croakings.

> SHARON
>
> No change.

> KARRAS
>
> Is Karl in his room?

> SHARON
>
> No, he's at the store. Excuse me, I've got to get this stuff in the washer.

Karras nods as she moves off toward the basement steps. Again the doorbell chimes.

> SHARON
>
> Would you get that, please, Father?

Karras opens the door, disclosing two young girls around Regan's age. Mindful of the demonic sounds, Karras steps outside, closing the door almost all the way.

EXTERIOR DOOR—MACNEIL HOUSE—DUSK

> FIRST YOUNG GIRL
>
> Hi. Has Regan come back from the hospital yet?

> KARRAS
>
> Yes.

> FIRST YOUNG GIRL
>
> Can we see her for a minute?

KARRAS

She's not in.

FIRST YOUNG GIRL

Well, couldjya tell her there's a party at my house Thursday night? It's for my birthday. I'm Cathie, Cathie Hofman. Will ya tell her?

KARRAS

Yes, I'll tell her.

SECOND YOUNG GIRL

She's supposed to bring a present.

Her companion nudges her sharply. She giggles, covering a mouthful of braces.

FIRST YOUNG GIRL

Thanks.

Karras watches them trip off, a tragic sadness in his eyes.

INTERIOR REGAN'S BEDROOM—DUSK

Karras enters. From off scene we hear demonic raging. As the camera tracks front with Karras, his head is lowered and he walks wearily to the chair where he had been sitting beside Merrin. During these moves:

REGAN/DEMON (*off scene*)

. . . would have lost! Would have lost and you knew it! You scum, Merrin! Bastard! Come back and let us finish! Come back! You were losing! You were losing! You were losing and you knew iiiit, you knew iiiit! Come baaaaaaackk!

A sound of throat clearing, then spitting. During this, Karras has picked up his copy of *The Roman Ritual* and then the blanket from the chair. And now as he turns, draping the blanket over his shoulders, he freezes, reacting with horror as he sees:

REGAN ON BED—MERRIN

Limp and disjointed, Merrin lies sprawled face down on the floor. He is on the far side of the bed and beside it. Regan/Demon watches intensely.

as Karras rushes to Merrin. Kneeling beside him, he turns him over, disclosing the bluish coloration of Merrin's face.

REGAN/DEMON (*off scene*)

Saintly flatulence! Die, will you? Die? Karras, heal him! Bring him back! Bring him back that we may finishhhhh iiiit!

Then inchoate croakings and moans of rage and frustration from off scene as Karras feels for Merrin's pulse and in a wrenching instant of anguish realizes that Merrin is dead. Groaning in a whisper:

KARRAS

Ah, God! God, no!

Karras sags back on his heels, an aching moan of grief rising up in his throat as he shuts his eyes fiercely, shaking his head in despair.

KARRAS

No!

Abruptly, Karras opens his eyes and leans forward, and the hand still gripping Merrin's wrist in search of a pulse now squeezes it savagely as if to force back the lost beat of life. After this, Karras sees something on the floor around Merrin: the pillbox and a scattering of nitroglycerin pills. Karras slowly picks up one of the pills and holds it to his eyes. His gaze then goes to Merrin's face, his expression filled with the realization of Merrin's conscious sacrifice; filled with tenderness and love.

REGAN/DEMON

Yes, he knew that exhaustion would kill him! He knew it! And yet he went on! Not out of goodness! Not charity! No! It was *pride!* Ah, Merrin, you preening, pious pig! Overweening excretion! Not even the worms will partake of your corruption!

Making a trembling effort to ignore the demon's words, Karras has gently and tenderly begun to place Merrin's hands on his chest in the form of a cross. And here, as Karras completes the move:

REGAN/DEMON (*off scene*)
Very good, Karras!

From off scene, the sound of spitting. An enormous, mucoid glob of yellowish spittle hits the dead man's eye.

ANGLE AT REGAN/DEMON

REGAN/DEMON (*mockingly*)
The last rites!

Throwing back its head, it laughs long, and wildly.

AT KARRAS—MERRIN'S FACE IN THE SHOT

As the off-scene laughter continues, Karras stares numbly at the spittle. His hands, the muscles of his neck are trembling. And then slowly, in quivering, up-angling jerks, he looks up at the demon (camera), disclosing a face that is a purpling snarl, an electrifying spasm of murderous rage. In a seething whisper:

KARRAS
You son of a bitch! You murdering bastard!

ANGLE AT REGAN/DEMON

as it stops laughing and stares warily at Karras.

ANGLE AT KARRAS

Though he is motionless, he gives an impression of un-coiling. The sinews of his neck are pulled taut, like cables.

KARRAS
You were losing! Yes! You were losing because you're a loser, because you've *always* been a loser!

A projectile stream of vomit from off scene strikes his face, but he is oblivious.

KARRAS
Yes, you're very good with children! Little girls!

255

Well, come on! Let's see you try something bigger!

Karras has his hands out like great fleshy hooks, beckoning, challenging.

KARRAS
Come on, loser! Try me! Leave the girl and take me! Come into me!

ANGLE AT REGAN/DEMON

In the demonic features there is now a trembling, wild-eyed rage, a fearsome struggle against some irresistible temptation.

KARRAS (*off scene*)
Take me! Come into me! Come into—!

QUICK CUT TO:

ANGLE AT KARRAS

He breaks off, his body jerking as if suddenly seized by an alien inner force. His hands go to his throat and he struggles to his feet. His actions are those of a man who is fighting for control of his own organism.

KARRAS (*chokingly*)
Good! Yes, you're stupid! Stupid! Loser!

He suddenly lurches toward the bed, then arrests his forward movement with:

KARRAS
No!

And now Karras jerks backward, fighting to get his own body to the shuttered window. On the move backward:

KARRAS
No! No, you're not going to harm them! No! Over here! Over—!

QUICK CUT TO:

INTERIOR KARL AND WILLIE'S BEDROOM—NIGHT

Religious statues. A Sacred Heart painting on the wall. Willie, in red-eyed, staring dejection, sits on the edge of the bed. She looks up toward the ceiling at the sound of a commotion upstairs. The camera moves into the small hall between Willie and Karl's room and kitchen, picking up Sharon coming up from the basement, and going into the kitchen where Chris, too, is staring at the ceiling. From above, off scene, we hear indistinct voices, one of them Karras's. The other is much like Karras's, but deeper, stronger, demonic. Chris and Sharon exchange quick glances, then race out of the kitchen.

ANGLE DOWN STAIRS—FROM SECOND-FLOOR LANDING

As Chris and Sharon race out from the kitchen area and up the stairs, we hear from Regan's bedroom a sound like shutters being ripped from their hinges. Also the voices.

ANGLE FROM NEAR REGAN'S BEDROOM DOOR

as Chris and Sharon rush toward us and we hear a shattering of glass.

INTERIOR REGAN'S BEDROOM—AT DOOR—NIGHT

Chris and Sharon burst in, halt. Sharon rushes forward toward the window. Chris follows with her eyes for a moment, then stares over toward the bed. She reacts with alarm and rushes forward.

ANGLE AT MERRIN

as Chris reaches him. She kneels beside him, reacting, shocked.

CHRIS

Oh, my God! Sharon! Shar, come here! Quick, come—!

ANGLE AT SHARON

looking down from the window. Hands to the sides of face, she is screaming.

ANOTHER ANGLE—TO INCLUDE CHRIS

as Sharon runs toward door.

> CHRIS
> Shar, what is it!

> SHARON (*running out*)
> Father Karras!

Chris rises and runs to the window.

SLIGHT UP ANGLE AT CHRIS FROM EXTERIOR WINDOW

She freezes at what she sees down below. Then from behind her, a small, wan voice calls tearfully.

> REGAN (*off scene*)
> Mother?

Chris half turns her head.

> REGAN (*off scene*)
> Mother, what's happening?

ANGLE AT CHRIS—FROM INTERIOR ROOM

She turns toward Regan, not daring to believe that this is not another trick of the demon.

> REGAN (*off scene*)
> Oh, please! Please, come here!

ANGLE AT REGAN WEEPING

> REGAN
> Mother, please! I'm afraid! Oh, mother, please! Oh, mother, please come here—

ANOTHER ANGLE

as Chris rushes forward to Regan, arms outstretched, weeping.

> CHRIS
> Rags! Oh, my baby, my baby!

She is on the bed embracing her daughter.

CHRIS
Oh, Rags! You've come back! You've come—!

QUICK CUT TO:

INTERIOR JESUIT RESIDENCE HALL—RECEP-
TION ROOM—NIGHT

A trembling Sharon is with Dyer, who is knotting the
sash around his cassock with feverish haste as:

DYER
Called an ambulance?

SHARON
Oh, my God! I didn't think!

Dyer turns to the switchboard operator, who has been
following the conversation with alarm.

DYER
Call Georgetown—!

Before he can say "hospital" she cuts him off, already
plugging in.

OPERATOR
I've got it! Go on! Go ahead!

EXTERIOR UP SHOT AT STEPS BESIDE THE
HOUSE FROM M STREET—NIGHT

Dyer is racing down the steps, Sharon behind him. We
hear an off-scene murmur of a crowd.

UP ANGLE AT A GATHERING OF PASSERSBY

at an accident scene. They are looking down at the
camera. A policeman shepherds them back.

We hear murmurs of the litany of indifference:

FIRST MAN (*off scene*)
What happened?

SECOND MAN (*off scene*)
Some guy fell down the steps.

FIRST WOMAN (*off scene*)
It's a priest.

FIRST MAN (*off scene*)
Christ, he must'a been drunk. See the vomit?

SECOND WOMAN (*off scene*)
Come on, Ed, we'll be late for the—

POLICEMAN
Come on, now, move it back, folks. Give him air.

Dyer is pushing through the crowd.

DYER
Let me through, please! Coming through! Coming—!

He breaks through and stares down at the camera point of view as if frozen in a timeless dimension of grief.

DYER'S POINT OF VIEW—AT KARRAS

Karras lies crumpled and twisted on his back, his head in the center of a growing pool of blood. He is staring vacantly to the side, mouth open, jaw slack. Then his eyes shift over to Dyer and leap alive, seeming to glow with some elation, some urgent plea. The camera now moves quickly forward and down to Karras as Dyer kneels beside him.

LOW ANGLE—AT DYER, KARRAS

Dyer puts a light and tender hand that is like a caress to the bruised, gashed face. Blood trickles from the corner of Karras's mouth.

DYER
Damien . . .

Dyer pauses to still the quaver in his throat; then:

DYER
Can you talk?

Slowly and painfully Karras reaches out his hand to Dyer's wrist and grips it, briefly squeezing. Fighting back the tears, Dyer leans his mouth close to Karras's ear.

DYER

> Do you want to make your confession now, Damien?

Karras squeezes Dyer's wrist again.

DYER

> Are you sorry for all of the sins of your life and for having offended almighty God?

Another squeeze. And now Dyer leans back and slowly traces the sign of the cross over Karras, reciting the words of absolution:

DYER

> *"Ego te absolvo . . ."*

CLOSE ANGLE AT KARRAS

as an enormous tear rolls down from the corner of his eye.

DYER (*off scene*)

> *". . . in nomine Patris, et Filii, et Spiritus Sancti. Amen."*

ANGLE AT DYER

as he again leans over, his mouth close to Karras's ear.

DYER

> Would you—?

He pauses, forcing the swelling from his throat. Then:

DYER

> Would you believe what that idiot Toomey did today? He made a . . .

He halts, slightly turning his head toward his wrist.

CLOSE ANGLE AT DYER'S WRIST

gripped by Karras. The grip is slackening, the hand slowly opening, then falling limp.

SIDE ANGLE AT DYER

as he slowly lifts his head and looks down at Karras.

CLOSE DOWN SHOT AT KARRAS (POINT OF VIEW)

He is dead. The eyes are open and filled with peace. And with something else: a glint of triumph and something mysteriously like joy.

SIDE ANGLE—DYER—KARRAS

Slowly and tenderly, Dyer slips Karras's eyelids down as we hear the wailing siren of an approaching ambulance.

> DYER
> Good night, Damien. Sleep—

He breaks down. He weeps.

INTERIOR AMBULANCE—NIGHT

As Karras is loaded aboard on a stretcher, Dyer climbs in and sits down beside an intern. He reaches over and takes Karras's hand, holding it in both of his as he stares down at the torn face.

> INTERN (*gently*)
> There's nothing you can do for him now, Father. Don't make it harder on yourself. Don't come.

Holding his gaze on Karras, Dyer mutely shakes his head. The intern looks up to the open rear of the ambulance where the driver is patiently waiting. The intern nods. As the driver starts to close the rear door, Chris races up and stares in at Karras.

> AMBULANCE DRIVER
> Excuse me, lady.

Her eyes still on Karras, Chris is forced to step back as the ambulance door is put up with a click.

ANGLE AT CHRIS—INTERIOR AMBULANCE POINT OF VIEW

as Sharon comes up beside her, both women staring at the ambulance.

> FOURTH MAN (*off scene*)
> What happened?

FIRST MAN (*off scene*)
.Who knows, buddy? Who the hell knows?

We hear the ambulance start away, and the camera
(ambulance point of view) pulls away from the scene,
continuing on until Chris, Sharon, and the spectators
are very far in the distance.

SLOWLY FADE OUT

FADE IN:

EXTERIOR PROSPECT STREET—FULL SHOT—
FEATURING THE HOUSE—DAY

A beautiful, bright sunny day with a steady stream of
students and professors on the move. Sharon exits from
the house carrying a suitcase which she places in the
trunk of the limo in front of the house.

INTERIOR MACNEIL HOUSE—CHRIS'S BED-
ROOM—DAY

While Karl stands by, Chris is folding a final item into
a suitcase open on her bed. She drops the lid.

CHRIS
OK, that's all of it.

Sharon enters, something in her hand.

SHARON
Chris, what about those stereo earphones?

CHRIS
Storage.

Karl has locked up the suitcase and exits.

SHARON
OK, we're all set then. Dulles Airport's pretty
far, Chris. You'd best allow an hour.

CHRIS
Gonna miss you.

SHARON
Same here, Chris.

CHRIS
You won't change your mind?

SHARON
People change.

She unclasps her hand, disclosing Karras's medal and chain which she holds up to Chris.

SHARON
Here, I found this in her room. It belonged to Father Karras.

Chris, after a pause, takes it from her.

SHARON (*glancing at her watch*)
You'd better hurry.

INTERIOR SECOND-FLOOR HALL—MACNEIL HOUSE—DAY

Chris approaches Regan's bedroom.

CHRIS (*calling*)
Hey, Rags, how ya comin'?

INTERIOR REGAN'S BEDROOM—FULL ANGLE AT REGAN

A little wan and gaunt, dark sacs beneath her eyes, Regan stands by her bed, holding two stuffed animals in her grip as she stares down with indecision and a child's discontent at an open, overpacked suitcase. From off scene, a sound of hammering.

CHRIS
How ya comin', hon? We're late.

REGAN
There's just not enough *room* in this thing!

CHRIS
Well, ya can't take it all now, sweetheart. Just leave it and Willie'll bring it later on. Come on, we've got to hurry or we're going to miss the plane.

Sound of door chime.

REGAN *(mildly pouting)*

Oh, OK.

CHRIS

That's my baby.

Chris exits, heading for the stairs. With a sigh of resignation, Regan looks down at the animals. Then she turns off scene toward the sound of hammering.

POINT-OF-VIEW SHOT—AT WINDOW

A carpenter is refitting it with new shutters.

ANGLE AT REGAN

She is staring at the window, angling her head slightly to one side. She frowns as if nagged by some elusive memory. She looks down in thought.

ANGLE AT WINDOW—CARPENTER WORKING

INTERIOR FRONT-DOOR AREA—MACNEIL HOUSE—DAY

Chris opens the door, disclosing Dyer in his cassock and Roman collar.

CHRIS

Oh, hi, Father. I was just about to call to say good-bye. Come on in.

DYER

Oh, well, just for a second. I know you're rushing.

CHRIS

Yeah, we're runnin' kinda late. But I'm really glad to see you.

Dyer nods a bit glumly. Karl passes through the door and out into the street with two suitcases, heading for Chris's car, which is parked on the street in front of the house.

CHRIS *(gently)*

She still can't remember what happened, Father.

DYER

Well, it's good that she can't, in a way.

CHRIS (*nodding, eyes down*)

Yeah, I guess.

DYER

I'm glad she's well.

CHRIS

Funny. He never even knew her.

Dyer looks up, and then so does Chris, their eyes meeting. After a pause:

DYER

What do *you* think happened? Do you think
she was really possessed?

CHRIS (*after a pause*)

If you're asking if I believe in the devil, the
answer is yes—yeah, that I believe. The devil
keeps doing commercials.

DYER

But if all of the evil in the world makes you
think that there might be a devil—then how do
you account for all of the good?

Chris's reaction reveals that this is a telling point. Then
into the scene comes Regan, dressed to go.

REGAN

OK, I finished.

CHRIS

Honey, this is Father Dyer. Say, "Hi."

REGAN

Hi.

DYER

Hi.
(*tousles her hair*)
All set to go?

CHRIS (*thoughtfully*)

You know, one thing, Father Dyer . . .

266

As Dyer looks to Chris, neither of them notice that Regan has begun to stare oddly at Dyer's Roman collar with that same frown, that same tugging remembrance in her eyes.

DYER

Yes, Chris?

CHRIS

You said . . .

A quick, aware glance to Regan, then back to Dyer.

CLOSE ANGLE AT REGAN STILL STARING AT COLLAR

CHRIS (*off scene*)
Well, you said that Father Karras had a problem with his faith.

CLOSE ANGLE AT DYER'S COLLAR

DYER (*off scene*)
Yes.

ANGLE AT CHRIS

She stares down at the floor, frowning, then shakes her head.

CHRIS

Boy, he sure didn't act like it, did he.

KARL (*off scene*)
All ready.

ANOTHER ANGLE TO INCLUDE ALL

CHRIS

OK, Karl.
(*taking Dyer's hand*)
Bye, Father. I'll call you from LA.

DYER

Good-bye, Chris.

Suddenly, impulsively, Regan reaches up to Dyer, pulls his head down and kisses his cheek. Then, looking puzzled at what she has done:

Good-bye.

DYER

Good-bye, dear.

Chris takes Regan's hand and draws her toward the car. Then she remembers the medal still in her hand. As she offers it to Dyer:

CHRIS

Oh, I forgot this. Here.

Dyer instantly recognizes the medal. For a moment he stares at it. Then:

DYER

Why don't *you* keep it?

A beat. Dyer sees that Chris's eyes are clouding up.

DYER

It's all right, Chris. For him, it's the beginning.

Chris holds his gaze, then nods.

CHRIS

C'mon. Rags. Gotta hurry.

As Chris and Regan leave the frame, the camera stays on Dyer as he turns to watch them.

CHRIS (*off scene*)
(*calling*)

Bye, Father!

POINT-OF-VIEW SHOT—AT CAR PULLING AWAY

and moving quickly down Prospect Street.

ANGLE AT DYER—WATCHING

Willie goes back inside the house. From off scene we hear the car brakes.

POINT-OF-VIEW SHOT—AT SQUAD CAR

Kinderman is emerging, hurrying toward Dyer.

268

KINDERMAN

I came to say good-bye.

DYER

You just missed them.

Kinderman stops. A beat. Then:

KINDERMAN

How's the girl?

DYER

She seemed fine.

KINDERMAN

Ah, that's good. Very good. Well, that's all that's important. Back to business. Back to work. Bye now, Father.

Kinderman turns and takes a step toward the squad car, then stops and stares back speculatively at Dyer.

KINDERMAN

You go to films, Father Dyer? You like them?

DYER

Oh, sure.

KINDERMAN

I get passes.
(*hesitates for a moment*)
In fact, I've got a pass for the Crest tomorrow night. You'd like to go?

DYER

What's playing?

KINDERMAN

Wuthering Heights.

DYER

Who's in it?

KINDERMAN

Heathcliffe, Jackie Gleason, and in the role Catherine Earnshaw, Lucille Ball.

DYER (*deadpan*)

I've seen it.

Kinderman stares limply for a moment, then looks away.

> KINDERMAN (*murmuring*)
> Another one.

The detective steps up to the sidewalk, hooks arms with Dyer and slowly starts walking him down the street. The camera tracks front.

> KINDERMAN (*fondly*)
> I'm reminded of a line in the film *Casablanca*. At the end Humphrey Bogart says to Claude Rains, "Louie—I think this is the beginning of a beautiful friendship."

FIXED REAR SHOT

as Kinderman and Dyer walk away from us.

> DYER
> You know, you *look* a little bit like Bogart.

> KINDERMAN
> You noticed.

Autumn leaves and laughing students traverse the frame as we gradually raise the camera angle to a high shot and the end music swells.

TO BLACK

TITLES

Why Changes Were Made in the Screenplay

Plainly speaking, I liked that script. Billy Friedkin didn't. He objected to its cinematic trickery, its flashbacks, and the opening montage. He felt that in a film which depended on whether or not the audience believes that the bed really is levitating, only disaster could result from drawing attention to cinematic techniques and mechanics. It was important, he argued, that the audience should in no way sense Frank Morgan behind the curtain working the controls of *The Wizard of Oz*. I cautiously agreed; and in the cold light of day, I had to admit that extending the credits over so many pages was an act of madness. But I must say I was altogether unprepared for Billy's major criticism of my screenplay: "It isn't faithful enough to the novel."

"Ah, Mephistopheles!" Seducer!

Billy was serious. In fact, he was so fixated on the novel that when in my first-draft screenplay I changed Regan's sculpture from the bird it had been in the novel to a bear,[1] Billy shrieked and demanded we go back to the bird. I asked him why, and he answered simply: "It's in the book."

The unarguable problem, of course, was length, for a timing of the script disclosed that it would make at least a four-hour film; this in spite of my carefully considered, time-saving montage, and my various gimmicks and tricks. So, we set to work on trimming the script. Each morning, Billy and I would meet at my office to discuss construction. Billy wanted the sequences of events to be exactly as they were in the novel, and he tried to ensure this by refusing to work from my first-draft screenplay. Instead, he worked from his note-laden copy of the novel. Sitting on a faded orange sofa in my office, Billy would bracket

---

[1] The cosmic significance behind this change was my youngest daughter's fondness for bears. In fact, she calls me "Papa Bear."

with a ball-point pen the scenes that we both agreed should be used in the film. Even where the changes I'd made in the dialogue were only slight, Billy would cringe and ask that I keep the dialogue exactly as it had been in the book.

The first major casualty of the rewrite was the Karl and Elvira subplot which threw suspicion on Karl. Out, too, went the lesser red herrings that pointed to Karras, and even to Sharon, as being somehow involved in the desecrations or in Dennings's death. Our reasoning was that by the time the film had been playing for a month, almost everyone in the audience would know from the outset—before they had purchased their tickets, in fact—that the butler didn't do it. Thus these subplots would not only add nothing to the forward movement of the plot but would doubtless frustrate and even antagonize an audience that would be approximately eighteen miles ahead of us. Although I particularly hated to lose Karras as a suspect, along with such concomitant intriguing touches as the desecrator's fluent knowledge of Latin, I agreed with the necessity of the excisions. But it hurt. Time is not a thief, he's a butcher.

Another victim of the rewrite was the extent of Kinderman's role in the original plot. For if the audience knew from the outset that Regan was the killer, the police investigation would be devoid of both mystery and suspense. The character of Kinderman presented yet another problem; namely, a television series called "Columbo." I cannot begin to convey the extent of my irritation when I read letters—and I get quite a few of them—asking if I based the character of Kinderman on Columbo. As any plagiarist would know, the novel was written long before Columbo debuted on TV. But the audience, we figured, would not be aware of this and would think that I'd copied my character from Columbo; furthermore, we feared that by the time our film came out approximately two years later, audiences would be so surfeited with Columbo's character and shtick that the Kinderman character would run the risk of being a cliché. Which was why we not only shortened the part but eliminated most of Kinderman's "mind-like-a-steel-trap-masked-by-phony-bumbling" aspects.

Some of the other scenes we cut, I didn't miss. For example, the first-draft depiction of Karras actually functioning as a psychiatrist, as opposed to his merely being described as one. We compensated for this loss with the very brief scene in which Karras is seen (largely in pantomime) deep in conversation with a troubled-looking priest. We also dropped the scene in which reference is made to a spectroanalysis of the paint on Regan's sculpture. While filming at the Georgetown location, we replaced it with the brief scene in which Kinderman finds a large fragment of sculpted clay at the bottom of the treacherous steps beside the MacNeil house.[2] Other less than monumental deletions included some lighter moments between Sharon and Chris; and a setup for the "help me" sequence, Chris's mention of an *L* and an *M* rising up on Regan's skin while she was under observation in the Barringer Clinic.

These trims, as I say, were very minor in terms of the film's impact. But the loss of other elements, whether in the script, on the set, or in the editing, still causes me to bleed varying quantities of blood. Some of these deletions and compressions—and our reasons for cutting them—are as follows, in an inverse order of importance:

1. The fuller exposition of Karras's crisis of faith in the scene where Dyer comforts him after his mother's death. Here, the problem was pace, as it was in the next point.

2. More fully developed interview/investigation scenes between Karras and the demon. Although these scenes contained very little action, I thought them

---

[2] To me, it is obvious that the fragment is from one of Regan's sculptures that was knocked from the window seat of her room by Dennings when she pushed him out of the window. But certain commentators on the film—both pro and con—have wondered in print how "a piece of the statue of the demon" confronted by Merrin in the prologue "got from northern Iraq to the bottom of the steps in Georgetown." Had that been the case, I must confess that I would wonder, too.

suspenseful within the context of the supernatural detective story, i.e., the mystery of whether or not Regan is really possessed (along with the implication: Is there a God?). These scenes provided verbal clues to the answer in terms of Regan's heightened intelligence, her language, and her pattern of association of ideas. And within these expanded scenes, the demon manifested—what shall we call it—personality? In short, the demon was given an opportunity to be more complex, to be more than merely vulgar. But Billy and I finally agreed that preliminary encounters with the demon should be kept to a minimum, thus ensuring a greater impact for the exorcism scene. And, of course, the need to cut a good seventy pages from somewhere in the script was very persuasive.

3. A more gradual revelation of the onset of Regan's disorder. Here the cuts were made in the editing room rather than in the script. By the time I'd reworked the script it was down to 133 pages. Even so, the film that we shot from it at first had a running time of over three hours. Billy was determined to pare it to two, for he was convinced that any film exceeding this length would have an unwanted effect on the collective posteriors of America's audiences. In other words, after two hours, people get restless; their concentration falls apart. And so Billy eliminated most of the "gradual onset" scenes. Anyway, quite frankly, they were boring, and again we reasoned that the audience, knowing up front that Regan was possessed rather than physiologically or psychologically ill, would be thinking, "Let's get on with it."[3]

---

[3] I still believe this decision was correct, although I do think that ideally revisions of this type should be made before you get to the set. If a screenplay is properly constructed, any substantial cut will inevitably create confusion, rough juxtapositions, and an appearance of sloppy work on the part of the author. Audiences are jarred when Chris refers out of nowhere to Regan taking pills "just like the doctor said" at a point in the film where they have yet to see Regan being examined by a doctor, are in the dark about why she might have gone if in fact she did, and have no idea what kind of pills she might be taking. Billy did agree to restore in the editing the appropriate medical scene that preceded the line about the pills, and he tried very hard to work it in, but after many unsuccessful efforts to do so without slowing down the pace and dissipating the building tension, he had to give it up.

4. The "beginning of a beautiful friendship" tag line between Kinderman and Dyer. By reprising Kinderman's playful discussion with Karras, I intended to suggest that Karras lived on through Dyer. I believed this suggestion of "carrying on" would provide a lift which the audience would need at that point. This scene was not a victim of the "two-hour" mandate, but was cut in the editing room by the unanimous vote of everyone (but me) who felt that the tag somehow took the ending past its station.

5. The demon's devastating psychological attacks on everyone in the household. These were implied by Merrin but never delivered in the final script. Billy felt that the exorcism scene should focus exclusively on the demon versus the two priests, and that therefore no one else should be present in the room. So the demon's attacks on Chris for her divorce and for putting her career ahead of her child's welfare, and on Sharon for her sexual fantasies concerning Karras, and on Karl by disclosing the secret of his daughter's drug addiction, are all missing.[4] And although Merrin *is* in the room, he is no longer subjected to the demon's attack on his fear of committing the sin of pride.[5]

6. The clear understanding that the demon in Regan is the same one that Merrin had met—and bested—in a previous exorcism in Africa. The African exorcism reference remains in the film. ("The exorcism lasted for months: I hear it damn near killed him.") But gone is the demon's crucial line to Merrin: "This time, you're going to lose." You will recall that in the first-draft script, the line was delivered by the demon off scene. In the final draft, it was the first line uttered by the demon as Merrin entered the room for the exorcism. This, plus other hints, created an aura of vendetta, and

---

[4]Karl was excluded from the room for still another reason: the earlier loss of the Elvira subplot. An accidental side effect of his absence kept unresolved a solution to a mystery in the film: the audience never finds out that it was Karl who placed the crucifix under Regan's pillow, because they never learn that he is Catholic, a fact revealed in the original draft when he blessed himself as the bed floated up off the ground during the exorcism.

[5]As was the case with Teilhard de Chardin, as revealed in some personal (though now published) correspondence.

further indicated that Regan's possession is a setup; that the target all along is Merrin—at least, as the demon has construed it. Though another way of construing it—and my own—would be that Karras was the target and that the demon himself was being used as the crucible of Karras's salvation. This added an extra dimension to the exorcism, an underpinning that clarified the prologue in northern Iraq and integrated it into the rest of the plot. But when the sequence was shot, the line wasn't used. Billy preferred that the demon be silent until after he spits in Merrin's face as the priest is reciting the Lord's Prayer.[6] With respect to dramatic tension, he was right. I should have found another place to insert the line. I didn't. No excuse.

7. The scene in which Merrin and Karras converse in the hall. Here we had an explicit articulation of the theme that gave the film clarity and a definite moral weight: clarity because it focused the story on Karras and his problem of faith; and moral weight because it put the obscene and repellent elements of the film into the context of evil's primary attack on mankind: namely, the inducement of despair. Moreover, without it, we lost the observation that once a demon leaves a host's body, it never returns to it.[7] So after Karras has offered himself to the demon in place of Regan, his only remaining problem is how to prevent the demon from using his (Karras's) body to murder Regan and possibly others in the household. As the demon (in Karras) moves to Regan to strangle her, Karras opts to take the demon out of the window. And with Karras's death, we know that the demon cannot reenter Regan.[8] Thus Karras's victory is complete. And we are allowed to feel glad; in fact, uplifted. The revised (and final) screen-

---

[6]Incidentally, most scriptural scholars would support our "deliver us from the evil one" ending to the prayer in place of the usual "deliver us from evil." The former seems the authentic translation.

[7]This has no basis in fact.

[8]As for the danger of him wandering about in search of an immediate new host—a speculation many viewers of the film have expressed—the fact is that in the Western world possession is so extraordinarily rare that to my knowledge there have only been three Church-approved exorcisms performed in America in the last forty or fifty years.

play retained the bare bones of the hallway scene. Then we cut it down further, although in rehearsal Max von Sydow argued for expanding on it somewhat. This was done and the scene was shot. But later it was cut from the film because Billy said it was a "showstopper," not in the usual sense but in that it stopped the action dead in its tracks by pausing for a "theological commercial." Regardless, I still disagree very strongly with the scene's absence from the film.

And here I suppose I should explain the relationship between the producer and the director with respect to the ultimate control of a film. Frequently, it depends upon the financing studio through which you produce and distribute the film. At some studios—Columbia Pictures, for example—producers are favored. Not so at Warner Brothers, however. Here, the director's word is final.

Billy Friedkin had no objection to the religious content of the story. Far from it. His opposition on showstopper grounds was not an unreasonable one. And both in the script and on the set Billy did retain other touches of "message," as in the scene I wrote between Dyer and Chris at the end of the film in which Dyer starts her thinking about God as the only explanation of goodness in the world and also when Chris cries over Karras's medal and Dyer comforts her with "For him, it's the beginning." In this ending in the script, Chris decides she will keep the medal, thus betokening that she is now open to faith. But we were not to see these moments in the film.

We had to drop the exchange in which Chris accepts the medal because it simply didn't work, which nobody noticed until we were editing. And inasmuch as the scene had been shot in Georgetown, it wasn't practical to revise and redo it, for the Georgetown City Council had given us fits about permission to shoot in the first place. Even if permisson were given, it would have taken us weeks to get it. So the medal exchange was dropped.

In still another instance, on the night before filming a scene Billy called me to his hotel room. There I found with him, Ellen Burstyn (Chris), Lee J. Cobb

(Kinderman), and Father William O'Malley, S.J., who played the part of Father Dyer. Billy had been rehearsing the scene with them, as was his custom the night before shooting. And he told me that the "good in the world" scene wasn't working; would I please listen and give him my opinion. The cast ran through the scene, coming apart at the place where Chris says "the devil keeps doing commercials." There wasn't a doubt that the scene did not work. And in my opinion, no remedy was possible. For the problem, I was convinced, was Ellen Burstyn's powerful subconscious block on the subject of Satan's existence. She'd objected to the line some weeks before in New York, and I'd already rewritten it for her several times. In the final script, the scene ran as follows:

DYER

What do you think happened? Do you think she was really possessed?

CHRIS

If you're asking if I believe in the devil, the answer is yes. Yeah. I do. Because the devil keeps doing commercials.

DYER

But if all of the evil in the world tends to make you believe in the devil, how do you account for all of the good?

And now in rehearsal, Ellen stiffened up on the line and made it stilted. In a word—"my hunch, my opinion," as Kinderman would say—she subconsciously took a dive and I felt that she'd do it again when we shot. So we scrapped the scene. This kind of thing had happened before. In the Barringer Clinic scene (in the film), Chris is asked by one of the doctors: "Do you have any religious beliefs?" Chris is supposed to answer a definite "No," for part of the dramatic tension in the story, as well as in the plot, depended upon Chris being an atheist. But instead of the "No," Ellen's block slipped in an ad-libbed response of, "Oh, well, maybe God." Ellen Burstyn's talents as an actress are no less than spectacular;[9] but we later looped in the "no."

Balancing out the minor losses were certain additions to my original script. One was the prologue in northern Iraq. I'd originally cut it because of the running-time problem, and because it didn't work very well with the montage opening in the first draft. Still another reason I cut it, I suppose, was the residual influence of Harper & Row's suggestion that I cut it from the novel. But Billy insisted we restore it, and it would turn out to be—for me, at least—the most beautiful section of the film. Billy also came up with the recently discovered arteriography technique for probing the brain, which turned into a very powerful scene in the film. And it was Billy's suggestion that we use Karras's visit to his mother, as in the novel. Billy had been very close to his mother, as I had been to mine, and he had taken her death very hard. He understood this scene very well. Another moment that I think works beautifully is Karras's dream of his mother, which Billy at a very late date suggested we restore from the novel.

One addition to the script was prompted by another —and unexpected—source. During rehearsals of the exorcism scene we had help from a technical expert, a priest, Father John J. Nicola, who was with us to ensure authenticity. Father Nicola, who opposed both the desecration and masturbation scenes, made but one comment concerning the exorcism. The only area that lacked authenticity, he told us, was the verbal obscenities uttered by the demon. While he never suggested that we change what we had, he did point out that in actual cases the language was far beyond what we had. On that day, I recall, I walked heavily up to my office, sat down at my typewriter and concentrated on writing a string of the worst filth I could possibly imagine. I then gave Billy multiple choices for every moment of the scene which required obscenities. He picked three. They are, of course, the worst in the film. And quite properly so. For *The Exorcist* film does not purport to be cop-out. Our demon was not someone with whom you could make a

_____

[9]She also came up with a couple of lines of dialogue which are among the best in the film.

pact; our demon was real, and since we were representing a reflection of ultimate evil we could not, as Stanley Kauffmann has noted, simply have Regan say "Darn," or have a Greek chorus enter and announce that Regan had done "some very naughty things" off camera.

Two other changes in the script, both of them suggested by Billy Friedkin, seem also an improvement. In the first draft script I'd shown Burke Dennings' head turned around; and at the start of the script I'd also shown Karras's mother dead. But I agreed when Billy suggested that perhaps there would be greater impact in disclosing both of these events in a casual manner and setting. Thus, the death of the mother would be announced in an almost offhand remark at the party; and the reference to Dennings's head being turned around and facing backward would be made by Kinderman when he and Karras were walking on the campus, past an active tennis court, the day being bright and sunny.

One final note. During the filming of the prologue on location in northern Iraq, by the ruins of Nineveh (which I did not attend), Billy Friedkin added a touch that has become comparable to the great "slab" controversy in *2001*. This is Merrin's discovery of a Christian holy medal in the dig at the exact spot where an amulet of the demon Pazuzu will be found a moment after. The medal—or one just like it—is later worn by Karras's mother. And at the end of the film it is Karras who is wearing it. How did the medal get from northern Iraq to Damien Karras's neck? Many people have asked me that question—and many critics have written about it in their reviews. Some have speculated that the finding of the medal beside the amulet is one of several symbolic foreshadowings of the coming conflict between Merrin and the demon, between good and evil. In fact, Billy's primary *conscious* reason for putting the medal there was simply to "add resonances" to the film. It certainly accomplished that objective. But a much better question for reviewers to have asked is how a contemporary Christian medal got into an archaeological ruin from pre-Christian Nineveh in the first place. I also commend to their consideration the following: How could Merrin, a crack archaeologist, a character

282

modeled on Teilhard de Chardin, fail to recognize a medal of St. Joseph when he sees it? I somehow doubt that we'll ever get an answer to this puzzle.[10]

The script that follows integrates the final shooting script, changes made while in rehearsal or by the cast while filming (whether intentionally or inadvertently), and changes effected in the cutting room. In a word, it is the film as seen in theaters. With the exception of the scene between Merrin and Karras in the hall, my disagreements are buried in the stunning impact the film delivers. Read the transcript and judge for yourself.

---

[10]Unless you speak Arabic. For though the English subtitle has Merrin saying merely, "This is strange," on being shown the medal, in Arabic he is in fact saying words to the effect of, "What's *this* doing here?"

with Scene Settings

WARNER BROS.

A WARNER COMMUNICATIONS COMPANY
PRESENTS

A
WILLIAM FRIEDKIN
FILM

WLLIAM PETER
BLATTY'S

THE
EXORCIST

The film opens at an archaeological excavation site at the ruins of Nineveh. An old man in khakis (Father Merrin) works at a section of the mound with an excavating pick. He looks up as a small boy shouts to him.

> BOY (*in Arabic*)
> They found something . . . small pieces.

> MERRIN (*in Arabic*)
> Where?

> BOY (*in Arabic*)
> At the base of the mound.

Merrin hurries over to the archaeologist who has made the find. He examines the artifacts, singling out a religious medal for close scrutiny.

ARCHAEOLOGIST (*in Arabic*)
Some interesting finds . . .

MERRIN (*in Arabic*)
Very good.

ARCHAEOLOGIST (*in Arabic*)
Lamps, arrowheads, coins . . .

MERRIN (*in Arabic, indicating medal*)
This is strange.

ARCHAEOLOGIST (*in Arabic*)
Not from the same period.

Merrin scratches at the mound and makes an additional find. He extracts it gingerly from the hardened clay and, as he begins to dust it off, his expression turns to dismay as he recognizes a green stone amulet in the figure of the demon Pazuzu.

At a streetside teahouse, an exhausted Merrin sits warming his trembling hands around a glass of steaming tea. On his face is an expression of foreboding.

WAITER (*in Arabic*)
Something else?

MERRIN (*in Arabic*)
No, thank you.

At the curator of antiquities' office, the tagged finds of the archaeological dig are now spread in neat rows on a long table. Merrin sits at a table to the side, examining the Pazuzu amulet while the curator writes in a ledger, listing the finds. After a moment, the curator looks over at the amulet.

CURATOR (*in Arabic*)
Evil against evil.

Merrin continues to stare down at it with a haunted expression.

CURATOR (*in Arabic*)
Father?

Merrin doesn't answer, but abruptly the clock on the wall stops ticking. In the sudden silence that follows, Merrin looks up at the curator, whose brow is furrowed.

CURATOR (*in Arabic*)
I wish you didn't have to go.

MERRIN (*in Arabic*)
There is something I must do.

CURATOR (*in Arabic, with regret*)
Good-bye.

Merrin leaves, stepping into the gathering gloom of the streets of Mosul. As the curator looks worriedly after him, he nearly collides with a fast-moving droshky.

At the Nineveh excavation site again, Merrin slowly and wearily walks amid the ruins of a former temple area. He is menacingly challenged by an Arab watchman, rifle at the ready until he recognizes Merrin. Merrin continues walking. He has the air of someone searching out vibrations, looking for something, yet afraid of finding it. At last he confronts it: a statue of the demon Pazuzu. He lowers his head, closing his eyes against a dread confirmation of his premonition. The statue's shadow lengthens and creeps onto his face as in the distance is heard the howls of wild dogs. Merrin lifts his head to gaze once more at the statue. But in his expression now is acceptance and grim determination. The statue and the old man confront each other, like two ancient enemies squared off in a massive arena.

The yelping of the wild dogs turns into the subdued barking of neighborhood dogs in the Georgetown area of Washington, D.C. In her upstairs bedroom, Chris MacNeil is sitting up in bed, studying a film script. She is distracted by the sound of light irregular rappings coming from somewhere outside the room. Her concentration broken, she tosses down the script and gets out of bed. The rappings grow louder as she approaches her daughter Regan's bedroom, then abruptly cease. Chris looks baffled as she enters the room and tiptoes

over to the bed. Regan is asleep, her blankets askew.
Chris shivers. Yet Regan's brow is covered with
perspiration. Puzzled, Chris rubs at her goose pimples.
The sounds begin again, this time softer, like tiny
claws scratching at the ceiling. Chris stares up for
a moment, then leans over and adjusts Regan's pillow.

> CHRIS (*in a whisper*)
> Sure do love you.

Bathrobed and sleepy-eyed, Chris joins Willie, her
middle-aged housekeeper, in the kitchen. Willie hastily
wipes her hands on a dishtowel.

> WILLIE (*German accent*)
> Good morning, Mrs. MacNeil.

> CHRIS
> How are you today?

> WILLIE
> Fine, thank you.

> CHRIS
> That's good.
> (*to Willie, indicating coffee*)
> It's OK, I've got it. Thanks.

Crusty-eyed, Chris moves sleepily about the kitchen,
getting milk for her coffee from the refrigerator as she
talks. A man enters: it is Karl, Willie's husband, very
Teutonic.

> KARL
> Good morning, ma'am.

> CHRIS
> Good morning, Karl . . . Oh, Karl, we've got
> rats in the attic. You better get some traps.

> KARL
> Rats?

> CHRIS
> Um-hum, 'fraid so.

> KARL
> But the attic is clean.

CHRIS

All right, then we've got clean rats.

KARL

No, no. No rats.

CHRIS

I just heard them, Karl.

KARL

Maybe plumbing.

CHRIS

Yeah, or maybe *rats*. Now will you just get the traps?

KARL

Yes, I go now.

CHRIS (*exasperated*)

Well don't go *now,* Karl. The stores aren't open yet.

KARL (*leaving*)

I will see.

WILLIE

They are closed.

A film is being shot on the Georgetown University campus. The usual equipment, cast, and crew are in evidence, as well as spectators made up of faculty and students. Chris, in jeans and a sweatshirt, calls to her director, an elfin Englishman named Burke Dennings. He looks as if he has been drinking and keeps swigging from a paper cup.

CHRIS

Burke! Oh, Burke!

FILM PRODUCER

Is the scene really essential, Burke?

DENNINGS

Chris . . .

FILM PRODUCER
Would you just consider it, whether or not we can do without it?

Burke leaves him and joins Chris.

CHRIS
Burke, take a look at this damn thing, will yuh? It just doesn't make sense.

DENNINGS
Why, it's perfectly plain. You're a teacher at the college. You don't want a building torn down.

CHRIS
Burke, come on, I can *read,* for crissakes.

DENNINGS
Well, what's wrong?

CHRIS
Well, *why* are they tearing the building down?

DENNINGS
Shall we summon the writer? He's in Paris, I believe.

CHRIS
Hiding?

DENNINGS
Fucking.

Chris collapses against Burke, laughing. She collects herself as she notices a priest (Karras) among the spectators, worried that he might be offended by the obscenity. But Karras is smiling as he walks away. He turns once to look back at the filming, then continues walking.

PRODUCTION ASSISTANT
Scene thirty-nine, hotel, take four.

DENNINGS (*through megaphone*)
All right, hustle background. Action!

PROTESTER (*through megaphone*)
Is this your campus? Let's get our defense de-

partment off this campus! It's our school. They have no right! I've seen enough killing in my life. There's no reason for it anymore!

The camera rolls and while extras cheer and boo at her approach, Chris marches up the steps of the building and seizes the bullhorn from the rebel student leader. In the ensuing melee, there is pushing and shoving. Police arrive on the scene.

CHRIS (through megaphone)

Wait a minute! Wait a minute . . . wait a minute! Hold it!

Some of the student factions are holding up signs and banners: "KEEP CLASSES OPEN," "FREE LOGIC!" "SHUT DOWN!" "CLOSE THE SCHOOL," and "BURN IT!" Other placards are blank. Many of the students in one sector are affecting shrouds and death masks.

CHRIS (through bullhorn)

Hey, come on, we're all concerned with human rights, for God's sake. But the kids who wanna get an education have a right, too!

The crowd erupts as Chris continues over the hubbub.

CHRIS

Wait, hold it, don't you understand? It's against your own principles for God's sake! You can't, you can't accomplish anything by shutting kids out of their school. Hold it! Hold it! If you want to effect any change, you have to do it within the system.

DENNINGS (through megaphone)

OK, cut, that's a wrap.

Chris is at the campus's main gate. Wearing a sweater and beret, she is addressing the driver of her limousine.

CHRIS

I think I'll walk home tonight, Mike.

OK.

She hands him an oversize leather bag she is carrying.

CHRIS

Here, take that and drop it by my house, huh?
Good night.

He nods. She starts walking home, weary and a little
preoccupied. As she walks by St. Mike's Church court-
yard, she sees Karras deep in conversation with a
troubled-looking priest. Chris pauses and watches curi-
ously, out of earshot.

PRIEST

I mean, there's not a day in my life that I don't
feel like a fraud. I mean, priests, doctors, law-
yers, I've talked to them all. I don't know anyone who hasn't felt that.

Chris seems pensive as she moves on.

In Chris's kitchen her secretary Sharon Spencer, a
pretty young woman, is sitting at a table, typing. A
stack of mail and messages is beside her. Chris comes
in the front door.

CHRIS

Hello.

SHARON

In here!

CHRIS (*entering the kitchen*)

Hi.

SHARON

Hi. How'd your day go?

CHRIS

Oh, not too bad. It was kinda like the Walt
Disney version of the *Ho Chi Minh Story,* but
other than that it was terrific.

Chris leafs through the mail and messages as Sharon
stops typing long enough to hand her an envelope.

CHRIS

What we got, anything exciting here?

SHARON

And also, you got an invitation.

CHRIS

What's this?

SHARON

Dinner at the White House!

CHRIS

You're kidding me? What is it, a big party or something?

SHARON

Uhn-uhn, it's five or six people.

CHRIS

Hm, Thursday, huh. Far out.

She is interrupted by the bounding entrance of Regan, her eleven-year-old daughter. Freckles. Ponytail. Arms outstretched, she races for her mother.

REGAN

Hi, mom!

Chris catches Regan in a bear hug.

CHRIS

Whatcha do today?

REGAN

Stuff.

CHRIS

What's that mean? Stuff.

REGAN

Well, ah, me an' Sharon played a game in the backyard.

CHRIS

You did?

REGAN

And we had a picnic down by the river.

CHRIS

That's nice. What else?

REGAN

Oh, mom, you should have seen, this man came along on this beautiful gray horse.

CHRIS

Really, what kind?

REGAN (*to Sharon*)

Wasn't he pretty?

SHARON

He was beautiful.

CHRIS

Was it a mare, a gelding, or what?

REGAN

I think it was a gelding.

CHRIS

Um-hum.

REGAN

It was gray, oh, it was so beautiful. And the guy let me ride it all around and everything.

CHRIS

No kidding.

SHARON

Yeah, she rode it for about a half an hour.

CHRIS

Oh, nice.

REGAN

Oh, I loved it. Oh, mom, *can't* we get a horse?

CHRIS

Well, not while we're in Washington, honey.

REGAN

Why not?

CHRIS

We'll see when we get home. OK?

When can I have one?

We'll see, Regan, we'll see.
(*to Sharon*)
Hey, listen, on the party invitation, I wanna
write a personal—
(*as Regan filches a cookie and runs off with it*)
Oh, Regan, don't touch that. Regan, come back
here! All right, give it up, give it up, give it to
me!

No!

You'll be sorry, come on!

Chris catches up with Regan, grabs her and hugs her.
They both sink to the floor, giggling.

A platform of a New York subway station, silent
except for the rumble of a passing train. Points of
light stretch down through the darkness of the tunnel,
like guides to hopelessness. The station appears to be
deserted except for Karras, who stands close to the
edge of the platform. He carries a valise resembling a
doctor's medical bag. His posture is dejected. Near him
lies an old wino, drunk, his back propped up against
the station wall.

Father, could you help an old altar boy? I'm a
Catholic.

Karras looks up startled and dismayed. There is pain
in his face. He shuts his eyes against the wino's intrusion and clutches at his coat lapels, pulling them together as if to hide the collar. A train rushes by.

Karras walks despondently along a New York street
studded with decrepit tenement buildings. He pauses
before one to watch some ragged, grimy, foul-mouthed
urchins pitching pennies against the stoop. Then he

297

climbs up the steps. At the end of a long dark hall inside the building, he stops at the door of an apartment and lightly raps. From within there is the faint sound of a radio turned to a news station. Karras waits for a moment, then digs out a key from his pants pocket and enters. The radio becomes more audible as he goes into a railroad-flat kitchen. Sparse and ancient furnishings. Karras breathes in an aching sigh as his gaze brushes around at the painful reminders of his past. Then he glances toward the sound of the radio, puts down his valise, and starts into the bedroom.

KARRAS

Mama? Mama . . .

No response. He goes into a very small living room where he sees his mother asleep in a chair.

KARRAS

Mama?

His mother awakens with a slight start. She is overjoyed to see him.

MAMA (*in a thick Mediterranean accent*)
Dimmy! Dimmy!

She hastily gets to her feet and throws her arms around Karras. She and Karras greet each other in Greek, then go back to speaking English.

KARRAS

I'm all right, mama.

MAMA

I'm so glad to see you.

KARRAS

You look good.

MAMA

I'm all right.

KARRAS

How's your leg?

MAMA

How 'bout you, Dimmy? You are all right?

298

KARRAS

I'm fine, mama, I'm fine.

Later, Karras eats alone at the table while his mother watches him from across the room.

MAMA

Your Uncle John passed by to visit me.

KARRAS

Oh really, when?

MAMA

Last month.

Karras bends to tighten a bandage on his mother's leg.

KARRAS

That too tight?

MAMA

No.

KARRAS

Now mama, you have to stay off it. You can't go up and down the stairs. Now you have to give it rest.

MAMA

OK.

KARRAS

Mama, I could take you somewhere where you'd be safe, you wouldn't be alone. There would be people around, you know? You wouldn't be sitting here listening to a radio.

MAMA (*in Greek, then in English*)

You understand me? This is my house and I'm not going noplace.

Karras murmurs resignedly as his mother scrutinizes him.

MAMA

Dimmy, you worry for something.

KARRAS

No, mama.

299

MAMA

You are not happy? Tell me, what is the matter?

KARRAS

Look, mama, I'm all right, I'm fine, really I am.

In the basement playroom of the MacNeil house, Regan sails a sculpted clay "worry bird" with a feather plume and a comically long painted nose across the room to Chris.

REGAN (*laughing*)

Here it comes . . . there!

CHRIS

Oh, look at that.

REGAN

You like it?

CHRIS (*laughing*)

Oh, is that funny! I better put him over here to dry though, he's still wet. Oh, here we go. There, he can dry there. Hey, where'd this come from?

She has noticed a Ouija board and planchette.

REGAN

I found it.

CHRIS

Where?

REGAN

Closet.

CHRIS

Have you been playing with it?

REGAN

Yep.

CHRIS

You know how?

REGAN

I'll show you.

CHRIS

Wait a minute, you need two.

REGAN

No, you don't. I do it all the time.

CHRIS

Oh yeah, well, let's both play.

Regan has her fingertips positioned on the planchette.
They sit down with it at the games table. As Chris
reaches out to put hers there, too, the planchette makes
a sudden, forceful move to the "NO" position on the
board.

CHRIS

You really don't want me to play, huh?

REGAN

No, I do! Captain Howdy said no.

CHRIS

Captain who?

REGAN

Captain Howdy.

CHRIS

Who's Captain Howdy?

REGAN

You know, I make the questions and he does
the answers.

CHRIS (*humoring her*)

Oh, Captain Howdy, I see.

REGAN

He's nice.

CHRIS

Oh, I bet he is.

REGAN

Here, I'll show yuh.

CHRIS

All right.

Regan stares at the board, her eyes shut tight in concentration.

> REGAN
>
> Captain Howdy, do you think my mom's pretty?

Seconds tick by. Nothing happens. Chris turns her head at an odd, creaking sound from the closet area. She stares for a moment, then looks back at the board.

> REGAN
>
> Captain Howdy?
> (*no response*)
> Captain Howdy, that isn't very nice.

> CHRIS
>
> Well, maybe he's sleeping.

> REGAN
>
> You think?

Regan is in bed reading a movie magazine featuring a picture of her and her mother as Chris walks in to tuck her good night and grabs the magazine from her.

> CHRIS
>
> What? Regan, why are you reading that stuff?

> REGAN
>
> 'Cause I like it.

> CHRIS
>
> It's not even a good picture of you. You look so mature.

> REGAN (*giggling*)
>
> I wouldn't talk.

> CHRIS (*hugging her, teasing*)
>
> You wouldn't talk?

> REGAN
>
> I wouldn't.

> CHRIS
>
> Well, I didn't have my makeup man there. Let me take an eyelash off your face. OK . . . no, I didn't get it.

Gently she brushes Regan's cheek, as Regan snuggles happily down into her bedcovers.

CHRIS

What are we gonna do on your birthday? Isn't it nice it's on Sunday this year? Um, no work. What can we do?

REGAN

I don't know.

CHRIS

Well, what would you *like* to do? Got any ideas?

REGAN

Huh-uh.

CHRIS

No? Let me think, let me think. What can we do? Hey, you know, we never finished seeing all the sights in Washington. Didn't get to the Lee Mansion, lots of stuff. Shall we do that? Go sightseeing? H'm? If it's a nice day?

REGAN

Yeah. It's OK.

CHRIS

And tomorrow night, I'll take you to a movie. OK?

REGAN (*reaching up to hug Chris*)
Oh, I love you!

CHRIS

I love you, Rags. We'll have a good day, yeah?

REGAN

You can bring Mr. Dennings, if you like.

CHRIS (*surprised*)
Mr. Dennings?

REGAN

Well, you know, it's OK.

CHRIS (*chuckling*)
Well, thank you very much. But why on earth would I wanna bring Burke on your birthday?

REGAN
Well, wellll, you like him . . .

CHRIS
Yeah, I like him. Don't you like him?

Regan looks away without responding.

CHRIS
Hey, what's goin' on, what is this, huh?

REGAN (*a bit sullenly*)
You're going to marry him, arent you?

CHRIS (*amused*)
Oh, you've gotta be kidding!

REGAN
Why?

CHRIS
Me marry Burke Dennings? Don't be silly, of course not. Where'd you ever get an idea like that?

REGAN
But you *like* him.

CHRIS
Of course I like him. I like pizzas, too, but I'm not gonna marry one.

REGAN
You don't like him like daddy?

CHRIS (*serious now*)
Regan, I love your daddy. I'll always love your daddy, honey. OK? Burke just comes around here a lot 'cause, well, he's lonely, don't got nothin' to do.

REGAN
Well, I heard—differently.

CHRIS

Oh you did. What did you hear, huh?

REGAN (*carefully noncommittal*)

I don't know.

CHRIS

Well, what?

REGAN

I just thought . . .

CHRIS

Well, you didn't think so good.

REGAN (*giggling again*)

How do you know?

CHRIS

Because Burke and I are just friends. OK? Really.

REGAN

OK.

CHRIS

You ready for sleep?

Chris kisses Regan and holds her close for a moment.

REGAN

Good night.

CHRIS

Good night, honey.

Karras sits in a booth at a crowded campus beer joint with "Tom," the president of Georgetown University.

KARRAS

It's my mother, Tom. She's alone and I never should have left her. At least in New York, I'd be near, I'd be closer to her.

TOM

I could see about a transfer, Damien.

305

I need reassignment, Tom. I want out of this job. It's wrong, it's no good.

TOM

You're the best we've got.

KARRAS

Am I really? It's more than psychiatry and you know that, Tom. Some of their problems come down to faith, their vocation, the meaning of their lives and I can't cut it any more. I need out, I'm unfit . . . I think I've lost my faith, Tom.

At night in her bedroom, Chris is pacing with the phone receiver to her ear, holding while talking to Sharon, who is seated on edge of bed, scribbling in a steno pad.

CHRIS (*exasperated, into the phone*)
Hello? Yes, this is Mrs. MacNeil. Operator, you have got to be kidding! I have been on this line for twenty minutes!
(*to Sharon*)
Jesus Christ, can you believe this?

Unseen by Chris or Sharon. Regan is eavesdropping on Chris's conversation. She is despondent.

CHRIS

He doesn't even call his daughter on her birthday, for crissakes.

SHARON

Well, maybe the circuit is busy.

CHRIS

Oh, circuits my ass! He doesn't give a shit!

Regan dejectedly goes into her bedroom.

SHARON

Look, why don't you let me—

CHRIS

No, I've got it, Sharon, that's all right.
(*into phone*)

306

Yes! No, operator, don't tell me there's no answer. It's the Hotel Excelsior in Rome! Would you try it again, please, and let it ring . . . Oh, hello. Yes? No, operator, I've given you the number four times! What, do you take an illiteracy test to get that job, for crissakes? Don't tell me to be calm, goddamn it! I've been on this fucking line for twenty minutes!

Chris is sound asleep in her bed. The phone rings. She gropes for it and mutters into the receiver.

CHRIS

Yeah? You're kidding me? . . . OK. I thought I just went to bed. Hey, what, what're we doing, scene sixty-one? OK. Oh, just remind Phil about that blue belt, huh? I'll see yuh.

She hangs up, gets out of bed, then notices that Regan is in bed with her, half awake.

CHRIS

What are you doing here?

REGAN

My bed was shaking. I can't get to sleep.

CHRIS

Ah, honey.

Chris wraps herself in a bathrobe and climbs the attic stairs, lighted candle in hand. She tries the light switch. It doesn't work. Slowly and nervously she is searching about the attic, avoiding the rat traps Karl has set when all at once the candle flame shoots up, then is instantly extinguished. Karl, who has created the draft by coming silently up the stairs after Chris, suddenly looms behind her, scaring her half to death.

CHRIS (gasping)

Jesus! Oh, Karl, Jesus Christ, Karl, don't do that.

KARL

Very sorry, but you see—no rats.

CHRIS (*recovering herself*)
No rats. Thanks a lot, that's terrific.

He goes back down the stairs. Chris stares after him for a moment, then releases a sigh of relief.

In the Dahlgren Chapel on the Georgetown University campus early one morning, the sacristan enters, carrying two vases of flowers. He genuflects in front of the main altar, then sets one vase at the side altar to the right. As he approaches the altar at the opposite side, he stops short and reacts with horror as he sees a desecrated statue of the Blessed Virgin. The Virgin has been transformed into a harlot. Glued to the appropriate spot is a sculpted clay phallus in erection. Sculpted naked breasts have also been attached.

SACRISTAN
Ohhhhh, my God!

In a hallway of Bellevue Hospital in New York, Karras and his uncle are conversing as they walk, their voices metallically reverberant. Karras is ruefully shaking his head; his uncle gestures helplessly, defensively.

UNCLE (*in a thick accent*)
The edema affected her brain, you understand, Dimmy? She don't let no doctor come near her. She was all the time screaming, even talking to the radio.

KARRAS (*tight-lipped*)
You should have called me the minute it happened.

UNCLE
Listen, regular hospital not gonna put up with that, Dimmy, understand? So we give her a shot and bring her here, till the doctors, they fix up her leg. Then we take her right out, Dimmy. Two or three months and she's out, good as new!

Karras and his uncle have halted outside the locked door of the neuropsychiatric ward.

UNCLE

Miss?

NURSE

Yes?

UNCLE

We want to see Mrs. Karras.

NURSE

Do you have an appointment?

UNCLE

Yes.

NURSE

Are you a relative?

UNCLE

Yes, I am her brother, he is her son.

NURSE

Just a minute.

UNCLE (*to Damien*)

You know, it's funny. If you wasn't a priest, you be famous psychiatrist now, Park Avenue. Your mother she'd be living in a penthouse instead of this— You go in, Dimmy, I wait for you outside.

The nurse unlocks the door. Demented cries and moans assault Karras's ears as he enters the ward.

SECOND NURSE

You'll find Mrs. Karras in the last bed on the left-hand side. (*to delirious patient*) No, no, come along. Try to relax, it's all right.

The patients are mostly elderly, and they clutch pathetically, supplicatingly, at Karras. He disengages himself from them and moves on, stopping finally before a bedded patient far down the row: his mother. Gaunt and hollow-eyed, she looks confused and disoriented.

KARRAS

It's Dimmy, mama.

Dimmy . . . why you did this to me, Dimmy?
Why?

Resolutely, she turns away from Karras, crooning pite-
ously in Greek.

KARRAS
Come on, I'm gonna take you outa here, mama.
Mama, I'm gonna take you home. It's all right,
mama, everything's gonna be all right, mama.
Mama, I'm gonna take you home.

Outside the hospital, he reproaches his uncle.

KARRAS
. . . couldn't you have put her someplace else?

UNCLE
Like what? Private hospital? Who got the money
for that, Dimmy? You?

At a gym, Karras, in boxer shorts and a T-shirt,
savagely works out at a large punching bag. He slams
fiercely at the bag with a mixture of rage and frustration.

In Chris MacNeil's living room, a party is in progress.
Some of the cast and crew of the motion picture and a
few Jesuits are present. There is a vibrant hum of conversation. Burke Dennings, glass in hand, sits chatting with a silver-maned senator and his wife. Burke
is drunk and irritable.

DENNINGS
There seems to be an alien pubic hair in my
drink.

SENATOR (*offended*)
I beg your pardon?

DENNINGS
Never seen it before in my life. Have you?

A more congenial conversation is taking place in another part of the room.
310

ASTRONAUT

Well, actually, Father, we're pretty comfortable up there, at least compared to the Gemini and Mercury programs, where they were tight for space. You see, we got about two hundred and ten cubic feet, so we can move around.

DYER

Listen, if you ever go up there again, will you take me along?

ASTRONAUT (*laughing*)

What for?

DYER

First missionary on Mars.

Karl approaches Burke's group with a drinks tray.

DENNINGS (*to Karl*)

Tell me, was it *public* relations you did for the Gestapo, or *community* relations?

KARL (*grimly*)

I'm Swiss.

DENNINGS (*drunkenly, sneering*)

Yes, of course. And you never went bowling with Goebbels either, I suppose, huh? Nazi bastard!

Holding his fury in check, Karl moves on, passing Chris and Father Dyer.

CHRIS

. . . over behind the church, you know where I mean, over there? It's a red brick wing.

DYER

St. Mike's.

CHRIS

What goes on there? I mean, who's the priest I keep seeing there? He's there all the time, he has black hair and he's very intense-looking. Who's that?

DYER

Damien Karras.

CHRIS

Karras?

DYER

That's his office, back of St. Mike's.

CHRIS

Oh.

DYER

He's our, our psychiatric counselor . . . He had a pretty rough knock last night, poor guy. His mother passed away. She was living by herself, and I guess she was dead a couple of days before they found her.

Moments later, Chris bursts into the kitchen as Dennings continues to rave at a stolid, carefully expressionless Karl, who stands immobile, arms akimbo, watching Dennings.

DENNINGS

Cunting hun! Bloody damned butchering Nazi pig!

KARL

Stop it, I kill you!

Sharon enters as Chris pushes a struggling Karl out of the room.

DENNINGS

What the hell makes you think you're so fucking superior?

CHRIS

Karl, Karl.

As soon as Karl has gone, Dennings becomes instantly composed and, as Chris turns to him after shoving Karl out of the door, he playfully rubs his hands together.

DENNINGS

What's for dessert?

Upstairs, Regan is in bed. Chris tucks in her bedcovers. The lights are out and Regan is turned on her side, her eyes closed. Chris pauses to look down fondly at her before rejoining her departing guests.

CHRIS

. . . you sleepy?

Back downstairs, Chris and Sharon gently and tactfully hustle an unsteady Burke to the front door.

CHRIS

That's right, OK. There you go. All right. Listen, Burke, your car's at the curb. Louie's waiting, it's nice and warm.

DENNINGS (*embracing her tightly*)

Bye.

As they shut the door behind him, Sharon and Chris exchange tolerantly amused looks.

SHARON (*to Chris*)

Boy, was he acting up.

CHRIS

Blind, that's what he was.

Father Dyer and the dean are in a group gathered around the piano, singing and playing amid much gaiety. Dyer hails Chris as she and Sharon return.

DYER

Hi, Chris. It's a great party.

CHRIS

Yeah, don't stop, keep goin'.

DYER

I don't need any encouragement. My idea of heaven is a solid white nightclub, with me as a headliner for all eternity, and they love me.

The group laughs and breaks into a hammy version of "Home, Sweet Home." But Dyer interrupts to indicate Regan, who is standing in the doorway in her night-

313

gown, staring up at the astronaut. Chris follows Dyer's look.

DYER
Hey, I think, I think we've got a guest.

REGAN (*portentously, to the astronaut*)
You're going to die up there.

As Regan begins urinating gushingly onto the rug, a sudden silence falls on the group. Chris gasps in shock and dismay. In an instant, Chris rushes over to Regan.

CHRIS
Regan . . . oh my God, honey. Honey, what's the matter?
(*to her guests*)
I'm sorry, she's been sick, she didn't know what she was saying.

ASTRONAUT
OK. It's OK.

CHRIS
Come upstairs now.

It is later. Regan sits in the bathtub like someone in a trance while Chris bathes her.

CHRIS
What made you say that, Regan? Do you know, sweetheart?

And still later, in bed, as moonlight streams in through the open window, Regan turns her face toward the wall, staring dully into space. A worried Chris sits on the edge of the bed. Through the window, from the street below, we hear the voices of the last of the departing guests. Chris gets up to leave the bedroom and is almost out of the door when she is arrested by Regan calling to her in a low, despairing, flat tone:

REGAN
Mother, what's wrong with me?

Chris is caught off guard, then recovers and goes back to her daughter's bed.

> CHRIS
> It's just like the doctor said, it's nerves. And that's all. OK? You just take your pills and you'll be fine, really. OK?

There is no answer from Regan. Chris waits. Troubled, she leaves the room and goes into the hall. There, she leans over the balustrade railing to look at Willie scrubbing the urine stains out of the carpet downstairs.

> CHRIS
> Is it coming out, Willie?

> WILLIE
> Yes, I think so.

> CHRIS
> Good.

Chris continues to stare for a moment more, then turns toward her bedroom and enters it, closing the door. There is silence for a moment, then from within Regan's bedroom, we hear metallic sounds, like bedsprings violently quivering. Tentative at first, they become more insistent.

> REGAN (*with increasing urgency*)
> Mother! *Mother!*

The bedspring sounds have become much louder. Regan's cries ring out, filled with terror now.

> REGAN
> Motherrrrr! Motherrrrrrrr!

Chris's door has already shot open, as she races for Regan's bedroom.

> REGAN
> Motherrrrrrr! Motherrrrrr!

Rushing in, Chris throws herself on the bed, which is pitching and shaking. She holds on to her terrified

315

daughter as they are both violently tossed about by the bed's movements.

CHRIS

Oh, my God!

REGAN

Make it stop. Mother, I'm scared. I'm scared!

Dyer heads down a corridor in the Jesuit residence hall. He passes an open door, through which the sounds of a poker game can be heard.

STUDENTS' VOICES

Big five. Another five with a pair. There's a ten with two, three clubs, and a six. Pair of threes still bet. All right, pot's right. Here they come. Threes are still the bet.

Later, in Karras's dimly lit room, he sits behind the desk. Karras, hunched on the edge of his cot, stubs out a cigarette in an ashtray on the floor next to an empty bottle of Scotch.

KARRAS

Yeah? Where'd yuh get the money for the Chivas Regal, the poor box?

DYER

Huh, that's an insult. I got a vow of poverty.

KARRAS

Where'd yuh get it then?

DYER

I stole it.

KARRAS

I believe you.

DYER

College presidents shouldn't drink. Tends to set a bad example. I figure I saved him from a big temptation.

Karras is nodding slightly, forcing a smile, when suddenly he bursts into sobs.

316

KARRAS

Oh, Christ, I should've been there. I wasn't there, I should've been there.

DYER

There was nothin' you could do. Lie down.

Karras does.

DYER

Gimme the butt . . . come on. Now you think you can sleep?

Dyer moves to the foot of the cot, undoes Karras's shoelaces, and removes his shoes.

KARRAS

Yeah . . . What're you gonna do, steal my shoes now?

DYER

No, I tell fortunes by reading the creases. Now shut up and go to sleep. Good night, Dims.

Dyer pauses at the door on his way out.

KARRAS

Stealing is a sin . . .
(*light snoring*)
Mama . . . ma . . .

In an examining room in a hospital, Chris and a nurse are forcibly restraining Regan as a doctor attempts to administer an injection.

REGAN (*screaming*)

I don't want it!

CHRIS

Regan, honey, it's to help you.

REGAN

I don't want it, I don't want it!

She spits in the doctor's face.

REGAN

You fuckin' bastard!

It is very early in the morning. Karras is at the main altar of Holy Trinity Church, saying mass. There is a scattering of worshipers in the church.

KARRAS

"Remember also, O Lord, Thy servant, Mary Karras, who has gone before us with the sign of faith, and sleeps the sleep of peace . . . Lord, I am not worthy to receive You. You will only say the word and I shall be healed. May the body of Christ bring me to everlasting life."

Dr. Klein, the doctor who had previously had such trouble giving Regan a shot, is now talking with a worried Chris in his office.

KLEIN

Well, it's a symptom of a type of disturbance in the chemicoelectrical activity of the brain. In the case of your daughter, in the temporal lobe. That's up here in the lateral part of the brain.

CHRIS

Uh-huh.

KLEIN

It's rare but it does cause bizarre hallucinations and usually just before a convulsion.

CHRIS

A convulsion?

KLEIN

The shaking of the bed. That's doubtless due to muscular spasms.

CHRIS

Oh no, no, no, that was no spasm, doctor. Look, I got on the bed, the whole bed was thumping and rising off the floor and shaking the whole thing! With me on it!

KLEIN

Mrs. MacNeil, the problem with your daughter is not her bed, it's her brain.

CHRIS

So, ah, what causes this—

KLEIN

Lesion. Lesion in the temporal lobe. It's a kind
of seizure disorder.

CHRIS

Uh, look, doc, I really don't understand how
her whole personality could change.

KLEIN

In temporal lobe it's very common.

CHRIS

It is?

KLEIN

It's ah, it can last for days, even weeks. It isn't
rare to find destructive, even criminal behavior.

CHRIS

Hey, do me a favor, will yuh? Tell me something good.

KLEIN

Don't be alarmed. If it's a lesion, in a way she's
fortunate. All we have to do is remove the scar.

In the radiological lab, Regan is having an arterio-
gram done on her brain.

INTERN

Regan, can you sit up, scoot over here? Near
me. A little more. Good. Regan, I'm just gonna
move you down a little on the table, OK? It's
just for a short time.

RADIOLOGIST

Very sticky. Now, Regan, you're going to feel
something a little cold and wet. OK. Now you're
gonna feel a little stickier. Don't move.

Regan gasps, then whimpers.

The radiologist and Dr. Tanney, a consulting neurologist, are looking at X rays of Regan's skull in a small

medical lab X-ray room. They seem puzzled by what they see.

TANNEY

. . . there's just nothing there. No vascular displacement at all. You want me to run another series?

KLEIN

I don't think so. I'd like you to see her again.

NURSE (*entering*)

Excuse me, doctor, Chris MacNeil's on the phone. She says it's urgent.

KLEIN (*to Tanney*)

Got some time?

TANNEY

Of course.

As Sharon admits Klein and Tanney to the MacNeil house, we hear Regan's moans of pain and screams of terror issuing from her bedroom upstairs.

SHARON

Dr. Klein.

KLEIN

Yes, I'm Dr. Klein. This is Dr. Tanney.

TANNEY

How do you do.

SHARON

I'm Sharon. Things have gotten worse since I phoned you, I think you better come upstairs.

They follow her hurriedly up the stairs.

KLEIN

Is she having the spasms again?

SHARON

Yeah, but they've gotten violent.

KLEIN

Did you give her the medication she needed?

SHARON

Yes.

TANNEY

What was that?

KLEIN

Thorazine. Before that it was ritalin.

Sharon opens the door to Regan's bedroom after calling in to Chris.

SHARON

Chris, doctors.

REGAN (*screaming*)

Mother, please!

KLEIN

Mrs. MacNeil, Dr. Tanney.

REGAN

Oh, mother, please make him stop! It's burning! It's burning!

CHRIS (*frantic*)

Do something, doctor, please help her.

REGAN

Please, mother! Make it stop, he's trying to kill me! Mother! Mother, make it . . .

Regan's throat abruptly swells up and emits a growllike sound.

KLEIN

All right now, Regan, let's see what's—

Suddenly Regan hits Klein, sending him hurtling across the room. And her voice is no longer that of a terrified child.

REGAN/DEMON

Keep away! The sow is mine! Fuck me! Fuck me! Fuck me!

KLEIN (*indicating his medical kit*)

My bag! Quick!

Klein hastily prepares a hypodermic injection.

REGAN

Stay away from me! Stay away! Mother, don't let them— Mother, please!

TANNEY

Hold still. Hold her tight . . .

Sharon pulls a nearly hysterical Chris out of the room as the doctors give Regan a shot to calm her. A moment later, a blessed silence falls and the doctors join Chris and Sharon who are waiting tensely in the hall. Chris dabs at her nose with a moist, balled-up handkerchief, her eyes red from crying.

KLEIN (*soothingly*)

She's heavily sedated. She'll probably sleep through tomorrow.

CHRIS

What was going on in there? How could she fly off the bed like that?

TANNEY

Pathological states can induce abnormal strength, accelerated motor performance. Uh, for example, say a ninety-pound woman sees her child pinned under the wheel of a truck, runs out and lifts the wheels a half a foot above the ground. You've heard the story, same thing here. Same principle, I mean.

CHRIS

So what's wrong with her?

KLEIN

We still think the temporal lobe.

CHRIS (*shouting*)

Oh, what're you *talking* about, for crissakes? Did you see her or not! She's acting like she's fucking out of her mind, psychotic, like a, a split personality or—what d'ya . . .
(*collecting herself*)
Jesus, I'm sorry.

TANNEY

There haven't been more than a hundred authentic cases of so-called split personality, Mrs. MacNeil. Now I know the temptation to leap to psychiatry, but any reasonable psychiatrist would exhaust the somatic possibilities first.

CHRIS

So what's next?

TANNEY

A pneumoencephelogram, I would think, to pin down the lesion. It will involve another spinal.

CHRIS (*a sob catching in her throat*)
Oh, Christ!

TANNEY

What we missed in the EEG and the arteriograms could conceivably turn up there. At least, it would eliminate certain other possibilities.

Later, Dr. Klein talks with Chris in his office, the X-rays forming a backdrop to their conversation.

KLEIN

Dr. Tanney says the X rays are negative. In other words, normal. You keep any drugs in your house?

CHRIS

No, of course not, nothing like that.

KLEIN

Are you sure?

CHRIS

Well, of course I'm sure. I'd tell you. Christ, I don't even smoke grass.

KLEIN

You planning to be home soon? I mean, to LA?

CHRIS (*haltingly*)
Uh, no, I, ah, I'm building a new house, my old one's been sold. I don't know.
(*she sniffles*)

I was gonna take . . . I was gonna take Regan
to Europe for a while after she finished school.
Why'd you ask?

KLEIN

I think it's time we started looking for a psychiatrist.

It is nighttime. Chris drives home, oblivious to a
nearby accident as she parks and enters her house
despondently. The lights in the house blink. Chris looks
up, perplexed and a little apprehensive. The phone rings
and she moves to answer it.

CHRIS (*into phone*)

Hello?

There is no one on the other end of the line. She hangs
up. The lights blink out again, this time for a longer
moment before coming on.

CHRIS

Shar? Jesus . . .

Chris goes upstairs to Regan's bedroom. Regan is
asleep. Chris hugs herself, shivering. She murmurs,
"Shit!" then, "God!" as she closes Regan's wide-open
window and goes back down to the living room. Sharon
enters through the front door, carrying a pharmacy bag.

CHRIS (*angrily*)

Sharon? What the hell do you mean going off
and leaving Regan by herself? Are you crazy?
Her window's wide open. The whole room is
freezing!

SHARON

What? Didn't he tell you?

CHRIS

Didn't *who* tell me?

SHARON

Burke, isn't—

CHRIS

What's Burke got to do with it?

324

SHARON

Look, there wasn't anybody here, so when I went to get the thorazine, I had him stay with her and— Oh, I should have known better, I'm sorry.

CHRIS

I guess you should have!

SHARON

How were the tests?

CHRIS

We have to start looking for a shrink.

As she speaks, Chris is answering a ring at the front door. It is the assistant director, ashen-faced.

CHRIS

Hi, Chuck, come on in.

CHUCK

I suppose you heard.

CHRIS

Heard what?

CHUCK

You haven't heard.
(*a pause*)
Burke's dead. He must've been drunk. He fell down from the top of the steps right outside. By the time he hit M Street, he broke his neck.

CHRIS (*gasping*)

Oh, God. No.

She breaks into sobs.

CHUCK (*comforting her*)
Yeah. I know.

In Chris's bedroom, a psychiatrist stands in front of Regan. Regan appears to be in a trance. Chris and Dr. Klein watch tensely.

PSYCHIATRIST

. . . when I touch your forehead, open your eyes. Are you comfortable, Regan?

REGAN (*softly; hypnotized*)

Yes.

PSYCHIATRIST

How old are you?

REGAN

Twelve.

PSYCHIATRIST

Is there someone inside you?

REGAN

Sometimes.

PSYCHIATRIST

Who is it?

REGAN

I don't know.

PSYCHIATRIST

Is it Captain Howdy?

REGAN

I don't know.

PSYCHIATRIST

If I ask him to tell me, will you let him answer?

REGAN

No.

PSYCHIATRIST

Why not?

REGAN

I'm afraid.

PSYCHIATRIST

If he talks to me, I think he'll leave you. Do you want him to leave you?

REGAN

Yes.

PSYCHIATRIST

I'm speaking to the person inside of Regan now.
If you are there, you too are hypnotized, and
must answer all my questions. Come forward
and answer me now.

As if in response, a picture falls from the mantel.
Regan's features contort into a malevolent mask and
she emits an odor so horrible that Chris and Dr. Klein
back away from her, grimacing. She begins wailing in
the coarse, guttural voice of the demon.

PSYCHIATRIST

Are you the person inside of Regan? Who are
you?

Regan reaches out and grabs the psychiatrist's scrotum
in an iron grip. He yelps in pain and they both fall to
the floor, struggling.

PSYCHIATRIST

Let go!

On an outdoor track of the Georgetown University
campus, Karras, in shorts and a T-shirt, is doing laps.
He is unaware that a portly, middle-aged man is watching him. It is Detective Kinderman. When Karras slows
to a walk, Kinderman approaches him.

KINDERMAN

Father Karras?

KARRAS

Have we met?

KINDERMAN

No, we haven't met, but they said I could tell,
'cause you look like a boxer. William F. Kinderman, homicide.

KARRAS

What's this all about?

KINDERMAN

Yeah, it's true, you do look like a boxer. Like
John Garfield in *Body and Soul*. Exactly John
Garfield. People tell you that, Father?

KARRAS

Do people tell you you look like Paul Newman?

KINDERMAN

Always.

As they talk, they walk through the campus, past tennis courts and strolling students.

KINDERMAN

Well, you know this director who was doing the film here? Burke Dennings?

KARRAS

I've seen him.

KINDERMAN

You've seen him. You're also familiar how last week he died?

KARRAS

Only what I read in the papers.

KINDERMAN

Father, what do you know on the subject of witchcraft? From the witching end, not the hunting.

KARRAS

I once did a paper on it.

KINDERMAN

Really?

KARRAS

From the psychiatric end.

KINDERMAN

I know, I read it. Father, this desecration in the church, you think this has anything to do with witchcraft?

KARRAS

Maybe. Some rituals used in Black Mass, maybe.

KINDERMAN

And now, Dennings, you, you read how he died?

KARRAS

In a fall.

KINDERMAN

Let me tell you how, and please, Father, confidential. Burke Dennings, good Father, was found at the bottom of those steps leading to M Street with his head turned completely around. Facing backward.

KARRAS

Didn't happen in the fall?

KINDERMAN

It's possible. Possible. However—

KARRAS

Unlikely.

KINDERMAN

Exactly. So on the one hand we've got a witchcraft kind of murder, and on the other hand, a Black Mass-type desecration in the church.

KARRAS

You think the killer and the desecrator are the same?

KINDERMAN

Maybe somebody crazy, somebody with a spite against the Church, some unconscious rebellion.

KARRAS

Sick priest, is that it?

KINDERMAN

Look, Father, this is hard for you, please, I understand. But for priests on the campus here, you're the psychiatrist, you'd know who was sick at the time, who wasn't. I mean, this kind of sickness, you'd know that.

329

KARRAS

I don't know anyone who fits that description.

KINDERMAN

Ah . . . doctor's ethics. If you knew, you wouldn't tell, huh?

KARRAS

No, I probably wouldn't.

KINDERMAN

Not to bother you with trivia, but a psychiatrist, in sunny California no less, was put in jail for not telling the police what he knew about a patient.

KARRAS

Is that a threat?

KINDERMAN

No, I mention it only in passing.

KARRAS

Incidentally, *I* mention it only in passing, I could always tell the judge it was a matter of confession.

KINDERMAN

Hey, hey, Father, wait a minute! D'you like movies?

KARRAS

Very much.

KINDERMAN

Well, I get passes to the best shows in town. Mrs. K, you know, she gets tired, you know, never likes to go.

KARRAS

That's too bad.

KINDERMAN

Yeah, I hate to go alone. You know, I love to talk film, to discuss, to critique. You wanna see a film with me? I got passes to the Crest, it's *Othello*.

KARRAS

Who's in it?

KINDERMAN

Who's in it? Debbie Reynolds, Desdemona, and Othello, Groucho Marx. Ya happy?

KARRAS (*deadpan*)

I've seen it.

KINDERMAN

One last time. You can think of some priest who fits the bill?

KARRAS

Come on.

KINDERMAN

No, answer the question, Father Paranoia.

KARRAS

All right, all right.
(*conspiratorially*)
You know who I think really did it?

KINDERMAN

Who?

KARRAS

The Dominicans, go pick on them.

His eyes twinkle as he turns and walks away from Kinderman toward the residence hall. Kinderman calls out after him.

KINDERMAN

I could have you deported, you know that?
(*no response from Karras*)
I lied! You look like Sal Mineo!

In a room at the Barringer Clinic, Chris, taut and drawn, sits with a group of doctors at a table. Regan's image, emitting gurgling, growling sounds, is projected on a closed circuit television screen.

CLINIC DIRECTOR

It looks like a type of disorder that's, uh, rarely

331

ever seen anymore, except in primitive cultures. We, we call it somnambuliform possession. Quite frankly, we really don't know much about it at all, except that it, it starts with a conflict or a guilt and it leads to the patient's delusion that his body has been invaded by some alien intelligence, uh, a spirit, if you will.

CHRIS

Look, I'm telling you again, and you'd better believe me, I am not going to lock her up in some goddamn asylum.

CLINIC DIRECTOR

Well, it's—

CHRIS

And I don't care what you call it, I'm not putting her away!

CLINIC DIRECTOR

I'm sorry.

CHRIS (*losing control*)

You're sorry? Jesus Christ, eighty-eight doctors and all you can tell me with all your bullshit is—

CLINIC DIRECTOR

Of course, there is one outside chance for a cure. It, ah, I think of it as a shock treatment. As I said, it's a very outside chance, but you're so—

CHRIS

Would you just name it, for God's sake? What is it?

1ST DOCTOR

Do you have any religious beliefs?

CHRIS

No.

WOMAN DOCTOR

What about your daughter?

332

No ... why?

CLINIC DIRECTOR
Have you ever heard of exorcism? ... Well, it's
a stylized ritual in which the, uh, rabbi, or the
priest, try to drive out the so-called invading
spirit. It's been pretty much discarded these
days, except by the, the Catholics, who keep
it in the closet as a sort of an embarrassment,
but, uh, it has worked, in fact, although not for
the reasons they think, of course. It's—it's, uh,
purely, uh, force of suggestion. The, uh, victim's
belief in possession is what helped cause it, so
in that same way, the belief in the power of
exorcism can make it disappear.

CHRIS (*incredulous*)
You're telling me that I should take my daughter to a witch doctor. Is that it?

Back in Regan's bedroom, Chris leans down to ad-
just her daughter's pillow. In doing so, she discovers a
crucifix hidden under it. Frowning, she picks it up and
goes downstairs, where she confronts Karl, Sharon, and
Willie with it.

CHRIS
Karl? Did you put this in Regan's bedroom?

KARL
She's going to be well?

CHRIS
Karl, if you put this in Regan's bedroom, I want
you to tell me. Now did you?

KARL
No, not me. I didn't.

Outside the MacNeil house, Kinderman catches sight
of a fragment of clay from a crudely made sculpture
lying at the foot of the steps. He picks it up and turns
it over thoughtfully in his hand as he climbs the steps.

CHRIS (*to Sharon*)

This was under Regan's pillow. Did you put it
there?

SHARON

Of course I didn't.

WILLIE

I didn't put it.

Karl reenters the living room after answering the
door chimes.

KARL

Excuse me, madam.

CHRIS (*to Willie*)

What?

KARL

A man to see you.

CHRIS

What man?

Chris and Kinderman are seated, drinking coffee and
talking.

KINDERMAN

Might your daughter remember, perhaps, if Mr.
Dennings was in her room that night?

CHRIS

Why do you ask?

KINDERMAN

Oh, might she remember?

CHRIS

No. No, she was heavily sedated.

KINDERMAN

It's serious?

CHRIS

Yes, I'm afraid it is.

KINDERMAN
May I ask—

CHRIS
We still don't know.

KINDERMAN
Watch out for drafts. A draft in the fall when the house is hot is a magic carpet for bacteria.

KARL (*entering*)
Excuse me, madam, anything else?

CHRIS
No, Karl, we're fine, thank you. It's all right, Karl.
(*to Kinderman*)
Why are you asking all this?

KINDERMAN
It's strange. The deceased comes to visit, stays only twenty minutes, and leaves all alone a very sick girl. And, speaking plainly, Mrs. MacNeil, it isn't likely he would fall from a window. Besides, a fall wouldn't do to his neck what we found, except maybe one chance in a thousand. No, my hunch, my opinion, he was killed by a very powerful man, point one. And the fracturing of his skull, point two. Plus the various other things we mentioned, would make it very probable . . . probable, not certain . . . that the deceased was killed and then pushed from your daughter's window. But nobody was in the room except your daughter, so how can this be? It could be one way. If someone came calling between the time Miss Spencer left and the time you returned.

CHRIS (*horrified comprehension dawning*)
Judas priest, just a second!

KINDERMAN
The servants, they have visitors?

335

CHRIS (*recovering herself*)

Not at all.

KINDERMAN

Or you were expecting a package that day? Some delivery?

CHRIS

None that I know of.

KINDERMAN

Groceries? Uh, cleaning? A package?

CHRIS

I really wouldn't know. See, Karl takes care of all that.

KINDERMAN

I see.

CHRIS

Would you like to ask him?

KINDERMAN

Hmm, no, never mind, it's—it's very remote. No, never mind. Nope.

CHRIS (*an insincere offer*)

Would you like some more coffee?

Kinderman surprises her by accepting. He has picked up a clay turtle obviously fashioned by a child.

KINDERMAN

That's cute. Your daughter, she's the artist? Thank you.
(*accepting coffee*)
Incidentally, um, you might ask your daughter if she remembers seeing Mr. Dennings in her room that night.

CHRIS

Look, he, he wouldn't have any reason in the world to go up to her room.

KINDERMAN

Oh, I know, I realize, but if certain British

doctors never asked what is this fungus, we
wouldn't today have penicillin. Correct?

CHRIS

Well, when she's better, I'll ask her.

She puts the turtle, which she has taken from Kinderman, into her pocket.

KINDERMAN

Yeah, couldn't hurt. Ah, in the meantime—

CHRIS

(*anything to get him to leave*)
That's OK.

KINDERMAN

I, I, I really hate to ask you this, but, for my
daughter, could you please give an autograph?

CHRIS (*relieved*)

Of course . . . uh, where's a pencil?

KINDERMAN

Right here, here. Oh, she'd love it.

CHRIS

Ah, and what's her name?

KINDERMAN (*embarrassed; confessing*)

I lied, it's for me. The spelling is on the back,
Kinderman.

CHRIS

OK.

KINDERMAN

Oh, you know that film you made? Uh, *Angel?*

CHRIS (*as she signs the card*)

Oh, yeah.

KINDERMAN

I saw that six times.

CHRIS

Really?

KINDERMAN

It was beautiful.
(*taking the card*)
Thank you. You're a very nice lady. Thank
you.

CHRIS (*warmly*)

You're a nice man.

KINDERMAN

Ah, I'll come back when she's feeling better.
Good-bye.

CHRIS

Bye.

Horrible sounds come from Regan's bedroom. This
time there are two distinct voices: that of a tearful and
terror-stricken Regan and that of someone else—a man
—with a powerful, deep bass voice. Regan is pleading;
the man commanding in obscene terms.

REGAN

Please, no!

REGAN/DEMON

Do it!

REGAN

Please don't!

REGAN/DEMON

You bitch, do it, do it!

REGAN

No, please, no!

REGAN/DEMON

Yes! Let Jesus fuck you! Let Jesus fuck you!
Let him fuck you!

Chris has raced into the room, but stops short when
she sees Regan sitting on the violently shaking bed,
legs apart, masturbating herself with a bloodied crucifix, clearly much against her will. Her features and
expression shift to match the voices that speak through
her mouth. Chris lunges toward Regan as a chair

flies across the room and slams the door shut, cutting off Sharon and Willie, who pound frantically at the closed door, shouting to be let in. Falling, Chris rolls out of the path of the bureau, which has hurtled toward her.

CHRIS (*grabbing for the cross*)
Give it, give it to me!

REGAN/DEMON
Lick me, lick me!

The Regan/Demon pulls Chris's head down, rubs her face sensually against her blood-smeared pelvis, then lifts Chris's head and smashes her a blow across the chest that sends her reeling across the room and crashing to a wall with stunning force. Chris is momentarily stunned, but then begins crawling painfully toward the bed.

REGAN/DENNINGS
Do you know what she did, your cunting daughter?

Wearing a belted coat and a scarf, and hiding her haggard, bruised face behind huge dark glasses, Chris is leaning over a bridge railing, staring moodily down. When she is approached by Karras, casually dressed in khakis, a Georgetown University sweater, and sneakers, she doesn't recognize him at first.

KARRAS
... Chris MacNeil?

CHRIS
Please go away.

KARRAS
I'm Father Karras.

CHRIS
I'm very sorry. Hello.

KARRAS
It's all right, I should've told you I wouldn't be in uniform.

CHRIS

Yeah, well, that would have helped. Have you got a cigarette, Father?

KARRAS

Sure . . .

CHRIS

Thanks.

While talking, they leave the bridge and stroll through a park, eventually winding up sitting on a bench. Chris sniffles.

KARRAS

Cold?

CHRIS

Yeah. Uh . . . how did a shrink ever get to be a priest?

KARRAS

It's the other way around. The Society sent me through medical school.

CHRIS

Oh, where?

KARRAS

Harvard, Bellevue, Johns Hopkins—places like that.

CHRIS

I see. You're a friend of Father Dyer's, right?

KARRAS

Yes, I am.

CHRIS

Pretty close?

KARRAS

Pretty close.

CHRIS

Did he talk to you about my party?

KARRAS

He sure did.

CHRIS

About my daughter?

KARRAS

No, I didn't know you had one.

CHRIS

He didn't mention her?

KARRAS

No.

CHRIS

Huh. He didn't tell you what she did?

KARRAS

He didn't mention her.

CHRIS

Priests are pretty tight-mouthed, then, huh?

KARRAS

That depends.

CHRIS

On what?

KARRAS

The priest.

CHRIS

Sure. I mean, what if a person, uh, came to, uh, you know, that was a murderer or a criminal of some kind and they, and they wanted some kind of help, I mean, would you have to turn them in?

KARRAS

Well, if he came to me for spiritual advice, I'd say no.

CHRIS

You wouldn't?

KARRAS

No, I wouldn't. But I would try to convince him to turn himself in.

CHRIS

Uh-huh. And, uh, how do you go about getting an exorcism?

KARRAS

I beg your pardon?

CHRIS

If a, if a person's, you know, possessed by a, a, a, a demon or something, how do they, how do they get an exorcism?

KARRAS

Well, the first thing, I'd have to get 'em into a time machine and get 'em back to the sixteenth century.

CHRIS

I didn't getcha.

KARRAS

Well, it just doesn't happen anymore, Miss MacNeil.

CHRIS

Yeah, since when?

KARRAS

Well, since we learned about mental illness, paranoia, schizophrenia, all those things they taught me at Harvard. Miss MacNeil, since the day I joined the Jesuits, I've never met one priest who has performed an exorcism. Not one.

CHRIS

Yeah, well, it just so happens that somebody very close to me is, is probably possessed. And needs an exorcist . . . Father Karras, it's my little girl.

Fighting back a sob, Chris slips off her sunglasses. Karras is visibly shocked at the desperation he sees reflected in her face.

KARRAS

Then that's all the more reason to forget about exorcism.

CHRIS

Why? I don't understand.

KARRAS

To begin with, it could only make things worse.

CHRIS

Oh? How?

KARRAS

Secondly, the Church, before it approves an exorcism, conducts an investigation to see if it's warranted. That takes time.

CHRIS

Oh, yeah.

KARRAS

Meanwhile, your daughter—

CHRIS (*breaking in*)

You could do it yourself, couldn't you?

KARRAS

No, I couldn't. I'd need Church approval and that's rarely given.

CHRIS

But . . . could you see her?

KARRAS

Yes, I could, I could see her as a psychiatrist, but I can't—

CHRIS (*interrupting again*)

Oh, not a psychiatrist! She needs a priest! She's already seen every fucking psychiatrist in the world and they sent me to you! Now are you gonna send me back to them? Jesus *Christ,* won't somebody *help* me?

Chris crumples against Karras's chest, giving in to her sobs. He tries awkwardly to comfort her.

KARRAS

Oh, you don't see, you don't understand. Your daughter . . .

CHRIS

. . . oh, God, can't you help her, just *help* her?

Later, Chris and Karras ascend the stairs to Regan's bedroom, Karras frowning at the sounds coming from it. They pass Karl, leaning against the wall in the hallway, head bowed.

KARL

It wants no straps.

Karras enters the bedroom. He freezes in horror at what he sees. Arms held down by a double set of restraining straps, the creature that lies on the bed is now more Demon than Regan. Nevertheless, Karras strives to maintain an affable, conversational tone.

KARRAS

Hello, Regan. I'm a friend of your mother's. I'd like to help you.

REGAN/DEMON

You might loosen these straps, then.

KARRAS

I'm afraid you might hurt yourself, Regan.

REGAN/DEMON

I'm not Regan.

KARRAS

I see. Well, then, let's introduce ourselves. I'm Damien Karras.

REGAN/DEMON

I am the devil. Now kindly undo these straps.

KARRAS

If you're the devil, why not make the straps disappear?

REGAN/DEMON

That's much too vulgar a display of power, Karras.

KARRAS

Where's Regan?

REGAN/DEMON
In here, with us.

KARRAS
Show me Regan and I'll loosen one of the straps.

REGAN/WINO
Could you help an old altar boy, Father?

REGAN/DEMON
Your mother's in here with us, Karras. Would you like to leave a message? I'll see that she gets it.

KARRAS
If that's true, then you must know my mother's maiden name. What is it?

There is only hissing for an answer.

KARRAS
What is it?

Suddenly, a stream of bile-green vomit spews forth from the Regan/Demon's mouth at Karras, hitting him directly in the face. Karras recoils.

In the playroom downstairs, Chris is ironing Karras's freshly washed sweater. She hands it to him.

KARRAS
Thank you . . . Look, I'm only against the possibility of doing your daughter more harm than good.

CHRIS
Nothing you could do could make it any worse.

KARRAS
I can't do it. I need evidence that the Church would accept as signs of possession.

CHRIS
Like what?

345

KARRAS

Like her speaking in a language she's never known or studied.

CHRIS

What else?

KARRAS

I don't know. I'd have to look it up.

CHRIS

I thought you were supposed to be an expert.

KARRAS

There are no experts. You probably know as much about possession as most priests. Look, your daughter doesn't say she's a demon, she says she's the devil himself. Now, if you've seen as many psychotics as I have, you'd realize that's the same thing as saying you're Napoleon Bonaparte. You asked me what I think is best for your daughter. Six months under observation in the best hospital you can find.

CHRIS

You show me Regan's double—same face, same voice, everything—and I'd know it wasn't Regan. I'd know it in my gut. And I'm telling you that that thing upstairs isn't my daughter. Now I want you to tell me that you know for a fact that there's nothing wrong with my daughter except in her mind! You tell me that you know for a fact that an exorcism wouldn't do any good! *You tell me that!*

Karras pauses on the steps outside the front door as he is taking leave of Chris. He keeps his tone casual.

KARRAS

Did Regan know a priest was coming over?

CHRIS

No.

KARRAS

Did you know my mother died recently?

CHRIS

Yes, I did. I'm very sorry.

KARRAS

No . . . Is Regan aware of it?

CHRIS

Not at all. Why'd you ask?

KARRAS

It's not important, good night.

Dressed in his vestments, Karras is at the altar of the chapel, saying mass. He is in the middle of the consecration. He breaks the Host.

KARRAS

". . . He broke the bread and gave it to His disciples and said: 'Take this, all of you, and eat it. For this is My body.' When the supper was ended, He took the cup, again He gave You thanks and praise. Gave the cup to His disciples and said, 'Take this, all of you, and drink from it. This is the cup of My blood, the blood of the new and everlasting covenant, the mystery of faith.' "

In Regan's bedroom again, Karras sits in his clerical robes at the foot of the bed. A tape recorder is running on the floor beside him.

REGAN/DEMON

What an excellent day for an exorcism.

KARRAS

You'd like that?

REGAN/DEMON

Intensely.

KARRAS

But wouldn't that drive you out of Regan?

REGAN/DEMON

It would bring us together.

347

                                    KARRAS
You and Regan?

                            REGAN/DEMON
You and us.

A bureau drawer flies open. The Regan/Demon bursts
into hysterical laughter.

                                    KARRAS
Did you do that?

                    REGAN/DEMON (*cackling*)
Uh-huh.

                                    KARRAS
Do it again.

                            REGAN/DEMON
In time.

                                    KARRAS
No, now.

                            REGAN/DEMON
In time. *Mirabile dictu,* don't you agree?

                                    KARRAS
You speak Latin?

                            REGAN/DEMON
Ego te absolvo.

                                    KARRAS
Quod nomen mihi est?

                            REGAN/DEMON
Bonjour!

                                    KARRAS
Quod nomen mihi est?

                            REGAN/DEMON
La plume de ma tante.

It laughs mockingly.

                                    KARRAS
How long are you planning to stay in Regan?

REGAN/DEMON
Until she rots and lies stinking in the earth.
(*Karras holds up a small vial of water*)
What's that?

KARRAS
Holy water.

He sprinkles some on her.

REGAN/DEMON (*howling in pain and terror*)
You keep it away! It burns . . . oh, it burns!

Karras looks disappointed at her reaction. The howling
ceases and Regan's head falls back on the pillow. The
whites of her eyes are exposed, as her eyes roll upward
into their sockets. She rolls her head feverishly from
side to side, muttering an indistinct gibberish.

KARRAS
Who are you?

REGAN/DEMON
eno on ma I. eno on ma I.

Intrigued by the gibberish, Karras moves closer to the
bed to listen and turns up the volume on the recorder.
The sounds cease. They are replaced by deep and raspy
breathing. Karras joins Chris downstairs. She is speaking softly, disjointedly, into the phone.

CHRIS
You know, I'm like, uh, in seclusion. No, I'm
just exhausted from work and . . . Um, she's,
she's all right. She just isn't, ah, I don't wanna
talk about it, OK? Um . . . OK, I'll talk to ya,
huh? I'll call ya as soon as it's over, all right?
(*a pause, as she listens*)
No, I just, I'm really, I'm going through something and I just have to, uh . . . No, no, no, no,
there's nothing. Hey, thanks a lot. By now.
(*to Karras*)
Want a drink?

KARRAS
Please.

CHRIS

What d'ya drink?

KARRAS

Ah, Scotch, ice, water.

CHRIS

OK.
(*she opens the ice bucket*)
No ice. I'll get some from the kitchen.

KARRAS

No, that's all right, I'll take it straight, that's
fine.

CHRIS

It's OK, no trouble.

KARRAS (*insisting*)

No, that's fine. Please, sit.

CHRIS

Really, you're sure?

KARRAS

Yeah, sit.
(*Chris does so*)
Where's her father?

CHRIS

In Europe.

KARRAS

Have you told him what's happening?

CHRIS

No.

KARRAS

Well, I think you should. I told Regan that was
holy water. I sprinkled it on her and she reacted
very violently . . . It's tap water.

CHRIS

What's the difference?

KARRAS

Holy water's blessed. And that doesn't help support a case for possession.

CHRIS (*blurting it out*)

She killed Burke Dennings.

KARRAS (*astonished*)

What?

CHRIS (*in a whisper*)

She killed Burke Dennings. She pushed him out her window.

Karras and the language lab director are in the language lab, listening to the end of the recording of Karras's last session with Regan. Karras is tense.

LANGUAGE LAB DIRECTOR

... it's a language, all right. It's English.

KARRAS

Whatta yuh mean, English?

LANGUAGE LAB DIRECTOR

Well, it's English in reverse. Listen.

It is late at night. Karras is back in his room, listening to more tapes backward.

REGAN/DEMON'S VOICE

Give us time. Let her die.

KARRAS'S VOICE

Uoy era ohw?

REGAN/DEMON'S VOICE

I am no one. I am no one. Fear the priest. Dimmy. Fear the priest. Merrin, Merrin—I am no one. Merrin, Merrin. Let her die. Give us time—

The phone rings and Karras jumps, startled.

KARRAS (*into phone*)

What? ... Yeah? ... Yeah. I'll be right there.

Sharon, holding a flashlight, has the front door of the MacNeil house open, awaiting Karras. As he comes up the steps, she puts a finger to her lips for quiet. She beckons him in and closes the door silently.

SHARON (*whispering*)
I don't want Chris to see this.

KARRAS
Well, what's wrong? What is it?

SHARON
Shhhhh.

They tiptoe upstairs. Sharon puts on a jacket before ushering him into Regan's icy bedroom. Regan, breathing heavily, seems to be in a coma. Sharon gently pulls open Regan's pajamas and shines the flashlight on her chest. There, in letters rising from her skin, are the words "help me."

Daytime. In the main building of Georgetown University, Karras and the bishop converse in the bishop's office.

BISHOP
You're convinced that it's genuine?

KARRAS (*pondering*)
I don't know. No, not really, I suppose. But I have made a prudent judgment that it meets the conditions set down in the *Ritual*.

BISHOP
You would want to do the exorcism yourself?

KARRAS
Yes.

BISHOP
It might be best to have a man with experience. Maybe someone who's spent time in the foreign missions.

KARRAS (*disappointed*)
I understand, Your Excellency.

BISHOP

Let's see who's around. In the meantime, I'll call you as soon as I know.

KARRAS

Thank you, Your Excellency.

In the Georgetown University president's office, he and the bishop discuss the case.

TOM

Well, he does know the background. I doubt there's any danger in just having him assist. There should be a psychiatrist present, anyway.

BISHOP

What about the exorcist? Have you any ideas?

TOM

How about Lankester Merrin?

BISHOP

Merrin? Why, I'd a notion he was over in Iraq. I think I read he was working on a dig near Nineveh.

TOM

Yeah, you're right, Mike, but he's finished. He came back three or four months ago. He's at Woodstock now.

BISHOP

What's he doing there? Teaching?

TOM

No, he's working on another book.

BISHOP

Don't you think he's too old, Tom? How's his health?

TOM

He must be all right, he's still running around digging up tombs. Besides, he's had experience.

BISHOP

I didn't know that.

Ten, twelve years ago, I think, in Africa. The exorcism supposedly lasted months. I heard it damn near killed him.

At Woodstock Seminary in Maryland, Merrin receives a telegram summoning him to perform an exorcism. He does not have to open the envelope. He already knows its contents.

At night, in a heavy fog, a cab pulls up to the Mac-Neil house and Father Merrin steps out, carrying a battered valise. Chris opens the door to admit him.

MERRIN

Mrs. MacNeil?

CHRIS

Yes.

MERRIN

I'm Father Merrin.

CHRIS

Come in.

MERRIN

Thank you. Is Father Karras here?

CHRIS

Yes, yes, he's here. He's here already.

KARRAS (*entering*)

Father?

MERRIN

Father Karras.

KARRAS

It's an honor to meet you, Father.

Howls from the Regan/Demon are heard from above.

MERRIN

Are you very tired?

KARRAS

No.

MERRIN

I'd like you to go quickly across to the Residence, Damien, and gather up a cassock for
myself, two surplices, a purple stole, and some
holy water, and, uh, your copy of *The Roman
Ritual,* the large one. I believe we should begin.

KARRAS

Do you want to hear the background of the
case first, Father?

MERRIN

Why?

While Chris sets staring vacantly, her needlepoint
ignored in her lap, Karras and Merrin are dressing in
the vestments Karras has just brought from the Residence hall.

MERRIN

Especially important is the warning to avoid
conversation with the demon. We may ask what
is relevant, but anything beyond that is dangerous. He's a liar, the demon is a liar! He will lie
to confuse us. But he will also mix lies with the
truth to attack us. The attack is psychological,
Damien. And powerful. So don't listen. Remember that. Do not listen!

KARRAS

I think it might be helpful if I gave you some
background on the different personalities that
Regan has manifested. So far, I'd say there seem
to be three. She's convinced that she's—

MERRIN (*authoritatively*)

There is only one.

Ready now, Merrin and Karras step into Regan's bedroom and move to the bed. The room is freezing. Their
breath is condensing in the frigid air. Regan licks a
wolfish, blackened tongue across cracked, dried lips.

Stick your cock up her ass, you motherfucking, worthless cocksucker!

MERRIN

Be silent!
(*praying*)
"Our Father Who art in heaven, hallowed be Thy Name—"

Regan spits and hits Merrin in the eye. The yellowish glob of mucus oozes slowly down his cheek. Serenely, Merrin takes out a handkerchief and wipes it away.

MERRIN

"—Thy kingdom come, Thy will be done, on earth as it is in heaven; give us this day our daily bread; forgive us our trespasses as we forgive those who trespass against us; and lead us not into temptation—"

KARRAS

"But deliver us from the evil one."

Karras looks up to see Regan's tongue flicking rapidly in and out of her mouth. He returns to his text to follow as Merrin prays.

MERRIN

"Save me, O God, by Thy Name, by Thy might, defend my cause; proud men have risen up against me, and men of violence seek my life; but God is my helper, and the Lord sustains my life, in every need He has delivered me. Glory be to the Father and to the Son and to the Holy Spirit—"

KARRAS

"As it was in the beginning, is now and ever shall be, world without end, amen.

MERRIN

"Save Your servant . . ."

KARRAS

"Who places her trust in Thee, my God."

MERRIN

"Be unto her, O Lord, a fortified tower."

KARRAS

"In the face of the enemy."

MERRIN

"Let the enemy have no power over her."

KARRAS

"And the son of iniquity be powerless to harm her."

REGAN/DEMON

Your mother sucks cocks in hell, Karras! You faithless slime!

MERRIN

"O Lord, hear my prayer."

KARRAS

"And let my cry come unto Thee—"

MERRIN

"The Lord be with you—"

KARRAS

"And also with you."

The lights in the icy room flicker off and on. Then, as Merrin continues to pray, the front legs of Regan's bed jerkily rise up off the floor, inches at a time, until they are almost a foot off the ground. The back legs come up also at that point and the bed continues to levitate nearly up to the ceiling, where it hovers briefly, then slowly descends. Karras is transfixed by this spectacle, his attention distracted from Merrin's prayer.

MERRIN

"Let us pray. Holy Lord, Almighty Father, everlasting God, and Father of our Lord, Jesus Christ, Who once and for all consigned that fallen tyrant to the flames of hell. Who sent Your only begotten Son into the world to crush that roaring lion, hasten to our call for help and snatch from ruination and from the clutches of the noonday devil, this human being, made in Your image and likeness. Strike terror, Lord, into the beast, now laying waste Your vineyard. Let Your mighty hand cast him out of Your servant, Regan Teresa MacNeil, so he may no longer hold captive this person whom it pleased You to make in Your image. And to redeem through Your Son, Who lives and reigns with You in the unity of the Holy Spirit, God, forever and ever."

KARRAS

"Amen."

MERRIN

"O Lord, hear my prayer . . ." Father Karras.

Merrin sees that Karras has not been listening. He pauses to regain his attention.

MERRIN

Father Karras . . . Damien . . . The response, please, Damien!

Damien manages to collect himself. Once again he looks down at the text.

KARRAS

"And let my cry come unto Thee."

MERRIN

"Almighty Lord, Word of God the Father, Jesus Christ, God the Lord of all creation; Who gave to Your holy apostles the power to tramp underfoot serpents and scorpions, grant me, Your unworthy servant, pardon for all my sins—"

REGAN/DEMON

Bastard! Scum!

MERRIN

"—and the power to confront this cruel demon."

KARRAS

"Amen."

Regan vomits copiously on the bed. Merrin cleans up with the purple stole, which he hands to Karras. Karras takes it into the bathroom, rinses out the vomit and brings it back to Merrin, who kisses it and puts it on.

MERRIN

"See the cross of the Lord. Begone, you hostile powers. O Lord, hear my prayer."

KARRAS

"And let my cry come unto Thee."

MERRIN

"The Lord be with you."

KARRAS

"And also with you, Father."

MERRIN (*coughing*)

"I cast you out, unclean spirit!"

Cracks appear in the door and ceiling.

REGAN/DEMON

Shove it up your ass, you faggot!

MERRIN

"In the name of our Lord, Jesus Christ! It is He Who commands you, He Who flung you from the heights of heaven to the depths of hell!"

REGAN/DEMON

Fuck him!

MERRIN

"Begone!"

REGAN/DEMON

Fuck him, Karras!

MERRIN

"From this creature of God, begone! In the name of the Father, and of the Son, and of the Holy Spirit. By this sign of the holy cross, of our Lord Jesus Christ, Who lives and reigns with the Father and the Holy Spirit."

Regan's head slowly swivels in an almost 360-degree arc as she sits on the bed. Once again Damien's attention is diverted and Merrin has to prompt him into giving the response.

MERRIN

Damien!

KARRAS

"Amen."

The entire room starts rocking violently. Furniture hurtles through the air and both priests are thrown off balance. Karras clings desperately to a padded bedpost, but Merrin still manages to retain his serenity.

MERRIN

"O God, Defender of the human race, look down in pity—"

REGAN/DEMON (*to Karras*)

You killed your mother, you left her alone to die!

KARRAS (*desperately*)

Shut up!

MERRIN

"Upon this Your servant, Regan Teresa Mac-Neil."

REGAN/DEMON

She'll never forgive you! Bastard! Bastard!

KARRAS

Shut up!

Karras and Merrin have been thrown to the floor. They watch as Regan's eyeballs roll up into her head; then they manage to collect themselves and stand up.

MERRIN

"I command you by the judge of the living and the dead to depart from this servant of God. It's the power—"
(*to Karras*)
—Holy water!

(sprinkling it)
"It is the power of Christ that compels you!"

MERRIN AND KARRAS *(in unison)*
"The power of Christ compels you!
The power of Christ compels you!
The power of Christ compels you!
The power of Christ compels you!"

During this adjuration, the priests' voices build to a crescendo as Regan's body begins slowly to rise into the air. It sways above the bed for a long moment, the skin on her legs splitting in bloody cracks.

MERRIN AND KARRAS *(in unison)*
"The power of Christ compels you!
The power of Christ compels you!
The power of Christ compels you!
The power of Christ compels you!
The power of Christ compels you!
The power of Christ compels you!
The power of Christ compels you!
The power of Christ compels you!
The power of Christ compels you!"

Regan's body has gradually descended. Karras hurries over to her, tears a strap off the bed and ties her hands together. As he turns away, she raises her tied hands and deals him a powerful blow on the back of his head. He falls to the floor.

"The power of Christ compels you!
He brought you low by His bloodstained cross!
Do not despise my command because you know me to be a sinner.
It is God Himself Who commands you!
The majestic Christ Who commands you!
God the Father commands you.
God the Son commands you!
God the Holy Spirit commands you!
The mystery of the cross commands you!
The blood of the martyrs commands you!
Give way to Christ, you prince of murderers.
You're guilty, before Almighty God, guilty, befor His Son, guilty before the whole human race.

It is the Lord Who expels you. He Who is coming to judge both the living and the dead and the world by fire."

Briefly Regan lifts herself toward an apparition of the demon Pazuzu. As Merrin kneels by the bed, Karras crawls over and covers Regan with a blanket. She shivers and huddles underneath it.

MERRIN (*to Karras*)
Are you tired?
(*Damien nods*)
Let us rest—before we start again . . .

An exhausted Merrin and Karras are sitting in the hallway outside the bedroom.

MERRIN
Will you excuse me, Damien?

Merrin moves off toward the bathroom, where he takes out a pillbox, extracts a nitroglycerin tablet, and places it under his tongue. Karras returns to the bedroom alone and is horrified to see for an instant an apparition of his mother, sitting on the bed in place of Regan. It vanishes. He sits by Regan, and is startled to hear his mother's voice.

REGAN/KARRAS'S MOTHER
Dimmy, why you do this to me? Please, Dimmy, I'm afraid.

KARRAS (*insistent*)
You're not my mother.

REGAN/KARRAS'S MOTHER
Dimmy, please!

Merrin has rejoined Karras, who holds a stethoscope to Regan's chest. Regan lies still, her breathing labored.

MERRIN
What is it?

KARRAS
Her heart.

362

MERRIN

Can you give her something?

KARRAS

She'll go into a coma.

Regan, in the voice of Karras's mother, speaks a few pleading phrases in Greek to Karras.

KARRAS (*frantic*)

You're not my mother!

MERRIN

Don't listen.

REGAN/KARRAS'S MOTHER

Why, Dimmy?

Karras breaks into convulsive sobbing.

MERRIN

Damien.

REGAN/KARRAS'S MOTHER

Dimmy, please!

MERRIN (*raising his voice*)

Damien! Get out!

Merrin leads Karras out, then reenters the room and, after sprinkling holy water, kneels by Regan's bedside.

MERRIN

"Our Father Who art in heaven, hallowed be Thy Name—"

Downstairs Karras sits brooding as Chris comes in.

CHRIS

Is it over?

Karras shakes his head negatively.

CHRIS

Is she gonna die?

KARRAS (*firmly*)

No.

He rises and starts upstairs with renewed conviction as Chris answers the door chimes admitting Kinderman. When Karras reenters Regan's bedroom, he sees Merrin sprawled face down on the floor on the far side of the bed. Regan is screeching and croaking. Karras dashes over to Merrin, kneels, and turns him face up. He feels for his pulse, tries frantically to pump life back into the priest with blows to his chest but gives up when he realizes Merrin is dead. He hears a giggle and turns on Regan, shaking and pummeling her onto the floor and nearly strangling her in his fury.

KARRAS

You son of a bitch! Take me! Come into me! Goddamn you, take me! Take me!

A gargantuan struggle is visible in the demonic features of Regan's face. She screams out as Karras's body jerks, apparently manipulated by some inner alien force which now reaches toward Regan to strangle her. But Karras fights this force for control of his body, and he wins, compelling it toward the window.

KARRAS

No!

With this last, anguished cry, Karras leaps out of the window. His cry is immediately followed by frightened sobs and whimpers that are unmistakably those of an ordinary little girl.

REGAN

Mother . . . Mother . . .
(sobbing)
Mother . . . Mother . . .

Chris rushes in, pausing an instant to make sure it's really Regan again. She is followed by Kinderman.

CHRIS

Rags?

She dashes over to where her daughter is cowering on the floor. She flings herself down on top of Regan, cradling her and crying in hysterical relief as Kinderman watches.

A crowd is gathering at the scene of an accident. Their attention is focused on a man lying twisted and crumpled in a pool of blood on the pavement at the foot of the steps under Regan's window. It is Karras.

MALE BYSTANDER
Somebody fell at the bottom of the steps here!

Father Dyer has pushed his way through the crowd and is kneeling beside Karras. Fighting back tears, he grasps Karras's wrist and leans close to whisper in his ear.

DYER
Do you want to make your confession? Are you sorry—
(*his voice catches*)
Are you sorry for having offended God with all the sins of your past life?
(*he breaks down for a moment, then starts administering the last rites*)
"*Ego te absolvo in nomine Patris, et Filii, et Spiritus Sancti. Amen.*"

As a wailing siren signals the approach of an ambulance, Dyer weeps openly.

On a bright, sunshiny day, Sharon and Chris are briskly packing up last-minute items before moving out of the house on Prospect Street.

SHARON
Where do you want this?

CHRIS
What is it?

SHARON
Phonograph.

CHRIS
Storage.

Sharon puts it in one of the large cardboard cartons that are standing about.

SHARON
That's everything.

CHRIS (*warmly*)
I'm gonna miss you.

SHARON (*with equal warmth*)
Same here.

CHRIS
You're sure you won't change your mind?

SHARON (*shaking her head "no"*)
I found this in her room.
(*she hands Chris Karras's medallion and chain*)
Better hurry—

Chris and Sharon embrace affectionately. A few minutes later, Chris, then Regan, go out of the front door for the last time. Chris is her old self, but Regan has not yet fully recovered from her ordeal. She looks wan, her face bearing traces of bruises. On their way down the steps, they run into Father Dyer, coming to bid them good-bye.

CHRIS
Regan, come on, honey, we have to get going.
(*aside, to Dyer*)
She doesn't remember any of it.

DYER
That's good.

REGAN (*catching up*)
All done.

CHRIS
OK. Honey, this is Father Dyer.

REGAN
Hi, Father.

DYER
Hello.

KARL
All ready, missus.

CHRIS
Good-bye, Father.

DYER
Good-bye.

CHRIS

I'll call you.

Regan has been staring up at Father Dyer's Roman collar, some vague memory apparently tugging at her. Suddenly, impulsively, she reaches up to Dyer, pulls his head down, and kisses his cheek. She runs off toward the waiting limousine, looking faintly embarrassed at her own unexpected gesture.

DYER (*moved*)

By.

WILLIE

Good-bye, Father.

DYER

I hope I see you again.

WILLIE

I hope so, too.

Chris follows Regan into the limousine and it starts to glide off. Then it stops. Chris rolls down her window and leans out.

CHRIS

Father Dyer? I thought you'd like to keep this.

She hands him the medallion Sharon has just given her —Karras's medallion. The car pulls away and is soon lost in traffic. Dyer slowly walks to the top of the steps beside the house. Sadly, he stares down. Then he turns away and toward life.

Screen Credits

THE
EXORCIST

DIRECTED BY
WILLIAM
FRIEDKIN

WRITTEN FOR THE SCREEN
AND PRODUCED BY
WILLIAM PETER
BLATTY
Based on His Novel

Executive Producer
NOEL MARSHALL

ELLEN BURSTYN
Chris MacNeil

MAX von SYDOW
Father Merrin

LEE J. COBB
Lieutenant Kinderman

KITTY WINN
Sharon

JACK MacGOWRAN
Burke Dennings

JASON MILLER
Father Karras

LINDA BLAIR
Regan

Reverend WILLIAM O'MALLEY, S.J.
BARTON HEYMAN
PETE MASTERSON
RUDOLF SCHUNDLER
GINA PETRUSHKA
ROBERT SYMONDS
ARTHUR STORCH
Reverend THOMAS BERMINGHAM, S.J.
VASILIKI MALIAROS
TITOS VANDIS

WALLACE ROONEY
RON FABER
DONNA MITCHELL
ROY COOPER
ROBERT GERRINGER
and
MERCEDES MacCAMBRIDGE

Associate Producer
DAVID SALVEN

Director of Photography
OWEN ROIZMAN

Makeup Artist
DICK SMITH

Special Effects
MARCEL VERCOUTERE

Production Design
BILL MALLEY

First Assistant Director
TERENCE A. DONNELLY

Set Decorator
JERRY WUNDERLICH

Music
KRZYSZTOF PENDERECKI

Kanon for Orchestra and Tape
Cello Concerto
        Courtesy of Angel Records
String Quartet (1960)
  Courtesy of Candid/Vox Productions, Inc.
Polymorphia
(Orchestra of the Cracow Philarmonia,
HENRYK CZYZ, Conductor)
        Courtesy of Philips Records
The Devils of Loudon
(Hamburg State Opera, MAREK JANOWSKI,
Conductor)
        Courtesy of Philips Records

Music (remains on screen)
HANS WERNER HENZE
Fantasia for Strings
    Courtesy of Deutsche Grammophon

GEORGE CRUMB
(Tutti) Threnody 1: Night of the Electric
Insects
    Courtesy of Composers Recordings, Inc.

ANTON WEBERN
Fliessend, Aüsserts Zart from Five Pieces
for Orchestra, Op. 10
        Courtesy of Angel Records

Music (remains on screen)
BEGINNINGS
From the Wind Harp
    Courtesy of United Artists Records

MIKE OLDFIELD
Tubular Bells
    Courtesy of Virgin Records

DAVID BORDEN
Study No. 1/Study No. 2

Additional Music Composed By
JACK NITZSCHE

IRAQ SEQUENCE

Director of Photography	BILLY WILLIAMS
Production Manager	WILLIAM KAPLAN
Sound	JEAN-LOUIS DUCARME
Film Editor	BUD SMITH
Assistant Film Editor	ROSS LEVY

Supervising Film Editor
JORDAN LEONDOPOULOS

Film Editors
EVAN LOTTMAN
NORMAN GAY

Assistant Film Editors
MICHAEL GOLDMAN   CRAIG McKAY
JONATHAN PONTELL

Sound
CHRIS NEWMAN

Dubbing Mixer
BUZZ KNUDSON

Sound Effects Editors
FRED BROWN
ROSS TAYLOR

Special Sound Effects
RON NAGLE   DOC SIEGEL
GONZALO GAVIRA   BOB FINE

Sound Consultant
HAL LANDAKER

Music Editor
GENE MARKS

Gaffer	DICK QUINLAN
Key Grip	EDDIE QUINN
Property Master	JOE CARACCIOLO
Script Supervisor	NICK SGARRO
Costume Designer	JOE FRETWELL
Hair Stylist	BILL FARLEY
Administrative Assistant	ALBERT SHAPIRO
Casting	NESSA HYAMS
	JULIET TAYLOR
	LOUIS Di GIAMO
Still Photographer	JOSH WEINER
Second Assistant Director	ALAN GREEN
Ladies' Wardrobe	FLORENCE FOY
Men's Wardrobe	BILL BEATTIE
Production Office Coordinator	ANNE MOONEY
Master Scenic Artist	EDDIE GARZERO

Technical Advisers
Reverend JOHN NICOLA, S.J.
Reverend THOMAS BERMINGHAM, S.J.
Reverend WILLIAM O'MALLEY, S.J.
NORMAN E. CHASE, M.D.
Professor of Radiology,
New York University Medical Center
HERBERT E. WALKER, M.D.
ARTHUR I. SNYDER, M.D.

Optical Effects	MARV YSTROM
Title Design	DAN PERRI
Color	METROCOLOR
Color Consultant	ROBERT M. McMILLAN
Photographic Equipment	PANAVISION
Jewelry Design	ALDO CIPULLO
	For Cartier, New York
Furs	REVILLON

A HOYA PRODUCTION

THE STORY, ALL NAMES, CHARACTERS, AND
INCIDENTS PORTRAYED IN THIS PRODUCTION
ARE FICTITIOUS. NO IDENTIFICATION WITH
ACTUAL PERSONS, PLACES, BUILDINGS, AND
PRODUCTS IS INTENDED OR SHOULD BE
INFERRED.

Distributed by WARNER BROS.
A WARNER COMMUNICATIONS COMPANY

ABOUT THE AUTHOR

WILLIAM PETER BLATTY was born in New York in 1928 and is a graduate of Georgetown University. After taking an M.A. in English literature at George Washington University, he served as an editor with the U.S. Information Agency in Lebanon and was Policy Branch Chief of the U.S. Air Force Psychological Warfare Division in Washington, D.C. He now lives in Aspen, Colorado and has published five previous books, including *The Exorcist*. He is also the author of numerous screenplays, among them *A Shot in the Dark*.

RELAX!
SIT DOWN
and Catch Up On Your Reading!

OTHER WORLDS.
OTHER REALITIES.

In fact and fiction, these extraordinary books bring the fascinating world of the supernatural down to earth. From ancient astronauts and black magic to witchcraft, voodoo and mysticism—these books look at other worlds and examine other realities.